Young Mr. Darcy in Love

Cover art by David Berg and Cherri Trotter

Young Mr. Darcy in Love

Jane Austen's
Pride and Prejudice
Continues

Marsha Altman

Laughing Man Publications

Dedication

For Jane Austen.

I'm surprised it took me this long to get around to that. Right?

Introduction

Once again, if you've bought this book without knowing that this is the seventh book in a series, you now have fair warning to return it. Or give it a shot, as you're in for a lot of fun.

Welcome returning readers! You'll all be happy to learn that our story is safely back in England. Two years have passed since the events of *The Knights of Derbyshire* and one since *Georgiana and the Wolf*. I have nothing else to say except that I sincerely hope you enjoy this book.

In our previous books:

In *The Darcys and the Bingleys* (Book 1), Elizabeth Bennet married Mr. Darcy (of being Mr. Darcy fame), and her older sister Jane Bennet married Mr. Bingley (of being Darcy's friend fame). Seriously, you did not read Pride and Prejudice? This was the book that made you regret not freshening up. At least take the movie out or something. Anyway, they proceeded to have a whole mess of kids. Fortunately, not all at the same time. The Darcys' oldest child is Geoffrey Darcy, and the Bingleys' oldest child is Georgiana Bingley.

Caroline Bingley, Charles's unwed sister, became involved with a Scottish earl, who then turned out to be a rake, and by that I mean a 19th-century scoundrel and not a gardening tool. This was all exposed in time for her to also reveal she was actually in love with the impoverished Dr. Daniel Maddox. Dr. Maddox had lost his social standing when his older brother Brian gambled away their family fortune. After some sword fighting and the bad guy getting clobbered with a candlestick, Dr. Maddox and Caroline Bingley were married, not leaving enough time in the book for them to have a mess of kids, but presumably that was coming.

In *The Plight of the Darcy Brothers* (Book 2), Mary Bennet, Jane and Elizabeth's unmarried sister, returned from studying in France with child, the father being an Italian seminary student. Darcy and Elizabeth traveled through Europe to find him, on the way discovering that Darcy had an illegitimate half-brother named Grégoire Bellamont-Darcy holed up in a French monastery. Mary's would-be suitor was found, and he offered her a settlement. Mary had a son, Joseph, and is currently unmarried and living with her parents. Darcy also discovered that George Wickham (the villain in Pride and Prejudice, who seduced and married Lydia Bennet, the youngest Bennet sister) was also his half-brother. Their family reunion went the worst possible way, with fratricide and a complete lack of potato salad. Lydia got over her husband's death rather quickly but was left with two children, George and Isabella Wickham.

Brother Grégoire, still a monk, went to live in Austria. Dr. Maddox and Caroline Bingley had a daughter, but also adopted a son, the bastard child of the Prince Regent and a prostitute, named Frederick (the son, not the prostitute).

In *Mr. Darcy's Great Escape* (Book 3), Napoleon invaded Russia, and in the tumult of war, Darcy lost track of his brother Grégoire, and Dr. Maddox lost track of his brother Brian, who was supposed to have married a Transylvanian princess but then disappeared. The two of them traveled to Austria to find them but ended up in a Transylvanian dungeon as hostages, and their wives ended up rescuing them after locating Grégoire. Brian Maddox and his wife, Princess Nadezhda, reappeared after being missing for two years, having taken the long way home through Russia, Japan, and then a boat ride to England. So it turns out they were fine all along. No one was thrilled to hear that. They brought with them a mixed-race Japanese convict named Mugin, whom I only mention because he pops up from time to time.

Lydia Bennet remarried and had a whole mess of kids with her new husband, Mr. Bradley. Kitty Bennet, the last remaining Bennet sister to be mentioned, got married to a Mr. Townsend over a whole page, because she isn't a very interesting character so I didn't spend a lot of time with her.

After the war, Grégoire Bellamont-Darcy moved to Spain, his previous monastery having been dissolved by Napoleon.

There is also a Bavarian saint named Sebald buried in Darcy's graveyard instead of his traditional home in Nuremburg, but there's a long story behind it, so just take it for what it is.

In *The Ballad of Grégoire Darcy* (Book 4), Grégoire Bellamont-Darcy was forced to leave his monastery for what seemed like largely political reasons, and moved to Ireland, where he met a peasant named Caitlin MacKenna and, this being a historical romance series, eventually married her but not before some dramatic things happened to pad out the book a little. They have a son named Patrick, and Grégoire is a schoolteacher.

Charles Bingley and Brian Maddox went into business together and traveled to India and the Far East, bringing back a monkey and Mugin. Unfortunately for Darcy the monkey remained, but Mugin was kicked out of England after Brian discovered he was teaching Georgiana Bingley how to fight. I'm probably bothering to mention this minor subplot for a reason.

Mary Bennet, the single mother of Joseph Bennet, married Dr. Andrew Bertrand, a doctor of French origin, and still lives in Longbourn. Mrs. Bennet died of a stroke, and after her passing, Mr. Bennet left Longbourn and took up residence in the library at Pemberley. So far, Darcy hasn't complained about any old people smells, probably because *everyone* smelled in Georgian England.

In *The Knights of Derbyshire* (Book 5), the Darcys held a party for their son Geoffrey Darcy, heir to Pemberley and Derbyshire, who turned eighteen and was about to leave for Cambridge. On the day after the party he ran afoul of an English Radical and was seriously wounded, kidnapped, and held for ransom by a man named Hatcher. When traditional negotiations for release were unsuccessful, he was rescued by a person dressed as a white wolf, later revealed to be Georgiana Bingley, the newly-out (in society, not the way you're thinking) eldest daughter of Charles and Jane. She was ultimately shot by Hatcher but rescued by her father and Geoffrey Darcy. To save her reputation, the affair was covered up. While recovering from a head injury that ultimately resulted in partial deafness, Geoffrey awkwardly confessed his feelings for Georgiana before rejecting her, leaving both would-be lovers in a bit of a spat, otherwise known as a cliffhanger. Geoffrey joined his older cousin George Wickham (son of George Wickham and Lydia Bennet) in Cambridge while Georgiana went to a seminary in France.

In *Georgiana and the Wolf* (Book 6), Georgiana Bingley spends a brief year of her stint in an English boarding school in rural France protecting her friend Lady Heather Littlefield from a malicious aristocratic suitor while aiding a French inspector named Robert Audley to solve a series of murders she may have sort of caused.

Family Trees

Bold face indicates living, *Italics* indicates deceased.

<u>The Darcys</u>

Henry Darcy
        (with unnamed wife)
        Gregory Darcy (never married)
        Geoffrey Darcy
                (children with *Lady Anne Fitzwilliam*)
                Fitzwilliam Darcy
                        (children with **Elizabeth Bennet**)
                        Geoffrey Darcy
                        Anne Darcy
                        Sarah Darcy
                        Cassandra Darcy
                Georgiana Darcy-Kincaid
                        (children with **Lord William Kincaid**)
                        Viscount Robert Kincaid
                (children with *Mrs. Wickham*)
                George Wickham
                        (children with **Lydia Bennet**)

George Wickham the Younger

Isabella Wickham
(children with *Miss Bellamont*)
Grégoire Bellamont-Darcy
(children with **Caitlin MacKenna**)
Patrick Bellamont

Assorted:
Lady Catherine de Bourgh – **Mr. Darcy's** aunt on his mother's side)
(children with *Sir Lewis de Bourgh*)
Anne de Bourgh-Fitzwilliam
(children with **Richard Fitzwilliam**, now Lord Matlock)
Edward Fitzwilliam, Viscount of Matlock

The Bingleys

Charles Bingley (I)
(children with *Mrs. Bingley*)
Louisa Bingley-Hurst
(married **Mr. Hurst**, no children)

Caroline Bingley-Maddox
(children with **Dr. Daniel Maddox**
– see *The Maddoxes*)
Charles Bingley (II)
(children with **Jane Bennet**)
Georgiana (Georgie) Bingley
Charles (Charlie) Bingley (III)
Elizabeth (Eliza) Bingley
Edmund Bingley

The Bennets

Edmund Bennet
(children with **Mrs. Bennet**)
Jane Bennet-Bingley
(children with **Mr. Bingley** – see
The Bingleys)
Elizabeth Bennet-Darcy
(children with **Mr. Darcy** – see *The
Darcys*)
Mary Bennet-Bertrand
(children with **Giovanni Mastai**)
Joseph Bennet
(children with **Dr. Andrew
Bertrand**)

Margaret Bertrand

Kitty Bennet-Townsend

Lydia Bennet-Bradley (formerly Wickham)

(children with *Mr. Wickham* – see *The Darcys*)

(children with **Mr. Bradley**)
Julie Bradley
Brandon Bradley

Assorted:

Mr. Collins – nephew of **Mr. Edmund Bennet**

(children with **Charlotte Lucas-Collins**)
Amelia Collins
Maria Collins
Eleanor Collins
Jane Collins

The Maddoxes

Stewart Maddox

(children with *Mrs. Maddox*)
Brian Maddox

(married to **Princess Nadezhda of Sibui**, no children)

Dr. Daniel Maddox

   (children with Caroline Bingley)

   Frederick Maddox (adopted, son of the **Prince of Wales** and *Lilly Garrison*)

   Emily Maddox (same age as Fredrick)

   Daniel Maddox the Younger

CHAPTER 1

Prologue

London, 1825

"You want to get in trouble, don't you? I have to answer to the Chief Councilor for this."

Liu Xiao took the tea from the English servant girl. She always seemed mystified when he left the saucer in her hands. "This? I haven't done anything yet."

"I have to answer to him for everything we do," Quon Jin said. "And I know you are going to do something."

"I can't help it if I'm bored," Liu said, and gagged on his tea. He immediately put the cup back in the saucer, saying in English to the servant, "More tea in tea!" She did her little knee-drop bow and scurried off. "That stuff is terrible," he said, returning his interests to further adjusting his attire in front of the gigantic mirror provided for him. He had already removed his blue silk shirt and everything else with any kind of imperial insignia that defined his status as an ambassador.

Quon Jin did his best to look imposing, which was very difficult. A man in his sixties, he was slumped over in a permanent bow (convenient on many other occasions), and his little black goatee was beginning to turn grey. He was almost a head shorter than Liu. "I don't care if you're bored or not and neither does the Grand Council! You were given a very honorable position because of your intelligence, and if you can manage not to ruin it by getting drunk with these monkeys, or heaven forbid something even worse, you might get a promotion. Or at least come home alive."

"All you think about is promotions," Liu said, and put on his hat. "I suppose that makes you a better officer than I." Liu knew very well he was too low-ranked for this mission and had only been acquired because he had a talent for languages, and could write in English. "You are a better diplomat, too, even if the king likes me better because I'm young."

A man entered and offered Quon Jin a stool. Their white servants always had such disrespectful posture, and their neckbands made them look all the more like animals puffing themselves up. Nonetheless, Ambassador Quon Jin took the seat. He was tired after a long night at Lord Liverpool's dinner party, even if, they had been assured, it had been an early night. "He likes anything new and shiny. Like a child. I did not leave for this filthy kingdom just to be paraded around like a puppet in front of delighted barbarians."

"Then go do something else," Liu Xiao said. "I am off. I will be back."

"When?"

"When I am needed."

Actually, Liu intended to be back before dawn, but that was not important to say. It wouldn't soothe Quon Jin, whom he liked for some strange reason. Jin had a sort of endearing quality to his insistent manner of doing things, like an overeager grandfather.

They had been in London for three months now, and Liu Xiao knew enough to not ask directions, at least while he was still in the western part of the city. To the east they had rarely ventured, except to talk to some merchants who had requested their audience, which actually was proving more successful than any negotiations with the ruler. The king was obscenely fat, obscenely drunk, and made no attempt to hide it, and the general consensus was that the entire kingdom was waiting for their ruler to die. This would not have been so unusual had it not been for a lack of structure beneath him. There was the Parliament, chosen not for their wisdom or their years of service, but by bribery, heredity, and commoner vote. It was a mass rabble no better than the ones on the market square. Liu, as a younger man, found it interesting to observe, but nonetheless frustratingly unproductive; in three months they had not succeeded in getting a single person to take them seriously, much less consider talking about or even looking at a proposed treaty. Instead, the Imperial diplomats went from dinner party to dinner party, where the women gossiped and laughed at the men, and the men made inebriated and failed attempts to talk of politics.

Liu was not enough of an administrator yet to be truly annoyed at the behavior of the local government. He had only completed his exams four years before. He had spent ten years studying for them, and it was worth every minute by anyone else's standards, but he could not help but think that there was something to be said for village life. At least most villagers were *doing* something.

The poor of London were easily found, mainly by the smell. Dressed respectably in black, but fooling no one as to his identity as a 'Chinaman,' he traveled the streets. He heard there were roving gangs, but he also heard they were all terrible fighters, and so went unhindered by anything except the minor responsibility not to get himself killed, as he spoke English much better than Quon Jin.

"Hey mister, I'll show yah where 'tis."

Liu looked away from the poster and down at the child, his face smeared with black soot, probably from his job. The poster on the brick wall had said something about a fight. "How much?" he said.

"Two shillin' be all 'tis, sir."

He laughed. "Two farthings are more appropriate, I believe, young master," he said, putting his fist in his other palm and bowing a little.

The boy did not look pleased that Liu understood the money system. "Two farthings 'tis, then."

Of course the boy did do him a service, as Liu found the directions hard to follow in this brick maze of a city, and he decided in the end it was worth two farthings, but certainly no more, and he paid the boy and entered the building.

A host of noises and smells assaulted him as he entered the crowd in the warehouse. Several gaslights burned over the center, where the hay had been cleared away and the crowd formed a ring. Inside that man-made ring, two peasants were pummeling each other with their fists, doing little to block and always going for the head. Liu watched with the first real fascination he'd felt in weeks as he melted into the crowd. These Englishmen were indeed so busy puffing themselves up that they stood perfectly straight and hit each other like poles with targets. It was logical – for an idiot – and undisciplined. It was also quite bloody, as the face bled especially easily, and finally one of them was hit hard enough that he fell to the ground. The apparent ringmaster began to call down from ten to one, and then declared the other man, rendered almost indistinguishable for all the red swelling and bleeding on his face, the winner.

"All takers! All takers! Half-pence on the current champion!"

There were takers, and they went down until one of them beat the champion in question, who at this point was probably done from sheer exhaustion. They were bloodthirsty creatures.

When there were no takers to the current man, as bulky as a horse, Liu stepped in. He had to look up to face the man, but he bowed politely. The money came down like rain around him, and the ringmaster had to run to collect all the bets before the fight could begin.

"I'll smash your face in, little man," said the champion, "and hang you by your ponytail."

Liu smiled and bowed again. "It is an honor." He turned to the crowd closing in behind him. "Please, back away. You are not in the fight."

The bell was rung and it began; the champion sent his fist flying. It would have bashed Liu's face in, if he had been stupid enough to leave his face there, but instead he knelt down and as the boxer's muscled chest came flying at him, Liu pushed his hand into the man's diaphragm. Forces of nature did the work for him; he had to kick out the man's legs to send him backwards and make sure he didn't just fall on Liu, who would not appreciate being crushed. The thud was audible even on the dirt floor as the man hit the ground, and Liu rose to his feet, his queue still swinging behind him.

There was a moment of silence before the ringmaster could even scramble to begin calling it. The champion was too stunned to rise. "Champion!" he said, pulling Liu's arm up into the air, and there was a lot of booing, but also a fair amount of cheering.

And so it began. Liu Xiao didn't even begin sweating before the fourth fight, and that was just from the heat in the room. His second opponent was more hesitant and it took a few more moves. The third even managed to get back on his feet a few times before Liu broke his leg, ensuring it would not happen again. So far, he had bloodied no one, and there was not a drop on him.

Now the crowd had learned to form a much larger ring, as there was far more movement between fighters. In fact, it was almost double its original size by the time Liu looked expectantly at the ringmaster, who turned to the man beside him and said, "Get Jack."

No contestants came forward for a long moment. Liu stood respectfully. He had no real desire to taunt them, as that would invite more trouble, and he really wanted to walk out without killing an opponent or seriously harming himself (especially as he had not heard good things about English medicine). Finally a space was cleared in front of them as someone emerged from the back, and the crowd began cheering as the man they shouted for stepped into the light.

'Jack' didn't seem much bigger than he was, nor particularly bulky, though his coat and scarf hid most of his body and therefore his build. He had wraps around his hands, so he was probably a somewhat regular fighter. Little was visible of his face because he wore a scarf despite the heat as well as a headband around his wild black hair.

Liu bowed, and Jack returned it, without the hand gesture. They both took a moment to size each other up, though Jack had had more of a chance, if he had been present for the past few rounds. Liu, however, was still trying to make out his opponent, who stood waiting, not for the bell but for Liu to do something, as if he were the type of fighter to sit on his heels until his opponent struck. Except, Liu noticed, looking at the heels, Jack wore sandals. Japanese geta shoes, male version. Liu was probably the only one who recognized them for what they were. But Jack was not Japanese. Or maybe he was. It was hard to tell.

The bell rang and Liu realized how lost he had been in contemplation. Jack stood and waited, giving no indication of a fighting stance. He would wait for Liu, and not make the same mistake of all the Englishmen Liu had already fought. "It is an honor," Liu said in Pinyin, his native tongue, but Jack either did not understand or decided not to acknowledge it.

Since Liu had to fight with his fists, he would. His fist came carefully but quickly, and Jack was ready. He moved to the side to block, something all of the other Englishmen had failed to do. He even tried to twist Liu's arm and break it, but Liu was too strong, and managed to spin him over. Jack wasn't very heavy and hit the ground, but was hardly incapacitated. He spun around to give himself the momentum to get up without his hands, and as he got back on his feet with a 'clonk' of his wooden shoes, the crowd cheered.

So it continued, for a long time, in fact. Jack was evasive – almost too much, and the crowd gave them a wide berth as Liu's punch connected with a box instead of Jack's neck, smashing the wood. Jack kicked Liu's other hand, catching it between the spokes of his geta, which were reinforced with metal, and then simply stepped down to catch Liu's arm.

"If I twist it," Jack whispered to him, "I'll break it."

Liu's other limbs were not pinned, and his left leg successfully knocked out one of Jack's. The Englishman went back down, freeing Liu, who used a similar tactic to grab the leg of his opponent. "The same," he said in English.

Jack growled and kicked Liu in the stomach, hard enough to free himself. The fight resumed with them both on their feet, even though it had never officially stopped.

This time, Liu assumed a formal tiger stance. Jack didn't bother with formalities and met it with a crane. Liu smiled; now he was truly back at home. Jack was no Englishman.

They came at each other with blocks and kicks and punches, but they were well-matched. Liu was no master, but neither was Jack. Liu was more powerful and aggressive; Jack more wily and inventive. Liu was stopped in a charge when a wooden sandal went flying at his face, hitting him square between the eyes just as Jack hit him in the stomach. Still not enough to knock him out, though Liu did cough, and the crowd, which had turned deadly silent, heard it and cheered.

This would not stand. Liu grabbed the sandal, tossed it back at Jack, and though it hit far more wildly, it gave Liu enough time to kick his legs out with enough force to leave serious bruises.

Liu put his slipper on Jack's chest, feeling his heaving breath. "You know the moves," he said, trying Japanese, "but you don't understand them."

"I won't give you this fight," Jack replied in the same language, though his accent was strange.

"If you don't, there will be serious consequences."

Jack sighed, and put his head back on the ground. He tapped the ground with his left hand, and the bell rang. "Winner!" the ringmaster said, and lifted up Liu's hand. Liu was perspiring, and though he could have continued beating Englishmen all night, he had other things on his mind. He offered a hand to Jack, who accepted it, and got back to his feet, collecting his geta sandal as he did.

"I want to fight you again," Liu said in Japanese.

"Good luck," Jack said, bowed in the Japanese style, and turned to leave. Liu was going to follow, but Jack was an expert at disappearing into the crowd as the ringmaster came to give Liu his winnings.

Since no one else would challenge Liu, the night was called. Everyone had won or lost enough, anyway. "High numbers tonight," the ringmaster said. "Will you be back tomorrow?"

"Where is Jack?" Liu said. "Where can I find him?"

"How should I know?"

"Is he here every night?"

"No. You got lucky."

Liu frowned and grabbed the ringmaster's arm. The old man stopped counting his money as Liu demanded, "Who is Jack?"

"For God's sake, I don't know!"

It was obvious that he didn't. The ringmaster hadn't fought Jack, hadn't figured out the most basic thing that distinguished the mystery fighter from every other person in the room.

"I may be back," he said, "maybe not." With that, Liu left with his money and a lot on his mind. As he stepped into the morning light, he brushed off his gown to catch the tiny hairs that had been caught in the buttons near his neck. He picked up the hairs and examined their beautiful shade of orange in the light.

Jack had been wearing a wig. The ringmaster didn't know that. He didn't know a lot of things, obviously. Liu wondered how many times he had held up Jack's arm, and noticed the hands were too small to be a man's.

CHAPTER 2

Anne's Ball

Two months later

Any man in want of a wife and thoroughly unacquainted with the father of the young lady in question, was seeking only one thing in July of 1825: an invitation to the Pemberley Ball. Anne Jane Darcy, the oldest of the Darcy sisters, was coming out, and not only would the affair be grand, but she was considered by many to be a beauty, and her inheritance would certainly be astronomical. However, if they had any inkling of what her father was feeling, every young man with a mother to warn him would have stayed far away.

Aside from his family, everyone at Pemberley steered clear of the master for the entire week approaching the ball. Though it was well known that he was a kind and generous master, and that whatever reserve he had could be softened by the presence of his wife or children, that particular week was a variation from the general rule. While Mr. Darcy had little interest in the specifics of the decorations and other plans, he kept a careful eye on the guest list. He was, until the day the invitations went out, marking people off the list with a brisk stroke of his pen.

"Darcy, we're *related* to them," his wife insisted.

"Distantly," he growled.

"It shall be even more distant if you do not invite them."

By mollifying him slowly in the way that only she could, Elizabeth Darcy returned names to the list, so that some people were actually invited.

A further comfort was the return of Geoffrey Darcy from his second year at Cambridge. The upcoming one would be his last. "How's Father?"

"Insane," his mother said. "Stay out of his way."

"I plan to," Geoffrey said with a smile. "Did you hear about George?"

"Through his sister. George is not one to boast in letters, but nonetheless we are very proud of him, if he would ever admit to it himself." Elizabeth shook her head. "A Darcy not admitting to something? Whoever thought that was possible?" she said with a sly glace at her husband as he entered the room.

"What have I done now?"

"Nothing, Father," Geoffrey said. "We were merely complimenting George on his fellowship, and chiding him for his lack of communication skills."

"There is no reason to boast about it in a letter," Darcy replied, and as their expressions melted into mirth, said, "Why are you laughing?"

There was much to be proud of. George Wickham, newly graduated from his baccalaureate work in Cambridge, had been awarded a fellowship, meaning he could while away the years in the dusty libraries of University as a Fellow if he so chose. They had always assumed he would seek further education, though he had not declared in what fashion he would do it, saying only that he was reluctant to go abroad and leave his sister behind. Isabella Wickham was a most eligible lady and heiress, and she was forever dragging him to balls when he was in Town, and then forever complaining the next day that all he did was stand in the corner and tell her not to dance with anyone because they were all suspicious – but the Darcys suspected she would not have had it any other way.

Their mother and stepfather, Mr. and Mrs. Bradley, were consumed with their children, all three of them. Isabel nobly tolerated living at home on Gracechurch Street because she loved her little sister Julie, who was now old enough to have talks with, her brother Brandon, and her youngest sister, Maria. She divided her time between Gracechurch Street and Chesterton, where she had a standing invitation with the Maddoxes to be at leisure there, and she was great friends with Emily Maddox.

Alternately Sir, Professor, and Dr. Daniel Maddox lived with his wife in Chesterton. He was now officially retired from the royal service and was the official anatomist professor of Cambridge University, lecturing at Trinity or King's College. When he was not lecturing himself, he was often seen attending other lectures. If he had had any part in the granting of George's fellowship, he said nothing. Lady Maddox concerned herself with her daughter, newly available but not quite ready for marriage, and her sons. Frederick would begin Cambridge in the fall, leaving young Danny behind at Eton. Daniel Maddox II was at first picked on for his glasses, but after a few lessons from his Uncle Brian, no one dared to come near him with an awful thought. He was excused from Anne's ball, being underage and uninterested. Most of the boys were, even those of age, except maybe Frederick Maddox. The Maddoxes themselves, of course, would be in attendance, along with Brian Maddox and Princess Nadezhda.

Darcy had only regained his ground in the study when a harried servant entered. "Sir Daniel Maddox to see you, sir."

"The doctor? Is he alone?"

"Yes, sir. We don't know quite what to do –
"

"– There is nothing to *do* with me," Dr. Maddox said, entering by himself with one hand running along the wall. "Darcy."

"Dr. Maddox," Darcy said, nodding for the servant to leave as he immediately rose and came to shake the doctor's hand, and thereby, guiding him to a seat. "It is wonderful to have you back at Pemberley at last. You are truly a –" He trailed off in horror.

"– sight for sore eyes, yes," Dr. Maddox said with a smile, setting his cane against his chest. "Yes, yes, those embarrassing turn of phrases seem to make everyone uncomfortable. Excepting myself, it seems."

"Would you like a drink?"

"I am rather fond of Pemberley's stock of brandy, thank you."

Darcy got the glass out and poured, handing it to the doctor, who stayed in his chair. It was hard to really read his expression, as his eyes were hidden behind black glasses.

"None for yourself?"

"Doctor's orders."

"I recall prescribing half a glass a day, if you were so inclined," Maddox said, taking a sip of his brandy.

"I am not inclined the night my daughter is entering society."

"Perhaps you should be. It will make the night more bearable," Dr. Maddox said. "The night Emily was presented at court I was terrified – and proud, mind you. She was very beautiful." It was an unspoken story that Emily had come out at quite a young age mainly because her father's sight was in rapid decline. "I am sure Anne will impress the crowd, as much or little as that pleases you."

"Both, I suppose. But mainly the latter, depending on their intentions," Darcy said, returning to his seat to take up his tea and some notes he had to finish before the evening. "You don't mind if I write? I am very happy to have your company. We have not seen each other since –" He knew he was to say Emily's first Season, but he couldn't bring himself to finish the sentence as soon as he said the word 'seen.'

But Dr. Maddox just smiled again. "And there we have it! I think everyone is more upset than I am."

"To be perfectly honest, Maddox, you seem positively jovial."

"To be blind? No," he said. "To have the terrible weight, which has been on my shoulders since I was a boy, of the worry about *going* blind lifted? Yes. No, I will not literally see my sons or daughter marry, but many parents aren't even present, and I shall be happy for the honor. I simply had no idea how much that fear drove all of my other thoughts. And now it's gone. I have nothing to do but laugh at other people when they say something around me that they think offends me." Dr. Maddox raised his glass before taking another a sip. "As for the other elephant in the room, Danny's condition is considered very stable in comparison to mine. He's worn spectacles now for two years with no further degrading and no cataracts. It is the assessment of the head of optometry at the University of St. Andrews, where the medical school has a decent staff beyond their anatomist, that he may just have myopia for the rest of his life, the same way someone is farsighted for the whole of their life. In that, we have been very lucky." He continued, "Speaking of children, Geoffrey seems to be doing well in University, in general and health-wise."

"Yes," Darcy said. "Be careful around him. He reads lips better than he will admit to."

"And my hearing is much improved. So be careful around the both of us, especially if we should decide to team up." Dr. Maddox reached over and found the table, where he set his drink down. "Between the two of us, we should be able to determine every whispered comment about how lovely your daughter looks tonight. And speaking of which, I shall take no more of your time, Mr. Darcy." He had risen before Darcy could get to him. "I will see you in a few hours, Darcy."

"Doctor."

~~~

Chatton House was a madhouse for its own reasons. As the Kincaids, the Fitzwilliams, the Townsends, and the Bradleys were all staying at Pemberley for the course of their visit, Mr. Bingley was charged with playing host to his sister, his brother-in-law (as Mr. Hurst was just coming out of mourning for Louisa), children, and relatives.

Accustomed to having many children to get out the door, Charles Bingley was ready early. He paused in front of the mirror as his manservant ran a lint brush over the coat one last time. "I do believe I've gotten old," he said to Jane as she entered. It was a hard statement to refute. His hair was graying, there were lines in his smile where there had not been previously, and there was the small matter of having two daughters of marriageable age and a son in University, with another soon to follow.

"I failed to notice," Jane said, "as you've hardly been acting the part. The day you retreat to your study with a glass of wine and a book instead of making conversation with your wife, I will declare you old."

"A fair bargain," he said, stepping off the platform and kissing her on the cheek. "How bad is it?" He gestured toward to door to indicate the situation in the rest of the house.

"Your heir has gone through three different outfits now, no one has heard from Brian or Nadezhda, and they are still trying to figure out *something* to do with Georgie's hair."

"By the established standards, we are doing well, then."

"Yes."

"And Lady Littlefield?"

Georgiana's friend from school was paying a visit and had been invited to the ball. Heather Littlefield seemed a fine young woman, and the Bingleys were glad to encourage Georgie to have at least one normal friendship. "She is fine," Jane answered. "She is helping with the Georgiana situation."

"So it is a *situation*."

"*Someone* apparently told her to try to put it up."

Bingley wrung his hands. "...And?"

"And then our beloved samurai brother-in-law suggested wax, as that is apparently how the Japanese maintain their hairstyles."

"But that's if –"

"And apparently we did not know the right kind of wax to be used on hair, and – Well, indulge me on one thing."

Bingley smiled. "Anything."

21

"I want to see the look on your face when you see it."

He could have reacted, but the door was open and Georgie's lady's-maid came rushing in. "Oh Mr. Bingley, sir, I am so sorry – I didn't want to burn her, and we had to get the wax out, and Her Highness said she didn't know a way –"

"I'm sure it will be fine," he said, and with one final nudge of his waistcoat, he followed her into Georgiana's chambers, where the already-dressed Lady Littlefield and various female servants curtseyed.

Georgiana rose from her dressing station and curtseyed to her father. "For the record, I wanted to leave it the way it was."

In recent years, Georgie had kept her hair exceptionally short, with the longest locks reaching only her ears, but now it was barely more than shaven. They'd done their best to style what was left, and their efforts were admirable.

"For Sarah's ball, if Darcy ever lets her out, we will cede to your authority," he said, and laughed. She did still manage to look beautiful – the rest of her certainly was. All of the girls were wearing white now, and nothing but, but it could be tastefully done, with the proper gloves and the unusual locket necklace around her neck. Bingley bowed politely to their guest. "Lady Littlefield." He excused himself, to be off to the next disaster, and was halted by the passing of a man he hardly knew. "Is that –"

Brian Maddox turned around. "Yes, I do remember how to dress properly," he said, putting a hand on his hip. Brian was, for the first time in recent memory, in proper evening attire, with a tight cravat, matching vest and coat, and even breeches. More importantly, he was sword-less – probably. "I promised Darcy."

"I imagine."

"Will you testify to my attire?"

"Testify?"

Brian knocked on the door he had stopped in front of, and it opened, to the protests of some servants inside. Daniel Maddox stood in the doorframe, one hand clutching it. "Yes?"

"Bingley, tell him."

"What?" Bingley said, distracted by the fact that Dr. Maddox wasn't wearing his glasses. "Oh, yes. Doctor Maddox, your brother is indeed an Englishman again. He looks quite fine."

"Glad to hear it," the doctor said with a smile. What Caroline had said in private was right, Bingley noticed – his gaze was unsettling. His pupils had settled looking upwards no matter where he might be inclined to look, and his eyes were cloudy from the cataracts, making the irises appear almost red. "Now, if we're all done being proud of a man in his fifties for being able to dress himself properly, I'd like to finish getting ready."

"I love you, too, Danny," Brian said, and the doctor smiled and closed the door.

~~~

"Why is it that fathers are more emotional than mothers about bringing their daughters out into society?" Elizabeth Darcy mused as she checked her bonnet last time. "I am the one who must fret over assuring her a good marriage."

"If we could not use 'daughter' and 'marriage' in the same sentence, I would be very appreciative," Darcy said. "Even by implication. I do recall you were ready to weep when Geoffrey left for Eton." He pulled her in front of him and kissed her gently on the forehead, so as not to disturb either of their carefully prepared outfits. "Besides, Anne will not worry for a good marriage."

"There is more to a marriage than a large inheritance."

"It is a very good start."

The high-pitched squealing in the hallway meant his younger girls were having their own start to the festivities. "Papa!"

He gave Elizabeth a nervous smile and opened the door to Cassandra, now twelve. "Yes?"

"Mrs. Annesley says Anne is ready."

"That doesn't mean I am," he said quietly as he followed his daughter down the hallway to his eldest's chambers. There on a stand, surrounded by her two sisters and Isabella Wickham, was Anne Jane Darcy, now seventeen and beautiful. Her brown hair, his shade, was so neatly put up it looked like nothing could take it down without ruining a masterpiece.

"Papa," she said. Even on the stand, she was still looking up to him, but not quite so much. "Mrs. Annesley says you shouldn't wear bracelets over gloves but –"

"But you want to wear your bracelet," Darcy said. "Well, you're a lady now. You may make your own clothing decisions – within reason."

The gold band sat nicely on her white gloves. "Did Grandmama really wear it?"

"To be honest, I have no idea. I found it among my father's personal effects. He may have given it to her and kept it with him after she died, he may have not. Either way, it was meant for someone's darling Anne," he said. Inscribed on the bracelet was 'To my darling Anne,' and it had been among his father's items in the old d'Arcy mansion in France, so he must have traveled with it, as a keepsake. "You were born just after we discovered it." That seemed so impossibly long ago, and yet he could remember it perfectly.

"Papa! Don't cry."

"I have something in my eye," he said, regaining his demeanor. "I believe your mother wishes to see you, and I've learned not to keep her waiting," he said and kissed his daughter on the cheek as Elizabeth entered, casting him a reassuring glance before turning her attentions to her daughter.

~~~

The evening came despite all the master of Pemberley's wishes that it would not, and Geoffrey Darcy found himself at ease in comparison to the rest of his family. All of the ladies in the house were busy with his mother obsessing over the last minute preparations of Anne's attire, and if there was any truth to Uncle Bingley's jokes (which there usually was), his father was off cleaning the last of his weaponry. The future master of Pemberley rarely made a clothing decision in his life, and when he did it was often terribly done, so he was dressed by his man-servant, and that was that. The only one to talk to was George Wickham, who was engrossed in a book in the library. He sat in Mr. Bennet's seat, as Mr. Bennet said he had never cared for balls as a father and now claimed the right of the elderly to avoid them entirely and was to stay upstairs with the younger children.

Restless, Geoffrey paced a bit while George continued to unintentionally ignore him, played with the fire, and then finally poured himself a glass of brandy.

"Just keep pouring," said Frederick Maddox from behind. The Chatton House party was apparently arriving. "I'd better be soused by ten if I'm to make it through this whole evening."

"Why? There'll be girls here."

"Too many of them my relatives," Frederick said, taking his own glass. "Well, not technically. Anyway, cheers." They clinked glasses.

"Congratulations on your graduation."

"Yes, I finally made it through Eton. I surprise even myself sometimes." He smiled with his usual rakish grin. "I wish I could go somewhere other than Cambridge. Just because it's expected. My first year away from home, and my father lives down the street."

"Just don't attend his lectures and you'll hardly see him," Geoffrey suggested. "Unless you are interested in medicine?"

"God, no."

"I like medicine," George said, announcing his presence rather abruptly to the room.

"Lot of good it did you at Oxford."

"I did just fine at Oxford," George said neutrally, not looking up from his book. "I was cum laude when I was dismissed."

"Are we ever going to get that story?"

"It's not polite to ask," said Charles Bingley the Third, entering and nodding to each of his cousins. "Geoffrey. Frederick. George."

"Want something?" Geoffrey offered.

"Yes." Charles nervously scratched his blond hair, thereby ruining the styling. "Chatton's a madhouse."

"*Chatton* is a madhouse? What about here? Have you *seen* my father lately?"

"My father hasn't," Frederick said, and Geoffrey snorted into his glass, Charles colored, and George buried himself in his book.

"I'm damned for laughing at that," Geoffrey said. "And you're double damned for saying it."

"You can't be *double* damned. There isn't a *double* hell. Besides, it's true."

"You're cruel," Charles said.

"What was cruel was being woken by all of the servants screaming at your sister," Frederick countered. "Though it was quite a riot."

"Eliza or Georgie?" Geoffrey said.

"Do you need to ask?"

"Oh," Geoffrey said. "Yes, I heard. I've not seen the evidence."

"Well, you won't. They're making her wear a wig."

Almost on cue, the door opened, and despite the very masculine sanctuary quality of the library, Georgiana Bingley entered, her hair pinned up beautifully for the ball, the trimmings of her dress subtly matching her green eyes. "Charles, whatever it is, stop blushing."

He wrung his hands. "You know I can't help it."

"Fred. George. Geoffrey," she curtseyed, and they bowed to her.

"I do, to be perfectly honest, think your hair looks very nice tonight, cousin," Frederick said. "Odd that it's a completely different shade of red from the normal shade. How did you manage that?"

"Just continue drinking until you pass out, Frederick, for all of us."

"Nice. And I was trying to be polite."

"You were failing," she said.

"It does – look nice," Geoffrey mumbled into his tumbler.

"Thank you," she said in sort of a half-grumble, half-appreciative tone. Frederick just snorted into his glass, Charles squirmed, and George rolled his eyes. In their families, it was impossible to not know that Geoffrey and Georgie were still barely on speaking terms.

"Is my sister almost ready?" Geoffrey asked.

"I wouldn't know," she replied, taking a glass of brandy from the table. "I am not going anywhere near four screaming girls, even if they are cousins."

"If I didn't know you better, I would say you have no heart," Frederick said.

"Good thing you do know me, then," she replied, "or I would say you'll be heading to the ball with a black eye."

If Frederick had a response, it was cut off by the bell. The guests were arriving, and that meant the ball was about to begin.

CHAPTER 3

The Dance

Anne Darcy, the first of three very beautiful and very eligible (and very wealthy) daughters of the Darcys of Pemberley, entered society in grand style. The ball was the event of the summer, even though it was held at Pemberley and not London, with a guest list restricted to people Darcy trusted. Families with summer houses often ill-used suddenly opened them for the summer. Even the Duke of Devonshire made a rare appearance in this part of his vast empire of English land to see how the other half of Derbyshire was doing.

She did not lack for dance partners; some were relatives (Charles Bingley the Third, who loved to dance and danced every set) and some not.

"Mama," Anne whispered, "ask Papa to stop glaring at every man who approaches me!"

Elizabeth laughed. "He's just being a father, dear. There little to do about it." She added, "Your grandpapa did the same for me. Now ignore him and go dance!"

But her husband had a good ear and snuck up behind her. "I have trouble imagining Mr. Bennet with a stern look on his face."

"Oh, he did, for me at least." She hadn't been invited when Jane came out, of course, but at her first assembly, her father was staring daggers into the hearts of any man who approached his favorite daughter. She didn't recall that so much for her younger sisters, but it had been that way for her.

"He knew what a prize you were," Darcy said with a smile.

"Mr. Darcy, you've now taken your eyes off your daughter for three seconds; she is already *waltzing* with the biggest rake in the county." When he simply *had* to look, she laughed.

On the other side of the room, Frederick and Geoffrey were spying on a pair of ladies who were whispering some distance away. "What are they saying?" Frederick asked.

"They're ... trying to determine which one of us is the Darcy heir," he said, focusing on their faces. "And who the other one is and if he's worth anything. Also, they suspect he may be a fop."

"You made that part up!"

"How do you know?" Geoffrey said. "All right, now they're wondering why I'm staring at them. I think we might actually have to dance."

"The blonde one's mine," Frederick said. "I'll pay you a sovereign to say I'm Mr. Darcy."

"Not for a quid, Maddox," he said and flagged the house manager Mr. Hawthorn (the M.C. for the evening) to introduce them. Geoffrey had no desire to dance, and as a student was not obligated, but this was his sister's debut, and his father demanded at least one dance of him. His partner was a dark-haired girl named Miss Hyde, but he made little conversation and learned little of her. He bowed perfunctorily and went back to his corner after the dance, only to find a scowling George watching his sister make conversation with the son of an earl.

"Tell me what he's saying," George demanded.

Geoffrey turned and focused on the pair in the distance, Izzy and Viscount Something-or-Other. "He's asked her to elope with him tonight, shortly before dinner."

"I'm in no mood for silliness, Darcy."

He rolled his eyes. "Fine. He asked her if she preferred the country over life in Town, and she said she had not decided. Am I to be everyone's spy tonight?"

"No. Dr. Maddox is doing his own share."

Dr. Maddox had not retreated like some of the other disabled or aged gentlemen to the card rooms. He took a seat out of the way of the floor as his wife danced with his brother. Brian and Caroline were both partner-less; Princess Nadezhda did not make public appearances unless begged, and certainly not to dance. The doctor settled in and focused on a couple of young men making conversation not far from where he sat, leaning on his cane.

"Which one is the cousin?"

"There are two cousins. The Bingleys."

"What, the tradesman at Chatton House?"

"Yes. Georgiana and Eliza. I don't know which is which, but they're both out," said the other young man. "I heard they each have fifty thousand pounds."

"For fifty thousand I would marry a tradesman's daughter," the other one said. "What about her? The one with red hair?"

"Please. That is obviously a wig."

"No! The other one. In that nice little bodice and yellow ribbons."

"Oh yes. Very lovely. What I wouldn't give for –"

Dr. Maddox interjected quietly, "That is Emily Maddox."

"Who's she?" said the first man.

"My daughter."

At that point they made no more conversation, at least not within earshot. In fact, he could positively hear them scurry away despite the noise of the dance.

"What are you laughing at?" his wife said, the dance now finished.

"Just enjoying eavesdropping on the brash young men in the crowd."

Caroline brushed her hand over his hair. "Sometimes I think you like being blind."

"It has its moments."

She leaned over and kissed him. "Mr. Darcy has offered to take some time away from following his daughter around with a shotgun to dance a set with me, if that meets your approval."

"Anything that makes you happy meets my approval."

On the opposite side, Jane leaned in to her husband. "Who is Eliza dancing with?"

"I believe that is ... Lord Brougham's son."

"She's danced two dances with him."

"As long as she stops there. At least it wasn't the first two."

"Some men like to show their affection by dancing with a woman twice at the first meeting."

He blushed at the reminder of their own long-ago meeting. "Well, he's Lord Brougham's son. It's not the end of the world. Besides, Charles has danced every dance and you haven't said anything."

"Because he dances with anyone. You know he just likes to dance."

"He is his father's son."

"Yes, setting lady's hearts dangerously aflutter while he's still ineligible."

"Are you going to discourage two of our children from dancing *at a ball* and then also comment on how Georgie hasn't accepted one offer?"

Jane smiled. "I suppose you've caught me on that one."

Georgiana was busy retreating to the corner where George and Geoffrey were standing. "Is this the hiding corner?"

"Only men are allowed to scowl away potential partners," George said.

"Besides, we're ineligible. Cap before the cradle and all that."

"Well, you won't be in a year, unless you're going for a Fellowship, Mr. Darcy. And if you think every girl in this room doesn't know that, you are fooling yourself."

"I assure you, I am aware," he grumbled.

"He's been reading lips all night," George said. "You would be surprised what people will say behind your back. Or just a certain distance away."

"I think I've strained my eyes. I have a splitting headache coming on, and we're still an hour from dinner and possible wine. And many hours from quiet."

"So I suppose we'll all be spoilsports together, then," George said.

Georgiana rolled her eyes. "Unfortunately, my father said I was obligated for one dance, and Charles is *always busy*, the flirt."

"He doesn't talk to them, so it barely counts as flirting," George said.

"If you are under such stringent obligations..." Geoffrey said, "May I have the next dance, Miss Bingley?"

"Are you serious?"

"I am."

After a long moment, she realized that he truly was serious. "You may." She curtseyed, he bowed, and she stepped toward the dance floor.

Geoffrey turned to George, who was smirking. "Well, at least it got the only smile out of you that will probably be seen this evening. Do I look all right?"

"How should I know? Ask the man who dressed you."

Geoffrey just gave his jacket a tug and followed Georgie. He could have been paying attention to the people who were staring at him, but he was too busy worrying about what he was doing, and hoping that she wouldn't notice his hands were shaking when they touched. The dance began. He knew all the steps without thinking, which was quite good, because his brain wasn't doing a lot of that.

"Your palms are sweating," Georgie said as they crossed.

"How did you know? I'm wearing gloves."

"Because you just confirmed it," she said with a little smirk. She hadn't given him a pleasant little smirk in two years.

Maybe he ought to dance with her more often.

"Are we supposed to converse while dancing?"

"I don't know," he answered. "You've danced more than I have."

"I've never had anything to say."

"Ridiculous," Geoffrey said, though he took the last turn a little too quickly, and he blinked to steady himself. "You always have something to say."

"All right, I've never had anything polite to say."

"Ah, the key difference."

They separated for the last time and took their positions. He bowed to her, but not very well. The dance was too fast for him, and he was too distracted. "Excuse me." And he left the ballroom.

"Did you see that?" Elizabeth said, pulling Darcy away from his current focus on where his daughter was going and whom she was speaking to.

"See what?"

"Our young Mr. Darcy danced with Miss Bingley. By choice!"

"That can't be. He can't stand her prattling. And he only dances when forced," he said. He turned his eyes fully away from his daughter for the first time in the evening, and towards his wife. "My, how he's changed."

~~~

Geoffrey Darcy made his excuses and did not return for the dinner. Darcy had been as careful with the seating arrangements as he had been with everything else, so that Anne was surrounded by family and not overeager bachelors. "I had no idea dancing was so exhausting!" she whispered to her mother.

"Then you haven't done enough of it," Elizabeth said. "But don't tell your father I said that."

Pemberley's food was only the finest, and it brought out the older crowd from the card rooms with exceptional speed. Then there was the white soup followed by the entertainment, which included some lovely playing of the pianoforte by

Eliza Bingley, games of whist and casino, and a chance for some gentlemen to smoke on the veranda. It was then that Anne finally had the chance to sneak away, bypassing her sisters, who were eager to talk to her, and open the door to Geoffrey's room.

He was lying on the floor with a pillow under his head, with only a single candle high on the shelf lighting the room. He stirred at the light from the hallway and the figure at the door. "What is it?"

"I came to see if you're all right."

"Anne! This is *your* ball."

"And you're *my* brother." She knelt next to him. "Are you going to be all right?"

"In the morning, I'll be fine. It was the last spin that got me. I should have picked a slower dance."

"It would have been more romantic."

"Hush! You're out five hours and suddenly you're all smart."

Anne smiled. "Feel better."

"I will."

"I'll send George up, if you want. He needs the excuse."

"You don't have –" but she was already gone, "– to."

~~~

A few minutes later, Geoffrey was disturbed again from his meditative attempts to stabilize his head. "Sorry. They sent the wrong George," Georgiana Bingley said in the doorframe.

"You're not angry with me?"

"For what?"

"For walking out immediately after our dance. I thought you might think I was running away." Geoffrey didn't want to say, *again*.

"It's rather easy to tell when your eyes cross," she said. "I shouldn't have pushed you."

"Pushed me? I requested the dance. And I had already appeased my parents' dancing requirements for the evening."

Georgie looked at her feet. "I should get back to the feast. After all, I must be chaperoned, lest my reputation be marred."

"If anyone thinks less of you as a woman for your perfect behavior as a dancer and your beautiful gown, as well as not being a gossiping chit, I will be very surprised." He added, "And I would be inclined to hit them, but I don't think I can get up right now."

"I'll delay my insults to society and propriety, then. Good night, Geoffrey. Feel better."

"Good night," he said, dreaming even though he was still awake.

~~~

Long after dinner and many card games, the festivities began to wind down, and mothers began to rein in their unruly and possibly tipsy sons before they embarrassed themselves, as everyone did at a good ball. As Anne's many new admirers drifted away, back into their carriages and gigs, Darcy began to relax, and shared a glass of wine with Bingley while the crowd finished up their card games.

"Well, brother, I think you succeeded in being sufficiently terrifying," Georgiana Kincaid said to Darcy, taking a seat beside him on the settee. "I remember thinking that you were delighted at my coming out ball."

"I was just as nervous, I assure you," Darcy said.

"And now, the court presentation," Lord Richard Fitzwilliam Matlock said.

"That's hardly anything. Quite brief, actually. And I don't think the king will be paying much attention."

"How is the king?"

Bingley kicked the leg of Dr. Bertrand's chair at the table, getting his attention. "How is His Majesty?"

Dr. Andrew Bertrand, now one of many staff attending the increasingly fat and ill king of

England, Scotland, and Ireland, said, "All I will say is the papers are not lying in their descriptions."

"You're as bad as Maddox!"

"What?" Brian said from over the din. "Whatever it is, I wasn't responsible."

"You weren't," his brother said. "They were talking about me. I treated the king when he was a bit less of a public laughingstock."

"More of a laughingstock and less pathetic!" Mr. Hurst proclaimed between drinks.

"Now, there's some sympathy to be had for a man who is stuck with a horrible wife, has lost his only daughter, and is still responsible for running the most powerful kingdom in the world," Dr. Maddox said. "I would offer up a kingdom *not* to be him, and instead be a well-paid physician and professor who is only obligated to teach one lecture a year."

"Hear, hear!" Bingley said and raised his glass.

~~~

Meanwhile, Anne's young male relatives, who had no other business at the close of the ball, had gathered again on the porch to pass around a bottle of excellent brandy.

"I thought you didn't start drinking again until your first lecture," Georgie said, joining the three of them with a shawl wrapped around her to shield her from the evening breeze.

"It's not all fun and games, you know," Charles defended, however meekly, as he passed her the bottle, which she took a gulp from. "The exams are in Latin. *And* Greek."

"Did they teach you the classics in that fancy seminary of yours?" Frederick asked.

"Are you serious? Those are hardly appropriate studies for a lady. Our small minds are not capable of grasping the complexities of dead languages and are more suited to think like living ones, *Maddok-Yarichin.*"

"What did she call me?" Frederick said to Charles.

He shrugged. "I don't understand Japanese. I can only recognize it."

"What good are you, then? I'll have to find someone else. What did you say again?"

"Are you crazy?" Georgiana said. "I'm not repeating it."

"That bad?" George said with a smile. "So what did the ladies have to say about us tonight?"

"Mainly, they discussed how much you were worth," she said. "Charles, they think you have about ten thousand a year. Frederick, they have no idea, but you're the son of a knight and the second cousin of an earl, so their fathers would approve. George, they couldn't believe how you just stood there silently when there were ladies waiting to dance. How rude!"

He shrugged unapologetically.

"The ladies do seem to have one-track minds," Frederick said, as if he was making a great observation.

"I would say that of men," George said, "but it's a different track."

~~~

At long last, when all of the guests except the very closest family had departed and many of the ladies had gone to bed, Mr. Bennet hobbled his way downstairs and joined them for a glass of port. "So then ... another thing I never thought I would be present for." He raised his glass to that and sipped.

"To a long life, Mr. Bennet," Darcy said, and they clinked glasses.

"Yes, I may even be so lucky as to see all my beautiful grandchildren *marry*," he said just as Darcy was trying to swallow. Darcy choked, of course, and lapsed into a coughing fit before he recovered. "Do be careful with your drink, Mr. Darcy. You never know when life will surprise you."

CHAPTER 4

Summer in London

Anne's formal presentation at court was a delightfully short affair. As predicted, the king took little interest in the matter and waved them through with the other girls who were declaring their stake on the polite world. From there they returned to Derbyshire, where the Darcy family as a whole would remain until Geoffrey left for Cambridge in October.

The official Season was well over, and those in Town were there for social calls and private balls or because they lived there. The Bingleys and the Maddoxes had entered the phase of their lives when Town could not be avoided, with eligible daughters that needed chaperoning and elder brothers who were often unavailable to do it. Jane, Edmund, and Charles the Third stayed at Chatton House, but Mr. Bingley was in Town, mainly for business, but also because he did not want to leave all of the care of his daughters to Dr. Maddox or George Wickham. Georgiana eased the burden by immediately taking off to Ireland for a few weeks, as she was quite fond of doing. Elizabeth Bingley, however, was a proper socialite and had friends in Town to call on and receive in the townhouse. Eliza, Emily Maddox, and Isabel Wickham were all about the same age and would often go to little assemblies and dances together, which only required one chaperone for all three girls. Since Dr. Maddox admitted he was useless for much beyond introductions, the duty fell to Bingley. He could have a trusted servant do it, but this was his daughter, and these were his nieces. He was not suspect of every friend they made, and none of them were serious about marriage yet, but they were dancing with men and learning the language of Town society, and he was going to oversee that.

When he wasn't available, George was there to take his place. George's Fellowship had no formal declaration, but he was informally apprenticed to Dr. Maddox, setting his sights on a medical career. Dr. Maddox insisted George needed clinical practice, and so George spent his days at clinics in observation and his nights following his sister to private balls. The busy schedule made him rather grumpy after a few weeks.

"Why does no one at these balls see me as a chaperone instead of a bachelor? Must I write 'Fellow' on my forehead?" he said to his Uncle Bingley one night.

"If you're not in your gown, you're not a Fellow as far as they're concerned. And they just want to dance."

"I don't want to dance. I want to watch my sister dance."

"Well," Bingley said with a sigh, "you could try dying your hair grey. That might throw them off."

Isabel loved dancing, and George loved to indulge her. Her experience standing at the altar in Gretna Green at fifteen had taught her caution, and she readily thanked her brother for his intervention. If anything, it gave her a few more years to be silly and worry about balls and gowns and ribbons and who asked her to dance and how many times. Marriage was a serious business.

On more than one occasion, George was tempted to ask Mr. Bradley to go in his stead, as Mr. Bradley was fully obligated to watch over his step-daughter, but it was not a reasonable expectation. George genuinely liked his stepfather, but he knew that he was too easily influenced by his mother, resulting in the mess in Scotland that almost ruined Isabel's life. So George didn't ask.

"George! It's not polite to fall asleep on Mr. Hart's stairs!"

He opened his eyes. "What? Oh, right." He managed a false smile for his sister.

"Do you want to go home?"

"I'm all right."

"I've had enough. Three sets are enough. We can go."

"Was it all with the same man?"

"Of course not! Though it could have been, with you nodding off like that. Why didn't you tell me you were tired?"

George didn't tell her he wasn't sleeping well. She didn't need it. He was the protector. Isabel was his responsibility, because no one else was there to take it, though there were moments when he wished someone would. There were people he could write to for help, but he didn't want to disturb Uncle Darcy, or further burden Uncle Bingley or Lady Maddox.

He requested a lightened schedule at the clinics and it was granted. Eliza and Isabel could be very persuasive, and he agreed to even dance, and not slight the ladies when men were short, as they increasingly were as the shooting season arrived. He danced several times with a lady named Miss Habersham, who seemed persistent despite his constant mentioning that he was not looking for a serious attachment.

~~~

"I thought gentlemen were called gentlemen because they did not have to work?"

Estelle teasingly asked George as he buttoned up his vest. "You've done it wrong."

"I may be a bit distracted," he said, noticing that he had indeed missed the first button and would have to do them all over again. She crawled over to his side of the bed and did it for him, which seemed to amuse her. He kissed her as thanks (beyond the payment left on the dresser). "Having a sister in society *is* work." And work it was. He'd cut back to two appointments a week at Harcourt. He had the time (he always managed to find time when he wanted to) but he lacked the energy. "And now women are courting *me*."

"You say that like it is such a terrible tragedy," she said, the 'is' a more pronounced 'izzz' with her French accent. He did like a courtesan with a French accent. It made the association seem more sophisticated. "Being a wanted bachelor."

"I don't like it." He felt like he could say that to her. Not that he wanted to make his regular courtesan his confidant, but something about sharing the most intimate physical process with a woman (repeatedly) made him a bit more open about non-physical intimacy. "I don't trust them."

"Not to trust a woman? That is a very important lesson to learn, *Monsieur Wickham*, and it seems you have already learned it."

Her joke put a smile on his face, but an uneasy one it was.

~~~

On Friday they attended yet another private ball, George dressed in his best outfit to escort his sister, only to discover, to his horror, that the hosts were none other than Mr. and Mrs. Habersham, parents of the young lady who had been so persistent that he had given in and danced with her. They were respectable members of society, but nonetheless not the people he wanted to be talking to. There were plenty of other people there, but George retreated into a corner and then into the library as soon as he found it. He was not just tired and irritated, but he was also nervous. He knew it because his hands were shaking when he poured himself whatever beverage was in a leftover pot; it turned out to be very sweet but cold tea.

"Mr. Wickham, I presume."

The voice that surprised him came from the person he had dreaded speaking to—his host. He bowed. "You presume correctly, Mr. Habersham."

"I've heard much about you, Mr. Wickham. Your father was not George Wickham, was he?"

Wondering if this would actually put the host's obvious intentions off, he said, "Yes, he was. My Christian name is also George."

"Well, well, enough of that," Mr. Habersham said, taking a seat. George hid his hands behind his back and stood by the window, occasionally looking out. "It seems you are a very mysterious person to my daughter."

"I believe I have made my…lack of intentions very clear."

"You have a living but intend on an academic career. Purely for your own amusement, I assume?"

"No, sir. I intend to become a physician, if I pass my exams. I've no intention of being an idle gentleman." If it would be taken as an insult, so be it. He didn't know how else to phrase it.

"A most noble endeavor. I know few men who've seen it through."

George just shrugged.

"I also understand you live with you family on Gracechurch Street."

He frowned. "Mr. Habersham, to be blunt, will you tell me where your conversation is heading? I apologize, but I am here to chaperone my younger sister, and I am remiss in my duties at the moment."

"She is quite well, I assure you. But if you wish to be so blunt about it, then we very well shall. My daughter has thirty thousand pounds, as you've probably discovered through your own channels.

Combined with your fortune, your family could do very well –"

"Money," George said, horrified but not surprised. "Is that all marriage is to you?"

"Of course not! Young men these days; so serious. That is only the practical side of the question. My daughter is smitten with you."

"I can't imagine why."

"Perhaps you are more likeable than you believe yourself to be, George."

He didn't like this conversation. He didn't like being called by his Christian name, and he had decided that he didn't like Mr. Habersham, to say nothing for his daughter. "With all due respect, Mr. Habersham, I thank you for a lovely evening, but I will be taking my leave now."

"Mr. Wickham! Surely the proposal –"

He stopped in the doorway. "A *proposal* is when I, after courting your daughter for some time after your permission, make her an offer of marriage of my own free will and desire. Not a meeting in a library. I apologize if I did not clarify that earlier, but now I believe we are on the same page. Good evening, Mr. Habersham."

His host had more to say, but George tuned it out and left the room as quickly as he could. He encountered none other than Miss Habersham in the hallway and, not remembering her Christian name, he bid her adieu in the most formal way, to show her he truly meant goodbye. The precise wording was lost on him later, because it was all a blur until he found Isabel, who thankfully was the only member of his family at the event, and pulled her aside.

"George! What's wrong?"

"We're leaving," he said. She was about to protest, he could see. "Can you please just do what I say?"

She nodded, hearing in his tone how important it was that she obey this one time. She trusted him. And with no proper good-byes, they took their leave. It was still early, but there would be no more socializing for the evening. George retreated to his room in the Gracechurch Street house, slamming the door behind him, and began to pace. How could Mr. Habersham possibly – no! He didn't want to hear that name again. He wanted to strike it from his mind. He would. He tried.

But he just couldn't.

~~~

For the first time in recent memory, George pleaded illness to Isabel's next request and asked that she find another chaperone – even Mr. Bradley would do, if Mr. Bingley was not in town (he wasn't). She had been hesitant in asking, knowing what a mood her brother had been in recently. She even put up with it a second time. He did not leave his room, except to go to the clinic and watch too many people be cut up and then die. He watched it with a morbid fascination and then went home, washed himself, and climbed into bed long before he found sleep. Some nights he didn't find it at all.

When his schoolbooks failed him, he pulled out his old favorites, some of them worn from years of use. He was only a quarter into Malory's first book when there was a knock on the door. "Come in."

Of course, it was Isabel. Neither of his parents had come near him in a week. She shut the door, and inquired as to his health and then caught him on his series of obvious lies. She knew him too well, and it irritated him.

"What about that girl you liked? Miss Habersham –"

"I didn't like her!" he said. "She just wants my money."

"You talked to her, even danced with her!"

"She's –" He broke off and put his hands over his head again. "Forget it."

"George."

"I said forget it!" he shouted, and Isabel stepped back. George never shouted. He seemed horrified at his outburst, and sunk further into the chair's cushions. "I apologize for my behavior."

"You do not have to apologize," she said softly, taking a seat on his bed. "Tell me what happened." Reassuringly she added, "You can tell me."

"We made conversation. To be fair, multiple times."

"I know, I saw. And you danced with her," she reminded him encouragingly.

"Yes. I suppose that says something." He sighed. "But despite it, I came to my conclusions through conversation with her and some very forward conversations with her father. While there may be some ... inherently good qualities in Miss Habersham, I do not want to spend the rest of my life with her. I didn't know how to tell her. I told her I was a Fellow, not interested in matrimony. I told her I had no intention of leaving Cambridge before passing the Tripos exams. There were so many ways –" George buried his face in his hands again. "I can't do this, Izzy."

"You can. Your only fault is your poor esteem of yourself."

"I can't play the game of society, going to these balls and making conversation with these people who look at me and wonder how much I'm worth and when I will be available– it's bad enough when they look at you, my baby sister. At least then I can stop them. Or try to look at them reasonably.

But I can't –" He put his hands down and shook his head.

She put her hand over his, which was now desperately clutching the wooden arm of the chair. "Fine. We won't go to any more balls and I'll talk to Miss Hab –"

"There's no need. I can assure you, she will not be pursuing me any longer, and let us leave it at that."

She decided to. Whatever he had said, it was bad enough. "No matter what, you're exhausted. I'll retire for the winter. I'll go to Chesterton in December and stay with Emily and Lady Maddox."

His eyes seemed to glitter with hope. "You should not put yourself in a position –"

"*George*," she said, "your health is more important than my social calendar."

"It shouldn't be."

"Of course it should. You're my brother," Isabel said. "But promise me you'll talk to Uncle Darcy."

"Uncle Darcy is busy enough."

"When has he ever been too busy for you?"

He just looked away, having no proper answer.

"At least talk to Dr. Maddox, then. As his student, you're obligated. And I doubt he's failed to notice it –"

"Why would you say that?"

"Because he's not blind," Isabel said, and then covered her mouth. "All right, he *is* blind, but you know –"

"– what was meant, yes," he said, cracking a weak smile. "I will talk to Dr. Maddox."

"Good." She hugged him. "You're my brother. You should not have to suffer."

"It is not your decision."

"I can at least try," she said, before turning on her heels and leaving him alone with his thoughts.

~~~

George waited until he was announced to invade Dr. Maddox's study. "Dr. Maddox."

"George. You're early," the doctor said, quietly dismissing his manservant, who had been reading him the paper when George entered. "Have a seat. My schedule is particularly quiet this morning. Did you breakfast?"

"I had something, yes."

"Good." The doctor sipped his coffee. "What brings you by?"

"I think you already know, Dr. Maddox."

The doctor set his cup down, stood up, and navigated his way to where George was sitting. He put his hand on George's forehead. "No fever, but your skin is rather clammy." He found George's hand. "Your hand is shaking. I assume you are not also covered with lesions?"

"No, sir."

The doctor let out a thoughtful "hmm," as he returned to his seat at the desk. Dr. Maddox was exceptionally good at getting around either of his houses without aid. "So. You've not been sleeping well."

"No."

"What about the sleeping brew?"

"I ... haven't been taking it."

Dr. Maddox didn't judge. Nothing about him looked judgmental. He was calm and relaxed in his chair. He didn't say anything.

The silence finally made George too anxious and he had to jump in, "I can't – I can't sleep with all of these thoughts in my head. Usually I can just dismiss them but –"

"But you won't take the brew."

"No. I know it is foolish. I cannot properly explain my actions, why I am so suspicious of it –"

"I can teach you the ingredients, if you wish to make it yourself," the doctor said. "But that is hardly the point, is it?"

"You treated my uncle, didn't you? After you returned from the Continent?"

Dr. Maddox sighed. "That was years ago, and the circumstances were different. In the years since then I've attempted to come to … some understanding of it, but every psychical doctor says the same nonsense. The mind is still a riddle to us."

George looked down and wrung his hands.

"That said," the doctor continued, "I've always been one for empirical research, and it is my conclusion based on reading various case studies and – well, to be frank, watching your uncle – that there is usually an exacerbating incident immediately preceding a rise in symptoms."

"And the treatments?"

"Hardly the issue, as it has been established that people always seem to get sicker when they apply them. Why I am the only one to come to this conclusion, I have no idea. That is why I restrict myself to the other organs, with which I have more success." He sighed. "With that said, how is the situation at home? And be assured, you may consider this a patient-doctor conversation, not a family question."

"Of course," George said, swallowing. "It's been – all right. I've contributed a bit to keep the place up, but I think it is fair, and Izzy doesn't want to leave because she loves the Bradley children, and Mother loves the help. All things considered, I think I am getting along well with my mother."

"Isabel and Emily are quite close," the doctor said. "They do appreciate your chaperoning them. There are balls and there are *balls*. You are not alone in your fears. Seventeen is not too young to be courted, but I dread the day a man comes to my door and asks my permission to court Emily. Or worse, does *not* ask my permission. These are the sorts of things that keep parents awake at night."

Instinctively, George nodded before answering, "I imagine."

"It is very hard to be a parent, or a brother, to a young lady. Even parenting a brother can be tough. It ruined Brian for many years. I was such a handful in so many ways. I didn't envy him, but I understand it now a bit better than I did at the time. I am sure Darcy will tell you the same thing concerning Lady Kincaid." He continued, "You are doing an exemplary job. You should know that."

"Thank you."

"It does not mean it is right that the entire burden should fall to you, but for Isabel's sake, the whole extended family are grateful. Now that that's all said – have you written to Darcy?"

"Not yet."

"Have you written to Grégoire?"

"I – hadn't thought of it."

"You've never been out of England, have you? I hear the weather is very lovely in Ireland this time of year, and Grégoire has a place on the coast. Miss Bingley is there now, but you may want to write and see if they would be willing to have more visitors. You know your uncle – he always is eager to see you. And your sister."

"Y-You don't mind? That I'd be gone? I promised –"

"I managed without your wonderful assistance for many years, Mr. Wickham. I believe I can manage to do so for a few more months. Just be back by October."

George smiled, genuinely, for the first time in days. "I will."

CHAPTER 5

The Emerald Isle

It took two weeks to arrange, allowing time for communications between Dublin and London, but Grégoire quickly replied to George's letter and said he would be happy to host the Wickhams. The trickier part was telling his parents, but George chose the strategy of telling Mr. Bradley first. George Wickham was one and twenty and under no obligation to give details of his comings and goings, but he was also taking his sister, about whom he owed them at least some explanation.

Mr. Bradley was not necessarily a man to be described as intelligent, but he could be intuitive, especially in the small space that was their home on Gracechurch Street, and he tactfully offered to break the news to Mrs. Bradley on George's behalf. In fact, the efforts were so successful that George and Isabel were out the door with only one painfully awkward reproach about abandoning their family, and their mother mainly used old material to do so, which made it bearable. Last-minute arrangements included a letter from Aunt and Uncle Darcy wishing them the best.

The travel itself was mercifully short, as George quickly discovered that reading on a ship made him nauseous. He had to put his book away and join his sister, who was watching Britain's other island come into view. "It's so green."

"It is called the Emerald Isle."

"Oh no! We forgot to get a birthday present for Patrick!"

He smiled. "That's weeks off. We'll pick something up in Dublin. "

She gave him a friendly tug of the arm. "This mist is a shame. You're so pale, George."

"So are you," he said, brushing off her concern for his health.

"Ladies are supposed to be pale. We are pristine creatures, too gentle for the rough hands of man."

George knew quite a few 'ladies' who had no problems dealing with the rough hands of men. However, none of that knowledge applied to his sister. "Then keep your bonnet on, Miss Wickham, or you might catch a tan from a ray of sunshine and crumble into dust."

Uncle Grégoire was there to greet them at the docks in Dublin. He hugged Isabel and shook George's hand. "It is so wonderful to have you." Grégoire looked the way he always looked – forever in the wrong century with his tunic and silver cross – and he was overjoyed to see them.

"I hope you will find the house to your liking," he said as they climbed into the carriage. "Then again, if my brother finds it suitable, I suppose anyone would." He congratulated George on his fellowship but said nothing in the carriage about their reasons for a sudden trip to Ireland, which George had only hinted at in the letter. Instead he made conversation with Isabel, who told him all about life in London and how the other girls of the family were doing. He knew very little about the Ton but still listened with great interest, giving George the opportunity to nod off. He had no idea how tired he'd been when, safe and secure with his uncle and sister, he could quiet his mind.

He was roused some hours later, when they arrived at a modest-sized country house that was indeed right on the water, only a short walk from the sea. Aunt Bellamont and their cousins Patrick Bellamont and Georgiana Bingley were there to greet them. "I tought we were gonna 'av ter wait al' day," Caitlin Bellamont said to her husband as he kissed her hello. "Patrick! Watch deh horses!"

Patrick, now almost six, had managed to escape his mother's grasp and came running to George, grabbing him around his waist and hugging it tight. "George!"

"Hello, Patrick." When he stepped forward to greet the others, Patrick refused to dislodge himself, like a barnacle on a hull. "You have another cousin here."

But Patrick was less inclined to run to a lady, only looked up and said, "Hello Izzy."

"Hello, Patrick."

"It seems you have something stuck to you, Mr. Wickham," Georgiana Bingley said as she greeted the new arrivals. "Miss Wickham."

"Miss Bingley," George said with a bow. "I imagine he'll eventually get bored and detach."

"Patrick! Yeh git yisser 'ole back 'ere!" Mrs. Bellamont shouted, and Patrick quickly obeyed, but without the slightest indication that he knew he was in any trouble. "Mr. Wickham. Miss Wickham. Welcum ter our home."

"Aunt Bellamont! Thank you so much for having us," Isabel said, embracing her aunt as George bowed and they were shown inside. The Bellamont house was grand by Gracechurch Street standards, but cluttered, especially compared to the stylishly graceful Pemberley, as it was filled with bookcases and portraits of saints.

Normally George felt uncomfortable in new surroundings, but this was his Uncle Grégoire's house, and Grégoire could make anyone comfortable. The familiar smell of leather binding and dusty book covers was also soothing to his particular tastes.

"I shuffled the books around," Grégoire said as George was shown to his room. "The ones to your liking should be in here, but honestly I cannot keep track of my own collection."

George pulled out a heavy tome. It was the second volume of Gibbon's *Decline and Fall of the Roman Empire*, probably an original. "Gregory Darcy," George said, reading the name scribbled on the inside cover.

"Yes. It's from your great-uncle's collection. Most of the books here are, actually. I even found some medical ones, though they may not be quite up to the latest medicinal standards," he said. "Supper is at eight, after Vespers. I go to Mass every morning at seven, though for some reason, all of my Protestant relatives seem reluctant to join me. Otherwise, your time is your own. Miss Bingley will be here for the next few weeks. Oh, and if your sister wishes to swim in the ocean, make sure someone watches her. There is a very strong undertow about twenty feet out."

"I will," George replied, looking out his window at the sea. "Thank you, Uncle Grégoire."

"You do not have to thank me, nephew."

"Well, I wish to, all the same," he said.

~~~

68

There was an easy rhythm to life at the Bellamont House. They had only a few servants, and Mrs. Bellamont spent most of her time cooking or playing with her son. Patrick Bellamont had inherited his mother's outgoing (to be polite about it) nature and his father's kindness, but it made him a handful. He could get away with all sorts of mischief in the presence of his father, who spent the day in prayer, writing, or out in the garden, unless it was one of the days he taught at the local orphanage.

The first night in his new surroundings, George awoke in an alarmed state before remembering where he was. He opened his window and listened to the sound of the ocean and found it quite soothing, so much so that he fell back to sleep in record time. The second night, and nearly every night after that, he slept soundly. As usual, when unsettled, he turned to reading, forcing new thoughts into his mind to replace the old ones, but sometimes he couldn't focus on the pages. At that point he would wander to try to clear his mind, glad for more space than the house at Gracechurch, where there were few halls and where his restlessness would disturb his parents. When he was there, he often left the house altogether, eventually ending up at Harcourt and not returning until early morning, which upset his sister and began the cycle anew – not because she knew where he went (she did not) – but because he was so unsettled and she worried. At Cambridge they locked the doors at nine, but there were plenty of ancient halls to wander and libraries to hole up in.

One night at Bellamont House, he decided to explore the main library, only to find Grégoire at his desk with his pen and ink, no doubt writing his next column. He did not seem disturbed at all by George's presence despite the hour. "Would you like some tea? Or some wine? Or are you a whiskey man? The local brew is very good, I'm told, but I'll always be a Frenchman when it comes to spirits."

"Whiskey, if it's not any trouble."

"No trouble," his uncle said, rising to open the cabinet not far and remove the bottle and a tumbler. "No trouble at all."

"How is a monk so acquainted with liquor?" George said as he sat down in the offered chair and took the whiskey. Grégoire was right; it was quite good.

"In Mon-Claire, where I was a Cistercian novice, their chief product was wine, and I became trained as a professional taster," Grégoire said, returning to his chair. He looked at his notes. "I believe I am finished working for tonight."

"Do you always write at this time?"

"Not always, but I do find it a very peaceful hour, after rising for Vigils," he said. "In other words, it is an hour when my son is asleep." They shared a chuckle. "So – how are you finding Ireland, Mr. Wickham?"

"I rather like it. Despite my energetic young cousin's best efforts, it is very peaceful."

"Yes. Miss Bingley feels the same way, though I believe she looks more for privacy than peace. How I came to be the family's hideaway holder, I will never know, but I am honored. It is a very important position." He took a sip of his tea, or whatever it was in the cup, and continued, "Everyone needs their place of solace, be it in the arms of another person or in actual solitude. Though, as I am not much of a monk after all, I would suggest the former over the latter. Too many extremes can weigh down on a man – or scar him. There are many people in this family who would tell you that. But finding the perfect balance can be very difficult."

"How do you seem to know what I'm thinking?"

"To be perfectly honest, because I know your uncle. So what would drive you away from society so readily is not such a mystery to me."

"But no one knows the cause of it."

"No more than we know the cause of anything related to the mind."

George had to put aside his immediate suspicions. This was his uncle, the one who had been with Uncle Darcy through bad times and had been so insistent on returning Uncle Gregory to England. He had every logical reason to understand – "You cannot possibly understand it."

"I apologize. I do not presume to."

George turned the glass in his hands, because it gave them something to do. "Sometimes I have thoughts that run away from me. Ideas I can't get out of my mind. Negative ones. Even when I know they're irrational, that does not mean they go away."

"Your great-uncle kept a journal. Did Darcy ever tell you that?"

"He did – some time ago. I've not thought of it since, and he's not brought it up."

"I think he means to protect you. It is not an easy read. Uncle Gregory was a suicide who was mistreated by his father and his doctors, and the only escape he found was leaving society entirely. Nonetheless," he said, opening up the desk, "you are your own man, and can make your own decisions." He removed a stack of worn journals, barely still held together by the loose binding. "Every man is ultimately the decider of his own fate, or at least, how he deals with life as it is presented to him. It has been my observation that it is easier to go through something when you feel someone else understands you." He passed the journals to George. "Even if he is dead."

~~~

"Are you sure you don't want to come in?" Isabel called. "You should at least get your feet wet!"

"That means getting these boots off and you know that's a half-hour process," George said, and obstinately returned to his reading, one eye still on his sister as she played ankle-deep in the water with Patrick.

"Is your sister still putting up with you being an obstinate git?" Georgiana Bingley said, announcing her presence as she sat down in the chair next to him.

"She has yet to be persuaded to do otherwise," he replied, not looking up from his reading. "I am beginning to suspect that it may actually be good for me to listen to her once in a while."

"Still hiding in your books?"

"Still hiding from Geoffrey?"

"You are a bastard. You know that?"

He smiled. "You haven't said 'no.'"

Georgie huffed and sunk into her chair, kicking off her wooden sandals so her feet rested on the grass.

"So what is going on between the two of you?"

"Why do you care?"

"Because I've spent two years of my life watching him mope all around Cambridge, and now Frederick will have to endure it as well."

She was not so quick to answer. For Georgiana, this was unusual. "Moping, really? What about drinking and cavorting and all of the things that makes town and gown relations so famously poor?"

"What little he has been responsible for, I am under no obligation to tell you. I will say that he has not been *cavorting* with the female species, and he has taken quite a ribbing for it." George added, "We also do *some* studying at University."

"Am I supposed to take solace in that?"

George closed his book and looked at Georgiana. "Do you really want to know my opinion? Because I have no wish to make idle conversation about topics that should be taken seriously."

"Fine. I will hear the opinion of the expert on women."

"I will ignore that," he said. "Despite your self-declared cynicism, you are a hopeless romantic, waiting for Geoffrey to declare his love for you and throw himself into your arms. Whatever occurred between you that brought you to this conclusion, I know not, but I know that you've failed to consider certain possibilities."

"*What* possibilities?" Georgie said, clearly frustrated.

"The possibility, for one, that Geoffrey is so in love with you that, were he to declare himself, you would probably be married inside a month by necessity. Which brings us to the first problem—disregarding the fact that he is supposed to be a celibate bachelor like all University students— that his father will have his hide if he fails to finish Cambridge. And *before you say it*, Geoffrey standing up to his father is quite different from you standing up to Uncle Bingley, and you know it. But suppose for a moment he put all that aside and you were married. Thus would begin a long series of social obligations that he might know he's not ready for and knows you would hate. And of course, the inevitable result of any situation, children. Do you expect to be training for some imaginary future battle while you're in confinement? Or nursing a child? I will not speculate on your own eagerness to be a mother, but I will say that Geoffrey Darcy, at twenty, is not ready to be a father."

Georgie looked away. "You *are* no good at talking to women."

"I never denied it. My propensity for the truth always causes enough damage," he said, and reopened his book. When he looked up again, he discovered that Georgiana had silently fled.

~~~

"*What* did you say to Georgie?" Isabel demanded, cornering him in the library just before supper. She looked ready to throttle him.

"She asked my honest opinion on a most important issue and I gave it."

"*George!* You're not supposed to do that!"

"I'm supposed to tell an outright lie, then?"

"You're not supposed to hurt a woman's feelings! What kind of gentleman doesn't know that?"

"So I'm to lie, then? You know I find it abhorrent to –"

"For heaven's sake, this isn't about what *you* don't like. This is about having some consideration for *other* people's feelings!"

He sighed. He did truly feel bad now, if it made his sister so upset by sheer adjacency. "I'm not good at that, Izzy."

"Well, maybe you should *try* some time."

She could not have cut him worse. It took the extent of his abilities to mask the emotion on his face before supper.

~~~

The Bellamonts were not late night people and made no pretense of being anything else. They were a couple with a young child, and they did not keep their adult guests up with singing or playing cards, nor did they own a pianoforte. Izzy and Georgie made an attempt to teach Caitlin whist while Grégoire said even more evening prayers, and then most people turned in. It was only when the servants were gone and everyone turned in that George safely opened the whiskey and began to pour.

Drinking for him was usually a solitary activity, out of sheer embarrassment. The smell reminded him of his home in Newcastle. In fact, it was one of the most distinct memories he had of it. He could only hazily recall his father drinking, but he could remember the smell, and the yelling, and his mother going on and on about how much he drank.

There was still something to be said for liquor, at least good whiskey. There were the affects of alcohol itself, so potent on him with his low tolerance. A glass or two and his world was so much warmer and fuzzier than it had been, and after the third glass he could even laugh at all of those terrible thoughts flying around in his head.

"Are you going to pour me one or am I going to have to do it myself?" Ah. Georgiana, of course.

He did succeed in getting most of the whiskey into her glass and not onto the table between them. When she had appeared, he had no idea. It was a rather small house, compared to hers or Pemberley, and he'd assumed he was likely the only one awake. "Sorry," he said, not able to disguise the slur in his voice. She giggled. "You – you laughing at me?"

"Yes, George. I am."

"Then – I don't know – 'sbetter than before." George grabbed the table end for support. "I shouldn' upset a lady. I'm – I'm so bad at talking to ladies!" He banged on the table. "Ow."

Georgie laughed and took a health sip from her own glass. "It is better when you're drunk. Which is, sadly, such a rare display."

"So – you're not – horribly angry with me?"

"Of course I am!" she shouted, then quickly lowered her voice. "But if you want the truth, which I know you love so much, I'm angrier with myself."

He had no answer to that. He poured himself another drink, but didn't take from it yet. "He loves you."

"I know."

"And you love him. It makes – sense," he put his fingers together in some attempt to interlace them. "It – goes. But it's frightening. To give ..." he stumbled in his speech. "To give yourself

78

to someone – to let anybody inside – it's scary. When it's not just sex. Or companionship. When it's like – love." George did take a drink, but couldn't finish it, and held the glass to his chest. "What'f you're wrong? And you gave yourself to someone and they hurt you and everyone betrays you and, you know - ?"

"No," she said. "I really don't."

"Of course it's – oh, forget it, it's one of my stupid things. Who were we talking about? Geoffrey? Wha – wha'ya wanna know about Geoffrey? That he won't look at another woman even when they're thrown in his face? That your brother is more experienced –"

"Stop!" Georgie said emphatically, although without any true harshness. "Wait – my brother?"

George nodded, which made him dizzy, so he put his head down on the table. He had splashed most of his drink on his waistcoat with the motion. "We got him drunk – "

"I don't think I want to know this."

" – an' we bought him a whore – a nice one – because he was being so obstinate about it, and we locked him in." He gestured with his hand. "I assume he came out wi'the expected results."

Georgie put her hand over her forehead. "But you didn't do that with – "

"Geoffrey? No. 's saving himself for you."

"Great. Now I feel horrible."

79

"What?"

She finished off her glass. "I'm not drunk enough to explain it. Not even to you, who knows everything anyway and is also too in the cups to remember half of what we're saying right now."

"Guilty as charged, Your Excellent – Excellency. Is it Excellency? I dunno – I haven' been in trouble."

"It's bad – being in trouble."

"I think I would like prison – if it had a big library."

"It would be lonely."

"I would be – you know – safe."

"George," she said, "prison is supposed to keep *you* away from *other people*."

"But it would work the other way," he said. "I would be safe." George smiled, and finished the glass. "No one could hurt me."

While he was contemplating this lovely idea, Georgie said, "You really are sick."

"You really are crazy."

"I'm not and you know it."

He swallowed. "You're just lonely."

"So are you."

"And so is Geoffrey. So we can all be lonely together," he said.

It was a very lonely thing to say.

~~~

Fortunately, his host was kind enough to treat George's splitting headache without commenting on it. By noon, George was recovered enough to leave his darkened room and be served a light luncheon, though he wasn't particularly hungry. Isabel was at the table, trying to keep Patrick from finger-painting with his mashed potatoes.

"Grégoire's teachin'," Aunt Bellamont said. "If you're lookin' fer 'im."

"Thank you. I think I might go for a walk," he announced.

"Thar's a patt behind de garden dat leads ter town, if yer folly it long enoof."

Fairly sure he had understood that, George nodded. "Thank you, Aunt Bellamont." He kissed his sister and put on his coat and hat before leaving. It was a beautiful day, and now that his headache had lessened sufficiently, he was able to appreciate the sunlight. The path led straight into the woods, and he walked briskly without paying his surroundings much notice.

In horror, he suddenly halted at the figure he came upon. He *was* in Ireland, so that set his recognition back a bit, but he finally realized it was in fact Georgiana, her overcoat discarded. While she was clothed, her clothing was shocking—a tunic and wide breeches and, of course, her sandals.

In the clearing some distance from the actual path, she had made a little space for herself and was so consumed by her bizarre set of movements that she did not notice his presence. Surely she would have said something. He had seen, on a visit, Brian Maddox move like that. He'd said it was an Oriental sort of exercise for practice, to do a particular set of movements. George just hadn't expected Georgiana to be doing it with a sword, or that it involved a back-flip that let her spin around and point it at his throat. "Hello," she said between breaths.

"...Miss Bingley," he said, backing away.

Georgie smirked and replaced her sword into the sheath hung over her back. It looked familiar somehow, but he couldn't place it. He hadn't seen it during the wolf incident.

"So –"

"My parents and I have an agreement," she said, picking a cloth up from her pile of discarded items and wiping the sweat off her face. "I can do whatever I want in private, as long as it stays that way."

"And have you kept your promise?" Actually, he was surprised that it had even been an offer on the table, but there had to be something that was keeping Georgie so in line since the wolf incident. She had been playing the part of the good daughter for two years now.

"I won't answer that unless you've had another three glasses of whiskey. Or any sort of spirit, really. Puts you right out."

He blushed. "I do apologize for ... whatever I said." He added, "What did I say?"

"You apologized for hurting my feelings in your own bumbling way, you wondered out loud what jail would be like, and you told me far too much about my brother's social life in University. That is all. Will you toss me my gown?"

Not accustomed to hearing such a thing from a relative, he choked up before she impatiently pointed to the gown that was hanging from a tree branch right next to him. He took it and did in fact toss it to her as requested.

"Now turn around. We must have some propriety."

He turned. "I believe propriety and these woods do not belong in the same conversation if this is what you've been doing with your time."

"Back to your old judgmental self, aren't you? I think I like you better drunk."

"I'm told I am more sociable."

"Then I recommend a steady diet of it. There. Will you walk me home?"

George turned, and she was once again in a proper gown, a sack over her shoulder, and the sword wrapped in a cloth in one hand. "Of course," he said, deciding he'd had enough walking for one day, or maybe one lifetime.

CHAPTER 6

Letters from Friends

To Mr. Geoffrey Darcy,

I have been instructed by Uncle Grégoire to send you these books, which you should find very enlightening on the particulars of translating high Latin.

Sincerely,
G Wickham

P.S. Ireland is very fine.

~~~

Dear Geoffrey,

Hello from Ireland! George and I are having a very pleasant trip. I don't know if you have ever visited Uncle Grégoire's place, but it is a most peculiar building. There are books in every room! Needless to say, George loves it, even if he won't say it—you know how he is! The sea is very beautiful. Patrick is a darling, but I dread being left in charge of him, as I am when they go to Sunday Mass, because he is a much faster runner than me (but not Georgiana, thank goodness!) and is determined to escape all authority whenever he can and make a mess of the kitchen. Of course his father won't discipline him, so Aunt Bellamont has to do it (those stories about the wild Irish are true!)

Speaking of Georgie, we had about two weeks together before she left for London. Her hair is starting to grow back. If you don't get a letter from her, then she has failed to keep her promise to me and you can berate her for it! (Just a little. And not when she's armed!)

I will see you this winter, as I will be in Chesterton with Lady M and Emily.

Your Loving Cousin,
Isabella Wickham

~~~

To Mr. Darcy, of Pemberley, Derbyshire, and King's College

I have been informed by Miss W that if I do not write you, you will take great offense. Hence, this letter.

Miss Georgiana Louisa Bingley

P.S. You may write me back, if you wish. I suppose you could discuss college and whatnot.

~~~

Dear Georgiana,

This may seem truly pathetic, but I have only been back in school two weeks and already I miss G Wickham's presence in our quarters. It may sound silly, but he was my roommate for two years, and was very polite and quiet, and more than once I tried to get him to finish my essays, and more than once he was not tricked and shooed me away. I know George rarely speaks his mind, and when he does, he tends to be abominably rude, but he got us out of more than one scrape without chastising us for it or ever mentioning it again (unless he did to you; I know not. I hope not).

87

GW was here for commencement, and then, as you probably know, immediately returned to London and I'm told will not be back until Dr. Maddox begins his lecture series. Fellows have a great deal more liberty than students, and they're paid (but poorly, I assure you), but I could not imagine lingering here for years, and I don't think Father would tolerate it unless I was serious about the church, which would be a difficult lie for me to tell at this point in my life and academic career. I will miss University in general terms, but not everything about it. The tutor Father selected is particularly talented, particularly expensive, and particularly brutal. I have no idea when complex algorithms (a theoretical form of mathematics that has no proper use, I assure you) will come up in my life again. Unlike the classics, I can't even make conversation about them. I would not have kind words for the man who decided to focus the curriculum away from logic and classicism and towards algebra and geometry (again, more types of mathematics).

Your brother is doing well, as always. CB is smarter than he thinks he is, especially when it comes to languages, and he seems to have fitted in nicely with some of the students of dramatics over at King's College. I know very little about them, but the few I've met are pleasant and outgoing and just the sort of people GW would despise but CB would love. They are not troublemakers, I am happy to report, as I imagine I would have to answer to Uncle B if something happened to him of a more serious nature. Every night they lock the gates at nine, which is terribly early, and though there are dozens of walls to climb and tunnels to escape through, it took your brother precisely one month to master one of the Heads' side door locks, and we've come and gone freely ever since.

As for the new member of our trio, FM continues to confound us by abusing all of the freedoms he finally has (I imagine growing up under his father could be very stifling) and yet somehow always emerges, often hung-over and still with yesterday's clothes, to ace every exam handed to him. He has frustrated his Tutor already, and I say FM is dangerously close to receiving every honor available (except, perhaps, good attendance at services, for which he already owes five shillings in fines). From such a learned household I suppose we should not be surprised, but it is not as if he lives in the library as GW does. CB's opinion is that the boy is simply brilliant, and that is the end of the matter. His father will be proud. (And no, I do not know if that rumor concerning his parents is true. Do you?)

There is not much else to say about University life. The hours are long, the Tutors self-righteous, the professors forever doing private research, and we all despise the morning bells, but I will miss it when it is over.

I've forgotten. There is some news! I have been admitted to the fencing society. It was easier when I finally admitted that I will never be what I once was, and that my abilities of sudden movements are limited, but I always try to remind myself that my father had to learn to fence with his left hand after so many years on his right. If I can spar with Father at Christmas, I will be most pleased. I could never beat you, but I never imagined that I would, and I confess that sometimes when the better (or just less handicapped) fencers are joking about me, I wish you were there to beat them one-handed. And blind-folded. Maybe hopping on one leg (you could do it, trust me).

Write when you can.

Sincerely,
Geoffrey Edward Darcy

~~~

To Mr. Darcy, of Pemberley, Derbyshire, and King's College

In answer to your first question, if GW has ever told me anything about your infamous escapades, I am sworn to secrecy. (As if George would do something that required secrecy and manage to pull it off).

In answer to your second, I do not know if the rumor is true. The more I think of it, the more I believe it is, because FM is so unlike Aunt M and

Uncle M in appearance, but if he is as intelligent as you so claim, he got it from somewhere, and we all know Uncle M is brilliant. It would not be polite to ask Emily about it. She must know there is a rumor on the wind, but she has said nothing of it, and I always try to stick to sensitive topics around the ladies.

Apologies. I meant 'other ladies.'

In answer to your third and I believe final question, I believe I could and would be willing to properly thrash any person who makes fun of your vertigo, if I could find some pretense to do it. You may not believe me when I say I am drawing short on ideas, but I did make a promise to behave while under my father's roof, and I do take my promises seriously.

As for GW, if you have any worries for him, be assured he is in a much better mood since his return from Ireland, and if you did not know he was in a melancholy state before, I suppose you will learn it now, because I was taught never to cross things out in a letter but to begin it from scratch, and I have no intention of doing either one of those things. Admittedly the other ladies had something to do with his mood, forever dragging him to parties and dances and balls so they could dance, which we both know is the worst torture in the world for him. I would be in a bad temper after a week of that, and he lasted nearly a month. I heard he even danced! But IW is coming with him later in the month to live at Chesterton, so he can throw himself back into his books, perhaps bodily. Be wary; he may try to hug the library stacks.

If you want a report on the situation of my own environs, I will oblige. I sleep in as late as I want, have a lazy breakfast, then perhaps call on Lady L, and we go shopping. Perhaps she drags me to an assembly, as she seems to trust my judgment on the character of men more than her own (meaning: she will never be married), and then we are home hopefully before the sun is up, depending on who is our chaperone. Papa is often in Town, but when he has had a long day and is tired himself, he sends his very bribe-able house manager, so we are not much bothered.

Now stop drooling and get back to your books!

Sincerely,
Georgiana Louisa Bingley

~~~

Dear Georgiana,

I believe I would be more receptive to your mocking if you had not told me on many occasions that the life of a Town lady in society is fantastically dull, as I have rarely known you to change your opinion on anything.

"Damnit!" Geoffrey said.

"Can't you be quiet while writing a letter? Some of us are trying to drink here," Frederick said from the armchair where he sat. In one hand was the book he was supposed to have memorized most of by the morning, and in the other, a bottle of brandy.

"What is it?" Charles said as he entered their living quarters. "What's going on?"

"Nothing. That is precisely the problem. I cannot finish this letter."

"Why not?"

"I cannot think of a thing to write."

"So, end the letter," Charles said, putting down his books and satchel. "There's no necessary length for letters."

"I know! But still ..." Not wanting to elucidate further on his eagerness to write Charles's sister, Geoffrey finally put the pen back in its holder. "It is probably too late for the mail anyway."

"It is. It just arrived." He opened his bag and removed a long box wrapped in paper. "Frederick."

"Is it from my father?"

"No." Charles turned it over. "There is no return."

Frederick's sudden interest, compared to his usual apathetic attitude, was something they were unaccustomed to. "Let me have it, then. What day is it?"

"Tuesday," Geoffrey said, temporarily distracted from his thoughts on the letter.

"Already?" Frederick opened his pocketknife and cut the cords holding the package together. He opened it to reveal a bottle of wine with a green bottle, and held it up to the light of the fireplace. "*Chateau de Loup*. 1778."

"Is that good?"

"Good?" Geoffrey said. "That is a very fine bottle of wine, Mr. Bingley. I think it might be worth fifty pounds."

"Fifty pounds!"

"Yes, Charles, you can stop being stunned at everything," Frederick said. "Well, should we have a drink?"

"With fifty-pound wine? You won't save it for an occasion?" Geoffrey asked.

Frederick took a corkscrew off the banister. "It is an occasion. Today is my birthday. How often does a man turn eighteen?"

"Don't be ridiculous, Fred, your birthday is –"

"*Emily's* birthday is in two weeks," he said, opening the wine and taking the glass Geoffrey offered. "Let it breathe. This is fine stuff. Anyway, today is my birthday. Or early tomorrow morning. We really don't know."

Charles swallowed. Geoffrey took the wine and set it down, and offered up another glass, which Frederick passed to Charles, "Yes, I am not the natural son of my parents. Congratulations, Inspector Bingley. I can't imagine what tipped you off. Now, may I have a glass of my own wine?"

Geoffrey passed him a third glass. "So your…natural parents send you a package?"

"My father does, I assume. My mother is dead." He did say this more somberly. "Father – Dr. Maddox – was the attending physician when she died of childbed fever."

"You've known this all your life?"

"Of course not. I had no idea. My parents very strategically told me after Emily came out," he said. "So, let us have a toast then, to my natural father to whom I owe my looks, my intelligence, and my penchant for revelry that Dr. Maddox would never indulge in." Before they could say otherwise, he clinked their glasses together and gulped down his wine in one swig. "Very good."

"You won't appreciate it if you drink it like that," Geoffrey said, sipping his. "This is a powerful vintage."

Frederick collapsed back in his seat, his book now abandoned, and poured himself another glass – and another after that. It was hard to get it away from him. He drank half the bottle within ten minutes before he stopped. Charles excused himself to go study in his private chambers, and Geoffrey made one last attempt at his letter and again found no words that were appropriate. He instead took the chair across from Frederick, finally availing himself of more of that wonderful wine. "You don't mind?"

Frederick waved it off. His mood, which hadn't been pleasant before, was briefly buoyed and then sunk as the wine level went down in the bottle.

"I suppose you know who he is," Geoffrey said, "if you are so lackadaisical about it."

Frederick took the bottle back and took a gulp right from it. "The official story is that he had no interest in my welfare, and that is that."

Geoffrey just nodded, realizing this was all Frederick would reveal at this moment. So he did know. "What about your mother?"

"What do you think? What kind of woman dies of childbed fever without a husband by her side? And, after three days, no man has made any attempt to claim the child or left her any funds for it? Have the satisfaction in knowing that every time you called me a bastard, you were right."

To that, Geoffrey had nothing to say, and he looked at the fire instead while taking another sip. Fine wine, indeed. Perhaps the best he'd ever had, and that was saying something. "He must feel guilty about it," he mused.

"I doubt he even thinks of me. He probably just assigned someone the task." He took yet another swig. "What am I talking about? He gave my father all of those honors. That wasn't for nothing." Frederick was definitely drunk, to be rambling on about such things.

Geoffrey did not answer. While he chewed on that particularly juicy piece of information, he hoped Frederick would incriminate himself, but he did not. *It couldn't possibly be ...* But he looked at Frederick and the younger man's face was all contempt and despair. "If it matters to you, Dr. Maddox and Lady Maddox have never given any indication that they see you as anything but their own son."

"So they tell me, and I believe it. But that doesn't make it true, does it?"

Another question he couldn't answer. He couldn't even imagine what it was like. Knowing his father existed but hadn't wanted him and still didn't. Knowing his mother was dead and forgotten.

"Don't tell Georgiana," Frederick announced, "in your love letter to her."

Geoffrey blushed. "It isn't –"

"I know very well what it is and what it isn't. But the point is I don't want her lording it over me. Not yet, anyway. That I'm the son of a laughingstock of a man and a common street

99

whore? She'd never let me forget that, would tease me constantly." He interrupted any attempted response on his companion's end. "No, forget I said that. She would never do something so contemptuous. Would she?" When there was no response, he repeated, "*Would she?*"

"I – I've no idea. I think not, but I have never presumed to understand her." Seeing Frederick was in no mood to talk, Geoffrey rose. "Happy Birthday."

Frederick made a noncommittal noise and Geoffrey took to his chambers, taking the letter and pen with him. There, he set the letter down. He would honor his promise to Frederick, at least until he was asked directly. He wanted to concentrate on prattling on about some inconsequential thing, but his heart wasn't in it. Instead he paced. Dr. Maddox was, besides his father, the most intelligent and distinguished person he knew. He certainly was the most learned. Whatever honors he had received – a living, knighthood, a professorship, a home in Chesterton – was surely of his own prowess as a physician and an intellectual.

Or had there been something else going on all along?

CHAPTER 7

Mr. Bingali

Mr. Bingley responded to the doorbell, thinking it might be the post. Instead, the footman informed him, "Lady Littlefield to see Miss Bingley, sir."

"Of course," he said, and bowed as she entered. "Lady Littlefield, how lovely to see you."

"Mr. Bingley."

Monkey scampered out of Bingley's office to greet the young lady, who had developed a certain fondness for him. She had learned that he knew how to hold out his hand on command for shaking, and she gladly took it. "Hello, Monkey!"

"If he bothers you, let me know. He has been rather fussy today."

"I am sure he will not, Mr. Bingley."

She excused herself to wait for Georgiana, who soon hurried down the steps to greet her friend, greeting her father with a brief, "Papa," as she passed.

Bingley smiled and returned to his study. He was enthusiastic about Georgie's friendship with Lady Littlefield, a slightly younger lady of a respectable family whom his daughter had met at the seminary in France. She was forever dragging Georgie shopping and to dances, which was something no one else had succeeded in doing. How their friendship had been forged, he had no idea, but he was not one to question the ways of women, nor would he question such a social friendship.

He emerged at half past two and briefly paused outside the sitting room.

"The viscount was even there!"

"Who, Lord Brougham's son? The one who has caught your fancy?"

"Georgie!"

"Well, don't mention him if you do not wish my commentary," Georgie said, and her father smiled.

"Fine. Yes, he was there. Do you know who else?"

"The Duke of Wellington."

"No! Better! That Mr. Dartmouth. The one you danced with –"

"Oh God ..."

Bingley could almost *hear* his daughter blushing.

"He really is a very interesting person, Georgie. His father is a manager in the East India Company. Perhaps your father knows him?"

"I'm *not* asking."

Feeling a bit guilty for eavesdropping on them, Bingley put on a clueless face and stepped into the room. "Lady Littlefield. Georgie."

"Mr. Bingley."

"Papa."

"I will be at the office until a bit before supper. If I am delayed, please don't wait up, and give my apologies to Eliza."

"All right, Papa."

"And don't feed Monkey." To which Monkey squealed, and Bingley gave him a hard stare. "You don't get an opinion."

~~~

"I am tired of walking these filthy streets with you," Quon Jin complained. "You won't even take a rickshaw!"

Liu Xiao was calmly encouraging. "They move too fast. I cannot see anyone from one of their rickshaws. If you don't like it, you can go home and prepare for the reception tonight.

"If I go home, you are sure to get in trouble!"

Liu laughed and bowed to a pair of passing ladies, who giggled and scampered off. "I have not been in trouble once this trip, no matter how boring it has been."

"You have come close. And now you bring us closer. You want to attract the attention of every monkey in this disgusting city?"

"No. I am only looking for one," he said.

"You are obsessed!" Quon Jin said. "I have half a mind to –"

But Liu put a hand against Quon's chest to stop his movement. "Look," he said gesturing his head in the direction of the river. Across the bridge, a couple was walking together. "The samurai and his wife."

"How do you know they're – Oh." Quon Jin squinted. "But they're white. They're playing dress up, like one of the king's parties."

"I don't think so," Liu said. "Look at him. He's not wearing those swords like props, like the generals do." He headed towards the bridge.

"Liu Xiao! Where are you going?"

"To meet them. What do you think?"

"On what pretext?"

"I'll make one up!" he shouted and kept going as Quon ran to catch up with him.

By the time he was on the bridge, the couple had noticed him, and with no apprehension, came to greet him. They were white, and though one of them at least was likely English, they had been speaking some unknown language. The samurai was dressed traditionally, his wife the same, except her hair was covered by a cloth. They were wearing tatami slippers, not geta shoes, he noted as he bowed. "I am Liu Xiao, Ambassador from the Imperial Court and Privy Council of the Forbidden City," he said in Japanese. As Quon caught up, he said, "This is Quon Jin."

"Maddox-san, and my wife, Nadi-sama," the samurai said in perfect Japanese, returning the bow.

"Do you speak pinyin?" Quon said.

"Very little," he answered in Chinese. "My partner, speak more." He switched back to Japanese. "We have a shipping company. We do business in Hong Kong and Nagasaki."

"Silk?"

"And other goods, yes. How do you find London, Ambassadors?"

"Very fine, but it seems the king has other things on his mind than relations with China."

"The king has very little on his mind," Maddox-san said with a laugh. "We are very interested to hear about your mission, unless it is private."

"It is not," he said, "except for some matters."

"I imagine you have had very few to talk with," the woman named Nadi-sama said. Liu was used to a woman speaking out of turn by now. "Ones who do not make a spectacle of you, that is."

"You are correct," he said, and quickly translated for Quon Jin, who did not speak much Japanese.

"If language is a problem," Maddox-san said, "my partner is more fluent than I am, and he is in the office right now."

"We would not wish to impose."

"Hardly," he said with an Englishman's smile. "He loves to practice his languages. He will be grateful." He turned and said something to his wife in their own language, and she returned it, and kissed his cheek before bowing to both ambassadors and leaving. "So, we go?"

The shipping area was not very far from the docks, but the office itself was in a bit better of a neighborhood. By now Liu was familiar with most of London, at least from the streets, but had rarely been inside a building in this neighborhood. The office was unmarked, but there was a little golden Buddha statue in the corner of the window.

"Bingley!" the samurai said as he entered the hallway, busy with employees were going to and fro. "Where is Bingley?" he said to the servant at the door.

"In his office, sir."

"Give me a moment," the samurai said to them in Japanese, before knocking and entering his partner's office.

Quon sat down on the nearest available stool. "This is a mistake. The wife isn't the fighter."

"No, of course not. She was the wrong size," Liu said, looking at the door that had been closed in front of him. There was a sign on it in Chinese – a death waiver for a fight with a wushu master named Ji Yuan and one *Humgao Guizi*. Liu laughed. "Do you think he knows what they wrote on this form?" Beneath it was an Englishman's signature. "They called him a demon all right. They even –" But the door opened, interrupting the thought, and he and Quon Jin entered the office.

The man—with very red hair, almost orange—sitting behind the desk rose to greet them. "Charles Bingley," he introduced himself with a bright smile.

Liu smiled. "I am honored to meet you."

Two hours and a pot of very good tea later, they had secured a friendship with these two businessmen and a dinner invitation for the following night at Bingley's house. Mr. Bingali was very inquisitive, Liu thought, and even more polite and outgoing than his samurai partner. He asked them dozens of questions about the Forbidden City, of which he had heard much, alternately flipping between Chinese, Japanese, and English as he needed to. Of him they learned that he had a small family – one wife, two sons, and two daughters.

107

Yes, they would come to dinner.

~~~

Elsewhere in London, the dinner hour was hastily approaching.

"Careful – careful. You don't want to mix too much in."

"What if I do?" George said nervously, holding the beaker over the glass jar with shaking hands.

"Well, then the house will blow up."

George dropped the beaker, which fortunately did not shatter but rolled along the table before he caught it; only half the contents were spilled out. He was still catching his breath when he heard Dr. Maddox laughing. "Please don't do that, sir."

The doctor smiled from his position in his chair. "You know very well that there is nothing so combustible in this house. Or if there were, I wouldn't have you messing with it with only me watching over you. I do not have a death wish, Mr. Wickham." He was still stifling his chuckling. "Now, if you've done it correctly, you should have something yellow and clear, not cloudy at all, and smells a bit like soap. It's very good for cleaning sores –" A knock on the door interrupted him. "Come."

The servant entered. "Dr. Bertrand to see you, sir."

"I've forgotten the time. Is he early?"

"A bit, sir. Mrs. Bertrand and Mr. Bennet have not yet arrived. He is, however, very eager to see you."

"Send him in then," the doctor said, and Dr. Andrew Bertrand entered. "Dr. Maddox. Mr. Wickham."

"Dr. Bertrand."

"I was giving Mr. Wickham a taste for mixing chemicals on his own, and so far, we have succeeded in not blowing ourselves up. A good start, I believe."

"Indeed," Dr. Bertrand said. "How are you, George?"

"Very well, Dr. Bertrand," George said, then left them alone. Bertrand shut the door securely behind him before taking a seat on the stool by the table.

"What brings you by, Andrew? I am sure you have better things to do," Dr. Maddox said.

"That does not mean I find them more pleasant," he said. "I am beginning to understand why you retired, Dr. Maddox."

To this, Maddox just chuckled. "Understood. What is it this time? Is His Majesty squabbling with his Prime Minister, Parliament, or his mistress?"

"None, actually. Or, not to the extent that's worth mentioning." He lowered his voice. "What do you know about Sir William Knighton?"

"Is he not His Majesty's new Private Secretary?"

"Not officially, no. They abolished the office to get rid of Bloomington." He sighed. "I know you always told me to steer clear of politics –

"

"– And I do stand by that, thank you."

"And I always have, but lately it's gotten rather hard to avoid. His Majesty is not well."

Dr. Maddox cautiously replied, "His Majesty has not been well in many respects for several years."

"I fear his isolation and increasing illness are turning him into a recluse. He listens to everything Sir Knighton says, even if he fusses about it like he does with the Prime Minister. Even Liverpool is concerned. Anyway, the reason I come to you is that he approached me today on my way out and asked me some very leading questions about you."

Now Maddox did not look quite his normal jovial self. "About me? Why ever would he be concerned about a retired physician? Is he not one himself?"

"He is. He wanted to know the usual things – what your party affiliation was, what your political views are, what meetings you attended – and at first, I said nothing. When he became more pressing, I asked him if I was being formally questioned. I meant it in jest."

"But you were."

"He said otherwise, but I know what he meant. So I told him that you had no particular political views, had never been to a session of Parliament or a Radical gathering in your life, and could not find the subject more boring." He added, "He also inquired as to your health."

"In the same…formal tone?"

"I hope you understand – I told him of your condition."

He nodded. "Anything else?"

"That was it. I was quite relieved when he was gone, actually."

Dr. Maddox took a moment to digest this new information. "I have no idea what he is up to, if he is up to anything, but I have nothing to hide from the king." Technically, not a lie. "Thank you for telling me."

"I will keep my ears open."

"Your eyes, too, as you have use of them," he said, rising and trying to restore his usual demeanor with his little jest. "Well, we'd best not keep the ladies waiting. I hear your wife arriving."

"You do? So the adage is true?"

"Of your other senses being heightened? Oh, yes. Quite beneficial. Especially in the bedroom."

"Dr. Maddox!"

"There had to be someone I could brag about it to," he said. "Well, I suppose if you make enough subtle hints, you may be relieved of your post, if it's become dangerous."

"The king has added more doctors to his staff."

"Without your consent?"

"Knighton's doing again. Well, there's Knighton himself, though he gave up his practice –"

"To gain the ear of a king, many men would."

"– and then there's that Prussian, Mr. Engel. Just a surgeon, I believe."

Dr. Maddox paused, stopping Bertrand's own step with his cane. "A Prussian doctor?"

"No, just a surgeon and apothecary. I've only met him once."

"What does he look like?"

"Short hair – black. Other than the spectacles he wears, not particularly noticeable." He realized that his companion was unusually silent. "Dr. Maddox, is something wrong?"

"No, no – there are thousands of Prussian doctors, I imagine – you said he has glasses?"

"Yes. Doctor, you've gone white, do you need –

"No, no, it's nothing," he said, but rested heavily on his cane. "A Prussian doctor operated on my hand once. Saved my life. I don't know why I'm not more grateful. It was just a bad time in my life. Brings up all sorts of memories."

"I'm sorry. I had no –"

"Forget it. It's nothing." He grabbed Bertrand's arm. "Come along. Don't want to keep the ladies waiting over nothing."

Dr. Maddox's shaky grip indicated that it wasn't.

~~~

Georgiana and Eliza Bingley had no engagements that evening, but Bingley found himself alone while going through some records after penning a letter to Jane. He would be joining her in a week, but it seemed such a long time, especially with her so close in Derbyshire with her sister. He would not be in London by choice, but his business and his daughters required it. It was good for them to socialize, but the notion that they might find someone to marry terrified him. He expressed his worries to Jane in written form, along with an account of recent events that included a bit about the ambassadors he had met.

After sealing the letter for the next day's post, he sat back in the armchair and stoked the fire.

"Papa?"

He looked up at his daughter. "Yes?"

Eliza Bingley sat down on the settee next to him. "How can you tell when a man likes you?"

"Why?" he asked emphatically, sitting forward in his chair, to which, she only giggled.

"Georgie said you would get like that if I said that," she said.

"Oh, I see. Baiting your father, are you now? I always wondered what terrible things would happened if the two of you teamed up," he said. "Now, answer my question. Who is this man?"

"There's no man! I mean, there are many men, but none which I would say are chasing me so affectionately. Viscount Brougham did dance two dances with me ... though it seems he did that with everyone."

"Yes, he seems quite the personality, doesn't he? Has he danced with Georgiana?"

"No. She'll hardly dance with anyone. The last person I saw her with was – Mr. Dartmouth."

"Mr. Dartmouth. And who is Mr. Dartmouth?"

"The son of a tradesman, has about sixty thousand pounds, a Cambridge man, and has just returned from two years abroad, including some travels in the east."

"You know quite a bit about this Mr. Dartmouth." He knew his youngest daughter was a bit of a flirt, but he was not quite sure where this was heading or whether he liked it.

"I know what everyone knows, Papa. You're trying to make something out of nothing."

"You're my daughter, and I'll be as protective as I please. So, Georgiana has danced with this Mr. Dartmouth."

"She does *occasionally* indulge the men who request a dance."

Monkey climbed up on to the arm of the chair, and rested on his arm as he stroked him. "So why all of this questioning? On behalf of your sister?"

"If I can figure one of them out – I could never figure her out."

"Elizabeth! That's not polite."

"I know, Papa, but it's true."

He sighed. "I suppose it is. So, you want to know how a man shows his affection."

"Yes."

"Well, the proposal of marriage is usually a fairly clear hint."

"*Papa.*"

"Or he could dance with a young lady two sets in a row. Preferably the first two sets. Perhaps he will spend the whole time staring at her while she happen to dance with other men, knowing he can't dance a third and still be considered a gentleman because of someone's stupid rules, but secretly hating all of the other men who dare to dance with her. And then he'll beg his sisters to call on her no matter how much they do not desire to do so, or perhaps he'd hold a ball just to have her over to his house –" He smiled. "There are many things. Or he could skulk in the corner, insult everyone he meets, and then corner one of them and propose marriage."

"You mean George?"

He laughed. "I mean your Uncle Darcy. Though if George has made any marriage proposals, I would be interested to hear of them."

She blushed. "I don't want to know how Uncle Darcy courted women."

"There was only one woman, and he is married to her. As for the other man, the one who dances two dances and then watches his beloved dance with other men with displeasure, who do you think *that* was?"

"...Uncle Maddox?"

"Now you are just avoiding the obvious. You know he has no sisters."

She attempted to bury herself in her shawl. "No! I cannot think of it!"

"And I cannot imagine my father courting my mother. But, there you have it. We were all young once. And foolish." He scratched Monkey, who gave a little whine and turned around. "But somehow, it all came together. And as for the rest of the tale, you are not old enough for *that*."

"Oh heavens, Papa! Don't!"

The sounds of her frightened laughter drowned out any loneliness he had been feeling before.

CHAPTER 8

The Dashing Dartmouth

More formally attired than at their first meeting, the samurai and his wife escorted Liu Xiao and Quon Jin from their apartment to the home of Mr. Bingley. "His older son is away at school, and his younger son is with his wife in the north. His two daughters you will likely be introduced to," Maddox-san explained. "If you are introduced, bow, but do not make conversation. If they try to engage you in some, respond politely, but do not look eager. You understand? There are ways to ruffle the feathers of even the most easy-going Englishman."

"We understand," Quon Jin said, and gave Liu a meaningful stare.

Mr. Bingley's house was in a very respectable neighborhood. They had been to houses with Oriental themes before, and even a few where the people seemed to have more of an obsession than an understanding, but the Bingley apartment was more tastefully done, with some truly rare jade and gold items on the cabinet shelves and no misplacement of set arrangements.

"Mr. Maddox. Your Highness," Mr. Bingley greeted his guests formally. The samurai's wife was obviously some kind of lower nobility. "Ambassador Jin, Ambassador Xiao, thank you for coming."

"Thank you, Mr. Bingali."

They were ushered into what was called the drawing room, even though there was never any drawing done in it to their understanding, where two girls who looked to be about the age of twenty, perhaps a little younger, stood before them, in their white gowns and long gloves. The blond one had her hair pinned up in the complicated style of a lady out in society, but the other – the one with orange hair like her father – had cut it very short, similar but not precisely like a man's.

"My daughters," Mr. Bingley said in English, "Miss Georgiana Bingley and Miss Elizabeth Bingley."

Liu bowed swiftly to Georgiana with a curious and piercing look, which was only briefly returned by a flash of green eyes before he turned to bow to her sister. Then he and Quon did as they had been told, and promptly went about politely ignoring the girls as they sat down for dinner. The conversation was in an alternating mixture of English, Japanese, and a little Chinese. Mr. Bingley was a pleasant host and was easily regaled by tales of the Forbidden City, which Liu told in English to be polite. The Englishman even wanted to know about his life before his exams. "When I was young, did not want to be official," he said. "I want be a wushu master."

"I fought one once," Mr. Bingley said. "It was a stunning success by my standards. In one of the three rounds, I managed to last maybe five seconds."

"Only because he let you," Mr. Maddox said in Japanese.

"At least he tried," Miss Georgiana answered back in the same language.

"Miss Bingley!" Bingley corrected, firmly but politely.

"What, Brian? You weren't good enough for the wushu master?" Nadezhda, ever on her side, said. Brian blushed and returned to his food.

Dinner was more properly spiced than the typically bland English fare they'd had in most places. After the meal, the girls disappeared with Mr. Maddox's wife, and the men drank hot sake from Japan. "It's all I have, I am afraid," Mr. Bingley said.

Of course, Liu would not have a chance to see either of the girls in private or speak to them again most likely – as if he had any further doubt. But his gracious (and apparently unsuspecting) host wanted to try his Chinese, and Liu was most thankful for this particular dinner and willing to return the favor. "Did you ever take an interest in wushu, Mr. Bingali?"

"I have never fought seriously. I shoot." He indicated raising a gun. "Birds, geese. That is all."

"Then why did you fight a master?"

"Because I thought it interesting," he replied. "Other than that, I am just a merchant."

"And we are just officials," Quon said in reply, and looked at Liu again, but his partner offered him nothing.

They made their polite good-byes, and Bingley requested further audience with them if they had the time (and they did), and they made their exit on their own.

"Well, I think you managed not to completely mess –"

"Shh," Liu said, putting his hand to his lips. Instead of continuing down the street, Liu pulled Quon into the alleyway, looking up at the rooftops. "Look."

But the figure was already gone, down onto the balcony and then more safely landing on the ground.

"Miss Bingley," Liu bowed, even though he couldn't see her properly.

"You said I didn't understand the moves," she replied in Japanese. "I studied them from a book. What do you expect?"

"I can expect nothing but surprises from you, obviously." Her smile seemed to glint in the gaslight. "I went through a lot of trouble to find you."

"A lot of trouble!" Quon said. "Too much!"

"He always says that," Liu assured her. "But I did find you."

"So?"

"So? I want to fight you again."

"Why?"

He decided to return her nonchalant attitude. "Because I'm bored. So?"

She laughed. "Fine. My Aunt, Nadi-sama, otherwise known as Her Highness, I'll tell her to contact you, say I heard you mention fighting tonight. You breathe one word about Jack to her and I'll slit your throat."

He bowed. "You have my word."

"I hope it's worth something," she said, and leapt back up the bin, onto the balcony, and over the side again with skilled precision.

"Liu Xiao!" Quon said, shaking him out of his stupor. "We have to go. You've gotten us in enough trouble already!"

Liu smiled. He had a feeling he'd hardly begun.

~~~

Isabel Wickham was leaving for Cambridge, to live with Lady Maddox and Emily in Chesterton for the winter, and the girls decided to celebrate. George even agreed to chaperone their night out, as they went bouncing from dance to dance – however informal or formal, as long as they could get an invitation. Between their combined dowries, the door was not shut very often.

"How are you?" Georgie asked her cousin George. She wanted to chide him for being responsible for some of this, but it was a bigger burden on him than her.

He shrugged and leaned against the bookshelf. "The last place had some fine brandy. Where was it?"

"Lord Shafford."

"Him? Why did I agree to go back *there*?" he blinked. "Oh, yes. Because the previous place had some fine wine."

She smiled. "Your sister appreciates it."

He shrugged again, and Lady Littlefield pulled her back in the direction of the dance floor. "Georgie, you have to dance at least one dance. It's practically rude not to."

"And it's rude not to be asked first," she said, eyeing the crowd of eager young bachelors, all of whom she was vaguely familiar with, at least by appearance. "And I would dance with George, but I think he's about to fall over."

"Nudge Mr. Dartmouth."

"Heather! What, is he here?"

"On command," he said from behind her. Mr. Dartmouth, one of the few men present who could say he had danced with Miss Bingley, had sandy brown hair and a very relaxed expression. "Miss Bingley. Lady Littlefield." He bowed.

They curtseyed. "Mr. Dartmouth," Georgie said. "As you could tell from your eavesdropping, we were discussing you, apparently."

"I'm honored." He smirked. "May I have the next dance?"

Georgie frowned. She didn't actually want to dance. If Heather hadn't dragged her out here –

"If you've not heard, I'm sworn to a young lady currently in Scotland. The daughter of a friend of my father's."

"You speak of her so lovingly."

He smiled a little bit. "I'm not falling over in desperation, nor am I upset with the arrangement. But that is hardly the point, as you've not answered my question."

Georgie felt Heather somewhat literally nudging her, and said, "You may."

He bowed and excused himself. Georgie glared at Littlefield, who was giggling and entirely unapologetic. "I'm making you dance with him next," was all Georgie had time to say before the current set ended, and she had to line up for her dance with Mr. Dartmouth. It was a slower dance, and she failed to hide her general feeling about it on her face as they began.

"Are you determined to spurn every man in this room?" Mr. Dartmouth said as they passed.

"Only the eligible bachelors."

"Even the handsome ones?"

"I don't bother to make distinctions."

They spun around the people next to them and returned to their place in line, facing each other as he said, "So he must be ineligible in order to court you?"

"I assume he would be aware of the impropriety of courting me if he was already engaged."

"Then you are assuming a lot about the integrity of men."

She had to suppress her urge to smile. "I suppose I am quite foolish in that regard."

He took her hand, as the dance required. "I can hardly fault you for it. We are in polite society. Though refusing to dance at a ball is not very polite."

"This particular crowd has learned not to ask."

He turned and circled the woman briefly next to him and she mirrored the moves. "Do you not care for dancing?"

"I am decidedly neutral."

"Then you do not care for this crowd of men."

"You are fond of making assumptions," she said.

"On the contrary, I have no assumptions about you, as all of my first impressions were dismissed. You are a riddle, Miss Bingley."

"Is that supposed to be a compliment, Mr. Dartmouth?"

"I can only hope you would take it as one."

They danced in silence for a few minutes, as she tried to decide if she was more annoyed that she had failed to scare him off or failed to successfully hide away in a corner as she did most evenings. Maybe she would have been better off in drunken George's company.

"I will make another dastardly assumption, which is that you would rather be doing other things than prancing about this room in a manner so established and yet so meaningless."

"And I will acknowledge that you are correct."

"So your friends put you up to this, then?"

"Why? Did yours?"

"No. Do you wish me to be plain?"

She wasn't sure she was, but she said, "Yes."

"I put myself up to this. I am a more social creature than is good for me and I enjoy a challenge."

She frowned. "And I am a challenge?"

"When you scowl as if you would bite the head off the first man to approach you, you are quite that. I assume you must mean to be. Have you a man in Scotland, Miss Bingley?"

"That's an inappropriate question and you know it," she said, gripping his hand a bit harder in anger. Well, not entirely anger. His face was too relaxed for her to not be forgiving. He seemed to be enjoying this, and not at all in a taunting way.

"I apologize. Unfortunately the dance does not make allowances for stopping to do so," he said as he passed her.

"Then it will have to wait," she said very resoundingly, and that seemed to work at silencing him for the rest of the dance. He had a tone that disturbed her in that she couldn't quite make it out.

The dance finally ended, and they bowed and stepped aside to leave space for more eager couples. "I apologize, Miss Bingley, if I have offended you," he said. "It was not my intention."

"Then what was your intention? To learn if I also have a mysterious paramour?"

"Susan is hardly my paramour, though I do like her very much, which by our standards is more than enough to make a marriage," he said.

"You have not answered my question."

He grinned. He had a very charming way of doing it. "I suppose not. My intention was to get some information about you other than what is currently being circulated, and I despise idle conversation about how you find Town and the weather and all that."

She looked over her shoulder. Heather, Eliza, and Isabel were all dancing in the next set. George was off on the other side of the room. She had no reason to not keep talking to him. "What is the information currently being circulated, if I may be so bold?"

"Merely that you are the daughter of a wealthy man from Derbyshire who owns an Oriental trading business, that you are probably around twenty and have fifty thousand pounds, and that you are the less approachable of the Bingley sisters. Also, I heard you have very short hair, but I've not had it confirmed."

She giggled, an unusual reaction to a young man's conversation. "It's grown back quite a bit, actually." Her hair was returning to its regular length to her ears, which was just a bit longer than her brother's.

"In India the monks shave their heads. I don't suppose you had a brief internship as a Buddhist?"

"No. It's a ridiculous story, actually. My mother was attempting to make it look longer by applying wax. The end result was I was wearing a wig until recently."

"They cut it shorter to remove the wax?"

"Well, they had to stop my scalp from trying to burn itself off, I suppose."

He squirmed in sympathy with her recounted pain. "I will venture another presumption, which is either that they did it very quickly or that you have an impressively high tolerance for pain."

"Both, actually." She had to smile in recollection. "My sole triumph was that no one has attempted to suggest anything about my choice of hairstyles since – which for me is quite advantageous."

"You have a terrible independence streak. Your mother must be very frustrated."

"Maybe you're right and maybe you're wrong," she said, not in the mood to be angry at him anymore. "Either way, I will not answer."

"Like the question about your own intended. From your response, I've only been able to gather that he probably exists, but is *not* in Scotland."

She folded her arms and turned away from him, but he followed her. Still, she answered, "Perhaps. And your interest?"

"Only that I am forced to go to these events by my mother, and you are the most interesting woman in the room, and all the men wish to talk about is sport or ladies, if they see any difference."

"Your mother opposes the match to this – Miss Susan?"

"Hardly. But she does wish me to be more social. And not to let years of expensive dancing skills go to waste, I suppose."

She thought he was social enough already, but she still had to look down to hide her smile. "So we are both forced to go to these gatherings and dance with those who might be deemed strangers, despite the fact our minds are decidedly elsewhere?"

"We have that in common, yes. Or maybe we're trying to make them jealous."

She looked up at him, and realized he was being slightly serious, at least in regards to her. He had such a clever look about him, but not in the seemingly-arrogant way George looked at people, which could be mistaken so easily for pride, even though it came from a man with such little esteem of himself. No, she would change her own assumptions about Mr. Dartmouth, for the time being. He said he liked a challenge, he said she was a riddle, and he implied he was bored. "You are a better socialite than you esteem yourself to be."

"Is that meant to be taken as a compliment?"

She rolled her eyes. "Could it be taken any other way?"

~~~

The evening ended when it became apparent that they would have to carry George home, probably in a wheelbarrow, if they did not end it there. A sleepy-eyed, mumbling George Wickham was let off with his sister at their house on Gracechurch Street before the carriage continued on with only Georgie and her friend inside.

"So?"

"So?" she replied to Heather's comment. "What? I danced with one man to satisfy you."

"You look rather satisfied."

She turned to look out the window of the carriage, her way of hiding her blush. "Don't make so much out of nothing. You know very well my heart is declared."

"And determined to make every minute until your proposed suitor appears into agonizing torture for yourself," Heather Littlefield said from across the carriage. "You had *fun*. If these dances were only about marriage *all* the time, no one would go. I danced twice with Viscount Brougham and I am not the only one who can say that this evening. It does not mean he will propose to me tomorrow."

Georgiana put her tired feet, cramped from the dancing slippers, up on the cushion next to Heather. "Maybe he will."

"If you would stop being disparaging for one moment you would know that that wasn't true. You must be the most intelligent person I know. You know a flirt from a man on the hunt for a bride."

She frowned. "Maybe I don't."

"I'll help you, then. I am so in your debt I might as well. Example, the first: Your brother is a flirt."

"Edmund? Maybe if he'd take his head out of his books."

Heather rolled her eyes. "You *know* whom I am referring to."

"Charles is a flirt," she said. "I concede that. If he were older and I more devious and less of a friend, perhaps I would attempt some matchmaking between you."

"Stop it!"

"*You* started this conversation."

"I hold you at fault for the contemptuous suggestion nonetheless. Not that Mr. Charles isn't a perfectly amiable person, but nonetheless I am uninterested, and I think he is as well."

"He's young."

"No matchmaking!"

Georgiana finally smiled. "I went through so much trouble to get you *out* of a match; you can hardly expect me to put you right back *in* one."

~~~

When Georgiana said her giggling good-byes to Heather and returned home, her father was waiting. "You can't expect me to *not* be," he said in response to her unasked question and kissed her good night – or more accurately, good day. There was natural light through the windows of her room when she entered and dismissed her maid.

She sat at her desk in her bedclothes, still awake from all of the activity and something else in the pit of her stomach that she didn't know how to identify. Instead of pondering it further, she pulled out a fresh piece of paper.

> *To Mr. Darcy, of Pemberley, Derbyshire, and King's College*

She smiled wickedly. Make him jealous, yes?

I am writing you now from a very early hour. We have been out all night dancing with Izzy, who is off to Chesterton in a few days and will miss all of this social life.

I admit I may even be becoming accustomed to it. Tonight I danced mostly of my own free will with a Mr. Dartmouth for the second time. He has an intended in Scotland but nonetheless has his own social requirements set by his family. He is quite the conversationalist.

I hope there is no serious news from Cambridge, where you all are supposed to be studying so hard and not drinking and fooling around. Say hello to my brother for me. And Frederick, I suppose.

Sincerely,
Georgiana Louisa Bingley

She set the letter aside and drew her drapes, allowing her some darkness as she fell into a deep and oddly contented sleep. The letter itself would remain on her desk for a full day before she had the courage to mail it.

CHAPTER 9

The Secret of Death Touch

Liu Xiao nearly tore apart the envelope when he received the letter from Her Highness, Princess Nadezhda Maddox. That was the way she signed her name in English, anyway. Thankfully he managed not to destroy the letter, an invitation to a very early meeting.

Dressed appropriately for fighting, he slipped out at about two in the morning, when Londoners were just beginning to think of going to sleep, and hired an English rickshaw to take him to the countryside. He had not been outside the city since his arrival, and the smell of nature overtook him in a very pleasant fashion.

The Maddox house was a small palace with a distinctly Japanese wing. Liu had only been to Japan once and spent only two weeks in Edo before his letter of passage was up, but he recognized its influence easily enough. Nadezhda Maddox greeted him and ushered him in to the sitting room with tatami mat floors and no servants in sight. She had her sword tucked into her obi, and she set the tea down between them as he knelt on the cushion across from her.

"My husband is in Town for all of today," she said. "On business."

He bowed and accepted the green tea she offered. It was properly made and very good.

"Jorgi-chan is my niece," she said, her manner harsher than it had been two days ago. "She is very dear to me, and I have overseen all of her training. Her parents are aware that she knows how to fight, but not to the extent she chooses to take it." She mixed her own tea. "I will make this clear now, Xiao-san. If you hurt her, even in the slightest way, I will take off your head."

He nodded respectfully. "I understand." When she did not begin talking again, he saw his opportunity. "May I ask who trained her, under your overseeing? I assume it was not your husband."

"Yes, he's too English, no matter how he dresses," she said. She had a strange accent, different from her husband, even when she spoke Japanese. "Her trainer was our guest here for a year when she was a child and then another when she was older. Now he is back in Japan, doing I don't know what. He may not even still be alive."

"So he was a warrior."

"He was a thug, to be plain. But he had a very intricate fighting style, and she took to it like water. He studied in China."

He still had not learned the name of her sensei, but that was not important. "He was trained in wushu?"

"Yes, I believe so. But he could not stay here."

He nodded.

"She will be here at dawn. No matter how hard she taunts you, remember my promise."

He bowed to her, and she left him alone in the room to wait.

~~~

The sun was just rising over the trees when he was invited outside. In the back, somewhat hidden by the trees, they had cleared a space and matted it well. There were even some training dummies lying about. This was where Maddox-san probably kept up his skills. The ring was quite large, and Nadezhda stood near Georgiana Bingley, who was squatting, dressed in her Jack costume without the wig and the scarf. From a distance, maybe, she could be mistaken for a boy. In her arms was a sword, Japanese but with a Chinese hilt.

She was so small and so fair, but her face betrayed none of that. He bowed to her. "Nadi-sama. Miss Bingali."

The women returned the bow. "You promised to teach me what the moves mean," Georgiana said, standing up.

"I made no such promise," he answered her in Japanese, apparently the language of the day. "I couldn't really tell you. I'm not a master, and I never will be, not if I trained my whole life. I know my limitations." He removed the sword from his belt before entering the ring. "Do you understand the basics of Bushido? Kendo?"

"The basics, yes."

"Then you already know why it doesn't work for you."

"I'm too small," she replied.

"Many respects, but yes," he said. "In Bushido, the blade is everything. It is hard, and it is the soul of the samurai. The body is merely an extension of that. In China, the blade is an extension of the body." He put the point of his sword into the ground and leaned on it. It bent with him. "Do you know what chi is?"

"A little."

"Tai chi, chi-gong – all of these things are meant to move it around, this energy that makes the universe." He put the sword back in its hilt and set it aside, approaching Georgiana. "All of the moves – the Japanese call them kata – are meant to harness it."

"Gravity," she said. "It can do the work for us."

"More than that. You know how to move, you know that it works, but you don't know why and how to make it better. How to make it even more to your favor. I heard the tale of an ancient master who could kill," he said, touching one finger to her upper chest just under her collarbone, "with this."

"With his hand?"

"That touch. Just as I did," he said. "That soft."

She looked at him skeptically. "You can teach me that?"

"I already told you, I am not a master. I only know it can be done. I've seen men come very close. But never close enough." He pointed to his head. "If you can make your mind match your body, you can do anything."

"Prove it."

He smiled. Maybe it was the idea of being a master with a student. Maybe it was that the student was a tiny Englishwoman with otherwise perfect manners (at least at the dinner table). Or maybe it was just that he had something to do, some mission to accomplish, but when he showed her how to slow down, calm her inner rage, and maybe achieve that state of being so tied to the universe that she could overcome anything, he wasn't bored by England anymore, at least not after the fight began.

Liu found it fascinating.

~~~

"I'll be gone a week at the most," Bingley said to his eldest daughter as the servants brought his and Eliza's trunks outside. "Are you sure you don't want to come? Your mother would love to see you." Thankfully, he did not give her time to answer. "Of course not; all of your friends are here."

"Papa, I'll be *fine*," Georgie insisted. She had been alone in London many times before her sister was out. There was a small army of servants and maids to assist her (and protect her). They were downright invasive sometimes, often a hindrance on what she actually wanted to do. "Say hello to everyone for me. Especially Mama."

"I'm fairly sure you are literate."

She smiled. "I'll write to her."

Bingley softened and kissed his daughter on the cheek before putting on his overcoat. Eliza waved good-bye from the carriage, and Georgie was free.

Of course, she still wasn't actually free, because she had no real contacts she cared to pass the time with unless she teamed up with Heather

Littlefield, who had her own personal guard, or went out with Emily Maddox, who was still in town for another few days. She was in the mood to do none of those things, though she did dine the first night at the Maddox house. No, she was not bored, she told them. She knew how to entertain herself.

Actually she did not, short of getting herself into some sort of trouble, and she had promised her father otherwise. She spent the first day ignoring the pile of cards in the basket and going through the library in his office in search of some book discussing what Liu had told her, but there was nothing in any languages she could read. There were some very interesting pictures of a seated man with arrows coming out of him in one of the books that she was fairly sure was in Hindustani, but all she could really do was admire the artwork.

By the second day, she admitted she was bored. It was hard to get out to Nadi-sama's house; on the first day she was too tired anyway, and on the second, the weather was foul until late in the afternoon. She had the normal options before her, limited somewhat by Heather's temporary absence to visit relatives. She could go to the theater or see a musical performance, but she had never cultivated a real interest in such things. In the back of her mind, she finally admitted, was the nagging guilt that it was not something she could enjoy with

Geoffrey, who was never quite willing to admit how deaf he really was.

That night, she supped at a reasonable hour, read by the fire in the sitting room for several hours, and went to her room to prepare for bed. She waited another hour, until every servant had gone to sleep, before putting on her black overcoat and sneaking across the hallway to Charles's room. His had the convenience of facing the alley and having a window that she made sure never made a creak. Once she was down the pipe, she wiped her hands on the rag she hid in the loose brick, readjusted her bonnet, and was off.

She had no real destination. She was still debating the merits of playing Jack tonight, or at least someone male enough to sneak in and observe a fight. The night was young, and she walked along the Thames, stopping to look over the water at St. James Gardens, lit up for the night and the hundreds of couples walking through it. Beyond it was Charlton Palace, once the home of the Prince Regent, before he became king and a fat reclusive over at Windsor Cottage.

"I hear they're going to tear it down."

The sudden intrusion on her quiet moment made her turn angrily to the person beside her. Her quick retort got cut off when she saw who stood there. "Good evening," she muttered instead.

"Excuse me. Miss Bingley," he said, bowing.

Now she curtseyed. "Mr. Dartmouth."

"If my presence upsets you, I will leave you be."

"Hardly as upsetting as your manner of behaving."

"I see a woman I know standing alone late at night on a dark street. Should I not come dashing to her aid?"

She suppressed her smile. "Your dashing is quite an amusing image."

"You think I'm incapable of it?"

"No, but that does not mean I am not capable of defending myself and therefore do not need the aid of a man, much less a young bachelor who by all appearances is unattached. Which is more important – my reputation or my life? I would say in polite society they're about even."

He chuckled. "I suppose you are right. No offer of a carriage ride home, then?"

"You wouldn't dare."

"I would if you tempt me like that."

"You are tempting me to punch you."

"And would you do such a thing?"

She punched him – not too fast or too hard. In fact, it was slow enough for him to catch it, but she pressed her knuckles into his palm.

"You're uncommonly strong, Miss Bingley." He now looked the smallest bit intimidated as he released her hand.

"Thank you," she said, withdrawing it.

"If you are so little concerned for your safety and so greatly concerned for your reputation, perhaps we should go somewhere with people so that it will not be marred by skulking in alleyways. To the gardens?"

She sighed. "To the gardens, then."

St. James Gardens had been redone yet again and were a sight to behold, so much so that they were open well past midnight and tickets still readily being sold.

"Why do people think flowers are so interesting?" Georgiana said. She was stifling under her coat from the heat of the gaslight but didn't want to take it off, as beneath her gown was her Jack costume.

"I have no idea, but neither can I stand for two hours to sit in a box and watch people sing in Italian. I suppose I am very uncultured."

"I suppose I am as uncultured as you in that respect, because even though I speak Italian, I am rather bored after two hours in a hot room."

"You speak Italian?" Mr. Dartmouth said. "You are more cultured than I."

"Says the man who lived in India."

"It makes me traveled. Not cultured." He looked at her. "Speaking of heat – would you like a drink, Miss Bingley? You look positively parched."

"It's the gaslights," she said. "Lemonade. Or something not very strong."

"Lemonade it is," he said and disappeared for a few moments before returning with her glass. It was almost November, so it was not hard to get ice. "Enjoy."

"None for you?"

"I am used to Indian weather."

She nodded and swallowed it all very quickly, and they returned the glass to the vendor. "I have seen enough of bushes and flowers, thank you very much," she said, "but I am entirely less bored now."

"I as well," he said. "It's hard to sit in a smelly, cramped city while your beloved is far away."

"I thought you weren't in love with her?"

"I was referring to yours."

Instead of getting angry, she blushed bright red, making her even hotter. Once they were past the gaslights and back to the square, there was at least a substantial fall breeze, and it seemed clear to Georgie that Mr. Dartmouth intended to walk her home. "What do you know of it?"

"Only that you will not tell me anything, so you must be deeply enamored of this man. Perhaps he does not even return your affections!"

"Don't say that!" she said, her voice louder than she would have liked it to be. Lowering her voice, she repeated, "Do not suppose to know my social life, try as you might. You may find I may tire quickly of your company."

He frowned. "That would indeed be upsetting, as you are the only interesting company I have had in weeks." He bowed. "I apologize, Miss Bingley."

"You are forgiven," she said in a very haughty voice, like a queen delivering orders. She felt like one. She felt almost giddy at the notion. "Provided you do not do it again."

"By accident or design, I make no guarantees. No man is perfect."

"That I will grant you. Certainly I have never met a man who did not stumble over his words or occasionally say the wrong thing. Or always say the wrong thing. Or never say anything at all when he very well should be speaking."

Mr. Dartmouth shook his head. "So judgmental."

"Why not? I have little else to do."

"While pining for your Scottish lover?"

She giggled. "He's in Cambridge, for your information."

"Ah, the student. You know men aren't ready to be married until they are at least a baccalaureate bachelor."

"But women are ready the day they are out, apparently." She looked at him. He had very

148

pleasing features, indeed. "Does that make any sense to you?"

"Perhaps women mature more quickly."

"Unfortunate for us, then, that we are the same age."

"Exactly?"

"I beat him by two weeks. And my father won five pounds on it."

"Childhood sweethearts?"

"Only if you suppose me a sweet little girl with ribbons in her hair and flowers in her cap." She did a little skip as they approached her house. "Oh goodness, I forgot!"

"What? Back at the garden – "

"No!" she said, giving him a little push. "Silly. I snuck *out*. Now I have to sneak *back in*."

He laughed. "You can't be serious."

"I can be serious!" she said, even though she did not feel particularly serious. She was too warm and too giddy and the situation too absurd. "I did sneak out. Now I have to get back up!"

"Up?" he said, and she dragged him into the alley and pointed to the open window. "How in the world do you get there?"

"By jumping. Now what are the rules for jumping? Are they like stairs, where the man always leads the lady down but walks up behind her? Or is it the other way around?"

"I've no idea," Mr. Dartmouth said with a shrug. "Do you wish a boost? It will be our secret."

She didn't feel particularly inclined to do her usual leaps. "Just catch me if I fall." She climbed up on the bins. Her usual balance seemed to be missing, and she nearly toppled over. He caught her just in time. "Thank you," she said, and with muffled laughter, they finally managed their way into Charles's room. "They'll hear," she said.

"Is there somewhere where they won't?"

She nodded, eager to show him all of the sudden. Normally she was not so impulsive about something so outrageously improper in her own home, but it was not a normal night, and at least it was interesting. They went down the hallway and up the stairs into the attic. There was a spare cot along with the various knick-knacks and trunks lying about. "Some of these are from the previous owners," she said, running a hand along the dust. "And that's mine," she said, pointing to the sack on the ground.

"You own a sack?"

"I own what's in the sack. I suppose someone else could have the sack if they really wanted it," she said, and removed Mugin's sword from it, carefully unwrapping it. "No," she said when he put a hand out for it. "It's mine."

"Like I've never held a sword before."

"Not one like this," she said and drew it, and he backed away, white as a sheet, as she pointed it very aimlessly at his throat. "See? I can defend myself!"

"You ... certainly can," he said. "Would you mind putting that down?"

She put it back in its sheath and wrapped it back up in its sack, pushing it under the cot. When she stood up, she nearly jumped as she discovered Mr. Dartmouth just behind her. "Don't do that! You scared me!"

"Not my intention," he said softly.

"You're always talking about your *intentions*," she said. "What if my intention was to lure you up here and chop your head off?"

"Then you would have succeeded," he said, laughing. "Thank God it wasn't!"

"Thank God!" she said, his laughter causing hers, until she was so dizzy from it that she had to sit down on the ground, with her back against the cot. He joined her. "Oh. I don't remember when I've laughed this hard. And at what? At nothing."

"Yes, of course," he said. "By now, you may have even realized that I've drugged you."

"What?"

"I suppose not. Thank goodness you put the sword away." He raised his eyebrows in the most adorable way. "I do have intentions, Miss

Bingley, but you make them abominably hard to perform."

"Because I'd kick your arse –"

"Yes. You would punch me if I were to say, you're a fool to love someone who will probably never show you any attention – "

"You – Don't say that about Geoffrey!" she said, both her ire and her amusement simultaneously raised, and she did throw a punch. It missed, and he caught her wrist and held it. "Why – when did you get so strong?"

"When did *you* get so strong?" he said, putting her wrist back down in her lap. "Did you wear your arms out playing the pianoforte?"

"I – I *hate* the pianoforte. I once ..." she sighed, the happy feeling warming her. "I once slammed the case down on my instructor's hands. She was my governess at the time."

"Ouch."

"She quit. I hated her anyway."

"You have a lot of anger, don't you? Partly at this Geoffrey fellow?"

"I wasn't always," she said. "But I was angry – I don't know. It's hard to explain the way I feel. I felt terrible when I killed Roux – "

"What?"

" – but not as bad when I killed the marquis. Somewhere between Roux and Maret I lost my feeling. My sense of humanity, even, if it was that easy. I know he was a terrible man, but ..." she looked down. "I suppose I am a monster."

They sat in silence. She felt her eyes drooping.

"Are you tired, Miss Bingley? May I call you Georgiana?"

"I – maybe a little."

He pulled out his pocket watch. "Well, you should be getting rather sleepy, and in about five minutes, you'll probably be right out."

She nodded. She didn't feel like doing much else.

He knelt beside her, stroking her hair. "Don't worry – I won't take you while you're asleep. I think that would be positively cruel."

"Thank you," she said, not really aware of what he had said, or much of anything. For the first time in a long time, she played the last moments of the life of the Marquis de Maret in her head over and over until it faded to black.

CHAPTER 10

Knight in Weathered Armor

"Who taught you how to fight? This Maret man?"

"No! Mugin, you git."

"Who's Mugin?"

"Mugin's ... I don't know, Mugin. It's his sword."

"And you used it to kill Maret?"

She nodded.

"Were there witnesses?"

"Heather and Robert?"

"Who?"

She elaborated, annoyed that her speech was so slurred and that she was distracted by the cramps in her arms. The pain became became more and more pressing and she finally opened her eyes to the dimly-lit room. Her arms hurt because they were tied to the cot. "What?" she said, forgetting his last question.

"We were talking about the Wolf. I should be writing this down. I find it very fascinating. I might not have to violate you after all. I may be able to get your inheritance without even marrying you."

"You won't marry me," she said, "Geoffrey will – "

"Yes, yes, we've been through that," he said. "About six times already."

"Sorry. I don' know what I've been – saying." She was tempted to nod off again, but he mentioned the Wolf. Since France, she hadn't talked about the Wolf to anyone, not even Heather. They occasionally talked around it, but never mentioned it directly. It was sacred to her, and Heather understood that. He came from the forest and then when he wasn't needed, he went back in. But they were so far away from the forest. They were in Town, in smelly London, and she was alone with him in her musty attic, tied to the musty cot that had belonged to the previous owners, who must have been musty themselves –

Wait, what?

"Miss Bingley?"

"Wha' have you done to me?"

"Hardly anything. Except drugged your drink, gotten myself alone with you in a place out of hearing distance of the servants, and had you tell me all of your secrets. I thought there might be something about a fistfight when you were younger or a dalliance with this lover of yours but – this is much better. You are a fascinating woman. The

Ton would love to hear of it. I wonder how much your father would pay for them *not* to hear of it. Would he pay the whole fifty thousand, or should I violate you as well? You said he's an amiable man. It may take a lot to get his blood up."

She frowned. She was trying to make sense of what she was hearing, but it was like the words kept slipping away from her. "Gimme my sword," she said.

"Absolutely not, Miss Bingley. Do you think me insane? Besides, you're more likely to hurt yourself right now."

"Give. Me. My. Sword," she said, with as little slurring as she could manage.

Mr. Dartmouth grinned in the lamplight. "Or you'll do what, exactly?"

She had her feet. Even without geta shoes, they'd never failed her, and even without her brain functioning, they would work. She managed to swing her legs around and grab his neck and give it a solid kick, knocking him over and into the pile of whatever was back there.

When he stood up he looked furious, his face red as he pulled loose his cravat and rubbed his neck. "I'll make you pay for that."

"Come nearer and I'll make you," she said.

"You're hardly in a position to do so," he said. "I know everything about you – I can't possibly imagine there's more – and you are in a very compromising position right now, if you have not realized it," he said, also removing his waistcoat. He went around her, out of range for her legs, and put his hand over her mouth. "Don't scream. And don't cry. I hate it when women – "

He would have said more, but the punch to his jaw sent him backwards hard enough that he hit the ground with a considerable thud.

~~~

Geoffrey Darcy considered himself a reasonable person. He was calm and patient, and not given to impulse. His father had taught him that, and he tried his best to keep his first reaction in check and judge the situation dispassionately. His hearing condition had also taught him considerable patience with other people and the world at large, because otherwise, he might have exploded in frustration long ago. Instead, he had come to accept that if the professor had a low voice and mumbled, he would have to use an ear horn and ignore the giggles of his classmates. Other people had it far worse than he did.

The last few weeks, however, he had been devouring the post with a certain passion. It began on the day of Georgiana's first letter to him and continued ever since. It wasn't worth his time to deny that each time he saw her handwriting and return address on the envelope he smiled, so he usually sorted his own mail before the others had the chance to see it.

It was such a day: Frederick was at a lecture, George still in London, and Charles had just returned from a meeting with his tutor when the mail arrived. Naturally, Geoffrey jumped up at the announcement, and Charles didn't bother to try to get in his way. Today his efforts were rewarded, for there under the letter from his father was another one on smaller, more feminine stationary, with handwriting he'd long-since memorized. He abandoned the rest of the pile by dumping it on Charles's lap in the common room and returned to his own.

To Mr. Darcy, of Pemberley, Derbyshire, and King's College

He frowned; he hated all of the formalities between them.

I am writing you now from a very early hour. We have been out all night dancing with Izzy, who is off to Chesterton in a few days and will miss all of this social life.

159

I admit I may even be becoming accustomed to it. Tonight I danced mostly of my own free will with a Mr. Dartmouth for the second time. He has an intended in Scotland, but nonetheless has his own social requirements set by his family. He is quite the conversationalist.

I hope there is no serious news from Cambridge, where you all are supposed to be studying so hard and not drinking and fooling around. Say hello to my brother for me. And Frederick, I suppose.

Sincerely,
Georgiana Louisa Bingley

He read the second paragraph several times before finishing the rest of the letter, which he paid little attention to after deciding its worth by comparison. She *what?* Who was Mr. Dartmouth? Had she made him up to taunt him? No, she would not be that cruel. He had to be real. And he was charming, and smart, and all of the things Geoffrey wasn't around to be and was afraid to be in front of her. It wasn't the first time he pined for the days when he could just talk to her without worrying about proprieties and social niceties, but this was the first time he was truly angry over it.

She intended this. Don't let it get to you. You have a lecture in two hours and a paper to hand in with your tutor tomorrow morning. He stood and paced, occasionally glancing in fury at the dreaded letter. *Don't let it get to you.*

But the image of Georgiana dancing, laughing, talking to another man did get to him. What if she let this Dartmouth man court her? No, she would never do that. She was loyal to him, no matter how little Geoffrey was loyal to her. Was she not permitted to have a social life?

No. Not with men, he thought before he could stop himself. Her plan had worked and he was jealous. She won, again. Why did this particular time make him so angry? *Oh Georgie – what have you done to me?*

He had to see her – talk to her. He didn't know what he would say, and he would probably mess it up or be forced into making the dreaded confession, and then he would have to propose, because there was no other logical way –

But he had to do *something*.

"Reynolds," he said, calling in his man. "I need a horse." He said it in such a tone that Reynolds looked at him, nodded once, and ran out of the room. He concerned himself only with throwing whatever items he thought he would need into his saddlebag, removing his robes and putting a coat on over his vest.

"Geoffrey? Is something wrong?" Charles sounded so calm and innocent compared to everything that was going on in his mind.

"No. It's fine." He took his half-finished paper and gave it Charles. "Will you give this to my tutor with my apologies? Lie and say it was a family emergency."

"Is it?"

"No. No, of course not," he said. *I just need to get to London very badly right now and I honestly can't explain why.*

Fortunately, Charles took the paper and let him leave without further questioning, and before Geoffrey knew it, Cambridge was disappearing behind him. It took the rest of the day and night to get to Town, and along the road he forced himself to stop, lest he kill the horse (and possibly himself). He swallowed some wine, ate a few rolls, and when his horse had rested a little, jumped back on it. He was sore by the time he saw the outskirts of London, and when he finally climbed off the saddle, his legs were quite cramped. He practically limped up the stairs of the Bingley townhouse and knocked on the door.

It was a long while before the footman answered. "Hello, Mr. Darcy. I am sorry, but the house is still abed."

"It doesn't – may I just come in?" He needed a drink, be it water or tea or anything. "My house is all shut up."

"Of course, Mr. Darcy," said the servant, removing Geoffrey's coat and bringing him a drink. "May I – "

But he had come too far. He swallowed the water in one gulp. If she was asleep, so be it. He charged up the stairs. "Georgie!" he yelled, banging on her door. Nothing. "Are you asleep?" A stupid question, but if she did not answer –

Wait. Why was Charles's door half-open? He wasn't at home. In fact, Geoffrey knew for a fact he was at Cambridge, having seen him there before leaving. He pushed the door gently open. No one was inside, but the window was open. "Huh." Still sweating from exertion, he paused contemplatively, and that was when he heard a crashing sound from above him. Someone was in the attic. Was that where she hid?

The servants had not yet caught him up when he ran towards the attic. He was well acquainted with the Bingley house, having played there in his youth, and he knew there was an attic with a small set of stairs leading up. He paused at the bottom, listening again mostly to his own heavy breathing, and heard muffled voices. Two people upstairs. Well, he would make it three. He was determined –

Whatever he was determined to do was derailed by the scene he found. Georgiana, tied to the cot. A man, unknown, was holding her down. He didn't care who the man was or what he was doing thereor bother to fashion a guess. All he cared about was the fact that the man's jaw was unbroken, and he was determined to fix that inconsistency by clocking him in the face as hard as he could. A day's ride had not robbed him of all of his strength, and the man hit the floor so hard he paused to see if he had killed him. No, the chest was still rising and falling; still alive. And now his hand hurt.

Then he heard her cry. It was more of a whimper, but he heard it nonetheless. "Georgie," he said, collecting himself and his thoughts enough to remove his pocketknife. "It's all right," he said, cutting her arms free and helping her sit up with her legs over the side of the cot. Thank God she was still clothed. "It's all right."

She did something he had never seen her do when not angry at him – she collapsed into sobs and incoherent mumbling. "Georgie," he said, putting his arm around her and drawing her head into his chest. "It's all right."

"'snot," she said, her voice slurred. "'snot. Never going to be. Why ... why did I – "

"Shhh."

"I did terrible things 'n France! And Derby – Derbyshire." She had trouble with the name, but she didn't seem drunk. He knew her drunken speech. Geoffrey lifted her head up and looked into her eyes and smelled her breath. Not drunk. Drugged, most likely. He let her rest her head on his chest again. "I told him everything. He – "

"Did he touch you?"

"Doesn' – matter. I'm no good as a lady – at being a good lady – at being any kind of lady."

"Georgie – did he touch you?"

She shook her head. "He didn't – he was going to – "

His sigh was heavy, and he glanced over at the unconscious young man, lacking a cravat and a waistcoat. His intentions were obvious. "Is that Mr. Dartmouth?" Geoffrey felt her trembling nod. "Did he give you something? Drug you?"

"I think – I thin' he said so. Oh God. Geoffrey, I broke so many promises, I promised Papa I would be good – "

"It's all right – "

"And I promised myself – I meant to be there for you," she pulled away and looked up at him, her eyes red. "You were supposed to be my first."

"He didn't harm you, Georgie. He was going to, but I stopped him."

"I – Robert. Oh God, I told him about that. I'm ruined. Even you – you'll hate me." She tugged at her hair. "You'll never want t'see me again."

"Who is Robert?" he said, putting his arms on her shoulders. "Georgie, I promise I won't get angry. Not at anything you say. I just want to know who hurt you."

She shook her head. "He didn't hurt me. We just kissed. You know. But he didn't mean to hurt me at all. He said he loved me. He said he wanted to marry me, but I told him to feck off, I was going to marry you, but I was so angry at you and lonely, and he was the only who cared whether I lived or died – "

He was beginning to grasp her meaning, and he didn't like it, but he would keep his promise. "When was this?"

"France. The Wolf. The marquis. The whole business." She shook her head again. "I'm a – am a bad person, Geoffrey. I'm not noble, and I'm not a warrior. I'm just a murderer. They were going to hurt Heather, and he hurt Sophie and he tried to kill me, so I killed him. I guess it was in self-defense, but it's so hard – why don't I feel worse? Why am I such an awful person?"

"You're not," he said.

"Geoffrey – how could you – "

166

"You are not an awful person," he said firmly. "You are the bravest, strongest, most clever person I know. And the most beautiful."

"You hate me."

"No."

"Because of Robert, and France, and now I got tricked by Dartmouth and you think – "

"Georgie, I don't hate you."

" – I didn't mean it, I didn't mean any of it, I wanted to hurt you then because I was so lonely, but I've always loved you, even if you hate me now and you hate me forever – "

"Georgie," he said, taking a firmer grasp of her. "I don't hate you. I love you."

She collapsed into his arms again, and wept. Why wouldn't she stop? How many tears could one woman have? "I love you, Georgie. I always have." He kissed the top of her head, stroking that lovely hair of hers. "I'll never hate you. Never."

She looked up at him with hope in her eyes for the first time.

"I love you," Geoffrey repeated and kissed her again, this time properly. There was an odd taste in her mouth, but it wasn't alcohol, and even if it had been, he didn't care. He didn't care about anything else at that exact moment – even breathing – except her.

It was a long time – and yet not long enough – before Geoffrey managed to pull away. The physical separation was painful as he rolled off her (because he had somehow got *on* her) and buried his head in the pillow.

"Geoffrey," she said, after a breathy silence. "You're bleeding." She seemed better now, as she slowly emerged from her drugged stupor.

She was right, he realized. His hand, which still stung, was scratched where the punch had connected. Though it was a small amount of blood, any amount of flexing hurt tremendously. "Ow!"

"Let me see it," she said, and he could hardly bring himself to contradict her as she sat up and examined his hand. She pulled each of his fingers, and he screamed. Well, it was more of yelp, or so he hoped. "It might be broken."

"We should probably ... get someone. I don't think I can ride with – ow! Okay, Georgie, we've established I'm injured. You can stop now."

She smiled and kissed him on the cheek. "Uncle Maddox."

"I hate to point out the obvious – "

Georgiana rolled her eyes. "He'll bring George."

"George?"

"He's been apprenticed. Where have you been?"

"Cambridge," he said. "And there's the matter of – " He gestured to Dartmouth, still unconscious on the floor.

"He might know what to do about him, too," she said. "Discreetly. So I'm not the talk of the Ton tomorrow. But I don't want - ," she stumbled. She was not back to her old self quite yet. How could she be? "Geoffrey, I don't want to marry him."

"His behavior really puts his reputation as a suitor beyond repair."

She fell into him. It was not want he wanted – Georgiana crying again – but the physical touch, he did not mind so much "Georgie," he whispered. "Believe me when I say, your father is not going to make you marry him. Whatever – did he - ?"

She shook her head rather fervently.

"Even *if*," he said. "Your father loves you too much to care about this propriety nonsense. He'll take care of it—send the man to jail, perhaps, and it will be okay – "

"My reputation will be tarnished," she whimpered. "Gone."

Geoffrey said, "Then I'll marry you."

He'd said it without thinking, without any consideration, and it hung there in the air, too awkward to address, too real to dismiss.

"Uncle Maddox," she said at last, after an unbearable silence.

169

"Uncle Maddox. Right." He stood and walked over to Mr. Dartmouth, kicking him in the side a bit, but there was no response. "If you write a note, I'll deliver it. Or see it delivered." His hand was now really starting to bother him, and he held it with his left hand. He doubted he could write legibly in this condition. Georgiana quickly opened up a pencil set and made up the note. "Give it to the footman."

"Do you want me to – "

"No," she said. "Don't leave me."

Of course, it was quite necessary not to leave Georgiana in the room with the man who had nearly forced himself on her, however disabled he was. That was entirely the reason, or so his head tried to reason as he sat on the stairs, not facing her, because he couldn't. They needed separation, he needed to think, he needed to ... He didn't know. He just didn't know.

The bleeding was so minor it had stopped by the time Doctor Maddox arrived with George Wickham in tow. "Georgiana?"

"Uncle!" she ran to him, embracing him as he finished climbing the stairs. "I'm so glad you're here. We didn't know who else to call."

"We?"

"Me," Geoffrey said. "I – came down. She might not have mentioned that. Also, I'm the reason Mr. Dartmouth is unconscious."

"He is?"

"On your left," said George, carrying the doctor's bag. "On the floor."

Doctor Maddox's cane eventually found the body. "Where's he hurt?"

"In the jaw," Geoffrey answered before George could. "Or, that's where I hit him."

Maddox gave a look in the general direction of Geoffrey's voice. "Are you all right, Mr. Darcy?"

"No, actually," Georgiana said quickly. "He hurt his hand. I think something's broken."

"George," the doctor said, "take care of your cousin first, Mr. Dartmouth second. Now," he scratched his head. "We must call the constable if what you said is true. When he arrives, I'll take care of it. Where are the servants?"

"I – I waited until they were asleep to go out." She buried her face in his coat. "I know, I shouldn't have. I brought this all on myself, Uncle."

"No," he said softly, but firmly. "No, you did not. You'll come home with me, and we'll sort this out and discover that nothing was your fault, my dear." He gently stroked her hair.

The constable was called and arrived in a timely fashion. As Dartmouth was taken away in irons, he talked quietly with the doctor. Georgiana was too upset to take notice of anything, but even in a haze of pain, Geoffrey could tell that his uncle

171

passed the man a bribe to keep this under wraps. George, who had earlier pronounced two of his fingers broken, waited until the constable left to remind Geoffrey, "You should punch with your knuckles, not your hand."

"Thank you for your advice," Geoffrey seethed.

"It can wait until we reach the house to be bound. Mr. Darcy, I assume you are in no condition to return to Cambridge tonight."

Geoffrey had the sense that his uncle would, if he could, have been giving him a very accusatory stare. "Yes, sir."

The Maddox townhouse was not very far away, and even though it was still quite early in the day, Lady Maddox was up and dressed—she had probably risen when her husband was called. "Georgiana! Oh – Geoffrey? Why are you not at University?"

"I believe it will all be explained in time," Doctor Maddox said to his wife, somehow succeeding in finding her arm. "First, please sit with Georgiana for a bit while we bind Geoffrey's hand."

His wife didn't question him, and Geoffrey was led into the laboratory, which the servants quickly lit up. Geoffrey's hand was placed on the table beside it. "There should be – George, there should be boards in the left cabinet, third drawer."

Dr. Maddox felt at the bottles, which were all differently sized, until he found the one he wanted and set it on the table. "And a spoon."

The servants brought them water, and the injured hand was cleaned and the small scratch patched before George set the hand aside and poured a spoonful of the green concoction. "Open up."

George fed it to him, and Geoffrey gagged.

"Yes, yes, it tastes terrible." Doctor Maddox took a seat across from him, resting his cane against his shoulder. "But it's very effective. George is going to set the bones, so you're going to appreciate it in a few minutes. That, and it will make my questioning of your sudden appearance in Town that much easier." He smiled. "It has a remarkable effect on Darcys, I've found."

"Can I possibly – have a real doctor do this?"

"Shut up," George said as he placed his hand into position, causing Geoffrey to cry out.

"Bedside manner, Mr. Wickham. Very important," his tutor reminded him. "And Geoffrey, George is very good at this. I've stumbled and broken things I don't know how many times as of late, so he's had practice. No matter how much I remind people not to move furniture around without telling me, they seem to do it anyway."

"I am sorry about that," George said.

173

"You haven't been the only one, I assure you. I think Frederick may be doing it intentionally at this point, despite the biblical injunction against stumbling blocks. Which fingers are broken?"

"The middle and the ring."

"Multiple places, or just once each?"

"I think just once each."

"Good. Proceed, then."

Those were not exactly words Geoffrey wanted to hear, but he managed to grit his teeth and keep from shouting as George set his fingers and bound them to boards so they would stay in place. "Try and keep your hand dry and clean."

"Have someone else take notes for you," Maddox said, "when you *do* return to University."

George disappeared. Not in a puff of smoke, but he slipped off to the side to begin packing up implements as Geoffrey withdrew his hand. His vision was a little blurred, his body suddenly exhausted, but the pain was lessened. All he could really concentrate on was the lamplight flickering off Uncle Maddox's black glasses.

"Very good, George," Maddox said to his assistant and called for a servant to help Geoffrey up. Walking was more of a bother than he wanted it to be, but it was only a townhouse, and the guest room was not terribly far away. He collapsed on the bed and was helped very carefully out of his waistcoat and boots.

"Now, I know all you want to do is go to sleep," the doctor said, announcing his presence, which honestly had escaped Geoffrey's limited notice, "but first you will be so kind as to explain to me, to the best of your abilities at the moment, how it is you came to be knocking the daylights out of Mr. Dartmouth."

"Well, he – "

"Yes, yes, that part I know," the doctor said. "But you'd best start at the beginning."

Slowly, Geoffrey retraced his steps and thoughts until he spotted the place and time in his mind. "I – received a letter. From Georgie."

"About Mr. Dartmouth?"

"Yes."

"What did it say?"

He was aware enough to tell he had no choice but to answer all questions. "That – that she's spoken with him, and she danced with him."

"What else?"

"That was it."

"When did you receive this missive?"

"Uhm – last morning, with the post."

Doctor Maddox cocked his head curiously. "At Cambridge?"

"Yes."

"So one must conclude that you, upon receiving a letter that contained nothing particularly unexpected or exceptional, immediately leapt on a horse and rode all the way to Town, went straight into the Bingley house, and punched Mr. Dartmouth."

Those were a lot of big words. Geoffrey frowned. "Yes."

"And why in the hell did you do that?"

He had never heard Uncle Maddox curse. Granted, it was rather minor, and not at all in a severe sort of voice, more amused, as if he were leading Geoffrey along. "... I don't know, sir."

His uncle settled back into the armchair, saying nothing for a moment, his expression unreadable. Geoffrey was tempted to close his eyes and maybe sleep, but the silence was at last broken again. "Did you ask Georgiana if she was compromised?"

"She wasn't."

"She said that or you were a witness to the entire event?"

"I came inside – he was forcing her down - ," his memory was getting muddled. "But no, she was not."

"So you performed a thorough inspection afterwards."

"No." Though, that was not entirely true. He certainly hadn't been a bystander to her personal condition while they were getting their senses about them. "I believe her, Uncle."

"I have no doubt. Nor do I doubt she wouldn't lie. Not to you, certainly." Maddox rose. "I shan't bother you any more tonight. You've given me enough to think on, Mr. Darcy."

Geoffrey could manage no further response. He closed his eyes, and all he heard was the tapping of the cane and the shutting of the heavy door before he was asleep.

~~~

"Daniel," his wife said, drawing his attention to the hallway as he left Geoffrey. He already knew she was there or at least in the general vicinity. He had memorized her scent – not her perfume, though he knew that well enough, but her personal scent, the very air about her. She joined him. "I've just helped Georgiana retire. She will probably go to Chatton House tomorrow."

"If she wishes," he said. "Did you lock the door?"

"Yes."

He kissed her on her forehead. "Clever thinking as always."

"What are we going to do?"

"Retire to our room as if nothing momentous has happened and deal with it later," he said. "Besides, my aim with a shotgun is terrible these days."

He let her, instead of the cane, guide him up the stairs. Stairs he always had trouble with, because space was so unpredictable once his foot was in it. Not like walls, which generally stayed where they were.

It was a chilly autumn, and there was a fire roaring in their room. Doctor Maddox was helped out of his waistcoat and then excused his manservant. "Did you speak with Georgiana?" he said to Caroline as he heard her emerge from her dressing room.

"No, we sat in silence for an hour. *Of course* I spoke with Georgiana," she said and took her place on the bed beside him as he removed his boots. At times, it was a laborious and frustrating task, and once he had gotten his own hands so knotted up in the laces that his wife wouldn't let him go about it for a week, but he would handle his own boots, thank you very much. However long it took him.

"How is she?" It was a very open question, he knew. He also knew she knew how to answer it. His hand strayed to the bed, and she held it.

"Appropriately shaken. Terrified. If Geoffrey hadn't shown up – " She leaned on his shoulder. "I thought she was doing all right."

"So did everyone. Except our young Master Darcy, who raced down here on instinct." But he did not give her time to respond. "I take it she is – "

"Yes."

"Thank God. Though, I had very little doubt of it. I asked Geoffrey."

"What? Did he give her a thorough inspection?"

He smiled. "I asked him the very same question. Clearly he did. He was probably blushing terribly. In a way, they owe Mr. Dartmouth a debt."

"That and a credit to the Darcy heritage of instinctively being the savior of all that is good in the world. Now matter how stupidly they must always go about it."

~~~

Geoffrey Darcy was quite sure he would have slept through the night if two things hadn't happened. First, at some point while he was still asleep, his pain medicine began to wither in strength. Second, he was startled awake by a voice, and that made him quite aware of the first thing. What in the world was Georgiana doing at Cambridge? Women weren't allowed in the dormitory – *officially*, anyway. Not that it mattered much to Frederick Maddox. But this was not Frederick Maddox, or Charles Bingley, or any other person other than her, and between her presence and the pain in his hand, he could piece together that he was not, in fact, at Cambridge. "Georgie?"

"When you call me that, I feel like I'm eight," she said. She was very close to him, but still above the covers, but he was having trouble adjusting his eyes to the dim light.

"Georgiana," his voice a little more emotional than he wanted it to be. "What – what are you doing here?"

"Can you believe that my own aunt locked me in my room?" she said. "Not that a lock would stop a Bingley."

He sat up abed, against the headboard. "Georgiana," he said with more authority. "You've – had a bad night."

"I know."

He swallowed. He knew he had to say it, and yet, he didn't want to tell her to go.

"I have bruises," she said. "I have little red spots. They'll be bruises in the morning. You know I bruise so easily."

He nodded.

"What I'm saying, you stupid git, is that I don't want to be alone tonight."

It took all of his self-control to muster, "That doesn't mean you should be with me."

"Would you like me to wake George?"

His eyes must have told the whole story of his sudden rage, because she giggled and leaned into him. This, he could not bring himself to stop. She lay by his side – on his side – and was very distracting from the pain in his hand. Thoroughly distracting.

"Why did you come to Town?"

It was so easy a question, so hard to answer. "I don't know."

"Geoffrey," she said, "you received my letter, didn't you? Tell me, what was going through your mind when you read it?"

He should have known she would piece together the timing of her letter with his sudden arrival. "I – I don't know how to phrase it," he said. "I ... guess ..." He trailed off, but she did not relent. She could have a terrifying gaze, even though it was obvious she wasn't the least bit angry with him. Finally he answered, "I couldn't stand the idea of you with Mr. Dartmouth."

"You didn't know Mr. Dartmouth."

"I suppose; then ... I couldn't stand to see you with someone – else."

"And by implication ..."

"The same as you, as you picked the lock and did the very improper thing of coming into a man's room in the middle of the night. Especially when you know he's drugged and has already, without the aid of medication, lost his head once tonight." He swallowed. "By implication, I love you. There, you have it. Again. Now go and leave me alone before I – "

"Before you what?"

He answered her with exactly *what* it was, which was a kiss. The kind that lasted, too; the kind where they were taking in each other's souls, not ending it until it became a physical necessity. It was followed by another, and then another, so much so that their physical positioning on the bed had changed. He only pulled away when the pain of trying to support himself with his hands reminded him he was not capable of doing so. And that they were in a very dangerous position. "Georgiana – "

She took his arm and steadied him so he did not have to weigh down the hand. "Thank you," he muttered. "Georgiana, you're making it very hard for me to be a gentleman."

"I don't want a gentleman," she said, her voice soft, exposed. "I want you."

Where was the Georgie that he knew and loved, and who was this daring woman before him? No, he shook his head, she had always been a daring woman, or a daring girl, always frightfully stubborn and secretive. Except to him; he was always different. He was always hers. "Marry me."

"This second?"

"I'm serious," he said, and he was not lying. "I can't – you know I can't. Shouldn't. Unless I'm dreaming this all, from the opium, or from some drink my cousin slipped me, and I really didn't ride all the way from Cambridge in the middle of the semester to see you because I couldn't stand the thought of another man even looking at you, much less – " But he couldn't bring up that memory. "Unless all that happened, I didn't realize that I won't stand it if you're not mine. Permanently."

"You know I am."

Was he taking advantage of her? It didn't seem like it. She wasn't crying or fighting him. She had snuck into *his* room while *he* was asleep. Yes, he was asking her for something very great, but it seemed like she was willing to give it. While he was contemplating all of this, she leaned in and kissed him again, whispering, "Yes, I will marry you." She wrapped her arms around him and pulled him down with her, and the last of his fortitude was gone. After all, they were now engaged, so some indiscretion was permissible? Emphasis on *some*.

It was all instinctual. All of the advice imparted to him, either awkwardly and subtly by his father, or openly and lewdly by his classmates, seemed to be irrelevant and, certainly, an unqualified comparison. If he fumbled, Georgiana gave no overt notice as she undid the buttons of his shirt, being the only one with two usable hands.

She was right – she did bruise easily, or it showed more easily because she was so pale. "Ow," she said as he ran his hand over her wrists and up her arm.

"Does it hurt?"

"A little. Not much."

"Do you want me to stop?"

"No."

That was all the incentive he needed and kissed her on her neck. Even though she'd been in London for weeks, she tasted like nature, like flowers and fields and all of the wild things that described her nature. Except maybe flowers.

"What're you giggling at?"

"Nothing," he said and silenced her with a kiss. "I love you." He could feel her tense when he said it, as though holding on to the moment, waiting to see if it was real or not. He could feel better than he could hear, and at the moment, it was doing him a world of good. "It's all right. I'm not leaving. I'm never leaving you again."

"I love you."

"I know."

When he was less distracted, he noticed the sky lightening, and despite his very strong desire for sleep, he whispered to the similarly-exhausted Georgiana, "I think you'd best be back in your room."

"Are you tossing me out?"

"I don't want to," he said as he kissed her neck. "But I think I have to."

"Is that the procedure? After being with a woman?"

"I don't know. I never have – had." He bore the brunt of her disbelieving look. "What? Is that so terrible a thing? Admittedly, I had to lie to Frederick about it so I wouldn't have to endure the endless ribbing he gives your brother about the same subject, but for some reason, other women didn't seem to – interest me."

"I will assume we are keeping this between us," she said, and then clarified, "the engagement, I mean. If you were serious about that."

"I was. And yes, our secret. Unless … it's not possible to keep."

She understood his meaning perfectly. Or, he hoped she did, as she kissed him once more, hurriedly dressed herself, and slid out of his room with the same stealth with which she had entered. The rooster was crowing by the time he was asleep.

CHAPTER 11

The Knight in Disgrace

Geoffrey rose late, which was not an overwhelming surprise. He did his best to quickly dress himself and sneak some coffee from the kitchen. He didn't immediately spot his hosts, and he knew Daniel Junior was at Eton, so that only left George Wickham, who found him easily enough.

"It looks swollen. Is it supposed to be?"

George untied the upper bandages, took a brief look, and retied them. "Yes, it can be a bit. Hurts like a bastard, does it not?"

"Didn't Uncle Maddox say something about your bedside manner?"

"He wants to talk to you in his study. *And* he says I shouldn't give you any pain medicine until you talk to him."

"Does that mean I'm in trouble?"

George gave him a wicked smile and walked off. Geoffrey huffed. There was no use putting it off, and he desperately wanted that pain medicine. He knocked on the study door. "Come." It was impressive that Doctor Maddox always rose to greet his guests when certainly he could be

187

excused from that convention in his condition. "Please, shut the door if you would." He walked around the desk and guided himself along the bookshelf. "Thank you, Mr. Darcy. Now, there should be a bookshelf about your level with a set of Chaucer's works in red binding. Do you see it?"

"Uh, yes, Uncle," Geoffrey said, looking to his left, confused but obedient.

"Would you do me the favor of standing against it?"

"All right," he said, and the doctor paced around without his cane, before finding him. "Thank you. Now – " Suddenly he rather violently grabbed Geoffrey's collar and pushed him against the bookcase. "*In my house.*"

"Uncle – "

"In *my* house! What am I going to say to my brother-in-law? My wife's *brother*?"

"Uncle, you're choking – "

"I am very aware of what I'm doing, thank you very much."

Geoffrey had frequently looked at his uncle with pity, as he was crippled, and now he was being reminded that Doctor Daniel Maddox was actually a fairly tall, robust man who, despite his blindness, was quite capable of picking up his nephew and throttling him. And that was to say nothing of those black glasses making it seem as if he always intensely stared at you.

"You know what you must do," the doctor said tightly.

"Sir?" Geoffrey rasped.

"You can't possibly be that stupid. Though, after last night, I am seriously questioning how much of your parents' intelligence you did inherit," the doctor said with full indignation. "Now, tell me, what is the proper procedure in this particular circumstance? I will give you a hint that involves Chatton House."

"Uncle, please, I can't – "

"Geoffrey Darcy! Of all the people!"

"I - ," he stammered, for it was getting hard – or at least painful – for him to breathe. " – I must go and ask Uncle Bingley for his consent."

Doctor Maddox finally released him with a long sigh. He reached out and found one of the desk chairs, and slumped into it as Geoffrey rubbed his neck. "I am sorry," Geoffrey said.

"I must admit – the outcome will probably be satisfying to all parties, but the way you went about it could not have been more foolish," his uncle said. "And your father will be furious if you do not finish at Cambridge, so that means a very long engagement. If Georgiana is capable of a long engagement. You had best pray that she is."

"I didn't - ," but he realized, there was no real use denying it. They had been alone, with the door closed, but there was only one reason why a woman went into the bedchambers of a man in the middle of the night and did not emerge for a length of time. Or maybe she had confessed it all to Lady Maddox; he really had no idea. "I don't know. About the engagement."

"Of course. But we will know in the next few weeks. The point is, you cannot wait that long. You must go to Bingley and tell him everything. *Everything*, Geoffrey."

Geoffrey swallowed. "She did consent. I did ask."

"Oh, how good of you." No attempt was made to hide his sarcasm and his disapproval.

"I love her." This part did not bring him any pain to say. "I do want her as my wife. I know – I'm not going to deny it—I was foolish. But I have no hesitation about my feelings."

"A young and foolish Darcy," the doctor sniggered. He seemed to be softening. "Now where have I heard that before? Oh, when I passed the time with your father in an Austrian prison by sharing all of our dirty secrets. I should tell you about your father's University days sometime – but not today, when you must ride to Derbyshire. Can you ride with one hand, Mr. Darcy?"

"Yes."

"Unfortunately, we can't give you a very strong dose or you'll be falling off your horse. I think your uncle the mystic would refer to it as a form of penance."

"I do apologize for my reprehensible behavior," Geoffrey said, bowing out of habit. "When my horse is ready, I will be gone. But – may I see Georgiana first?"

"I believe she is with her aunt, and I will leave that decision up to my wife. Something you'd best learn to do." However, he did smile. "Good luck, Master Geoffrey. You're going to need it."

He had no doubt of that.

~~~

He found Georgiana taking a mid-morning tea with her Aunt Caroline. Geoffrey felt himself choking up as he was introduced.

They rose and curtseyed, and he very awkwardly greeted them. And upon seeing Georgiana, not emotionally stricken but rather fresh-faced, he immediately bowed again to cover his blush.

"Mr. Darcy," Mrs. Maddox said, "we've just been discussing you."

Oh, I'm quite sure about that. "Thank you for your hospitality, Lady Maddox, but I'm afraid I must take my leave for Chatton House as soon as possible. May I have a moment – "

He did not have to explain himself. He couldn't decipher the riddle of his aunt's smile as she strode off in an accomplished fashion. The doors remained open, but they were at least out of earshot. It prevented any physical touch that he found himself rather desperate for, but that would come in time – and he had done enough damage as it was. "Georgiana – I apologize for my behavior."

"Do you regret it?"

"I'm going to get hell and damnation from the family, but no," he said. "No, I do not. But do you wish to marry me?"

"You've already asked."

He felt his blush only deepen until his ears were burning. "I was a little – forceful – when I applied for your hand. I want to do it now, with all civility. I love you, Georgiana. I've always loved you, but it took the horrible Mr. Dartmouth to make me realize that I want you to be my wife. I want you to be – *mine*."

Georgiana took his unbroken hand. Inappropriate, but no one was rushing in to stop her. "I have been waiting twenty years for you to say that."

"If I kiss you, I will probably get in more trouble than I already am."

"Then allow me," she said, and kissed his hand, as one would a superior. "Papa is a pushover.

He may be angry at the circumstances, but he has a terribly romantic heart."

"When will I see you again?"

"There's no reason for me to remain in Town now, so ... perhaps in a few days, when you are bruised and bloodied after Uncle Darcy hears about this."

"Thank you so much for reminding me."

~~~

It took him a day and a half, several changes of horses, and one night spent in an inn where exhaustion overtook pain and let him sleep before Geoffrey reached Chatton House. Unshaven, his hand bound and tied up, and covered in grime from the road, he must have been an alarming figure indeed. "Geoffrey!" Unfortunately, the first person who discovered him was his Aunt Jane. "My goodness! What happened to you?"

"I'm fine," he said even though it was plainly a lie. "A little tired, maybe."

"You're soaking wet! And there's no color in you at all! Geoffrey Darcy, you'll make yourself sick! And why are you not in Cambridge? Do your parents know where you are?"

"No," he said. "I – I need to talk to my uncle."

"What's wrong? What's happened?"

Geoffrey sighed. Something significant had happened to her daughter, his interference and latter actions aside. But there was no way he could conceive of telling her the story without her worming all of it out of him. "I'm the only one hurt." *Aside from Mr. Dartmouth.* "I promise – it will all be explained. But I must speak with Uncle Bingley."

"Why don't you have a seat in his study while I fetch him? And you should have something to eat. You look awful." She kissed him on the cheek. "Should I send for your parents?"

"No! I mean, no, not yet. Thank you, Aunt Bingley." He bowed stiffly and escaped to his uncle's study, though he knew it would not be an escape for long. Like his father's study, it was filled with books. Unlike his father's study, the books overflowed the shelves so much that some were simply stacked against the wall or piled precariously on the desk.

Geoffrey slumped into one of the chairs, and his exhaustion finally overcame him. Even though every part of his body seemed to hurt from riding, he'd had enough sense not to take a vial of Maddox's concoction before attempting to seek Georgiana's hand in marriage. He had no appetite for the food brought in for him and was actually beginning to drift off when Mr. Bingley finally entered. "Geoffrey?"

He leapt to his feet, despite the massive physical exertion it required of him. "Uncle Bingley." He bowed, trying very hard not to topple over.

"Mr. Darcy, what in the world has happened? Look at you – you're barely holding up. Should I call for a doctor?"

"No, I've just seen one. George Wickham patched me up."

"Yes, I've heard Doctor Maddox has taken him under his wing. Wait – what were you doing in Town? Did something happen in Cambridge?" His uncle's expression was appropriately confused. "Please, sit."

"I prefer to stand, sir," he said. That was proper, wasn't it? "I – I don't know how to begin this story."

"I often find chronologically is best," Bingley said, taking his seat.

Geoffrey exhaled, unconsciously leaning against the bookcase for support as he began with the letter he'd received about Mr. Dartmouth. "I cannot, at this point, explain my actions. I will attempt to do so later in the tale, I promise." He then proceeded to narrate the terrible events of the evening in question, pausing after his fight with

Dartmouth, to allow his uncle to absorb the terrible events.

Mr. Bingley was obviously distressed at the news of the near-violation of his eldest daughter. He ran his hands through his graying hair. "But – you saved her."

"Yes. I suppose."

"You – you suppose?"

He continued with his tale, not being completely descriptive about how exactly he had comforted her before they called Doctor Maddox. That would come later. He stopped at his retiring for the night, the first time.

There was a very uncomfortable silence as he watched his uncle rub his hands together and try to absorb all of this information. "I've been a terrible father."

"No – "

"Entirely inexcusable. I showed more concern with my sister's suitors than my own daughter's. We can now only hope that Mr. Dartmouth can be reasoned with."

"You're – intending to talk to him?"

"We certainly cannot press charges without it all coming out. In fact, I will be forced to bribe him to be assured of his silence if Georgiana is to have any hope of a reputation. But the chance of her having one at all is all thanks to you, Mr. Darcy. I am in your debt." He managed a weak smile.

Geoffrey shuddered. "You are not, sir."

"I don't understand your meaning."

"Uncle Bingley," he said, "I've come to Chatton House not only to deliver this news, but to ask for your consent. I wish to marry Georgiana."

"And – *what*?"

"I love her and she loves me. I asked her if she wanted to be my wife, and she consented." He hung his head. "I'm not quite finished with the story, if you would, sir."

Bingley, too stunned to do otherwise, nodded.

With as few descriptive words as possible, Geoffrey kept his promise to Doctor Maddox and explained how, mutually, they had come to realize their love for each other, and not as cousins. He tried to make it sound as though neither was in the wrong, or at the very least, that it was only he that was responsible for their joint actions, though he was not willing to go as far as to admit to forcing her. If anything, in truth, she had forced herself upon him, but he certainly wasn't going to say *that* either.

The expression on his uncle's face was enough to give him the strong temptation to run, but he did not. First, he doubted he had the strength to. Second, it certainly would not be the best for his application for Georgiana's hand.

Finally, after much pacing about, his uncle said, "What am I supposed to tell Darcy?"

"It's my responsibility, sir."

"You take a lot on yourself," Bingley said. He lumbered about, as if lost in his own study. "It does ... explain your actions."

"What does, sir?"

"Riding from Cambridge on the mere mention of a suitor for Georgiana. Not that you lack your father's instincts for being the gentleman savior, but he usually did it with a bit more investigation first." Bingley paced as he talked. "And – I can't say that you are ill-matched. Georgiana spoke her first words to you."

"She – she did?"

"I suppose you don't remember it. I can hardly blame you, as you were two, but we were quite concerned that she was not as articulate as you or other children her age. But it turned out she was perfectly capable but chose to talk only to you, or so you once told your mother, and she related the story to me much later and with much amusement." He smiled idly at the memory, if only briefly. "In fact, despite the manner in which this came about, I can't think of a single reason to object to such a union. If you would, there's a bottle in the – "

Geoffrey instantly reached for the false case and pulled it aside to reveal a spare bottle of brandy and several tumblers.

"You constantly surprise me. I suppose I don't wish to hear the story behind how you became so acquainted with the infamous shelf. Just pour me a glass. And one for yourself, perhaps."

Geoffrey thought well of the idea. He was parched and sore and happily settled into the chair next to his uncle and handed him a glass.

"Cheers," Uncle Bingley said. "To the final union of our families."

"You – you consent?"

"Of course I consent. I'd be a fool not to, breaking Georgiana's heart after the trauma she's been through. Now don't waste that brandy, Mr. Darcy. It's very expensive, and it looks like you need a stiff drink."

Geoffrey downed his drink in a way that would have impressed even Frederick Maddox. When he looked up, his uncle was smiling. "So – you hurt your hand?"

"Two fingers broken. I should have punched with my knuckles, not my fingers. Or so George told me. And it's swollen and throbbing now."

"Did the doctor – or Mr. Wickham, I suppose – give you something for it?"

"I didn't want to take it before speaking to you. Muddle my senses," he confessed, producing the vial from the pocket of his waistcoat.

"Ah yes, the famous concoction; works better than laudanum, but far less tasty, or so I've been told. I've never tasted either. I had a few doses for a benign tumor Doctor Maddox took off my knee some years ago. A product of getting old – which I must be, if I'm now in the position to be marrying off my daughters." His gentle and pleasant attitude made Geoffrey think that perhaps he was a hopeless romantic after all. More at ease, he finally uncorked and swallowed the vial's contents, chasing it down with the last of his brandy.

"So Miss Bingley will finally become Mrs. Darcy," Bingley said, chuckling. "After all these years."

Geoffrey could not figure out what he meant, but he felt a sudden lethargy and decided not to inquire further. Uncle Bingley did ramble on some more, but not all of it was coherent, until Bingley shook him a bit and said, "Geoffrey – son – I think you'd best lie down for a while."

"I ha-have to go – three more miles – to ... you know," he waved his hands about as if he could make the shape of Pemberley.

"I doubt you could make the journey in your present state, and should approach your parents when you are better acquainted with your senses. Come, Mr. Darcy," he said and pulled him up, because Geoffrey found he did not quite have the ability to stand on his own, not with sudden movement at least. "You Darcys have always been such lushes."

Geoffrey could find no suitable argument to that.

CHAPTER 12

Mr. Darcy and Miss Bingley

Darcy was already waiting on the bench at the halfway point between the estates of Pemberley and Chatton House with his hunting rifle in his lap. It was his custom to meet with Bingley when the weather was fine and brisk for some shooting, and he would admit only to himself that perhaps he was looking forward to having more time to do it when Geoffrey returned from school and, perhaps after a year or two of traveling the Continent, began to take a further role in the managing of Pemberley and the lands of the Darcy family. Darcy had been manager and master for nearly thirty years now and, while his tireless efforts did not come to naught, the idea of someone else shouldering some of the burden he had assumed at three and twenty became more appealing as the years passed.

"You're late," he said to Bingley as the other man approached, lacking a rifle and without his dogs. "What is the matter?" He had suddenly gotten a proper look at his friend's face.

"Your son is sleeping in my guest wing, having exhausted himself from riding two days from Town with a broken hand to see me. Otherwise, I believe, he would have continued immediately on to Pemberley, but I did not oblige him to ride the extra three miles and decided to fetch you myself."

Darcy looked up, trying to more accurately read Bingley's expression. He was most definitely serious. "And his purpose in seeing you?"

"Young Master Geoffrey has just asked me for my consent to marry my daughter."

"*Now?*" That was the first clarification Darcy needed, not which daughter and why.

"While in Town, he ensured that the matter of matrimony should not be delayed," Bingley said. "But not without saving her life first, which was very strategic in terms of assuring my good opinion of him."

Darcy stood up, handed his rifle to his man, and took a walking stick from him. The huntsman was dismissed. "I think my mind is failing me this morning, as nothing you've said makes any sense."

"It makes very little to me, I assure you," Bingley said with a wan smile. "Shall we walk? Geoffrey is soundly asleep and somewhat deserving of it, so perhaps we should allow him such a respite before demanding answers."

Darcy nodded numbly, and they began the walk to Chatton House. "My son is to be engaged to your daughter. Now."

"Yes."

"You granted your consent?"

"I had little option. Besides, I cannot say I am overly surprised or disappointed at the prospect of the match. Georgiana has spent most of her life making it clear that she will have no one else."

Darcy's mind was racing, but Bingley wasn't much help. His brother-in-law was abnormally subdued. "He needs *my* consent." Geoffrey would not be one and twenty for another four months. "You said he broke his hand?"

"Not beyond repairing. He will be fine. Nonetheless, I thought you might wish to talk to him first before informing Mrs. Darcy."

"Yes," Darcy grumbled. "I should have seen it coming. The timing is poor." His frown deepened. "Must they be married?"

"Eventually. The timing, we're not sure of. Georgie is due back tomorrow. She did not race up here like your son," he said. "Darcy, he saved my daughter's virtue and maybe her life. And he's in love. Be kind."

"It was hardly gentlemanly behavior."

"Sometimes harsher measures are called for."

Darcy sighed. "I do wish him to finish University."

"I believe he can, even if he marries."

He shook his head. "Why are *you* saying 'to be kind'? This is your daughter we are discussing."

"He saved her life and her virtue from an unsavory suitor, who is now sitting in a London jail and must be dealt with as soon as dealings here are concluded. I am not looking forward to it." He managed a smile. "But should I not be happy? My little girl is getting married."

"I confess I would not be so happy about it if it were Anne."

"With all due respects to you and my Georgie, Anne is not the type of girl you worry about."

Darcy stopped himself from correcting him. He did worry about his daughters – their safety, their comfort, their happiness, their future prospects – but this was not what Bingley was speaking of.

Bingley briefly related the tale as he knew it, beginning with the would-be courtship of Mr. Dartmouth and Geoffrey's appearance in Town, but he seemed reluctant to linger over the details, and Darcy was reluctant to press him on it. If Geoffrey were to act as a man, he would need to take responsibility for his actions, and part of that would be properly explaining himself to the concerned parents involved.

Of course, most of Darcy's resolve melted upon seeing his son, who was roused and called into the study shortly after their arrival. Geoffrey was shaken, unwashed, and barely put together at all. His arm was in a sling, the hand bandaged, and he barely seemed to be standing up straight, though he did make the attempt to hold himself up presentably and even managed a feeble bow. "Father. Uncle Bingley." He had no energy to hide his terror.

Bingley excused himself from his own study while Darcy tried to fashion his resolve. This was his son, and he had acted irresponsibly. His entire life would now be determined by the events of one night.

"Geoffrey," he began. "How is your hand?"

"A bit bothersome."

He gestured for him to sit. "Which fingers did you break?"

"The middle and the ring. They should heal nicely." He added, "George set the bones."

"Our George?"

"Yes, sir."

He nodded. "Bingley has informed me of some of the particulars, and he has granted his consent – after all, he has little option to do otherwise – but I would like to hear the complete story."

Geoffrey audibly sighed. Slowly, and with great attention to selecting particular details to share (and some clearly withheld), he told the story from the arrival of the letter in Cambridge to the conversation with Bingley a few hours before. Darcy rose and paced.

"I know my behavior was unacceptable," Geoffrey said, "and it was not my intention to – end the evening that way. That said, I did wish to make her my wife, and I asked her again in the morning, and she accepted again. I am aware of my obligation to Pemberley – " at which point, Darcy looked out the window and played with his signet ring. " – and perhaps Geor – Miss Bingley – would not be your first choice to be the future mistress of Pemberley. However, she will be *my* wife and *my* Mrs. Darcy, and she has never failed at anything she has tried to do, so the decision is mine to make; with all due respect, sir."

Darcy turned back to him. "You would go against me and be wed in Gretna Green if I did not grant my consent?"

The tired, wounded, and frightened boy before him answered immediately and with conviction, "Yes."

"Without a moment's hesitation, you would put your entire future in jeopardy because of an instinct?"

"It is more than instinct, but yes, I would." Geoffrey added, "I love her. I will not have anyone else."

"You are decided?"

"Yes."

His father smirked. "Then you are ready to be married. And perhaps to be a father." Darcy swatted at his son's very messy locks. "But hopefully not too soon, yes?"

"So I have your consent?"

"I wouldn't think of denying it," he said, and embraced his son, patting him on the back. "My son, married." He added, "Quite possibly, red-headed heirs. Goodness. If my grandson has Bingley's smile, we will be having some words." He let him go. "You should tell your mother yourself. And then, please, get yourself cleaned up."

"Of course, Father. Thank you, sir." Geoffrey smiled.

He called Bingley back in and they called for a carriage. Darcy, having seen his son enter as a boy, watched him leave the study thoroughly a man.

~~~

Geoffrey emerged, relieved, only to be assaulted by his aunt.

"Promise me you'll make her happy."

"I will do my very best, Aunt Bingley."

"Thank goodness you offered," she said, "for I don't think she'd accept an offer from anyone else in this world." She let him loose and wiped her eyes.

Next he encountered Edmund, who had begged his way out of attending Eton so he could focus on his own studies with private tutors, as he was more inclined to mathematics and business management than the classics. "Nice job," he said. "Good luck with her."

"Thanks," Geoffrey said, his mood lightened considerably after the approval of the man who was least likely to grant it. "I'll tell her you said that."

"I'm sure she will be pleased."

He climbed into the waiting carriage. "I will be along shortly," Darcy said. His father would likely stay to talk to Bingley about what was said. Georgie would say they were like gossiping wives sometimes. The thought put a smile on his face as he nodded off in the very short carriage ride home.

His mother greeted him as he emerged from the carriage, hatless, his overcoat still soiled from the road, and his arm in a sling. Someone had apprised her of at least some of the situation. "My baby," she whispered as she embraced him.

"I'm hardly a baby, no matter what commentary someone might have about my behavior," he said with a smile.

"Geoffrey, you will always be my baby boy," she said. "Even if you are taller than me and look more like your father every day." She kissed him on the cheek. "What happened to you?"

"I am engaged. That is the good news," he said.

"And how is Georgiana?"

He blushed. "Was I the last person to know we were to be married? Because it seems that way."

"You were the last person to make it official," she said reassuringly. "What is the bad news?"

He saw his sisters and the servants in the hallway, not far off. "I don't want to say it now," he whispered, "but she was assaulted. Fortunately, she had written me beforehand of someone's interest in her, and I dashed to London like a fool."

"Or like your father," she said. "I will ask him for the details. And I'll tell your sisters. But there is someone who deserves to be properly told, and he is in the library."

He nodded. "Thank you, Mother." The prospect of facing all three sisters and probably the servants, as soon as they found out, with their congratulations was intimidating. "Father will be along shortly, he said."

"Gossiping with Bingley?"

Geoffrey chuckled. That was enough of a response, and he bowed a brief greeting to his sisters. "Anne. Sarah. Cassandra. Excuse me, I am very tired, so direct your questions to Mother."

They rolled their eyes, but they did give in and raced to their poor mother as he bypassed the servants' curious glances and entered the library.

"Grandfather," he bowed, and Mr. Bennet put down his paper with a genuinely surprised look on his face. "I am to inform you shortly before I fall asleep on my feet that I am engaged to be married to Miss Bingley."

"She gave you that hard a time about it? Really twisted your arm, eh?"

"I only wish it was that simple."

"Oh, I'm sure it is a long and complex story," Mr. Bennet said, amused as always. "These sorts of things are better sorted out around people who smell better. By all means, go have a bath and some sleep, Grandson, and then I will listen to whatever tale awaits me. And congratulations."

"Thank you, Grandfather," he said and, with relief, managed his way up the great steps of Pemberley, where a horde of servants awaited him and unquestioningly maneuvered him to a warm bath. Reynolds was still at Cambridge, but he could manage without him, as all he wanted to do was bathe, and after he was done with that, he wasn't surprised that all he wanted to do was sleep.

His mother, unbeknownst to him, had called for the family emergency surgeon. Mr. Dunhill checked his hand, said the boards were intact but changed the bindings, and gave him a bottle of laudanum to help him sleep and told the servants to be liberal with the dosage. Geoffrey was accustomed to the throbbing in his hand and was reluctant to be drugged until he had at least eaten. He was excused from dinner and took a tray in his room before finally taking the laudanum, whereupon his body gave in to the physical and emotional exhaustion, and he slept.

~~~

Back at Chatton House, there was very little sleeping.

"Our daughter is getting married," Jane Bingley said to her husband after being given several moments to form a coherent response to the information he had just told her.

"I am aware."

"Our daughter is getting married," she said, her voice more emotional, but a very joyous emotional. "We have to get a dress! We have to get her – "

"The flowers won't be ready," he said, "even if it waits until July. I've never had much success with them."

"We are *not* having an Indian wedding, Charles."

"So I should cancel the Punjab musicians and the Mughal priest?"

She was too happy to raise issue with him. "Our daughter is getting married."

"And you've developed some kind of physical problem, if that's all you intend to say until she actually does, and I may have to put you away." He kissed her. "I am honestly surprised they waited this long."

"Geoffrey is a boy."

"He's a man *now*."

"I wish that was the worst of it," she said, suddenly serious, leaning on his shoulder. "What about this Mr. Dartmouth?"

"He's in a cell in London. As soon as Georgiana arrives and we get sorted out here, I have to go and see to him. I don't know what to say or do to this man." He put his hand over hers. "It will all be sorted out. Just let us thank God that Geoffrey is his father's son and instinctively knows when the people he loves are in trouble." Bingley sighed. "I shouldn't have left her there alone. I should have at least sent her to her uncle's house – "

"The servants should have been awake. You left an army to protect her there."

"An army is useless if the soldiers are all asleep."

"But then Geoffrey could not have made his dramatic entrance and broken his hand."

He laughed. "The Darcys must always be so dramatic, mustn't they?"

"I suppose they must. But it does get the job done."

~~~

Darcy returned to Pemberley and was received first not by his wife but by his three daughters, all of whom seemed to have especially shrill voices all of the sudden. "Is Geoffrey really getting *married*?"

"Do you distrust your mother so?" he replied.

"Can he still go to school?"

"When is the wedding?"

"Is it going to be here or in Cambridge?"

"Can Uncle Grégoire perform the ceremony? I know he isn't a priest – "

"It would be so *romantic* – "

Only Elizabeth could save him from the torrent of questions and ponderings from his daughters. "Girls," she said with a little force. "I would request a quiet moment with your Papa, if it is possible."

They scurried off, and he barely had enough time to pull her into the sitting room, away from the prying eyes of servants, before she embraced him. "Our baby is getting married."

"I know," he said, lacking a more formidable response.

"I told him you would tell me the particulars. Was it something dramatic?"

"Yes. A bit too dramatic, in my opinion, but what's to be done?" He kissed her on the cheek. "His request for my consent was most impressive, all things considered."

"You can be very intimidating when you want to be."

"It comes in handy," Darcy said. "So Miss Bingley is to be the next mistress of Pemberley."

"Lady Maddox may appreciate the irony of that."

He laughed. "I confess, I had not noticed it. I was a bit distracted."

"I cannot imagine what would have been on your mind," she teased, as was often her response.

CHAPTER 13

Bingley's Enlightenment

Georgiana arrived, escorted by Lady Maddox, the very next day. She nervously greeted her father and was excused to weep on her mother's shoulder, the stress of it all finally reaching a climax.

"The good news is they're going to have a very long engagement," Caroline Maddox said to her brother. "Though it might not seem like good news to them."

"It's possible to wait?"

She nodded.

"How is she?"

"I think she's more than a bit shaken from the experience with Mr. Dartmouth. She said she was ashamed that she let it happen."

"This is not her fault. She knows that."

"Perhaps on a rational level, yes. But Georgiana believes herself in charge of everything she says and does. No one's ever gotten the upper hand on her like that. She's very embarrassed about the whole thing."

"I'll talk to her," Bingley said. "And then I'll go to London and speak to this Mr. Dartmouth."

"I imagine he is expecting a bribe. He could not have seriously thought that after all he did, you would make her marry him."

"No, certainly not." He gave her a hopeful look. "I'm sure he can be reasoned with. Or, I'm sure I can ask the Maddoxes to use their particular form of persuasion, and *then* he can be reasoned with."

"Sometimes, they are very convenient relations to have."

He frowned. "Sometimes."

~~~

Back in the house, behind the closed doors of the sitting room, Jane embraced her daughter. It pained her that she could not recall the last time she had done so, except perhaps after the wolf incident, and then it had not been this emotional or prolonged. At the same time, this was her daughter, and she was upset and needed her mama, and that was one thing Jane knew how to be. She asked nothing of her.

"I didn't want to face Papa," Georgie said after some time. "I feel so bad. Did he – "

"He granted his consent, of course. As did Darcy," Jane said, stroking Georgiana's hair.

Fortunately, enough of it had grown back to do that. "He will always do what's best for you. That is his purpose in life."

"I thought maybe Uncle Darcy – I don't know what I thought," her daughter said. "I was so foolish – "

Jane wondered what specific part of the incident she felt so foolish about. Mr. Dartmouth had gotten the advantage of her but had gone through insane lengths to do it. On the other hand, sneaking into Geoffrey's chambers was perhaps not the best of choices, but could she be blamed? Geoffrey had done the noble thing, from what she could tell of Bingley's retelling, and placed all the blame on himself, despite the fact he had been injured, drugged, and locked in his room. He took the responsibility, which was exactly what a gentleman and responsible future husband should do for his wife. *His wife.* Georgie was going to be a wife. She didn't want to hear that it was such a relief to her mother, so Jane didn't say it. She knew that much about her own daughter. "You are not responsible."

"I let my guard down – "

"Georgiana," she said, looking into her eyes, "you may not believe it, but you are not, in fact, invincible." She gave her a reassuring smile. "None of us are. Especially the servants, who should have done something – "

"It was my fault. Please be kind to them – I snuck out – "

"And it was their responsibility to make sure you didn't do that, or at least to be aware when you came home – "

"It's not their fault."

"Very well. I will be kind to the servants – and to your Papa, who left you all alone in Town, if you agree to look at it with some rationality and realize you were not responsible by anyone's standards for what occurred between you and that awful man." But Georgie still looked weak. "And it had only the happiest of outcomes. You are engaged to the man you love."

"You're not upset – "

"That my eldest daughter is to be wed? It is my job in life to make that happen, and it has." Now she really did smile. "You deserve to be happy, and Geoffrey seems to be the only one who can make you so. That it took him this long to realize it can only be attributed to his sex, which is known to be rather obtuse." When Georgie finally cracked a smile, Jane hugged her again. "I am so proud of you for being so strong. And so happy for you. So is your father, although he was a bit put out when I told him we won't be having an Indian wedding."

"Mama!"

"It would have to be outside as I understand it, and you will be married in a church like a proper Englishwoman, and I don't care whether all of those flowers he planted have come in or not – it will be perfect anyway." She looked down at the sound of a squeak. "See? Even Monkey wants to give his congratulations."

For there was Monkey, his tiny hands pulling at the hem of her gown. "Monkey!" Georgiana cried. "*Kinasi!*" And he leapt up into her arms. "Ow – Monkey, not my nose – "

Jane laughed, which made her daughter laugh, which made Monkey howl with annoyance that he wasn't in on the joke, which made them both laugh again. So it took a small foreign animal and a handsome, half-deaf cousin to make Georgiana happy. They were probably rather minimal requirements in comparison to the rest of the girls she knew.

"You're really not upset?" Georgiana asked when they had recovered.

"At you? No. At Mr. Dartmouth? Let us just say, if he were in the room, I would strangle him until he turned blue." Georgie looked doubtful. "What? I've strangled your father on any number of occasions."

"Mama!"

"Ask him if you don't believe me," Jane said with a smirk.

~~~

On her way upstairs to clean herself up from the road, Georgiana first encountered her brother. "He was a real gentleman, even if he could barely stand."

"Who, Geoffrey?"

"Who else?" Edmund said, leaning against the doorframe. "He came in caked in mud and exhausted, told Father everything, and then fell fast asleep as soon as he had the consent. Faced Uncle Darcy, too. And remains alive, so I assume it went well. Congratulations."

"Thank you," she said. "How did Father take it?"

"All right, I suppose. He was quieter than usual last night. I guess he had a lot to think about. And Mother's in wedding mode, even though you won't be married until July at least. Expect to hear a lot about dresses."

"If that's the least I have to go through, I'll be glad," she said, but doubted it.

Eliza was standing in front of the doorway to Georgiana's room. "You're getting married!" she squealed.

"I suppose they didn't tell you anything," Georgie said. She had to release Monkey to make way for her little sister practically manhandling her into a hug. "The bad things, I mean."

"Posh. You got Geoffrey to propose. You've been trying to do that for *years* now."

She blushed. "Was I that obvious about it?"

"*Yes.*"

She half-scowled at her sister and retreated to her room, where the servants waited to attend to her. The level of attention from her family made her a little uncomfortable, but she finally had some time to relax and get the grime from traveling off of her. She had not had a moment alone since the incident, as her Aunt Maddox had traveled with her. Even if no conversation was made for long periods of time, it hadn't allowed her the solitude she craved. Nor would she have it for long. She was eager to see Geoffrey, and she had to face the Darcys to see him, and she could not begin to imagine how Uncle Darcy would receive her. But she let all that go for a little while and rested in her chaise, eventually drifting off into the peaceful sleep of not being in a carriage any longer.

When she rose, it was after noon, and she could not believe how tired she had been. She dressed and returned downstairs, with Monkey protectively trailing her, to find her mother and Aunt Maddox in conversation, at which point it was heavily implied that it was time to face her father.

"Papa," she said as she entered the study and curtseyed to her father as Monkey climbed up on the desk. The door was shut, and she felt more intimidated than she ever had been, even if her father had only a comforting look on her face.

"Georgiana," he said, "Congratulations."

"You approve?"

"How could I not?" he said. "That is, if we're talking of Geoffrey, and not of my stupidly leaving you unattended in London or expecting the servants to be competent enough to keep track of you. No, there are other people to blame for the bad end of it."

She sat and looked at her hands. "You are going to go to London?"

"Yes, to find out what Mr. Dartmouth's demands are and whether to pay him the full amount or not."

This was the part she had dreaded, the part she had spent two days working herself up to. Yes, she loved Geoffrey (even physically) and made no apologies for it. Yes, her choices were not always wise. But Papa was so forgiving – she'd known he'd forgive her behavior, until he heard the rest. "Papa …"

"What is it?"

"Perhaps – I should tell you what happened."

"It is not required, if you don't wish to. Geoffrey was accurate enough," he said kindly. "Mr. Dartmouth drugged you with some lemonade, intent on taking your virtue, and Geoffrey punched him in the jaw. There are other details, but I won't make you go into them."

"There are," she said. "He knows – " She broke off in a sob. She hadn't wanted to cry.

Maybe she wasn't really ready for this. She could only glance at her father, who was suddenly far more concerned. "Georgie – "

She blurted it out. "I told him everything. About Hatcher, about the Wolf, about – some things even you don't know about."

Now she dared to look up, and her father was frowning. Not in a harsh way, but any frown seemed harsh on *his* face. "Are you sure of what you said?"

"No. There are parts I don't – I don't remember. But whatever I did say was enough."

"And you want to tell me all of it, now. So I don't have to hear about it from the despicable cad sitting in a London jail."

She nodded.

Bingley sighed and leaned back in his chair. "I would appreciate hearing it from you. That much is true. Is there anything I don't already know about the wolf incident, as we shall put it?"

"No." Monkey, sensing her discomfort somehow, climbed into her arms again, and she held him tight. "Except there was a second one."

To this he had no immediate response. Several emotions passed over his face, but he did not respond harshly when he said, "In France?"

"Yes."

He seemed to be sorting the details out in his head. "It probably had something to do with Lady Littlefield, or ... Didn't I meet an inspector at your graduation?"

"You did."

"He was involved?"

"Papa, I'm so sorry," she whimpered. She was not trying to wipe the tears from her face. She was just letting them fall. "I didn't know how to tell you, but I couldn't *not* help Heather."

"You could have written me. I could have helped her."

"It was none of your business, and you couldn't have. Or maybe you could have – but certainly not in time, and anyway, that was not as it happened." She had told Geoffrey that she didn't care what her father thought, but now that she sat there facing him, she knew she did care very much. She knew she was going to break her father's heart, that he would likely never trust her again. "If I could have done it differently – "

"But you didn't," he said calmly. "You're being very brave by telling me, I've no doubt." He gave her an encouraging smile. That was because he didn't know yet.

He withheld comment as she explained, in every detail, how she came to know Heather Littlefield as a roommate, then as a friend, then as a victim of a cruel engagement to the worst kind of man. And Simon Roux, the man who threatened girls from her school and tried to rape her, and how she dealt with that. She didn't mince words; she was a murderer. Roux was dead, several of the bandits were dead, and the marquis was dead – and it was her fault.

What was worse? Hearing of the marquis or that Brian Maddox was involved and clearly had failed to mention it to his friend, relative, and business partner? "He didn't tell you in order to protect me," she said. "Please don't blame him."

To this, he hardened his expression but said nothing, indicating for her to go on.

Audley: she was fairly sure she told Dartmouth about it, because she remembered telling Geoffrey that she'd told Dartmouth, so there was no hiding it. By now, Bingley's face was unreadable. "He offered to marry me. I told him no. It was my doing. It was all me. Please don't be mad at Inspector Audley – "

"Why do you care if I'm mad at a man I'll likely never see again, nor will you?" he answered.

"Because it's *my* fault."

"Was he rendered senseless the entirety of the time he spent in town? Was he, as a man and detective, incapable of making his own decisions? Give him some of the credit and some of the blame, Georgiana."

She couldn't make him out. For once, her father was completely unreadable. And just when he thought it was over, there was more. Jack. She had to tell him about Jack. Damn Mr. Dartmouth! Why did the drugs make her tell him *everything?* And about Liu, to which her father did show a good deal of shock. A man he had brought into their home, a man he had trusted – and then Nadezhda again.

"I'll stop now. I'm sorry."

He just looked overwhelmed. "Is there *more?*" There was active fear in his voice.

"No. That is the entirety of it, I swear. Everything." She dared to look up at him, but he just rose, and poured himself a glass of brandy. To her surprise, he poured one for her as well, which she gladly accepted, immediately taking a sip. He walked around the room with a dazed expression as she sat there, mainly looking at the floor.

"...I can't tell your mother," he said at last, his voice broken. "I don't know how. I don't know

... what to say." He turned to her. "Does Geoffrey know?"

She nodded.

"Everything?"

"He will. When I see him next."

"Thank God you are to be married," her father said and downed his drink. "Thank God."

"Papa – "

"You're not a murderer," he said. "Perhaps technically, yes, but Geoffrey shot Hatcher, and I don't think of him as a murderer who deserves the gallows. Heavens, Darcy killed his own brother, and I don't imagine the word stamped to his forehead. I can't imagine how he makes peace with it, even if none of us blame him, except perhaps your Aunt Bradley. And Brian – well, maybe you've heard the unabridged version of his adventures in Japan and maybe you haven't, I don't know, but it was quite unsettling." He leaned against the desk. "And yet, life goes on." He swallowed the last of his brandy and put down the glass. "I once thought no one was good enough for either of my daughters. No one on earth. Darcy feels the same way about his; he just does it more openly. But if Geoffrey Darcy is good enough to understand you – something I have tried on many occasions and utterly failed – then he is worthy of you."

"I'm so sorry," she cried. "I just could not face your rejection – after France."

"My rejection? Oh yes, I suppose some fathers would disown their daughters, or at the very least, send them to a convent or to Bedlam for far lesser charges," Bingley said. "But I am not other fathers. I never wanted to be other fathers. No, despite your numerous unintentional attempts to be otherwise, you will always be my sweet little baby who drove us crazy when she was two because she didn't speak, then drove us crazy when she was three because she would only speak to her cousin Geoffrey, then drove us crazy when she was a young girl because she wouldn't wear ribbons and wanted to play with her aunt and that dangerous convict who seemed to be hanging around, and then drove us crazy when she took to dressing as animals and outdoing us on the job of protecting our own children. Now you have Geoffrey to drive crazy, though I imagine you've succeeded in doing so for years now." He leaned over and kissed her on her forehead. "You're my baby girl, and I will always love you. Even if ... I am occasionally – or frequently – confounded." He stood up straight. "I will make a bargain with you, one I hope you will keep to this time."

"I promise," she said, as overwhelmed as she was by his speech.

"What was just said will stay between us – and Geoffrey, I suppose – provided that until the day I give you away, you tell me everything. *Everything*, Georgiana."

"I promise," she repeated.

"Are you still planning on training with Liu Xiao?"

"If you let me," she said.

"Correct answer," he said, though he didn't say he would grant permission. He was pacing again, not fully settled with all the information he had. "No more fights."

"I promise, Papa."

"I just don't want you hurt, Georgie. You see now how it can happen?" he said, and she nodded. "I wish I had been there for you in France. I wish I could have taken all of your pain away when Hatcher shot you. But it seems all I am capable of is *begging* you to stay out of harm's way. For your papa."

She nodded.

"If you can hold to that, I will be proud of you. As for the rest ... I must think on it. All I know now is that Brian Maddox owes me a much bigger favor than he previously did, which will be some help with Mr. Dartmouth." He turned back to her. "I do appreciate you coming to me first. This is not information I would have appreciated hearing as threats from a man such as he is."

"I imagine," she said guiltily.

"Only good must come of it," Bingley said. "After all, you arc to be married. Geoffrey may have blundered into it, but he did get the courage to ask for your hand, which vastly improves the situation." He sighed. "Now, we must put our good faces on. The Darcys are expecting us."

Georgie rose. "Then ..."

He embraced her. "Did you truly believe I would shun you or further disparage you? You've done it enough to yourself already." He wiped her tears away. "You're a mess, and I won't have it. My daughter, finally engaged, and sobbing over it. It's not right. You deserve to be happy. As for the rest ... it's done. Somehow, I will find a way to make my peace with it. But give me some time."

"Of course, Papa." She leaned into his embrace, still shocked at the reception. He was hurting; she could tell that much. "I will be good."

"You will be honest; that is good enough for now," he replied.

~~~

Any lingering doubts Georgiana might have had about the Darcys' reaction to her engagement with their son evaporated when they received her at Pemberley. The future mistress of Pemberley was received by the current mistress of

Pemberley with a warm embrace before she could even enter. "You've made us so happy."

She smiled nervously. "Thank you."

Uncle Darcy of course was more restrained. "Miss Bingley. Congratulations on your engagement."

"Thank you, Uncle Darcy."

"Geoffrey is eager to see you," Aunt Darcy said.

Geoffrey was restricted to bed rest, but some accommodations had to be made for all of the people who wished to see him, not least of whom was Georgiana, so he was permitted to lie down in the sitting room. He begged for privacy with his bride to be. Of course they wouldn't grant it, but eventually his father agreed to close the glass doors so they could at least talk to each other without being overheard.

"I would get up – "

"I know," Georgie said, sitting down and taking his good hand. "How do you feel?"

"Tired, for reasons not far beyond my understanding." He smiled. "Listen, I know I was a bit rash – "

"About coming to rescue me? I can hardly fault you for that."

He shook his head. "I had better plans for proposing. Ones that would have been a bit less demanding – "

"Geoffrey, I *want* to marry you. I wouldn't have said so otherwise."

"And be Mrs. Darcy?"

"As long as *you* don't call me that, yes."

Geoffrey squeezed her hand. "While we have a moment – I don't wish to put you out, for asking these questions – "

"What I said in the attic? About France?"

He was glad he didn't have to say it. "Yes."

"You promised not to be angry," she said, her voice surprisingly meek.

"I'm not. But I do think I am deserving of an explanation nonetheless."

Behind their barrier of wood and glass, Georgiana Bingley confessed fully to all of her adventures in France, including Brian Maddox's part in it, from the death of Simon Roux to her graduation. Geoffrey laid there with an impassive expression on his face.

In a quiet voice he responded, "Does your father know? I assume not."

"I told him today."

"What does he think?"

"I don't know. It doesn't matter. I care about you - ," she broke off. "I didn't mean to hurt you. All right, I did, but I was stupid and hurt and lonely. But that does not mean – "

"We were not betrothed. In theory, there was not the least bit of connection between us, because of what *I* said and did here first. What you may have done in your own time ..." he sighed and wiped the tear from her cheek. "It was your own decision."

"You forgive me?"

"I am not in the position to say you need my forgiveness."

She took his hand back and kissed it desperately.

"By all rights," he said, "we should be married by Sunday. But if we can wait -"

"We can."

"You're sure?"

"Yes."

He sighed.

"Not that it says anything about you."

"I just ... Father wants us to wait until I graduate."

Georgie frowned. "That is a very long time."

"Yes."

"I would prefer not to wait so long, but all things being what they are, I am more inclined to impress your father."

"He can be foul when he doesn't have his way."

"Like a child."

"Or a woman scorned."

They shared a laugh, glad to have relieved some of the tension between them.

~~~

Before he was ready to retire for the night, Darcy had some paperwork to finish in the study, and promised Elizabeth he would join her shortly. There was the small matter of his son being betrothed, though it had no immediacy to it. How would they manage?

Perhaps they'll act like respectable adults.

But he couldn't help but remember calling on Longbourn almost every day of his engagement. His son wouldn't have that luxury—he would be at University, while Georgiana would likely be in Town or Derbyshire. Only the knock on the door could distract him from that dilemma.

"Master Darcy," Mrs. Annesley said, curtseying to him.

"Mrs. Annesley."

"I just wanted to inform you that there's been some gossiping among the servants as to Master Geoffrey ..."

"Yes," he said. "I won't deny it. If all goes as planned, Miss Bingley will be the next mistress of Pemberley." He paused and said, almost to himself, "That still does sound very odd." Directing his attention back to her, he continued, "Nonetheless, if the servants are … concerned, assure them that I'm sure Miss Bingley will be a wonderful mistress." He added, "And God willing, it will not be for a very long time."

She did indeed look assured.

CHAPTER 14

The Legacy of Mrs. Bennet

Georgiana rose later than was her custom the next morning, still tired from everything that had occurred. The Darcys had all been warm to her, and she thought she could still hear the combined efforts of the three Darcy sisters and Eliza squealing at the idea of the wedding ringing in her ears. She sighed and rang for the maid, was dressed, and went to breakfast.

"You're getting married!" her mother said in a girlish squeal, pinched her cheek, and left the table as Georgiana entered.

"Is she going to be like this until the wedding?" she asked.

"Oh yes. She'll drive us both batty," Bingley said, sitting at the head of the table. "But you should have seen Mrs. Bennet. That was ... a bit terrifying." He sipped his coffee. "Very terrifying."

"Charles! Are you insulting my mother?" Jane called out from the other room.

"No, of course not," he shouted back in reply and rolled his eyes at Georgie, who stifled a giggle and sat down. "Your Grandmother was at

Netherfield practically every day I didn't call on Longbourn first," he said in a hushed voice, "suggesting things."

"To Aunt Townsend's house?"

"Yes. I used to live there – it was how I met your mother. We moved to Derbyshire to be closer to the Darcys – and further away from Mrs. Bennet."

"Charles! I can't hear you but I know you're saying something about my mother!"

Georgie covered her mouth as Jane Bingley entered the room with some indignation.

"I was relating our history at Netherfield Park," he said, "and telling Georgiana about Mrs. Bennet's extensive interest in it."

"That is true," Jane said. "But not in front of the children."

"There is only one here, and she's hardly a child," he said.

"I'm counting Monkey."

"He's a fully-grown monkey, darling."

"But he behaves like a child," Jane said, to which Monkey replied by banging on the table from his perch on the top of a chair.

"Monkey, quiet," Bingley said. "I'm in enough trouble as it is." He gestured for Jane to come over, and kissed her. "I love you. And I did love my mother-in-law, and her incredible concern for your comfort at Netherfield."

"I know you did. Hence, we're in Derbyshire," she said, but seemed to accept his apology and left the room again.

"Stop laughing," Bingley said to his daughter. "If you think this is not what married life is, you will soon be proven wrong. Or worse, the conversations do not end so gracefully with your husband admitting defeat."

"Is that the extent of your marital advice?"

"Sadly, I think it is," he said. After a moment in which the only sounds were those of breakfast being eaten, he continued, "Geoffrey is to return to Cambridge as soon as he is well enough to travel, and I must go to London. You are not obliged to go with me."

She looked down. "I suppose I shouldn't ask about Cambridge."

"You cannot stay with the Maddoxes, no. They have, of course, extended the offer, but Geoffrey cannot call on you. He is in school. Theoretically doing school*work*, though that may be mainly in theory." He added sympathetically, "Christmas is not so far away."

"Papa, it's November."

"So, two months. Less, really." He shrugged. "I would not take Darcy to task on this one. He is very decided – and so am I."

She nodded in understanding and swallowed her coffee – and her pride.

~~~

Because Geoffrey was unable to call on Georgiana at Chatton House, she, her mother, and her Aunt Maddox made an appearance at Pemberley.

"Come to discuss redecorating the place, have you?" Mr. Bennet said when his granddaughter greeted him in his usual place in the library. "Or maybe your mother will comment on how expensive the furnishings must be."

"Papa!" Jane said.

"I thought that was what mothers did," he said with a wink. "Forgive my innocence on the subject."

"Don't say a word," Jane said to Caroline, who then closed her mouth.

Geoffrey made an appearance, looking a little dazed as he was settled into an armchair. Everyone on the Bingley side gave their general comments regarding his good health, to which he nodded politely and looked very much like he was fighting sleep. Eventually, they closed glass doors again to give the newly engaged couple a modicum of privacy.

"They're acting so strange," Georgie said to him. "And so are *you*."

"Laudanum."

"Oh. You're still taking it?"

"'snice."

"You doper!"

Geoffrey grinned. "I love you." He took her hand and kissed it.

"We'll be in trouble."

"When have you ever been afraid of being in trouble?" he said in a slurred voice.

She smiled. "True. When are they going to make you go back to Cambridge?"

"Soon." He frowned. "I suppose ... I have to finish the last two terms. Maybe after Christmas ... Mother said something about you possibly visiting Chesterton. I don't know." He squeezed her hand. "I'll write." He looked at his other hand, still in a sling. "I will have someone else write. It'll be awkward. I s'pose I shouldn' ask Frederick to do it. Normally he'd do anything for coin."

"I do not want a love letter written by Frederick Maddox, even if it is your words, thank you very much."

"Glad we agree on that," he said with a warm smile. "So are you well?"

"Yes."

"It's Uncle Bingley – he's upset, but not at you."

She wrapped her fingers around his. His hand was warm. "He deserves to be angry with me. I told him everything."

"But he's not – he's *Uncle Bingley*. He doesn't normally get angry."

"He does get upset. And worried about me."

"I'll protect you."

"You? The man who can't even punch someone without breaking his hand? You're supposed to use your knuckles, not your fingers, dummy."

He laughed. "George said the same thing."

"You are truly affected."

"No," he said, clearing his throat. "Just happy. I missed you."

"I was gone for one night."

"You know what I mean."

She looked at their hands. "I missed you, too."

"I'm sorry – sorry for making you wait," he said. "To hear that I loved you."

"I understand."

"You do?"

"There's so much – everyone is so upset or excited or confused –" she stumbled, and he squeezed her hand. "I took it too lightly. Marriage."

"Why shouldn't you? You've never been married before. An' didn't it say in all those advice books to get married quickly, and to a rich man?" he said. "An' my father was lecturing me about responsibility. He was nine and twenty when he married." He chuckled. "Maybe he was scared of it."

"Your father? Scared of anything?"

"He puts on a good show," Geoffrey said, "but he's – he's a normal person. When I was hurt after the thing with Hatcher and I woke up and I couldn't hear anything, I kept trying to pull out this thing they had in my ear – I could see it. He was so terrified." He swallowed. "It was scary, seeing him like that. I wanted to tell him I would be all right, but I didn't know if that was true. And I couldn't hear, so I didn't know if the words would come out right. I knew Mother would be upset, but this was different. When I was better, but still deaf, I had a lot of time to think, and I realized that parents could have emotions beyond just disapproval and reassurance. They are whole people who went through all of this trauma when we scraped our knees or got sick, but they always had to hide it." He shook his head. "Everyone jokes about how controlling Father's been of Anne's going out, but he's so afraid of giving her up. He has to give his daughter away to some man he doesn't even know yet. What if it doesn't work? What if something bad happens? At least Uncle Bingley *knows* me. He knows I'll take care of you." He paused. "Did any of that make sense? I honestly have forgotten half of what I said."

"Everything did," Georgie said. "You need to rest." He did look tired. She rose and kissed him on the cheek. "Promise me you won't leave for Cambridge without seeing me again."

He smiled. "Wouldn't dream of it."

~~~

On the other side of the glass door, Darcy crossed his arms and said, "He needs to go back to Cambridge. And cool his ... heels."

"You're positively cruel," Elizabeth said.

"If he's to finish Cambridge, they'll need a long engagement," Bingley said, sitting next to his wife on the settee. "Though it is cruel."

"No it isn't," Darcy defended.

"Name one day you didn't call on Longbourn during your engagement," Jane said.

"And arrangements in London do not count," Elizabeth chimed in.

Darcy frowned. "There was ... some day, I think Mr. Bennet was ill."

"And you were in Meryton, shopping all day," Bingley said to his wife. "That's right. We didn't call that day and you didn't come to Netherfield that day." He snickered. "Now I think we are being cruel."

"But practical," Darcy said with increasing indignation. "Besides, he's much younger than we were then. I feel soundly Geoffrey should wait until he's one and twenty."

Elizabeth glanced at her sister, then back at her husband. "Fair enough. Men do mature so much more slowly than women."

Darcy opened his mouth but stopped himself before he openly agreed with her.

~~~

The engagement would not be formally announced until Geoffrey graduated or a few months before, but there were rounds of letters to write to relatives, like Grégoire and Caitlin in Ireland, and Lord and Lady Kincaid in Scotland. Darcy did not pen them himself, as Elizabeth took greater pleasure in it, but he did look on to see what she wrote.

When Geoffrey came off the laudanum, it was decreed that he would spend the rest of his recovery at his college, as attendance was important to his graduation (it was practically the only thing of real importance to his graduation), and he could receive the best medical care there. Elizabeth thought he took the news very well.

The bigger surprise was that Georgiana said she wished to return to London with her father instead of staying in Derbyshire. She did not make her reasons public, but it wasn't questioned.

"I'll write," she said to Geoffrey as the carriage pulled up for him. "And you'll find someone respectable to write for you. And *not* Reynolds. I don't want his knowing stares."

"It depends on the content of my writing," he said, and kissed her. "I love you."

"I love you." She added, "December is only a month away."

He gave her a reassuring smile and was helped into the carriage, and then he was gone.

After many hugs from her mother and sister, Georgiana Bingley left the next day, joining her father on the long ride to Town.

"You won't have to see Mr. Dartmouth," he said. "It won't go to trial."

"I know," she said. "But I want to make sure you don't try to murder Uncle Brian and Nadi-sama."

"I'm within my right to do so."

"That said, I don't think you would be successful at it."

"You've no faith in me, then?"

"Papa, how long did you last when you fought the wushu master in China?"

He couldn't resist smiling. "We'll talk."

"I talked them into the things they did," she said.

"As persuasive as you think you are, that does not excuse them. They are capable of making their own decisions," he said. "Why do you really want to go to London?"

"I want to apologize to Mr. Xiao," she said, "for involving him in something that I should not have."

He nodded.

"And I suppose I'd like to say my goodbyes."

"Why?"

She looked at him.

"I'm upset about the secrecy," he said, "not the training."

"But you won't sanction it continuing."

"I wouldn't sanction my not being present when it happened," he said. "Ambassador or not, if he is going to beat my daughter, I should at least have some recourse."

"Fighting is not always about winning or losing, Papa."

"You say that because you've mostly won. I, on the other hand, hold a record of five seconds before being knocked over," he said with a wicked grin. "For the record."

"You're serious."

"Since you're so intent on continuing your hobbies, I think I might do better to at least be present to oversee them," he replied.

"Papa!" she squealed and climbed across the carriage to embrace him.

"And here I was, thinking I would be hated forever for this long engagement business," he said.

"I could never hate you."

He could not express the extent of his relief in hearing her say that. "I would not want to be at the receiving end of your wrath anyway, father or not."

~~~

A day later, a very rattled and tired Geoffrey Darcy arrived in Cambridge. Reynolds, having been informed by the horseman riding ahead, was waiting for him at the entrance to Trinity College. "Good to see you, sir." And he did look relieved.

"I am engaged," he stammered in exhaustion. "To Miss Bingley."

"Congratulations, Master Geoffrey. Though, I would remark, the letters to Mr. Bingley and Mr. Maddox came yesterday."

"Good to know," he said, entering the dormitory. He was only halfway properly into the sitting room when he doubled over from the unpleasant experience of being punched in the gut. Fortunately, it was not hard enough to make him lose his stomach. He heard Frederick laughing in the background.

"That's for my sister," Charles Bingley the Third said.

"I gathered," Geoffrey said, as Reynolds helped him to his feet. To his surprise, Charles did as well.

"I'm sorry," he said. "Family honor demanded it."

Geoffrey decided not to comment on the competency of the punch and said instead, "I would have done the same for Anne."

"He was planning it since the letter arrived," Frederick said from the armchair. He raised his glass in Geoffrey's direction. "Congratulations on your engagement and your future marriage to a crazy woman."

"Frederick!"

Geoffrey raised his eyebrows at Charles. "Enough. You can't expect him not to say it." He said to Frederick, "Crazy but deadly. You would be wise to remember that on occasion."

"Have I ever done anything wisely?" Frederick replied. "Now sit down and have a drink. You are back at University, and it's after one in the afternoon, so you've some obligation to get cup-shot."

"You're lucky George lives in the Fellow quarters," Charles said. "He was always going on about academic obligations."

"Yes, we've become more lackadaisical about them since he left our direct presence," Geoffrey said, taking a seat. It felt good to be seated. It felt terrific to be back.

CHAPTER 15

The Princess's Revenge

It was very hard to catch Brian Maddox unarmed. He always had at least one sword in his belt, unless, like now, he was answering the door very early in the morning. He was also still half-asleep, so his senses were not completely clear when Bingley decked him.

"Papa!"

"Sorry, Georgie," Bingley said to his daughter as she came up behind him. "Oh goodness, he's out cold. I didn't think I was that strong." He swallowed as Nadezhda ran forward. "It is not what it looks like."

"Actually, it is," Georgiana said.

"You're not helping."

Nadezhda knelt beside her husband, then looked up and said, "What did he do now?"

"He made an unauthorized trip to France," he replied. "And introduced me to Liu Xiao. Brought him into my home. Perhaps you know something of it? We should discuss this, no?"

~~~

"Ow. Thank you," Brian said to the servant who helped him apply the steak to his face, covering one of his eyes. With the other eye, he had to face Bingley's stare from across the dining room table. "In my limited defense, I did not know about Liu's intentions."

"But you did know about the French count's intentions."

"You mean the marquis?" he said. "Actually, I had no concept of the enormity of the situation until I was there. I went to deliver a sword. That hardly excuses it, but still."

Bingley turned his unrelenting gaze to Nadezhda.

"Mugin left the sword for her," she said, very matter of fact, though very apologetic as well. "And you did permit her to continue her training."

"With *you*. Not with the Chinese ambassador!" Bingley sighed and lowered his voice to normal levels. "It is the deception that bothers me, Your Highness. Do you think I would not have wanted to know if a man openly threatened to kill my daughter?"

"Papa, I told you I asked them not to tell," Georgiana said.

"They should have known not to listen to you!"

He was shouting again, and in the early morning quiet it had a surprising effect. It terrified him how affected Brian and Nadezhda were; he had never seen them so openly defenseless. And he had not even told them about Mr. Dartmouth yet.

"I've tremendously dishonored my family," Brian said. "Thank God we are not in Japan, or drastic measures would be called for."

"Drastic measures are called for," Bingley said, "but I'd rather put your skills to better use."

Brian looked up. "What do you mean?"

"I need a favor," he said, "and for me to even *contemplate* forgiving both of you, I believe you are in my debt."

~~~

"No arguments," Bingley said to the unasked question as Georgiana stood in the hallway as the footman put on his coat. "You'll have no part in this. I should be back by supper."

"Papa, don't – "

"I will do as I see fit," he said, his voice rising in volume. Seeing her frightened face, he stepped towards her and kissed her on the cheek. "I'm not a violent man. You know that. Except when it comes to my daughters. However, I am still a rather ineffectual violent man, and I didn't bring

Darcy, so Brian and Nadezhda Maddox will have to do."

"I'll tell Uncle Darcy you said that."

"I've known him for much longer than you, and I can assure you it would not be wise," he said with a smile, doffing his hat.

After meeting the Maddoxes, the ride to the jail was surprisingly short. There was a certain stench when they entered the front doors, even worse than what was out on the street.

The constable looked a bit intimidated by Brian's appearance but tried to hide it as he spoke with Bingley, explaining the situation. "We can't keep him any longer if you refuse to press charges, sir."

"And there's no way to press charges without making it public."

"It will go to trial." He added under his breath, "I recommend a sound bribe."

"This man drugged and tried to violate my daughter," Bingley replied. "You expect me to *reward* him?"

"Says you and every other father who's come by 'cause of a gentleman in a cell who didn't act too gentlemanly," he replied. "You can knock him around a little, but if you or your bodyguard – "

"Brother-in-law," Bingley corrected.

" –does anything serious, he'll press charges, and they might stick."

"We're just here for intimidation," Brian assured him.

"Keep your head about you," the constable said. "Ma'am, if you'd like – "

"I will go with them," she said in her very intimidating Transylvanian accent.

The constable shrugged and escorted them down the stairs, past rows of overstuffed cells with the very worst of London hooting and hollering at them. The noise was finally shut out by a door as they were led into a small room with only a chair, a little table, and some candlelight. "Try not to kill him. Or set the place on fire," the constable said, disappearing out the door to collect the prisoner.

"They'll really let us do this?" Brian asked.

"You've never visited a jail before?"

"Have you?" he said, to which, Bingley shook his head. "Well, I will say, I've never been roughed up by a gentleman. They always used hired thugs."

"What do you think you are?" Bingley answered as the door reopened and a shackled young man in filthy but very fine clothing was pushed in and seated.

"You have as long as you like," the constable said, and left.

257

"Mr. Bingley, I presume," said the young man. He looked tired, but not terrified. "And you must be the crazy aunt and uncle." He pointed (as best he could, with his hands shackled) to Brian's swords. "If you use either of those on me, you'll be in a worse position than I am. My father will have your head."

"Your father is in India," Bingley said. "Even if he was sympathetic to your plight, he would be in no condition to save you."

"And that's all you have to propose? Murdering me with a constable on the other side of the door? You must have more intelligence than that," he said, almost laughing. "Your hands I believe you're permitted to use. Maybe your walking stick, Mr. Bingley. And I'm willing to take a beating for fifty thousand pounds, if that's what it takes."

"Fifty thousand pounds?" Bingley said. "And may I ask where you came up with such an outrageous sum?"

"You know very well its source," Mr. Dartmouth said. "And you'll pay every farthing. I was going to start at ten, but I'm a busy man, and I want to go home and have a bath. Of course, that was also if you were merely trying to cover up that your daughter had been in a scandalous situation. Even I admit that I would have a hard argument in saying I took her virtue, and that would hardly put a good light on me. But for a girl who killed a French noble? You're lucky I'm *only* asking for her inheritance."

"You've no proof," Brian said.

"Have I need of any? The concern here is *talk*. And this will be something to talk about – the gentleman from the North with a murderous daughter who kills people like a Turkish assassin. And then offers herself up to the investigating inspector like a common whore – "

Bingley had told himself he would be good and let Brian do the legwork. But right now, his personal honor responded too quickly, and he punched Mr. Dartmouth in the face. The boy nearly toppled over, grabbing the table's edge to prevent himself from doing so. "You feck! You want to make it worse?" He laughed as he recovered. "Don't you know I'm still sore? I might even have a concussion – and despite what the constable may have told you, you will have to answer for a comatose prisoner."

Bingley clenched his sore fist in anger but said nothing.

"Now," Mr. Dartmouth said casually, "if we are done with the insults and want to *rationally* discuss the terms – take your hand off those." He pointed to Brian, whose hand rested gently on his katana. "You're making me nervous." Though it didn't look like he was nervous at all.

"Fine." Bingley sighed. "After much consideration, I have decided on the generous portion of a thousand pounds and – at my own expense – a ticket to the Bahamas."

"And what the shite am I supposed to do in the Bahamas?" Dartmouth laughed. "With a thousand pounds? Do you know how much it costs to buy land there now?"

"I've no idea and no intention of doing your research for you. I'm sure someone will be happy to tell you when you're there," Bingley said. "I recommend you take this offer, Dartmouth."

"Or what? You'll make me take it? And how do you suppose you'll do that?"

Bingley glanced at Brian, who shrugged. "You're right. My hands are tied. I'd best leave this to the professional."

With that, he and Brian left, closing the door behind them. The constable looked at them with surprise.

"That trick doesn't work," he said.

"Trick? Are you making assumptions about my wife, sir?" Brian said, this time his hands really on his swords. The constable backed away.

~~~

Nadezhda had dressed in a simple red kimono. She carried a tanto sword with a glossy

260

white sheath and no hilt, so beautiful that it did not look very much like a sword, and got lost in her complicated and beautiful obi next to the fan. She drew it with one hand and grabbed Dartmouth's hand with the other, planting it on the table. "How many fingers do you want to leave with?"

For the first time, Mr. Dartmouth did look genuinely stunned, and a little frightened. "You can't be serious. How will this look?"

"How will what look? Do you plan on telling all of your friends – if you have any – that a foreign woman tortured you until you gave in? Will they even believe you?" She cut very lightly into the flesh of his pinky finger, and he cried out. "Oh, be quiet. How badly do you need all five?"

"Stop it!"

"I haven't even hit bone yet, Mr. Dartmouth."

"You *whore!*"

"If that is your best accusation, you are in an unfortunate circumstance, Mr. Dartmouth," she said, and raised his hand above the table, slicing along the finger and into the palm. It was a surface wound, and his scream was only as severe as the wound. She wasn't damaging anything. "The flesh will grow back," she assured him as it fell away. It had the desired effect of little damage but a lot of blood, which began to drip down onto the table.

"What are you – "

She squeezed his hand, and the drip became a flow. She said nothing and watched the color slowly drain from his face. He was a man – he had seen blood before, no doubt, even if he had been a gentleman all his life. Not like blood as she knew it, after all she had seen in Japan. "It's not serious," she said, "but frightening, isn't it, to lose so much blood? You think it is very much, but then, you have so much. And your body makes more. Look at it."

He was transfixed. He was also biting his lip so hard there was blood from that as well. She was elaborately patient. She did not put away her knife but did not harm him again.

"Your body is filled with it," she said. "Like a fountain. It can be that way, when you cut a man's head off. You must have seen it, in India, what they do to men who steal? When they cut their hands off?"

He shook his head. "I've never – "

"The first time I cut a man's head off, it was like a geyser. I was standing too close. It ruined my dress. I didn't care. That was how my father must have done it." She felt him trying to pull away from her a little, but her grip was too strong. "He did it himself to the men who wouldn't marry me. And to my mother. He hurt the people who were close to him. He put their heads on spikes, like our

262

ancestor, Vladimir the Impaler. He thought it made a statement."

"Look, lady – "

"He would hurt anyone who hurt him. Or hurt anything he cared about. He had them killed. It insulted his manhood when my mother couldn't give him a son, like it was her fault, so he killed her. He did it with the axe in his own hands." She was lying; she had no memory of it, since she had been very young, and he likely had ordered someone to do the actual killing of his wife. She was not accustomed to thinking of her mother, who had never been a figure in her life. She was never mentioned, and Brian didn't ask about her, because she didn't know, and it brought up so many painful memories of her father and his cruelty. But she had to be dispassionate now, in this room, for this man. "Georgiana is like a daughter to me. Did you know that? Did she tell you that after you drugged her? Or before? How did you do it?"

"Do what?" he said, his voice a little shaky.

"Drug her. You must have planned it. You knew you couldn't get control of her otherwise. She was too fast, too smart for you. So how did you do it?"

"It was simple. I bought her lemonade," he said, "and drugged it." When he said it, she twisted his hand, and he yelped. "If you think – I don't know what you're thinking – I didn't violate her. She invited me in. She is a whore – "

"Georgiana is not a whore!" she shouted and dug her fingers into his injury. Now he screamed. "She would not sell herself for anything. She would fight to the end. So she said something to you when she was drugged, when you talked her into saying whatever she said. People can say terrible things when they lose control of themselves. They'll say anything. You should be more careful; you might learn something terrible." She squeezed his hand as she would an orange, and more blood came forth in a fascinating red. No wonder her father had been so obsessed with it. "Mr. Bingley is trying to be nice. I don't know why; it's this stupid English nonsense of saying one thing and meaning another because of propriety and good sense and all of the things that keep us from doing the things we want to do. If I had always done the things I was supposed to do instead of the things I wanted to do, my father would have murdered my husband and then me. Instead, I stood up for myself." She added, "You should take his offer."

"It's practically nothing – "

"A thousand pounds more than you deserve. That's the English system – rewarding criminals. Paying men who hurt little girls," she said. "I am glad I am not English. In my country, you would already be dead."

"We are not in your country."

"It makes little difference to me. You take your thousand pounds and your ticket and you never show your face in England again. I never want to see you, and neither does any member of this family – and we travel widely. You know Georgiana is dangerous – she said so herself. You think she won't kill you if she were to get the chance? Some night, when this is long past, and you've snuck back to England thinking we've forgotten and gone into one of your dark alleys to wait and plot to take another girl's honor, you think Miss Bingley won't slit your throat? I would be *disappointed* in her if she did not."

"I don't need to be in England to talk."

She released his hand. "This is true." In one move, she grabbed his head, forced his mouth open with her blade, and grabbed his tongue. It was disgusting, more disgusting than the blood had been, but this was for Georgiana. Her baby. "This is going to hurt," she said, and cut off the tip of his tongue. She then stepped back as he doubled over, his restrained hands trying to cover his mouth as he spewed blood. "Don't choke," she ordered. "Have enough decency not to die."

He coughed and she patted him on the back. She didn't want him to die for all of the reasons Bingley and Brian hadn't killed him. They couldn't kill him, not now. Not on English soil, for even with the most discretion, there would be an investigation. They didn't want that. "Be calm or you'll choke on your own blood. Either swallow it or spit it out." She picked the candlestick up from its place on the wall. "Do you want me to burn the end off, so the bleeding will stop?"

He shook his head in a fit of panic and fury.

"Are you sure?" Now she was worried. He needed not to die. She opened his mouth again.

"And this, my Nadezhda, is how you insure someone's silence," her father said, and the servant screamed, but after that, he did not bleed and he did not speak.

The memory startled her; at least after all these years, her father was good for something. She cauterized the end, and the bleeding stopped. He spat the rest of the blood on the floor and looked up at her, his eyes full of suffered tears.

"You'll speak; I didn't cut that much. Probably with a stammer, though," she said. "And you'll be on that boat. A thousand pounds will take you far in the Bahamas. I hear the sugar plantations are doing very well. They have very lovely weather there, not like where I am from, in Austria," she said. "You will like it."

She put his hand down, pulled loose his cravat, and wound it around his hand. "Press hard with your other hand."

He was breathing heavily when she knocked on the door, a signal for the constable to enter. He took a step backwards at the blood-covered table and the shivering young man.

"He will heal," was all she said and left the room. He didn't stop her.

~~~

Bingley reentered the room and nearly lost his stomach right there. Mr. Dartmouth's lower face and chest were covered in blood, and he was holding one of his hands tightly. There was such a difference from wanting someone to suffer and seeing it. "Are we agreed, Mr. Dartmouth, to the terms?"

The boy nodded fiercely.

"We'll be there," Brian said as Mr. Dartmouth tried to leave. "Making sure you're on that boat. Good day, Mr. Dartmouth."

The place smelled of sweat and blood, and they were glad to be gone. Bingley looked painfully at Nadezhda. "Thank you."

"All I desire is your forgiveness."

"You have it," he said, honestly afraid not to give it. "There is, however, one more thing."

~~~

For a gentleman of the Ton, Charles Bingley was up very early that morning, but he had a boat to catch. More specifically, he had a boat to see off, and with it, so much unpleasantness. Fortunately, the constable was good to his word and delivered Mr. Dartmouth, who had been cleaned up a bit and given a change of clothes. The boy just put his head down and nodded politely to Bingley before he boarded the ship, with his banknotes and some of his things they had collected from his house the night before. Without a word, he was gone, and Bingley sighed.

"Thank you," he whispered again to Nadezhda. "At noon?"

"Just about, yes."

He nodded and climbed into his carriage, eager to be home. The townhouse was still quiet, and he was penning a note to Jane when Georgiana entered, a robe over her bedclothes. "Papa."

He smiled sadly at her in reassurance. "Georgiana." He welcomed her into his arms. "No more tears." He found he was saying it for himself as well. "It's done." He added, "Only good came of it in the end. After all, you finally got Geoffrey to propose."

"*Papa*," she said in a more normal tone, which in itself was a relief.

"Now go wash up. We have to be out of Town by half past eleven!"

She curtseyed and scurried out. The smile on her face took a weight off his chest that he hadn't realized had been there until it was gone.

It did not take them long to reach their destination. The weather was a bit brisk, but it didn't seem to bother Georgie, and Bingley was determined not to let it bother him. Fortunately, Brian welcomed them indoors quickly to a large room they had never seen before, with matting on the floor.

"You can't be serious," he said to Brian.

"I can be serious. It's cold outside," Brian replied. "And it's only going to get colder. Nady, have you seen my – "

From the other corner, Nadezhda tossed him a helmet. "So Liu doesn't bash me," he said. "Heaven forbid I lose what little brains I have."

"I wasn't going to say it out loud," Bingley said.

"I was," Nadezhda said, and Georgiana giggled.

Liu Xiao arrived not long after that and was ushered into the dojo, approaching Bingley with intense humility. "Mr. Bingali. Miss Bingali."

"Mr. Xiao."

"I am so very sorry – "

Bingley offered his hand to shake, and Liu accepted. "Enough apologies. You're here to beat Mr. Maddox senseless, are you not?"

"*Hey!*"

"Yes, I believe so," Liu said. "Thank you, Mr. Bingali."

Make my daughter happy and you can have all the thanks you wish, Bingley thought as he and Georgie were seated. Liu's weapon was three long sticks all linked together by chain, and Brian's was a wooden sword. He took his long sword off his belt and handed it to Nadezhda. "All right, Ambassador. Give me what you've got."

"Many good wishes, samurai."

Brian was a very good fighter, and he was better than Bingley remembered him being in India, faster with more complex movements. He knew he trained relentlessly, even when he had no trainer. Liu was just younger and even more skilled and, Bingley realized, fought very much like Mugin. Or maybe Mugin had fought like him. Wasn't Mugin a wushu master? He'd forgotten in his anger. He was still pondering it when Brian took a strike to the head hard enough to make him tumble over. "Ow," he said very un-dramatically, his voice muffled by his headgear. "All right, match. Nady, tell him he won."

"He understands English, dear."

Liu helped Brian to his feet. "Good match."

"Good – match. Yes." A dazed Brian removed his helmet. "Bingley. Get up here and embarrass yourself."

"Absolutely not! I learned that lesson in China, thank you. There's only one place for a fighter in the Bingley clan, and sadly it is taken." He gestured his head in Liu's direction. "Go."

"Papa, I love you," she said, kissing him on the cheek before running up to her uncle, who began to hand off his armor to her.

"He won't hurt her," Nadezhda said, taking a seat next to Bingley. "I told him I will kill him."

"Once again, you would be doing my work for me," he said. "What am I going to tell Jane?"

"That I cannot answer for you, Mr. Bingley."

"That is very unfortunate," he said as he watched his daughter be suited up like a samurai, "because I've not the faintest idea."

CHAPTER 16

The Monarch in Winter

Dear Georgiana,

I'm sorry for my penmanship. My right hand is still unusable so this is my left. I hope you don't mind. I cannot express how I miss you and have always missed you though I feel it more keenly now. These scribbles will have to do until the bindings come off but they say it may be as late as Christmas – when I will see you anyway! I have never been so excited for the holiday in my life Now you see why I didn't want anyone else to write this? Sorry my hand is very tired so I should stop. I love you very much.

Geoffrey Darcy

~~~

Dear Geoffrey,

Please do not fret on my account. All right, you may fret a little, but do not hurt yourself beyond what you have already succeeded in doing. I would prefer if at least some of you were functional when I see you next.

I am still in Town with my father, and everyone is gone to their homes already so I have little companionship other than Monkey and occasionally the Maddoxes, but I will complain only in the respect that I am unable to see you. Papa says that it is not an option for me to live in Chesterton with Aunt Maddox for your next term, but I think I am slowly wearing down his defenses. To be honest, it would have been done already, but Papa is very sensitive right now, even though the business with Mr. D____ is settled. I think he knows that when we return to the country, Mama and Eliza will monopolize my time, to speak nothing of Aunt Darcy and your sisters a mere three miles away, so he is not rushing back to Derbyshire. I do wish he would stop calling me his little girl, because I am neither, though I will admit to being on the short side, but respectable I think for a lady. Still, it makes him smile, and there has been so much to make him melancholy, especially after I told him everything about France, and you became the least of his worries. You can have no fear about having him as a father, for he is thrilled at the prospect of us 'finally' coming together as if it was planned in our cradles! He always has a knowing smirk when he says it, too.

There is little to report, as the weather has turned ill, and we hardly venture out to the Maddoxes now. We dined with the Bertrands yesterday. I know that piece of information is absolutely fascinating to you and you are poring over my every social engagement as if it were an adventure novel, but there is a point in my mentioning this, which I have now come to: Joseph Bennet intends to join the church! He will begin Cambridge next fall, he has decided, and though he probably is better versed in Latin and Greek than most churchmen, he has a long road of study ahead of him.

Do you remember when your parents went to France? Or was it Italy? It was to find

Joseph's father. I remember something about him being promised to the church, but I cannot properly recall it and I cannot think of whom to ask. And is that rumor about Frederick true?

Yours,
Georgiana Bingley

<center>~~~</center>

Dearest Georgie,
Sorry again for brevity. I do remember that his father was Roman, or at least Italian, because they did go to Rome. That is where Uncle Grégoire got his cross. My parents have never spoken of it to me but I am fairly sure he (Joseph's father) was a churchman or was to be and that was likely why they did not marry.

To answer your other question, the rumor about FM is true. He was born two weeks before his sister and he got drunk – more than his usual drunk – on his birthday. Beyond that I am sworn to secrecy. I do apologize but he made me swear and he specifically mentioned you so I must abide by my oath.

For the record I do like it when you call me yours, however unintentional it may have been.

Love
Geoffrey Darcy

~~~

To Miss Georgiana Bingley,

Please be assured that Geoffrey is in good health and his hand is mending nicely, even if he expresses his frustration as to being unable to use it at this time. I thought you would like to know.

Sincerely,
Mr. G Wickham

~~~

To Mr. G Wickham,
Thank you very much for

"Monkey!" Georgiana screamed as the primate grabbed her pen with his mouth and retreated up onto the bookcase. "Bring that back!

Why are you so fussy today?" But Monkey just howled at her. "Are you hungry? Fine, if it will quiet you, I'll get you *something*." She covered her unfinished letter to George and let him leap into her arms, rewrapping her shawl more tightly around her shoulders to protect from the winter draft in the house.

As she entered the study, she noticed and greeted her father's guests. "Papa. Mr. Xiao. Mr. Jin." Monkey leapt from her arms and onto her father's desk, where he helped himself to the bowl of figs. "I'm sorry. He must be hungry."

"I fed him an hour ago," Bingley said, explaining to the other men, "He gets like this in the winter."

"Mughal monkey?" Jin said.

"Indian, yes."

"Cold weather, bad for monkey."

"He's been all right for the past few years," Bingley said. "Except in the very cold months."

"Bath," Jin said.

"What?"

"You give him a hot bath," Liu Xiao said in his superior English. "Like snow monkeys. They bathe in hot springs."

"It might be a good idea," Georgie said.

"Or a disaster," Bingley said. "And I'll have to answer to Mrs. Bingley for yet again almost destroying Chatton House."

"Papa, look at him," she said, and almost on cue, Monkey looked up at his owner with wide eyes.

"Stop it," Bingley said. "You know what that look does to me." Monkey squawked. "You don't even know what you're asking for, animal."

"Papa, why are you being so cruel?"

"If I must choose between him and your mother, I will always choose her." Then he floundered. "Perhaps something can be arranged. Now go bother someone else!" He almost literally pushed him off the table, which Monkey took as enough of a hint to grab as many figs as he could and go scampering out the door. Bingley sighed. "Georgiana, I was just telling Mr. Jin and Mr. Xiao that this is our last meeting until sometime in the spring. March at the earliest." To her expression he said, "They are not supposed to leave London, and I suppose it is harder to do actual diplomacy from Derbyshire."

They rose and bowed to her. "It has been an honor, Miss Bingley," Liu said.

"Thank you, Mr. Xiao." She curtseyed.

Their goodbyes were cut short by the time. There were things to be packed, and they both had to prepare to leave for supper. "Can I see Liu Xiao in the spring?" Georgie asked her father as they disappeared down the street.

"If you're not married by then," he said, and to her unasked question only provided a very knowing glance before going up to dress for their final night in Town.

~~~

Mr. Bingley and his eldest daughter were welcomed into the Bertrand home, already beginning to be covered in Christmas decorations, again. "The Bradleys will be joining us," Mary Bertrand said to her brother-in-law. "That should be distracting enough." They had been invited to Derbyshire for the holiday, but Dr. Bertrand's travel was increasingly restricted as he tended to the ailing (and probably dying) king.

"Wish them our best," Bingley said as his daughter was assaulted by her cousin Margaret, still a toddler, and every bit determined to show off everything she was learning to do.

"Uncle Bingley. Miss Bingley," Mr. Joseph Bennet had attained a good height, his features had matured into a young man's, and he had a slight air of seriousness about him, reminding Bingley more of Edmund than of Charles. His skin and hair were a bit darker than the rest of the family's, but there was nothing bizarre in his appearance. "Maggie, how many times has Mother told you not to attack your cousins on sight?"

"Lots!" she said.

"She's no trouble, Mr. Bennet," Georgie assured him as they heard a wail from upstairs.

"Excuse me – that's James," Mary said and disappeared upstairs. James Bertrand was only three months of age.

"Bring him down so we can see him!" Bingley shouted as she departed. "So – where is the eminent doctor?"

"He was delayed in coming home and is still preparing himself. He apologizes for his lateness," Joseph said. Moments later, Mary joined them again, this time bearing a bundle that was Bingley's newest nephew.

Little James had only a tuft of hair, light brown like his father's. The boy was passed to Georgie, who sat down with her cousin, his tiny limbs flailing and catching the lace of her dress. "Are you bothering your mother?" she said in the sweetest voice she had.

"Of course he isn't," Mary said as Joseph and Bingley watched on.

Bingley felt an odd unsettlement in his stomach upon watching his daughter, a skilled fighter and normally very aggressive young lady, properly cradle James's tiny head and whisper cooing sounds right back to him. *Thank God she's not with child*, he repeated over again in his head. He didn't think he could take it if she was. She was *his* baby. Charles Bingley had not overly concerned himself with his daughters entering society, at least not to the outrageous extent that Darcy did, but now at least he could understand his friend's feelings.

"Mr. Bingley. Are you all right?" Dr. Bertrand said, approaching from behind. "You look a bit pale."

"Just a drink, please," he said.

"If we're not in a rush..." Dr. Bertrand showed him into his study and poured Bingley a glass of brandy. "I apologize – "

"Joseph told us. We understand," he said, and sipped his drink. "Your job must be very demanding."

"Increasingly so. I can see why Dr. Maddox retired when he did," he said. He was far younger than Maddox had been when he left London and took the professorship, but he was still a man with a family and the responsibilities that came with it. "I am also considering an early retirement from this particular post."

"I thought you might be."

"This position made my reputation as a doctor," he said. "I would not be lacking in patients to fill my schedule. And the hours might be better. But of course, His Majesty is always in an off mood when I'm called, so it is very hard to broach the topic. Sir Maddox was always so brave with the king."

"He knew him when he was only the Prince," Bingley said. "And when his health was better."

"With Joseph leaving in the fall for Cambridge, and of course with a new infant, I wish I had more time to spend at home just now." Dr. Bertrand treated Joseph Bennet like his own son, and the birth of his biological children had not changed that. "But a man has his duties."

"To his occupation *and* his family."

Dr. Bertrand smiled. "I thought gentlemen had no occupation."

"Apparently being landlord or investor does not count, no matter how many hours you put into it," Bingley replied. "And I foolishly had to go into foreign shipping. Do you know how hard the language of China is?"

"You would give it up if you didn't enjoy it."

"You've caught me there," Bingley said.

The bell rang for supper, and they joined the others. Dinner was a celebratory affair, toasting to Georgiana's engagement (though they had done it before) and Joseph's plans for school, and the holidays in general. It was cut short only by a messenger from Windsor Cottage, and Dr. Bertrand reluctantly excused himself. The guests,

283

who would not see their hosts for several months, were not asked to leave in the absence of the doctor, so Bingley continued his chat with Joseph and Mary, and Georgiana was able spend more time with James.

When they finally left, Georgiana joined her father in the coach with a scowl on her face. "Never leave me alone with Aunt Bertrand again."

Personally, he thought Mary had mellowed considerably over the years, more so with each child. "What did she say?"

"Nothing I want to repeat to my father," she said, adding in a mumble, "Some unappreciated marital advice."

Nor did she appreciate his laughter, but he did it all the same.

~~~

Dr. Andrew Bertrand arrived at Windsor Cottage in a state of some consternation. He had left the king after many hours of watching over him during his daily ride around the gardens and treating his skin problems (mainly bedsores) and had not intended to return, specifically mentioning to the king's man that he was hosting a dinner party. It was not that other doctors were not on call for the ailing monarch, but His Majesty seemed to be random in the manner in which he demanded them.

"Lady Conyngham," he bowed as the lady passed him, going the opposite direction.

"Dr. Bertrand," the king's latest mistress replied with the briefest of curtseys. She was in no mood to talk and he was in no mood to press her.

Bag in hand he was ushered into the king's chambers, where his Royal Highness King George IV was bent over the side of the bed, hacking into a pot held by Dr. Engel. That His Majesty had succeeded in getting himself upright was a minor miracle, especially at this hour. "When did he start coughing?" he asked Sir Knighton, who was the only other person of authority in the room. Dr. Engel was not on the regular staff; Bertrand was not sure precisely why he was there.

"About an hour ago," Knighton said. "He's specifically demanded you."

He imagined. He looked at the pot and then up at the king. "Your Majesty."

The king grabbed him by his coat, pulling him uncomfortably close with swollen, fat fingers. "Tell me I'm not dying."

"I do not believe you are. If you were hacking blood, I would be more concerned, but you are not." He gestured towards the pot, then pressed his hand against the king's forehead. "No fever. You most likely have a cold." *And you didn't need me to tell you that. Dr. Engel is perfectly competent and he's right there,* he thought. "I can give you tonics to soothe your throat and recommend – "

The king grabbed him with both hands and shook him. "*What did you tell them?*"

"Tell whom, Your Majesty?"

"Them. Anyone." He softened at the prospect that he did not have an answer. George IV, once the silver-tongued Prince of Wales, was always frustrated when his words were lacking. "Have you betrayed me?"

Dr. Bertrand swallowed. He was right; he did not have Dr. Maddox's willpower or courage, which he needed at this moment, and made some attempt to call it up. "With all due respect, sir, I have nothing to betray you *with.*"

"Answer the question!"

"Sir, I have never and will never betray you. I have no secrets to provide, and if I did, I would never relinquish them, upon pain of death," he said, and the king partially released him.

His Majesty put a hand over his eyes and began to sob. This was not unusual behavior, and something Dr. Bertrand was more prepared to deal with. The king rapidly became incoherent again, and after drinking a tonic, settled down into a stupor that could be called sleep, at which point the doctors were dismissed by the ever-hovering

286

Knighton, who gave Bertrand a cold look as he departed.

"What was that about?" Dr. Bertrand whispered to Engel as they made their escape. The Prussian doctor was probably twenty years older than him and more an associate of Knighton's than an official member of the staff, but never failed to be competent when he did appear.

"I have no idea. I was called by Sir Knighton to attend His Majesty." He added, "I do not believe he is in good mental health."

"What do you expect?" Bertrand said, and they parted ways at the doorway to the Windsor complex.

It was not a long way back to his home, and Dr. Bertrand returned in enough time to see his children being put to bed. He kissed his daughter goodnight, said good evening to Joseph, who was still up studying, and joined his wife in her chambers. James was not sleeping through the night yet, and the cradle was by her side of the bed.

"How was it?" Mary asked as he kissed her, then his son, still in her arms from being fed.

His response was a very tense smile. She nodded in understanding and joined him in bed. Mrs. Bertrand found sleep much faster than her husband did.

CHAPTER 17

Mistress of Pemberley

Geoffrey could not remember a time when he was more eager for Christmas. He was counting the days, then the hours, then the minutes until it was time at last to leave for Pemberley. He wanted to take a horse, but it was too cold, and it was a standing order that he would take a proper carriage in the winter trek from Cambridge to Derbyshire. He did not want to make conversation with his traveling companion, Charles Bingley. That was not the Bingley he was interested in, and a few disparaging comments in response to any attempt to start a conversation made that obvious enough. Even though he didn't truly mean to be rude, it probably came off that way, he thought with a sigh, turning away from the window to look at Charles, who just smiled at him and returned to his book. Charles Bingley was not oblivious, just forgiving.

Within the boundaries of proper society, there was little he was allowed to do with Georgiana, but he was still her cousin, and besides, he thought, he had already done everything beyond the boundaries except leave her with child. So when they were surrounded by only family, he did not hesitate to embrace her. "Georgiana."

"I can't curtsey with you holding me like this."

He smiled. "Do you want me to let go?"

"No."

Still, they were in front of their parents and their various aunts and uncles, so the pair made an attempt at decorum. As the day went on, they were mostly chaperoned by brothers and sisters, so for the most part it didn't get in the way of anything but real intimacy, which as much as he craved it, would be a dangerous step. Still, he could let her lean on him as they sat on the settee together and think, *She's finally mine.*

Geoffrey wasn't sure where this almost animalistic possessiveness suddenly came from, but he had long since given up questioning his instincts. He was busy keeping the worst of them in check, keeping himself from bribing Charles, taking her up to his room, and having his way with her until they were both exhausted. He was also fairly sure she would not object, which made it all the worse. She had always been intimidating, even to him.

When the Kincaids and the Maddoxes arrived, things were easier because there were too many guests constantly moving between the two houses for everyone to be properly kept track of, and Frederick was more than happy to leave them alone in a sitting room for a sovereign.

"They should have known better than to put Frederick in charge of us," Georgie said.

"I know," he replied, and kissed her. Geoffrey knew she was hardly a porcelain doll – in fact, the very opposite of one, as much as that was possible – but her skin was so white and so soft that it was hard not to think of her as something that needed gentle care. Then there were her hands, as calloused as his or maybe more so, to remind him. Parts of her remained unscarred, unblemished by time or physical exertions.

"Georgie," he whispered after several minutes, "I have to stop."

It didn't need an explanation. "All right," she said between breaths. "We can't do this."

"You weren't finding it so objectionable – "

"I mean we can't pretend that we want to wait until you graduate."

Geoffrey detached himself from her and leaned back into the cushion. "I know. What are we supposed to do?"

"Well, what do those whores do?"

"How would I know?" he said, and she giggled. "What's so funny?"

"You're blushing."

"Because it's embarrassing."

"Why?"

"Well – you don't talk about such things. One would hope."

"I thought that was what happened at University."

"Yes, but not to me, and not to Charles. You would have to ask George."

She cocked her head. "George? George Wickham?"

"Yes."

"George Wickham, who goes to assemblies with his sister and never even looks at a woman, much less asks her to dance? George Wickham, who owns more books than the rest of us combined and has mastered Greek, Latin, and French just to read them?"

It was Geoffrey's turn to laugh. "Yes, that George Wickham. I am sad to shatter your image of him, but he is not the monk you believe him to be. Two years of living with him taught me that."

"He's good with women?"

"He's terrible. He's everything you have described. With that said, George Wickham always has a standing appointment with a courtesan in any major city he happens to visit."

Georgie covered her mouth. "Why didn't I know this?"

"Because he's so discreet about it. I think Charles knows, but do you think Charles would tell you something like that?"

"You would."

"Well, I have," he said, pulling her into him again. "Now I can tell you all of my dirty secrets from college, though there aren't that many, and that was the main one. There was also the time we got too drunk to remember the way home and ended up falling asleep in the quad of the wrong college, but that's hardly such a scandal for University students." He loved the feeling of having her in his arms, her back against his chest. She was so much smaller than him, her limbs so deceptively tiny. "George must have gone out to see this woman – I don't recall, maybe three or four times a week."

"He kept a mistress?"

"No. He didn't want the emotional attachment. He said he saw the same woman because it was the most sanitary thing to do and the easiest thing to arrange."

"God," she said, "even when he's shelling out shillings for prostitutes, he's still so *George* about it."

"Precisely. Though I don't know how I would approach him on the subject without some long tirade about social propriety – "

"I'll do it," she said.

"I do not believe he will want to answer you, if he even knows how they do it."

293

"I'll make him answer. And if he does not know, I will make him ask." She looked up at him. "That is a promise."

He kissed her. "I will hold you to it."

~~~

It was still two days to Christmas and Derbyshire was covered in a light snowfall. Thankfully, not enough to hold up the mail, whereupon all of the letters from relatives afar and abroad came in. The Bellamonts sent their love and promised their regular spring visit. George and Isabella Wickham were in London with their mother and the Bradleys, and Brian and Nadezhda decided to spend the holiday in Paris.

The post came very early, and Bingley was still in his Indian costume pajamas when he was told that Mr. Darcy had called. "Let him come," he said and took a seat in his study. "Darcy."

"Bingley." They had seen each other the night before. He nodded toward the letters his friend was sorting through. "Anything in the post?"

"Thank goodness, nothing terribly surprising," he replied, gesturing for Darcy to take a seat as coffee was served. "Mr. Maddox and Her Highness sent their good wishes."

"Ran all the way to France, did they?"

"The excuse given was, 'Her Highness has always wanted to see Midnight Mass at Notre Dame, and I am eager to oblige her,'" he read. "In my defense, I did not *tell* them to go to the Continent."

"Because a defense must be given."

Bingley just smiled at him. "Any news from the Darcy side?"

"We've been invited by the Vicar Collins and his wife to attend the wedding of one of their daughters, Miss Maria Collins, in March at Kent."

"How many do they have?"

"Four. This will be the second married."

"Is he intending to inherit Longbourn with any daughters left to worry about?"

"He is a wise planner in that respect," Darcy said. "And I suppose he has some consolation that the most likely purchaser of the old Bennet estate upon his death will be a nephew who has followed him in his profession."

"And his father's profession."

"You didn't have to say it," Darcy said. "I heard a rumor – "

" – whatever it is, she didn't do it."

Darcy just frowned at him indignantly. "I meant about your son."

"Whatever it is, he didn't do it."

"For God's sake, man, can you just let me finish a sentence?" he grumbled. "I heard a rumor that Edmund is considering Oxford."

"Oh." Bingley sighed in relief. "Yes. It is appropriate, as he does intend a career in business, and he is probably qualified to pass the entrance exams, but I am somewhat reluctant to grant my blessing. He is young yet, and I would prefer not to lose two children in one year."

"She'll be three miles away," Darcy said. "Though, you'd be better not to mention it often in front of my servants, or I won't have a staff come summer."

"Are you implying that my eldest daughter can be intimidating?"

"I hope that was rhetorical and I don't have to actually answer it," Darcy replied, to which Bingley laughed. "Let me say that they are ... relieved that Elizabeth is in good health."

"You are not being completely fair. Georgiana is a respectable lady, can even act like one when she wants to, and is very kind to her servants for someone of her age and stature."

"I am having a flashback – it may have been a dream I had about a long stream of governesses..."

"*Other* than governesses," Bingley fumed.

Darcy stood and paced by the fire, a smirk on his face. "They will come around, as they have plenty of time to do it." He sighed. "I did intend for Geoffrey to tour the Continent after his graduation."

"Did you ever let Geoffrey himself in on your intentions?"

"I won't dignify that with an answer."

"As you will," Bingley said. "If he still has the interest, I don't see why they shouldn't go together. I've never known a safer time to travel. Besides, it's unlikely they'll listen to us anyway once Geoffrey reaches majority, especially with a sudden flush of fifty thousand pounds. They never have before, and I doubt they'll start now." He looked up at Darcy and his expression. "You'd best make peace with it. It makes you feel less guilty when your children do remarkably stupid or dangerous things."

On this, Darcy could not contradict him.

~~~

Dear Georgiana,

I confess that it has been a great distress to me that I have been unavailable and therefore unable to see you at such a crucial time in your life. And to think that you will soon be married! My mother says I should not call on you at all for the first few months if I have any decorum.

The only way to relieve the suffering of a lost acquaintance is for you to visit me in Teversham. I will be staying there with my aunt and uncle for the better part of the winter, and if the roads are open, you are free to come anytime after Christmas. I insist!

Your Friend,
Lady Heather Littlefield

The letter (or that part of it) was read by the recipient to a very skeptical audience of Mr. and Mrs. Bingley. They both knew full well that Teversham was barely five miles from Chesterton and Cambridge. Georgiana knew that they knew. It was merely a question of their response.

"So," Bingley began, "you would be chaperoned by her uncle? And I suppose you would also insist on visiting the Maddoxes?"

"Papa, they're my relatives. Besides, Emily is there."

"So she is."

There was a silence.

"Why do you think me so untrustworthy?" she demanded.

"I can't possibly imagine," Jane replied, her arms still folded.

"There are downsides to having a reputation as a skilled sneak," her father said.

"I promise to be good!"

"And I have no doubt you will stretch the definition of the word 'good' to its limits," Bingley said. "If you can find a chaperone I can trust, you can go."

"Now you're being cruel. Mama, please! Did Papa not call on you during your engagement?"

"He was not twenty year old student at the time," she said, "studying, sharing the company of men – "

"Drinking, sharing the company of women –," Her father paused and looked over at her mother. "Geoffrey might be better off with her there."

"Charles! You're not helping!"

Georgiana scrambled for an answer. "Edmund could go."

This posed more questions than answers, as evident by the look on their faces.

"Well – you know how he just sits in his room and studies his own books, and he wants to go to Oxford next year, so he might benefit from discovering what is expected of him at University," she said. "And he's figured out more of my schemes than Charles and Eliza combined."

Her parents exchanged glances, then mumbled the eternal answer: "We'll think about it."

~~~

On Christmas Eve, the Darcys, the Bingleys, Mr. Bennet and the Maddoxes (minus a few members) came together for a long meal and time together before midnight services.

"So the chief mental anatomist says to the blue mass expert –"

"Darling, no one understands your jokes," Caroline Maddox said, handing her husband a glass of brandy. Fortunately, in the months since his condition was made official, the Pemberley staff had become more accustomed to Dr. Maddox and tended to surround him less with suggestions and instructions.

"We like the ones we understand," Bingley said. "The ones that aren't disgusting."

"That would be a small percentage, I'm afraid," Mr. Bennet said.

"I never said I was good at parties," Dr. Maddox replied.

"What about the one with the man returning from Waterloo – "

"Not in mixed company," Darcy said to Bingley, cutting him off.

"Yes, our fair maiden ears must be saved." Elizabeth rolled her eyes.

"It involves a lot of pus," Dr. Maddox explained.

Bingley sunk into the seat next to his wife. "I thought it was funny."

"I'm sure you did," Jane said.

"I think it's funny," Dr. Maddox said. "We could vote on it, the people who've heard."

"Vote? This isn't Parliament."

"Of course. Not enough gin or shouting."

"The two things do go well in combination," Mr. Bennet observed. "Speaking of excessive intoxication and shouting, where are my rowdy University student set of grandchildren?"

"Getting soused before having to face their elders," Elizabeth suggested, wondering just how right she might be.

~~~

"Pass the whiskey. Now!" Frederick was having none of Geoffrey's distracted hosting. "If I'm not cup shot before the sermon, I will be very upset."

"And we wouldn't want Frederick Maddox to be very upset," Georgie said.

"Do you want me to start singing, 'Here comes the bride' again?"

"Do you want to keep your vital organs?"

"It's Christmas!" Charles insisted, as Geoffrey was lost in a lovesick haze, and they had all given up on him an hour ago. "Or have you forgotten?"

"So?"

"So?"

"It means that Christ was born," Eliza Bingley said, "and maybe He'd appreciate it if you would take a night off from threatening mental or bodily harm to other family members?"

"She may be right," Geoffrey said as he returned to Georgie's side. She gave him a little punch in the arm, to which he responded by kissing her on the cheek.

"Disgusting. I think I liked them better when they were fighting," Emily Maddox said.

"Then you have a very short memory," her brother said. "It was definitely worse."

~~~

Afterward, Geoffrey remembered nothing from the Christmas service. He heard not a word of the sermon, and not because of his impairment.

The Darcys sat close enough and the Rector was loud enough; Geoffrey's *mind* was elsewhere. Part of it was unfortunately on the people staring at him. The heir to Pemberley was accustomed to being an attraction at services, but he noticed more and more heads were turning towards Anne, the eligible lady with fifty thousand pounds. Anne, marrying? A wave of dread washed over him, followed by a wave of guilt.

Is this what Father feels like about me?

He glanced at his father, but the master of Pemberley's eyes were set as they always were, firmly on the speaker or his prayer book.

Oh, God. Uncle Bingley.

The Bingleys were seated in a row across the aisle. Mr. Bingley was seated next to a soundly-sleeping Mr. Bennet. His expression was unfortunately unreadable, even for Geoffrey. Surely he wasn't thinking about it all the time? Or was that what it was like for a man to give up his daughter? Even the idea that Anne, only his sister, would be married and the property of some man who was not a Darcy, and bear children in some other name, and keep her own household ... It was frightening. And then Sarah would follow, and then Cassandra. He would be the only Darcy left. Even with both his parents alive and well and his own marriage intentions secured, it was a lonely concept.

At least he would have someone to be lonely *with*.

His view of Georgiana was obstructed by taller congregants. He had to wait until after services, when he found her immediately. "Happy Christmas."

"Happy Christmas," she said, giving him a little smile. She never gave him a real smile, except in privacy. "I think you just cut our whole family by racing to me."

"They'll recover," he said and kissed her hand.

~~~

The Christmas meal was on the late side the next day, as it was a late night for the older crowd and a mean morning for the hung-over younger crowd. With no one in the crowd well under ten, gift-giving was a far more private and subdued affair than it had been among the screaming children of yesteryear.

"Why are you – " Darcy said as he watched Bingley play with one of Danny Maddox's toys, a puzzle piece involving getting hoops through each other. "Forget it."

"What?"

"It's not worth asking," he said and sipped his wine as Elizabeth giggled.

The younger children were sitting over a board game where they could only advance if they answered questions on 'Universal History and Chronology.' Danny Maddox, Cassandra and Sarah Darcy, and even Edmund Bingley found this beyond their grasp and immediately began querying their parents for help, to which they responded that it was cheating to avoid having to admit they didn't know the answer.

They had almost abandoned it when Frederick Maddox, without even looking up from his book or his spirits said, "84."

"What?"

"A.D. 84 was the year the Romans defeated Calgacus at Ardoch. Who *doesn't* know that?"

"Oh yeah?" Edmund picked up another card. "So when did Joan of Arc die?"

"1431. Don't you read?"

"I told you Frederick was the smartest of us," Geoffrey said to Georgie as they watched the game from the relative privacy of a window seat. "Book-smart, that is. He's brilliant."

"So I should tell him you said that?"

"Please, no. He'd never let me live it down."

"When does he ever let anyone live anything down?" she said. "I didn't give you your present."

"No."

"You look depressed."

"I was hoping it would be a more private gift."

She rolled her eyes and handed him the letter. He read it and looked up in confusion. "Teversham is – "

"Five miles from Cambridge, if that. And guess who begged her parents hard enough for them to let her go?" she said. "Though we'll have to find a way to ditch Edmund."

"I'm sure we'll manage," he said. "Thank you. Now what I got you will seem ... material."

"That's what Christmas presents are supposed to be, right? Things?"

He pulled a small container out of his pocket and handed it to her. She opened up the little lacquered tube to reveal a scroll, with Japanese writing in bold strokes across it. "This is ... an engagement announcement. Of Darcy Jeffrey and Bingley Jorgiana."

"Thank goodness. I had no idea if it really said that."

She snuck a kiss. "Nadi-sama?"

"Uncle Brian, if you believe it."

"I do." She embraced him. "What kind of announcement is written in a language only I can read?"

"You're the only one I wanted to read it," he said, which earned him another fast kiss and a clearing of his father's throat, even though he was facing in the other direction. The latter, Geoffrey decided, was worth it.

CHAPTER 18

George Wickham's No-Good, Very Bad Day

The new year, 1826, came in without incident. The students returned to Cambridge, and the harshest weeks of winter passed quickly. Finally, with an embarrassing amount of hugs and kisses for both of them, Georgiana and her brother Edmund Bingley were sent to Teversham.

Duke and Duchess Bell welcomed them with an overbearing grace, but it was quickly made up for by the enthusiasm of their niece, Lady Littlefield. "I'm sorry," she said as they were escorted on a long and winding tour of a house that had once been great, probably in the 1600's, but had not been properly renovated, only well-dusted. The Bells were aristocracy and the Bingley children weren't, and it was obvious that that would not be forgotten for a second. Fortunately, they were released when Edmund mentioned an interest in the history of the estate, and Duke Bell's eyes practically lit up and he took the boy off. Heather Littlefield offered to show Georgiana the gardens herself, and the Duchess looked relieved.

"I really hope we aren't a bother," Georgie said as they stepped into the sunshine.

"You aren't! They're that way with everyone. The whole family is. I think it gives them something to do." They shared a laugh. "Tell me all about your Mr. Darcy!"

"He's tall, brown hair, very respectable demeanor when he's not doing something stupid, heir to the great fortune of Pemberley and half of Derbyshire – "

"Georgie!"

" – and has suddenly turned into a hopeless romantic."

"It must have been your response to his proposal."

"Yes." Georgiana blushed. "It *might* have been that."

"Well, I helped with your arrangements. You have to let me meet him!"

"Heather! When did you get so mercenary?"

"Since you got engaged to the man you ... well, refused to talk about it in the way that a woman might when really she just wants to rattle on and on about him." She added, "Actually, I think you've been that way since as long as I've known you."

"Heather," she said firmly.

But Heather only took her arm, leading her down the landscaped path around the pond. "You are betrothed. You can be even more honest now than ever. What admirable qualities does he have that swayed the complex person that is Miss Bingley?"

"He doesn't refer to me as a complex person, and he doesn't call me Miss Bingley," was her answer as she saw a flash of red against the trees. Her brother appeared before them, still heaving from running as fast as he could.

He bowed. "Lady Littlefield." He turned to his sister. "You have to get me out of here."

"You *asked* about the noble lineage of this family."

"And he asked me if Geoffrey had any brothers. When I said no, he inquired about my father's connections, then – " He paused. "I shouldn't say this in front of Her Ladyship."

"He tried to arrange my marriage to you?" Heather said, and the girls laughed at a furious Edmund, who tried to look imposing despite his slimness and lack of height. "Did you tell him your age?"

"I – didn't get that far. Before I left," he said. "Why are you laughing? He was talking about your marriage."

"Because he's desperate to outdo my mother, his sister, in the speed of the arrangements.

311

What a prize that would be! Even if he can't be married for ... "

" ... Six years. Maybe five," Georgie finished. "Edmund, I think you should be proud that he considered you such an eligible bachelor despite your age. A second son, and of a tradesman no less? You must have impressed him with something."

"You are in my debt beyond all abilities of mankind to measure," he said and stomped off, which only caused more laughter on their end.

~~~

"Why are we going to see George?" Edmund finally asked as their carriage approached the outskirts of Cambridge proper.

"I'm going to see George. You're going to do ... I don't know, whatever. Escort Heather to the park or something."

"Why do you need to see George? You're not marrying *him*."

Heather giggled; Georgiana snarled. "I like my cousin. Maybe I just want to talk to him."

"About what?"

"About his possible interest in Heather," she said.

"Or, that's what we told my aunt," Heather Littlefield said as the carriage came to a stop on an excessively bumpy road. All of the stones seemed to be misshapen. "One hour or two?"

"One," Georgiana said and, without further explanation, stepped out of the carriage, and it continued on to the market.

"I've never heard my sister giggle so much," Edmund said to Heather. "Or at all."

"She's in love."

"She's been in love for years."

"It's different."

Edmund shrugged. Some things were just beyond him.

~~~

George Wickham was already running late – in his mind, at least. He had no appointments, but he had at least six hours of reading to do before dinner with the other Fellows, and he had set aside the time, but the books weren't open yet. He spent the morning with a hangover that prevented him from serious study, after being offered a particularly wonderful glass of whiskey by his female companion – who was then so amused by his altered state that she offered him another one. It was the only time he could remember spending the night at her establishment before stumbling back to his apartment.

Needless to say, Georgiana's sudden visit was not readily welcomed, even though decorum dictated that he not shut the door in her face and turn his nose back to his books.

"I need advice," she said.

"Don't bother a Fellow."

But of course, she didn't listen. She let herself into his little parlor, and his servant offered her some refreshment before disappearing. She swallowed it in one gulp and set it down. "It's a delicate question."

George shut the doors, just for good measure. He had a pretty good guess as to what she meant. "You'd better not already be – "

"I'm not," she said quickly, "and I don't want to be. So here I am."

He stared at her blankly.

"George, don't do this to me."

"Do what?" he said. "I've no horribly immoral advice to offer you. I'm not an expert on not ... getting with child."

"But you know people who are."

"No."

"Don't deny it."

"I'm not," he said, uncomfortable with the flush on his face and her unrelenting stare. She was a head shorter than him and he was terrified all the same. "I'm saying I won't help you, even if I could."

"You could."

314

"Georgie, no."

"You could ask your…lady – "

"*No.*"

She was prepared for this. "Fine." She turned on her heels. "I'll just drink that potion – what is it? Tansy and quinine?"

Georgie turned to leave, and he actually grabbed her arm. "Promise me you won't."

"Oh, suddenly you do know *something.*"

"I'm studying medicine, Georgie. I know that stuff can hurt you. *Permanently.* Even kill you." He released his grip but kept the intensity in his voice. "Promise me you won't drink tansy, savin, or quinine. Promise me you won't drink any tonic you might have heard something about."

"I don't know. We Bingleys have a long tradition of doing stupid things because it seemed like a good idea at the time."

"I'm serious." He sighed. "What do you want?"

"Precisely what I asked for in the first place."

"And if I refuse?"

"Then you've left me with little option."

"Or you could – " But he knew he wasn't going to get anywhere, doing this. "Fine. Promise me you won't drink anything or do anything before I talk to you, and I'll ask her."

"You have my word."

"*Promise?*"

"God, George, yes. I'm not as stupid as you think." She curtseyed, and without further conversation, showed herself out.

"Sometimes I still think you are," he said aloud to the empty room.

~~~

George Wickham was nearing success – he was almost through his book in half the expected time, with the next one beside it on the desk – when there was a knock on the door again.

His servant approached. "Geoffrey Darcy to see you, sir."

He did not hide his groan as his cousin entered. "Geoffrey." He excused the servant.

"George," Geoffrey said, waiting until the man was gone before speaking, "I need some advice."

George just nodded hesitantly.

"You know ... things." He played with the gloves in his hands. "About ... pleasing a woman."

"Oh God." He hid none of his displeasure. "I can't do this with *both* of you. There are limits."

Geoffrey blushed. "G-Georgie was here?"

"Yes." George swallowed his brandy from the bottle opened after Georgiana's visit and sat down, "because I seem to be the resident expert at everything unmentionable. These things are unmentionable because they violate all laws of propriety between an unmarried couple – "

" – which you're so apt at doing."

George took the bottle and poured himself another full glass of brandy with no hesitation. "If you even try and threaten to go to my sister with that information, you should know that I've already been threatened once today by your betrothed and will not tolerate another."

"Today? Damn! Wait, why would she ask you -"

"She asked me something else, equally inappropriate."

"What are we supposed to do?"

"Make sure that the altar can wait until the completion of your degree. Or I believe Uncle Darcy will have your head."

"I have no idea how you came to be on your high horse about physical propriety, but – look," he rubbed his eyes. "Will you give me advice or not?"

George sighed. Geoffrey's pathetically pleading eyes told him he was about to lose another battle with both his morals and his cousin. It was just not his day.

~~~

317

It took a frustrating week to arrange it. First, Georgie had to say she was ready (and he knew better than to inquire how she knew), and then Geoffrey had to figure out a suitable alibi for her, not to mention how to get rid of his roommates. Frederick usually went right back to sleep after chapel, nursing a hangover, and didn't emerge again until mid-afternoon. Charles sometimes went off with his crowd of dramatist friends or was absorbed with studying, but he liked to study in his room far too often. And Georgiana had no business being in Cambridge with her friend at night. Oh, and they had to rid themselves of her chaperoning younger brother. She at least promised to manage that, arranging for Edmund to suddenly encounter that economics professor he had been so eager to meet on the road, leaving her with Heather, whom she would then dispose of by proposing to need to visit George again.

He had an easier time than he imagined just with an outright bribe to Frederick. He required no explanation as to why Geoffrey needed their place cleared and when he needed it. Geoffrey didn't care much for the wicked smile and the raised glass in pseudo-toast that Frederick gave him, but he shrugged it off.

There was one last piece of business. "Reynolds," Geoffrey said, putting a sovereign on the table. "Why don't you take off for a few hours? Give yourself a treat. It is your birthday soon, is it not?"

"In three more months, sir."

"That's why I said, soon. I mean, it's coming up."

Reynolds raised his eyebrow, took the money, and left without another word. It wasn't uncommon to ask discretion of a manservant, but Geoffrey had never done it before and so had been rather nervous about it. He steeled himself with a glass of wine, sipping slowly until there was a knock at the door. He opened it himself. "Hel –"

His expected guest seized him by the lining of his waistcoat and pushed him into a kiss that started at the door and ended up against the wall next to the fireplace.

"I – there could have been someone here," he said after he caught his breath.

"Then me showing up at all would have been a big enough surprise to scare them away," she said. Her red hair looked especially bright in the dark room, probably because it went against her borrowed black collegial robe. "Hopefully."

"Hopefully." He grinned and ran to shut and bolt the door. "We are alone. Reynolds gave me a look, but he did leave."

"And my brother?"

"Paid Frederick to distract him."

"Why is Frederick so money-hungry?"

"I think he's more mischief-hungry, and this is the only way he gets it. Especially in the Maddox household. Not exactly the woods of Derbyshire."

Georgiana looked around the main room, which had little to offer but old furniture, stone walls blackened by years of dirt, and a roaring fireplace. And lots of empty wine bottles. "This is where you live?"

"This is Cambridge. It's older than Pemberley. You can hardly expect them to keep the place up."

"Not even the chambers for the Fellows?"

"Oh, those are much worse. Hence, George resides elsewhere."

"It is convenient."

"It is." Realizing he had a guest, he scrambled to his senses. "Would you like a drink? Or refreshment? Or something – "

"Not now, thank you."

"You spoke – you spoke to George."

Georgiana Bingley blushed at him. "Oh God. He told you, that bastard?"

"Only when he was pleading with me to leave. He'd apparently had his limit of embarrassing questions."

"And what could you possibly have to ask him?"

Now he was blushing. "I love you."

"You can't use that line *every* time you wish to distract me."

"I can try."

They did not have a lot of time. They did not have as much time as he wished, though he supposed the day did not consist of enough hours to meet that requirement. Georgiana was due back well before dinner, and he honestly did not know if his roommates would enter at any moment, however embarrassing that might be. Still, Geoffrey did not want to rush. The first time had been a blur, and the next months an exercise in extreme frustration of every kind he could imagine. George had managed to be embarrassingly instructive about the benefits of not rushing, even if they were not newlyweds in a certain sense of the term.

"You're nervous," she said.

"You drive me insane." He smiled. "You don't deny it?"

"I would have a very weak defense."

Where she had managed to find undergraduate robes, he had no idea. His only concern once they were in his room was how quickly he could unbutton them. Thank God she wasn't wearing a corset. He couldn't even imagine how to manage one of those things.

Despite what was probably both their intentions, they were entwined from the moment they shed their clothing and collapsed in a huff not five minutes later. The long wait toward matrimony, intended to give them distance, was doing little good.

Not that, at that moment, he particularly minded. Geoffrey was too dazed and content to be in a truly self-castigating mood. And Georgie clinging to his side as they lay in bed made it all the better.

"When did you first fall in love with me?" he said after a long and easy silence.

"That's a stupid question."

"I meant it seriously."

"It's still a stupid question," she huffed. "I have always been in love with you."

He propped himself up so he could see her face properly. "You know what I mean. When did you stop looking at me like a cousin and start looking at me like someone you would think about marrying? And don't say you always knew. You can pretend with everyone else that you know everything," he said, ending it with a soft kiss, "but not with me."

She looked away. She was not used to questions she did not have a quick answer to. "I don't know. It must have been too gradual for me to notice." She turned back to him. "Why? Do you have a specific date and time?"

"Unfortunately, yes. Or a specific moment, at least, though I don't recall the date and time. I was sixteen, and it was summer."

"And you just came to a realization? An epiphany?"

He smiled. "No. And – it's embarrassing." He felt his cheeks grow hot. "A man doesn't talk about his baser instincts to a woman."

"Despite the fact that he's lying next to her, completely – "

"All right! Why do you want to know so badly?"

"Because you started this conversation," she said, kissing him on the shoulder. "Silly."

"Fine. I was – well, I told you, I was sixteen, and men – we have these dreams – and while we're having them, we don't really have control over our bodies."

"Really." It was not disbelief, it was new information to her that sounded in her voice.

"Unfortunately. And one night I had a rather ... erotic dream about you, and I woke up, and suddenly you were this woman instead of my best friend, and all I wanted to do was hold you like this and make you my wife, to put it in the most polite terms. I was devastated by this revelation and tried to put it out of my mind, but it was hard to do that with stained sheets." He said to her giggle, "Don't laugh at me. Do you know what it's like to

323

suddenly want to bed your best friend? Whom you spend all of your time with?" He stroked her hair. "I always loved your hair, but even more when you cut it."

"Because I look like a boy?"

"You don't look like a boy. Even if you had the haircut of a boy, which you don't, you would never -," he said, kissing her collarbone, " – ever – look like a boy." He loved the way she giggled when he kissed her neck. She so rarely laughed when not at someone else's expense. This wasn't making fun – it was just joy. She hadn't known enough joy in her life, even though she'd always done exactly as she pleased. It had earned her nothing. His hand strayed to the scar on her side, where Hatcher had shot her. The pain she must have gone through – but she never discussed it. All of the focus had been on him then, and his injuries, and his deafness. No time for the real hero.

"What are you thinking about?"

Had she just admitted she didn't know something? "You." Knowing that would not satisfy her, he continued, "I never see you happy."

"Are you completely daft?"

He smiled wickedly. "I mean – prior to our engagement. And tonight. Why are you so unhappy? If I didn't know George, you would be the most morbid and deadening person I know."

"What's this about George?"

"Even George has secrets. Darcy family stuff."

"The illness no one talks about but George obviously has?"

He nodded.

"Do you know about it? Will you tell me about it?"

"If you answer my question."

Again, she had to think. Fortunately, she did her thinking while nestled into the crook of his arm, which suited him just fine. "I was lonely. No one has ever understood me. Everyone tries, and then they just give up in frustration."

"So I am rewarded for not trying? Because I think you're perfect as you are?"

"Yes," she said. "Now answer my question."

Geoffrey swallowed. He could feel her heart beating against his chest. "I don't know the whole of it, but it starts with our Great-Uncle Gregory. Yes, the mad one no one talks about. He was worse than George and worse than my father. Or, they think he was made worse by the treatments, when the doctors bled him nearly to death. So Grandfather Darcy never had my father treated, and Father made sure George never saw a psychical doctor. They do more harm than good. Even Dr. Maddox will tell you that." He supposed this was the only way he would ever be comfortable talking about it. "It goes beyond what you can see – how

George avoids socializing and never sees women, therefore doesn't keep a mistress, and must resort to prostitutes. He distrusts mostly everyone he does not know well, and he told me – this did not come from me."

"I won't say a word."

"He told me he has stray thoughts. Dr. Maddox, who treated my father to some extent when he returned from captivity in Austria and was not himself, calls it paranoia. That people are plotting against him. That people mean to harm him. He knows they're nonsensical, but he says that doesn't make them go away."

Georgie was silent for a moment as she sunk into him and his words sunk into her mind. Biting her lip, she said, "He needs a good woman."

"He pays exquisitely for them."

"I *mean* he needs a wife. I would bet Uncle Darcy goes to Aunt Darcy when he needs someone to tell him his imagination has run away again, doesn't he?"

"I have little idea," he said. "Perhaps he does."

"Well, I still hold to it. George needs a woman – to hold him and tell him he's mad, and she loves him anyway, and he can trust her. And it's not going to be me, because I am spoken for."

"Glad to hear it."

CHAPTER 19

Missive from Ireland

If not for the previous meeting, the highlight of Geoffrey's week would have been Sunday supper with the Maddoxes. Unfortunately, he arrived to discover that only Edmund had come. Georgie was under the weather (nothing to be alarmed about, he was assured) and stayed back in Teversham. With Geoffrey's mind already set on his later plans, the meal was grueling, though he did his best to hide it. Sir Daniel did not hold him long afterwards and dismissed him with an uncomfortably knowing smirk.

As soon as he was back at University, Geoffrey found Reynolds. "I need servant's clothes. Fancy ones."

"How fancy?"

"I need a wig."

Reynolds just nodded. The man was similar to him in height, so Geoffrey managed to suitably fit into his manservant's best attire.

"Forgive me," Reynolds said after breaking out into a bout of laughter at the sight of Geoffrey Darcy in a servant's coat and wig.

"Easily," Geoffrey said. "Thank you." He felt he owed Reynolds a second birthday present. "My horse, please."

~~~

Even without knowing the way, it only took him an hour to find Teversham, despite a few stops for directions. He tied his horse to a tree in sight of the Bell estate and made his way across the small stream by jumping stones. It was dark, and he was no Georgie when it came to sneaking about, so by the time he reached the servants' entrance, his white socks were well-muddied and his wig was barely staying on. "Where is Miss Bingley staying?" he said breathlessly to a man chopping wood just outside, slipping him a sovereign. *That* earned him very precise directions, so precise he felt he could open the door without knocking, as that would only leave him standing longer in the hallway, a mysterious servant in non-matching attire.

"How dare you – Who are you?" the young lady in the chair, who rose at his entrance, sputtered indignantly. He bowed quickly and shut the door behind him.

"Oh my God," Georgie said from the bed. "Window. Geoffrey, you're supposed to go through the *window*. Did you not see the grate?"

"No." He bowed again. "Lady Littlefield."

She curtseyed. "Mr. Darcy. *Excuse me* for inquiring – "

"I heard she was ill." He added, "This is a social call. Forgive my intrusion, Your Ladyship."

"Heather, it's all right," Georgie insisted. "Not that I asked him to make a fool of himself, but it is still fine." Her voice sounded a little ragged, but she was certainly not beyond the point of conversation.

Heather Littlefield said, "I can't leave you alone. Couldn't even if he were just a servant."

"Can you give us some room?" Georgie begged. "*Please?*"

Geoffrey could not remember hearing Georgiana begging before. It must be a woman thing.

"Very well." Lady Littlefield covered the smile on her face as she retreated to the very far corner of the room. Geoffrey sighed and took her seat next to Georgiana, taking her hand.

"I would remove the wig," he said, "but I don't think I could get it back on again."

"Is it Reynolds'?"

"Yes. How are you?"

"Not with child." She looked at him knowingly.

He felt his face flush. "That wasn't why I raced here."

"Still good to know, is it not?"

He kissed her hand. "What's wrong, then?"

"I got my courses and my stomach is upset. Is that more than you wished to know?"

But she did not look entirely well. She was pale, her skin cold. He had three sisters, and none of them were restricted to their beds during any time they might have their courses, or he would have known about it, and that was really enough for him to know about it. "What's wrong?"

"I told you."

"Did you eat something?"

She looked away.

He tightened his grip for emphasis. "Tell me."

"I – drank something." She added, "It's nothing. I don't have the dosage right. The doctor came and I'm fine. I was just ill all day, and now I'm tired. That's really it. You should stop worrying – "

"I'm never going to stop worrying about you," he said. "What did you drink?"

Georgie covered her face with her free hand. "Geoffrey," she whispered, "I don't want to be with child."

The little he knew about the lengths that women would go to fight Mother Nature – all from asking some very embarrassing questions or overhearing them at particularly drunken nights at the bar – was alarming. "Georgie – "

"I don't want a child," she said. Her voice was muffled, and her eyes were red. "We're not married, and even if we were, I'm not ready."

"Georgie, you can hurt yourself. You've already done it."

"Nothing permanent."

"I don't care. I won't let you hurt yourself."

"It's the best way."

He frowned. "It's not." Geoffrey looked over his shoulder at Heather, who was doing needlepoint and humming loudly in the corner, then leaned into Georgiana. "We'll wait."

"Until *July?*"

"I'm not thrilled at the prospect either, but I will not let you hurt yourself." He ran his hand through her hair. It was gloved, but it was more for her than for him. "You have to promise never to do this again. If you don't, well ..." He tried to give her a smile. "July is not as far away as it seems."

"There were some other things to do, but I wanted to be sure."

"Nothing is a certainty, Georgie. You must know that."

She nodded into the pillow.

"We'll manage," he said. "I promise." He leaned over and kissed her on the cheek. "I love you."

"You smell like wig powder."

He giggled. "I suppose I do."

"Good thing I love you anyway."

He kissed her again and rose. "Feel better."

"I already do."

He bowed to Heather. "Good evening, Lady Littlefield."

"Good evening, Mr. Darcy. Perhaps next time we can meet in less inauspicious circumstances."

"Perhaps," he said, and made his escape.

~~~

"Mama!" Cassandra Darcy said, running into Elizabeth's study, where she was composing a letter. "Papa won't let me go to Lambton!"

"Did he say why?"

"He said it was too cold!"

Elizabeth sighed. It was a particularly frosty February day, colder than it had been in the past week, and she could not blame him. "It would be inconsiderate to ask the servants to escort you unless you have very pressing business in Lambton. Do you have very pressing business in Lambton?"

Her younger daughter swung back and forth in her shoes. "Maybe."

"Maybe?"

"No. But Papa's been so cross – "

"He's not been *cross*," she corrected. "Has he really been so mean?"

Her daughter finally began to waver. "I suppose not."

"What is your pressing business in Lambton? Buying ribbons and lace?" Elizabeth said. "Well, I promise you will get your opportunity, but it shall not be today, and that is not your father's fault. Nonetheless, I will have a talk with him."

"Thank you!" Cassandra seemed perpetually overexcited and ran over to give her mother a quick kiss on the cheek before running out.

Elizabeth set aside her letter, now too distracted to continue her correspondence with Charlotte. Darcy had been out-of-sorts since the new year; it was not worth denying it. Over their many years together, she had noticed and become accustomed to the fact that his mood would sink in the winter, when it was so cold and dark. Even with a roaring fire and no distractions, he did not always find sleep easily, and sometimes she woke in the middle of the night to find him not in bed but sitting in the armchair, stoking the fire. Despite this melancholy being so engrained in his character, he never let it excuse him from being polite and kind, never spoke a cross word to anyone, certainly not his children.

Nonetheless, this year was different. He was more given to silence. When his face was a mask, to her it was obvious introspection, probably more than was needed at the time. She would not call it a dark mood as much as a nervous one, and if it reached as far as her daughters, something needed to be done.

She inquired after her husband and was told he was alone in his study. He answered her knock, meaning he was willing to be disturbed, and Elizabeth found him at his desk, calmly sorting the post. "Elizabeth." He gave her a little smile.

"Darcy." She took a seat.

His manner was not cold, nor did it exude the usual warmth toward her. "Is this about Cassandra?"

"I explained to her about the cold. I assume that was your reason for not sending her to Lambton."

He nodded.

"I do not think she meant to say it, but she has noticed your behavior as of late."

"My behavior?" He always reacted differently when the discussion involved his daughters. "Have I said something to offend?"

"No. I am only implying that they are clever enough to know that something is bothering you."

"The instinct must be from your side," Darcy said. He set aside the mail and leaned back in the chair. "I don't precisely know what you mean."

"Perhaps you've not decided for yourself, but certainly something has been on your mind." Speaking out loud let her sort out more of her thoughts. "Is this about Geoffrey getting married?"

"Why should it be? Granted, he is marrying young, and to a woman many people would not hesitate to lock in Bedlam, but she is of exceedingly good connections, and there is no doubt that it's more than a passing fancy."

"You say it so logically," she said, "and without emotion."

"I am not without emotion."

"Hardly. You choose not to show it."

"Precisely."

She stood up and walked around the desk, putting her arms around her husband. "You at least are not giving a daughter away."

"No," he said. After a long pause, he continued. "When I was one and twenty, I was done with Cambridge and the world had opened to me. I spent a year traveling the Continent, both because it was fashionable and because I wanted to do it before I settled down in Pemberley."

"Though you are quite the homebody."

"I will not deny it. But – I knew my father was sick. He was not as ill as he would be when I returned, but he was never the same after Mother died. I knew I would return home to my formal training to run the estate, and two years later, I was father to my sister. My intentions were good, but at three and twenty, I was not ready to be a father."

She kissed the top of his head. "It was different. Georgiana had lost her real father when you assumed the role and had never known her mother."

"I was so overwhelmed, I lingered in bachelorhood. Even when I went with Bingley to see Netherfield, I had no desire to court or be courted."

"That you made abundantly clear."

At this he did smile and turned to face her. "Obviously, I made it far too clear. Nevertheless, I was still not a father before I was thirty. And the time that we had before you were increasing – when it was just us -" Darcy took her hand in his own. "I know we were both hoping for a child, and we were rewarded, but that time was perhaps the best of my life."

"It was happenstance. I could have been with child after our wedding night," she said. But that was neither here nor there. He had explained himself. "Geoffrey is very mature for his age, with all he has had to go through. No one likes to sit at a lecture with an ear horn. They must tease him. And he has always been an astute pupil of yours."

"He has."

"Geoffrey has always lived up to expectations – or exceeded them." But she could understand Darcy's fears – their baby was going to have to grow up, fast. Even faster if and when Georgiana was with child. "There's no helping the matter. They're in love. Would you want to repeat the agony of being in love with a woman and not being able to have her?"

Darcy looked up at her. "No, I certainly would not."

"Then we are agreed?"

"We are." He kissed her. "And now, the post awaits."

"You got something from Ireland," she said, recognizing the envelope type and the Dublin stamp. Relieved that he had finally unloaded his thoughts on her, and seeing that it had done him a world of good to do so, Elizabeth rose to leave. She was only halfway out the door when he called to her.

"Do you wish to accompany me to Ireland?"

"Have we been invited?" she asked casually, but when she turned again, his face had darkened considerably. "What has happened?"

"My brother is under investigation by the church," he said, handing her the letter. "Read it yourself."

To Mr. Darcy of Pemberley and Derbyshire,

I am writing this as an act of charity and friendship. I am a member of the clergy here in Dublin and have been party to the knowledge that a formal investigation has been launched against your brother, Grégoire Bellamont, author of the 'A Poor Sinner' columns. One of the bishops has become jealous of his popularity and has begun a discussion of possible charges of heresy. Though I have been a reader for years and am well aware that Mr. Bellamont has no beliefs that are not in line with church doctrine, the discussion has just grown larger and larger, and now they are thinking of bringing in a Dominican for a formal inquisition. I have not alerted your brother, as that would be too direct for my own safety. I trust that you will be able to alert him as soon as you can.

Bishop Landa
Dublin

"We must go to Ireland at once," she said. "You will write a letter in case it can reach him first?"

"Yes. Will you inform the children?"

Elizabeth nodded. "He will be all right."

338

Working together, they packed, took a light supper, kissed their daughters goodbye, and were on the road by sundown. They slept in the carriage that would carry them to the coast, their minds now singularly connected with a new worry.

~~~

"Brian," Nadezhda called from the bed, one arm outstretched. "Come back to me."

Brian Maddox wiped the shaving cream from his chin. "I am happy to oblige." He climbed back in the warm bed, even though it was now mid-morning and they had been awake for some time.

"One would think you are tiring of the view," she said. He had been staring out the window at the Paris skyline with a look of despair. "Has Paris lost its charm?"

"No, I suppose. I just woke up with an odd feeling this morning. Maybe English homesickness."

"I don't know why that would be, as there are more Englishmen here than in London I think."

Brian laughed and kissed her. "Perhaps. Do you think Bingley is still angry at us?"

"You know him better than I," she said. "But, no, I think not. The man couldn't stay angry for more than a couple days at most. And I confess I am eager to be home for the wedding."

"The wedding is in July, my dear."

"Do you really think it will wait until July? With all of that English propriety nonsense?"

"Says the woman whose father kept her locked in a castle and who won't show her hair in public. But I suppose you do have a point." He sighed at the knock at the door. "I'll get it."

He threw on his kimono, belted his obi, and entered the main room of their hotel apartment. With a hand on his sword, he opened the door. "Hello?"

It was a courier. "M-Message for you, sir. Express."

"Thank you," he said, paid the frightened man, and shut the door, taking the letter with him. The return was Transylvania and it was addressed to Nadezhda. "Your Highness." He presented her with the letter, which she sat up to read. His written Romanian was rusty.

"It is from my uncle," she explained. "He says there is some business to clear up at the castle."

"The one that belongs to us?"

"It is his now, but yes."

He rubbed her back. "You've no desire to go back there, do you?"

"He writes with some urgency," she said. "But ... perhaps I will write him first and ask more, and we will stay in Paris until he replies."

He mustered a smile. "So much of my life involves the speed of the mail. Still, I will not argue with the ultimate outcome," he said, and drew her into him. The letter was, for the moment, forgotten.

CHAPTER 20

A Voice Not Forgotten

More mundane reasons to see Geoffrey were easier to invent. They were engaged to be married, and had every reason to take (chaperoned) walks together when his schedule permitted it. Edmund trailed them as Georgie and Geoffrey strolled along the more scenic roads of Cambridge. Georgie was surprised at how much time he did seem to have.

"And I imagine your illustrious roommates are dutifully studying with their tutors, as opposed to yourself?"

Geoffrey grinned. "When I left, Frederick was still asleep. He's terrible to wake for services. He must have the worst attendance record at chapel – barely on the line of even Cambridge acceptability."

"But they keep him on because of his father."

"They keep him because his papers are outstanding and he has the best marks in his year at Trinity. Even if he doesn't try." He added, "We're all a bit jealous of him. Especially George."

"Frederick the scholar. Who knew?"

"It is an unnatural gift," Geoffrey said. "George thinks he's wasting his talents by not sitting for the Tripos."

"And Uncle Maddox?"

"I haven't asked Dr. Maddox his opinion."

"His real father must have been brilliant."

"Or his mother. I've no idea." He added guiltily, "Well, I have some idea, but I promised I wouldn't tell."

She nudged him. "Geoffrey."

"I promised! Well, I didn't promise him I wouldn't tell Mrs. Darcy, so I suppose I could find an appropriate time in the future." He added, "It's no one you know, personally. And even then it's just my guess, not a personal knowledge on the subject. He only discusses it when he's drunk."

"Which is most of the time."

"True."

They paused by the water. Edmund was reading as he walked, and this gave him a bit of a chance to keep up. It was worthless to adhere to propriety if they weren't going to prove they were doing it.

"And my brother?" Georgiana asked.

"Off with his friends."

"The dramatists?"

He nodded.

"While it is a relief, you must feel a bit betrayed at the abandonment."

"Charles is not the Bingley who holds my greatest interest," he said, which made her smile. He loved making her smile. "They're very polite, very sociable, and I don't think they're into any sort of trouble, as far as what is considered trouble by our standards. If he switched his studies to drama, Uncle Bingley would likely have an apoplexy, but I don't believe he intends to."

She was, as always, very astute. "But they're not your friends."

"We're acquaintances, not friends. No real reason that I can discern. Lack of mutual interests, I suppose. They want to talk about theater and the arts, and I want to sneak over to Teversham," he said. "I did see a performance of Charles' good friend Guy, who played Iago in a performance of *Othello*. They were very considerate to get me a seat near the front. Those box seats are a waste of money – horrible view in comparison."

"Maybe we'll try to sit near the orchestra in London sometime," she said. "If you wish."

"We should see the Scottish play next time it is performed," he said. "Macbeth."

"Why that one?"

"I believe it is the Bard's play with the most swordfights, so you're less likely to be bored."

She swatted him with her fan.

~~~

It was not George Wickham's week. He was
late to services, only halfway through his current
literature, and most, importantly, he was late to
attend Dr. Maddox. Only by a few minutes, by his
pocket watch, but his fear of ever disappointing the
eminent professor was enough to nearly drive him
to fits by the time the office door was in sight.
Though he despised the notion, the chief anatomist
of Cambridge had an assistant with him at all times
to write on the chalkboard, keep notes on the
students, and other general administrative duties.
George usually readily volunteered for the task,
even if it meant pouring tea and other servants'
work. He owed Daniel Maddox more than that.

"Good; you've arrived," the doctor said as
George entered and bowed. It was then he noticed
the professorial robes were removed, and Dr.
Maddox's manservant was helping him put on his
overcoat. "Mr. Wickham, I need you to be the
bearer of the terrible news that this week's lecture is
cancelled. I'm sure the students will be upset. They
may even be in tears as they run to the taverns."

"Professor Maddox, is everything all right?"

"Fine, fine. I've just been called to Windsor
to attend His Majesty. For consultation; I don't
think even he is so delusional to imagine I can do

346

more than that. Either way, one does not refuse a summons from the crown." Dr. Maddox said to his man, "My hat is ... somewhere; the grey one, please." He turned back in George's general direction. "You might as well sit down. It will be a minute until the carriage gets here, and we've not talked properly in some time. There's no tea, I'm afraid."

"I've had something, thank you." He did set his books down and take a seat. "I apologize for my tardiness – "

"I did not notice." In truth, George had only been a few minutes late. "So – I am to Town, and Caroline is in Chesterton, so I assume this means Frederick will try his best to harm himself in a drunken carriage race."

"I think he gave that up."

"Too near a scrape?"

"He kept losing. The Viscount Brougham is better."

Dr. Maddox chuckled. "He does not tolerate failures, particularly his own. None of us do, I suppose. Except perhaps Mr. Bellamont, who is so ridiculously humble he expects them all."

"I heard he's in a spot," George said. "Aunt and Uncle Darcy have set off to Dublin about some church investigation."

"Is it serious?"

"Geoffrey said that his father's letter implied it was; his mother's implied that it was nothing Uncle Darcy couldn't handle."

"It has been what, four, five years? No, more. And without a hint of trouble for the family mystic. I believe this is a record," the doctor replied. "As long as he is not wounded or incarcerated, he is not in trouble."

"I do not believe he is. Geoffrey would have said something when I spoke with him."

The doctor just nodded. "How is Geoffrey?"

George always wondered if Dr. Maddox could sense him blush. "He's fine."

"Lovesick?"

"I suppose."

"You suppose? My wife says she's seen puppies with a less sickeningly sweet expression than his when Georgiana's name comes into conversation. I will temper that by saying that Lady Maddox is not endeared to small animals, but I somehow don't doubt her. Or that I was any different and that she didn't appreciate it at the time."

"Professor!"

"Oh, you'll know the feeling someday. Oh, that is a sight I will be sad to miss. The young George Wickham, trailing some fine lady around like an abandoned pet. Someone will be describing that to me in great detail." With the bell, he rose from his seat, his manservant taking his arm. "I must be off to visit His Majesty and likely comfort him on his current woes. I'll send post as to my return in case any students are actually inclined to ask."

"I will inform them," George said. Despite Dr. Maddox's skepticism, many of his students were more attached to him than they were to other professors. Perhaps it was because he actually taught. "Good luck, Professor Maddox."

"Maddoxes try not to rely on luck, Mr. Wickham," he said as George opened the door for him. "It nearly always leads us astray."

~~~

Darcy had no appreciation for the rustic charms of Dublin, the few that were offered beneath the dirt and soot. He was not fond of cities, especially foreign ones, and would have happily started immediately on the road south to Grégoire's home but sent a messenger instead. "We've a stop to make," he told Elizabeth.

After several sets of directions in several different brogues that neither of them could make heads or tails of, they finally found their way to a little street not far from town center, where a sign with the local paper's name was barely legible. He pounded on the door with his walking stick, which earned him a stream of Irish curses and then finally an answer. "'ello?"

"I am here to speak to the editor of your paper," he said. "My name is Mr. Darcy, and this is my wife, Mrs. Darcy."

"'e's inside. Name's Arthur." He stepped back to allow them entrance. Below the floorboards, they could hear the mechanic sounds of what had to be the printing press. There were only a few rooms, all offices, and the very first held a spectacled man with red hair and an accent that had some English influence. "You are here to see me?" He rose. "Mr. Darcy, is it? Mrs. Darcy, welcome." He bowed, then immediately sat back down. His desk was covered in old newspapers. "What can I do for you?"

"I am inquiring after my brother," Darcy said. "Grégoire Bellamont. I believe he is a columnist here."

"Yer the fancy English brother, eh?" he said. "Not dat he used t'at precise terminology. Well, you've found him."

"I know he does not live in Dublin."

"No, I mean, 'e's here today. Came in for a few days. Does it every now and again to proof t'ings before dey go out for print." He gestured. "Second door."

Darcy turned to Elizabeth, who looked similarly surprised. "We'll see him, then," he said. They were not aware of his regular schedule, and it was an unexpected shock finding him here. Or perhaps he knew something the editor did not?

The knock brought the gentle "Come" in the voice of mixed accents they were so familiar with. Grégoire Bellamont was sitting quietly at another man's desk, wearing his spectacles and dutifully making notes on the page in front of him, an open Latin book at his side. His face registered complete surprise and delight. "Brother!" There was so little room in the office he almost had to climb over the desk to hug Darcy before stepping back down and bowing to Elizabeth. "Mrs. Darcy."

"Grégoire," she said, "this is an unexpected pleasure. We thought we'd have to travel out to your home to find you."

"I ... cannot imagine why you would be here, but it is indeed a pleasure," Grégoire said.

"The reason we are here is not so pleasant," Darcy said, passing Grégoire the letter. "We sent word to your house, assuming you were there."

"Caitlin is. But she would just put it in my pile." He opened the letter. It did not take him long to read. "This cannot be."

"After all you've written on religion – "

" – not a word of it blasphemy! And they know it. I have been investigated – not formally –

351

several times, Darcy. They've eventually informed me each time. In fact, many of the bishops here are fans of my writing. The reason that this letter is so incomprehensible is not the reason you think. Simply put, there is no such person as Bishop Landa."

~~~

"Who?" said the archbishop of Dublin. "Let me see," he said to Grégoire, who would refuse him nothing of course, and handed over the letter written to Darcy as they were seated in the spacious offices of the bishopric and served wine. "No, no, this is not anyone I know. Wait – I do know the Bishop Landa." The old man leaned back, his face scrunched up in concentration. He had been pleasant with them and actually quite informal with Grégoire, whom he seemed to know and respect. "Diego de Landa. The bishop of Yucatán."

"Then what is he doing in Dublin?" Elizabeth asked.

"Nothing. I only know of him because he wrote extensively about his missionary work among the Indians," he said. "The man's been dead for over two centuries."

~~~

Only on a few occasions had Dr. Maddox been to Windsor. He had been once to the castle proper to meet King George III, on the then-Prince's request that the grandfather meet his grandson, however unknowing Frederick's involvement. The wait up to it was terrifying, but the encounter itself was surprisingly not. George III had been blind and mad but very calm and polite, and most amusing when he did make sense, which even he seemed to know.

Now Windsor Castle was under renovations for the new king, though few thought he would live to see it completed. George IV had been in poor health when his father was still alive, and in the six years since his ascension to the throne, it had only declined. Dr. Maddox had seen him last, now almost two years ago, when Emily was presented at court. The doctor's attention had been on his daughter, and even with very heavy glasses he had to work to focus his eyes, so the little he'd seen of his king and former employer was through an ever-thickening blur. The king resembled a blob, or a chair with extra legs, and from other people's conversation, their own perspectives did not lead them to vastly different conclusions. The king was known to be excessively fat, beyond any norm, and a drunk, and probably addicted to laudanum. He hardly went outside anymore, and even then, it was to ride around the gardens in a carriage. He lived in Windsor Cottage, a temporary lodging while the castle was fitted up to his own grand schemes (for he did love architecture and grandeur). To the cottage in its current conditions, Dr. Maddox had never been. His manservant was not permitted to accompany him, and he had to rely instead on the servant to his left. He did hate being shuttled about but resigned himself to it as best he could.

Still, there was something unnerving about the darkness he was led through tonight. It was a late visit, well into the evening. The Prince of Wales was known for late nights. King George IV was not.

"Sir Daniel Maddox," said a voice in the darkness. "I am Sir William Knighton."

He bowed. "Sir William."

"Please be seated."

He did not like being pushed down onto a seat, but that was the way they always did it, like he was some helpless lump. Well, he was only mostly helpless, not entirely. His ears were keen enough to know that there were other people in the room, but the king was likely not one of them. George had always been a heavy breather. "I come at the request of the crown."

"Yes."

Unsure of the situation, he asked, "Does His Majesty wish to see me? Or are you requesting some medicinal advice that I might have?"

There was a long pause. His question was ignored. "Dr. Bertrand has been dismissed."

"Dr. Bertrand is a fine doctor," Dr. Maddox said. "With excellent training." He suddenly remembered that awful conversation with Bertrand – he would not perjure him. He knew he needed to speak carefully. "He is a man I hold in great respect."

"And he was trained by you to serve the king, was he not?"

"Yes. I did select him, based on his clinical experience," he said. "I do not understand this line of questioning. May I inquire as to why he was dismissed?"

"I thought it would be better, given his association to you, that he be separated from the crown. For his political safety. He is indeed a very fine physician and will make an excellent private doctor. Or perhaps Cambridge will offer him a position." Knighton's tone was a little patronizing.

But Maddox's heart had long-since sunk. He clenched his fist around his cane. "I know we have not been previously acquainted, Sir William, so I will inform you now that I despise politics, and that if we are to have a conversation, it would be suitable to both of us if the point was declared more expediently."

"What do you think?" Knighton said, to someone else, who answered back only in whispers. "Sir Daniel, we hate to trouble you further – "

"I would appreciate being told, given my limited abilities to know otherwise, who is addressing me."

"I do not believe you have met Dr. Engel."

The name did seem somehow familiar, but he couldn't place it. "No, I have not. Is he to be Dr. Bertrand's replacement? Forgive me, Doctor, if you are in this room, but we've not been introduced, so I am at a loss." He rose, apparently allowed to walk freely, stood up properly and bowed.

"I told you I shouldn't be here for zis," said the other man, the Prussian doctor. Yes, of course, Dr. Bertrand had mentioned him, called him Dr. Engel. He was speaking in a low voice, to Knighton.

"I confess I do have one advantage," Dr. Maddox said, stepping a bit to the side, nearer to the voice and further from Knighton, he was fairly sure. "My hearing, I have found, is definitely increased since the onset my visual impairment. So there is no need to make the attempt to hide from me." He needed to hear that voice again. He needed to confirm it.

"Apologies, Herr Doktor." The foreign voice sounded as familiar as he had thought.

Oh, he was trying to sound humble. Old and humble. Had he put grey in his hair? Was his back arched? Did he stutter or shuffle about? How much had he disguised himself, to come so far? And for what – to terrify an old, blind professor?

No. Daniel Maddox would not be terrified, ever again. He had faced torture, infection, blindness, and come perilously close to death. If that did not store up some ounce of bravery in him, nothing would. "You – " he said, his voice heavy with emotion, more than he wanted it to be, " – have no right to begin to apologize to me, Trommler." And with that, he struck, hitting the man somewhere vital enough for Trommler to cry out. The wood of his cane splintered and broke from the force of it, and he hoped bones broke, too. He hoped he shattered Trommler's whole arm, or back, or whatever he had hit. Whatever toppled Trommler was a sick satisfaction to him, so much so that he was utterly distracted when the guards overwhelmed him.

CHAPTER 21

The Great Escape

The knock on the door was very insistent. "Come on! Some of us have busy schedules!"

"For what? Drinking?" Georgie said to Geoffrey as they separated. "What's he on about?"

Geoffrey took a deep breath. "We probably should stop anyway." Could he hold her in his arms and *not* be affected in the most inconvenient way? Apparently not. July seemed so terribly far away, especially at this moment. "When will I see you again?"

"I'm due at Chesterton for supper tomorrow."

"I have a lecture." He grimaced. "I can miss it."

"Should you? It's just dinner. And Uncle Maddox is in London, so it'll just be Aunt Maddox staring at you."

"Are you saying you don't want to see me?"

She kissed him. "Of course not. I just want you to graduate."

"Geoffrey!" Frederick called out again, and they straightened their clothing before opening the

359

door. "God. How long am I supposed to talk to Heather Littlefield?"

"I thought you liked talking to women?" Georgie said.

"The way he talks to women is different from the way you talk to someone like Lady Littlefield," Geoffrey said, which earned him a glare from Frederick and a smile from Georgiana as she kissed him goodbye.

"No necking in front of me!"

"I'm sure you're well-compensated for your suffering," Georgie said unsympathetically, leaving to rejoin Lady Littlefield and return to Teversham.

"Is she really all that bad?" Geoffrey said as they walked back to their college.

"Georgie's always been that way to me."

"I mean Lady Littlefield."

"No." And that was all he said on the matter. "Did you hear from your father?"

"No. He's likely in Dublin by now. Why?"

"My father's still in London, and Uncle Brian is in Paris. It occurred to me if we were in some kind of trouble, Uncle Bingley would have to come to our rescue."

"Or Georgie would do it herself. Though it depends on what sort of trouble you mean, I suppose. Why, what are you planning?"

Frederick grinned. "You always think the worst of me."

"And so does the Head, apparently," Geoffrey gestured to the dean of Trinity, who was for some reason waiting at the entrance despite the hour. It was late, but certainly not anywhere close to curfew.

"Mr. Darcy," said the Head, "I am obliged to fine you if you do not return to your dormitory immediately."

"What?" He didn't know seeing a woman would get him in so much trouble. It hadn't stopped anyone else at University.

"*Now*, Mr. Darcy."

Geoffrey didn't leave until he noticed the guards, which he didn't recognize as University men. So he walked down the hallway and turned around the corner but stayed within earshot, even for his damaged hearing.

"Frederick Maddox?"

"That's me. Sir – "

"Mr. Maddox," the Head said grimly, "Your family is under house arrest. You can choose to take sanctuary in the college with the understanding that you will not leave Trinity grounds or you can join your family in Chesterton."

"It's your choice," said one of the guards. He sounded dangerously official when he said it.

"Where's my father?"

"We're not allowed to give you that information unless you come with us," said the guard.

'Don't do it!' Gregory thought urgently.

"Am I under arrest? On what charges?"

"Your family is to be held in your home, sir. You are not charged with any crimes."

"Then why – "

"You must make a decision, Mr. Maddox," the Head said.

"Fine. I'll go along. But someone must write *Uncle Bingley* and –"

"That's enough, Mr. Maddox. If you would just come along – "

That was all Geoffrey needed to hear. He returned to the dorm to find it empty; Charles was out again.

But what if Uncle Bingley couldn't help? Why did his father have to be away? And why was Frederick being held without charges? What did it mean that the entire Maddox family was under house arrest? "Reynolds, paper." He threw off his outer robes and sat down to write a very important letter.

~~~

The guards did not attempt to bind him or even really intimidate him. They did not offer explanation, either. They merely put him in the carriage and sent him off to the Maddox home. The ride was short, especially at this time of night, and he arrived to find guards at the front door and all of the lights lit.

"Frederick!"

Emily Maddox, his so-called twin sister, was in his arms before he could properly assess anything else about the situation. She hugged him so tightly it hurt. She hadn't done that since they were children. "You shouldn't have come," she said. "Maybe you were safer at the college."

"They told me there were no charges against me, personally. What does it matter where I am?" he said. "What's happened?"

"Mama's with the investigator," she said. "Papa's been arrested for treason."

"*What?*"

She looked up at him. She had been crying a long time, and it was starting afresh as she nodded. His dear sister, crying, said, "We don't know why. Maybe the constable will tell us."

"Where's Danny?"

As he asked, young Daniel Maddox appeared at the top of the stairs. He resembled what his father might have as a child in every way but two – his frizzled hair was red, and just now he was wearing one of the little Japanese training outfits like Uncle Brian wore.

363

"Danny," Frederick said, and welcomed his brother into his arms. Danny hadn't had his growth spurt yet and only reached his chest. "What did father say about wearing your glasses?"

"What does it matter? Father's going to *die*."

"Danny!" Emily cried. "How can you say that?"

"It's true! That's what they do to people who do treason."

"Father did not commit treason," Frederick said with as much authority as he could muster. It did not escape him that he was the man of the house now. "It must be a misunderstanding of some kind. It will be cleared up, and he will be released. Father has never done anything wrong in his life."

"Then why was he arrested?" his brother said anxiously.

"Maybe the constable will tell us," he assured him as the door opened, but the constable did not say anything. He crossed the room, ignoring them completely, and ordered his men to begin searching the house. Frederick was distracted, though, when his mother emerged from the study. Her normally perfect composure was broken, her hair falling down in places, her white skin flushed red from crying.

"Frederick," she said. "What are you doing here?"

"They came to Trinity," he explained. "I had to come."

Both she and the doctor were taller than him. Only Emily and Danny were shorter, and it probably wouldn't last with Danny. And right now, the way his mother kept her hair up, it made him feel even smaller as she took her eldest son in her arms.

"Mother," he said, "what's happened?"

"Your father was arrested when he arrived in London. That is all they will tell me. They don't have to tell me anything." She whispered, "If it's treason, it doesn't even have to go to trial."

He just nodded. He didn't know what else to do.

His mother made some attempt at recovering, chiding her younger son, "Danny, where are your glasses?"

Danny Maddox huffed and ran back upstairs either to get them or to hide. The three remaining Maddoxes went back into the study, which was a mess. All of the drawers had been pulled out, and many of the books had been tossed onto the floor during a frantic search. Frederick took the opportunity to pour himself a glass of brandy from his father's stock and offered one to his mother. To his surprise, she accepted.

"May I ask a question?" Emily addressed no one in particular, closing the door behind them to block out the sight of all of the servants scurrying in fear from the guards tearing apart the place.

"Of course," Frederick said, sitting down on the edge of his father's desk.

"Do you think, Fred – maybe, this has something to do with you?"

He turned to his mother. "I – I don't see why," his mother said, composing herself. "Not after all this time. And to take your father and leave Frederick alone?" She shook her head. "The last time Daniel saw the king was when you were presented at court. When we all saw the king. It was only a few minutes."

Frederick hadn't known at the time. He might have requested to go along if he had, but they told him afterwards. He had some understanding of their decision. "If they wouldn't let me stay at Trinity today, they don't care about me," he concluded. "What else could it possibly be about?"

"I cannot imagine," his mother said. "I just …Where is everyone? Are the Darcys still in Ireland?"

Frederick nodded.

"And Brian is in Paris. He wouldn't be of much use, but Her Highness could be with her title's authority. And if I could write Dr. Bertrand..."

"I told Geoffrey to write Uncle Bingley," he said. "Even if he didn't hear, he saw me being arrested. He will do something. Is Uncle Hurst still in Wales?"

"Yes, but he has no influence anywhere, even if he knew." Lady Maddox took the handkerchief her daughter offered her and wiped her nose. "No one can plead your father's case. We don't know anyone with the authority. Not if the charges aren't made public."

Frederick set down his glass after swallowing the last of his drink. Brandy was always hot in his throat, like liquid fire. "Is there anything in this house – any records – that might be bad ... for us?"

"Your father's case files, maybe – if they can read them. He wrote his notes in code. They did make me give them the laboratory key."

"The opium is in there – it's not illegal, is it?"

She shook her head. "Not for a physician."

He needed to think. No – he needed to act. His mother was right – if the crime was serious enough, real or imagined, there did not have to be a trial. What would someone nobler do? What would Geoffrey Darcy do? Or George Wickham? Why couldn't he be like them?

367

He kissed his mother and sister and excused himself. Ignoring the soldiers going through their rooms, he entered his own and sat down to write a letter.

"Frederick?"

He looked up. Danny was finally wearing his glasses and carrying one of the wooden swords that Brian used when teaching him. Frederick preferred more traditional English fencing. "What is it?"

"Father didn't do anything wrong," Danny said with unusually strong conviction for someone whose voice had yet to drop. "I know it. He's the best man I know."

Frederick smiled. "He is."

"If it's all a mistake, why are they doing this?"

"That's what mistakes are – people doing things wrong." He folded the letter and handed it to Danny. "Will you give this to Mother?"

His brother nodded and tucked it into the fold of his kimono. "Where are you going?"

"To London, to try to do some good," he said, opening his window.

"You can't get down that way," Danny interrupted. "My room is easier."

"Daniel Maddox, how do you know that?"

"Uncle Brian taught me."

"He teaches you all kinds of things, doesn't he?"

Danny nodded. "I'll show you."

"You shouldn't get in trouble."

"We're *all* in trouble already. What does it matter?"

The boy had a point. He couldn't fault him for that. "Lead the way."

They crossed the hallway into Danny's room, which was full of schoolbooks and Japanese items. Danny was right; the window led out to the kitchen roof and was a much smaller drop.

"Hey! You!" A soldier entered. "Kid! What are you doing?"

Fortunately, the sudden dilemma was solved by Danny's insistence. "Go."

"I can't leave – "

"Go!" Danny shouted. His voice was suddenly deep and it carried. It was almost frightening as he turned away from the window, raising his wooden sword.

"Boy, this is not a joke – "

But in a flash Danny was there, knocking the pistol out of its holster, disarming the soldier. The man grabbed for him, but Danny dropped to his knees, out of reach, and slammed the knob edge into the man's stomach.

Frederick heard shouts, but he was already climbing out the window, onto the roof, and dropping to the ground. In the ensuing commotion, no one noticed him slip away into the night.

~~~

That night, Georgiana Bingley was up as well, but for different reasons. The Duke and Duchess had retired, leaving Heather and Georgie to do as they pleased, with a legion of servants protecting them (from escaping). Not that it would stop Georgie, but she had promised her father she would be 'good,' and she was going to do her best to hold to that. Besides, getting into Trinity College would be difficult. It was practically a castle, and they were accustomed to students sneaking in and out (with or without women), so they would be on the watch. Not that she didn't contemplate it.

She had thought seeing Geoffrey today would satiate her for the time being, but it didn't. Despite their mutual understanding of the gravity of the situation, withdrawing from intimacy was easier said than done. If only she'd trusted all of the other preventions and not gone through with the quinine. The thing had been a disaster. Not only did it bring her courses, but it made her monstrously sick for a brief but sudden period of time, and the Duchess insisted on a doctor. She had a few very shameful words with the physician, who realized her position with uncanny ease, and put coin in his hand to make sure he said nothing to her hosts and passed it off as something she had eaten. He said there was no permanent damage, but he was serious in his insistence that she not try again. She was too small for any dosage, and repeated attempts could render her barren, or so he said, and she sensed it wasn't so much a scare tactic as the truth. Though she'd been happy to see him, she was exhausted in every way when Geoffrey arrived that night in his ridiculous servant costume, and she readily gave in to his very solid terms. All right, so she was no good at keeping her word to her father. So she would go back on her promise to George in a moment of panic. Geoffrey was different. He looked at her with such concern that she could not ignore him. The sadness on his face at the danger she'd put herself in – and his blaming himself for his part in it, no doubt – remained etched in her memory for days afterwards.

He had been right all those years ago. It was too hard to declare oneself and then expect no physical consequences. She had never taken her love for Geoffrey lightly, but he was better at these considerations than her. He was the level-headed one. She would cede that realization to him, if only in her mind and not out loud. And he wouldn't make her say it out loud, and she loved him for it.

Heather seemed perpetually amused by the whole thing. Perhaps Georgiana really was acting like a lovesick fool, but Heather Littlefield was a happy observer to someone else's success. Heather was younger than her by two years and still not rushing to the marriage market. Instead, she was taking in all of the dancing and flirting that a young girl was allowed and that she had been denied when she came out, being already engaged to a man she had never met.

"I'm not putting you out, am I?" Georgie asked, even though she knew she was, at least on some level.

"No. I never get to go out on my own, especially not to Cambridge."

"But you have to do it with Edmund. Or Frederick. I wish it were Charles, but I know he won't go along with it. He's far too noble." She said that last word with a tiny sneer.

"Georgie! That's your brother!"

"So? He is too noble right now. If I want to do sneaky things, I don't ask someone who doesn't know how to lie for me about it," she said. "Thank God Edmund will do it. I should talk with him about being nicer to you."

"He's not mean," Heather insisted. "He's young. He doesn't know how to talk to women."

"And then you have Frederick – "

"Mr. Maddox? He's not so bad."

Georgiana looked up from her tea. "Be serious."

"He can be charming when he wants to be," Heather said with a sly little grin. "And he's brilliant."

"I know, and I know," Georgie grumbled. "If he tries anything, I'll cut little bits off of him."

"*Georgie.*"

"Important bits."

"Georgiana Bingley!"

But Georgiana didn't have to answer because there was a knock at the door. "Come," Heather said, and the lady-maid entered her sitting room. "A Mr. Maddox to see Miss Bingley, marm. He says it is an emergency."

They exchanged glances before Heather said, "Send him in."

The charming Frederick Maddox they had been discussing was not the man who entered the room. This man was serious in demeanor, and there was a gash on his face, dried blood smeared across some of it. "Lady Littlefield. Georgie."

"Frederick!"

"Do you – "

"No doctor," he said. "I just fell and hit my head on the grate. It's not deep. Trust me – I'm a Maddox. I know wounds." He put his hand up to stop them from rushing to call the servants. "Lady

Littlefield, I apologize for my intrusion, but I need to speak with my cousin. Now."

Heather, realizing the seriousness of whatever was happening, curtseyed and excused herself from her own sitting room.

Frederick was a mess. Even though it was relatively mild for a winter's night, it was obvious he had unwisely come this far without a coat, because his waistcoat was muddy and wet and his hair was soaked. "My father's been arrested for treason."

"What?"

"I don't know why. He was called to London, and when he got there, they put him in jail. If it's high treason, there might not even be a trial. Mother, Emily, and Danny are under house arrest in Chesterton, and they're not allowed to write."

"And you?"

"I'm supposed to be with them, but I left. As you can see, it was a bit complicated." He had a seriousness about him she had never seen before. "I need your help."

It was the sort of 'I need your help' that, asked or unasked, she never said no to. "What do you need?"

"Do you have your – things with you? Your sword and all that?"

"I have the sword, yes."

"Good," he said. "I hate to put you out, but I need to get to the king."

"The king?"

"Yes."

"In his palace?"

"In his cottage. At Windsor. It's well-guarded, but once we get in, I can do the rest. I just can't get past the guards."

She raised an eyebrow. "That's a rather extreme way of putting me out."

"If you don't want to do it – "

"I'll need help," she said, "but I know where to get it."

"On the way?"

"In Town, actually. So yes, precisely on the way. When do you want to leave?"

"What are you going to say to – "

"What does it matter?" Georgie rose, calmly putting aside her tea and her needlework. "I'll come up with something, and I need to get my things from my trunk. Then I can leave."

"You – you're really going to do this for me?"

"Break into the King of England's residence, risking my life - or at the very least my freedom and reputation? Of course I will. Don't be silly," she said. "I just hope they perform marriage ceremonies in prison, or Geoffrey will be very disappointed."

375

"Get me to the king, and it won't come to that."

She hoped he was right.

CHAPTER 22

High Treason

Frederick was surprised at how fast Georgiana could move. She collected her belongings, made up a story for Heather that did not involve storming a castle, and had a carriage ready within a few minutes.

"What?" Georgie said as he stared at her as she finally climbed in with him, dressed in baggy male clothing with a scarf around her neck. "Why do you look so shocked?"

"It takes my sister an hour to do what you just did."

"How often do you ask your sister to do what I'm doing?"

"I meant the getting ready, but point taken," he said. She handed him a towel to wipe his face and a blanket for the carriage ride. He didn't even have an overcoat, just what he was wearing when he leapt out of the window. He held the cold cloth against the wound from his fall.

"Speaking of, are Emily and Danny all right? Is Aunt Maddox under arrest?"

"Only house arrest. Danny fended the guards off while I escaped."

"*Danny?*"

"He must be taking those lessons from Uncle Brian very seriously. Toppled a soldier without even trying." He sighed. "When I see the king, this will be all sorted out."

"So you keep saying. Have you ever met him?"

"Once, when I was five. He visited my father after he returned from Austria."

"Did you know who he was?"

He leaned back against the seat cushion, preparing himself for the ride. "I did not understand the gravity of the situation, no." He felt compelled after a moment to add, "*You* understand what we're about to do is high treason, correct?"

"Provided your plan doesn't work, yes. So let us hope that it will."

Georgiana's confidence was not mirrored in him. He had no idea where she got it from. Maybe she had really lost her mind, but at this exact moment, he could only be grateful that he had such a cousin.

~~~

The carriage stopped only to rest the horses and the driver. Frederick, who was probably sought after, did not venture far beyond the carriage the next morning except to stretch his legs while Georgiana went into the little hamlet to buy them some food. If the weather held, they would be in London by nightfall.

"I hope you like cheese," Georgie said. "That was practically all they had. And it smells awful, so we'd best eat it quick."

Despite her proclamation, it tasted delicious, and he washed it down with some wine before they were back on the road. A fast carriage ride did not lend itself to a good rest, but he tried his best, and Georgie was inclined to do the same. She had surprisingly few questions about the insanity of their mission. Instead, she curled up in her seat and went to sleep, clutching her sword at her side.

The sky was growing dark as the carriage finally rolled over the bumpy cobblestone roads that led into Town. Georgie gave the driver directions, and he stopped before an unfamiliar apartment, at which point he was told his services would no longer be needed. They were not far from Regent Park.

"Just follow my lead and act like you know what you're doing for once," she hissed as she rang the bell. He wondered if a woman dressed as a man and wearing wooden sandals knew what she was doing.

The doorman seemed to recognize Georgie, despite her dress (or lack of it). "Miss Bingley. The Ambassador – "

"I need to see Mr. Xiao. If he is not home at present, I would like to know where he is."

There was yelling in some very unfamiliar foreign tongue that sounded almost like someone couldn't finish their words, cutting them off in very insistent points, and then an Oriental emerged in jade robes. "Please come in, Miss Bingali."

They were ushered into a relatively nice but bare house.

"Ambassador Xiao, this is my cousin, Frederick Maddox," Georgie said, and Xiao bowed to him. "He needs our help."

"Mister Maddocsh," Mr. Xiao said. "How may I be of service?"

"How many crazy Orientals do you know?" Frederick whispered to Georgie.

"Just be glad this one isn't a criminal."

~~~

Frederick wasn't sure what strings she pulled or promises she made, but Georgie seemed to have very persuasive powers over Mr. Xiao, whom she familiarly called Liu. A Chinese ambassador, breaking into the royal palace!

"Filial piety," she explained.

"What?"

"You're doing this to save your father. I'm doing this to save my uncle. It's a big deal in China. Just don't mention it to the other ambassador."

Frederick had no intention to. Nor did he have a real plan; he was relying on them to get him into Windsor Cottage and the king's chambers. His Majesty rarely emerged to the public and was most likely there. They tried to pick a time when he might be alone but awake. Xiao, fortunately, knew his way about the cottage, having been there for many meetings. Georgie gave Frederick a black scarf to cover his face.

"Do I even want to know why you seem to have all these things on you?"

"No," Georgie answered. "Liu can navigate to the royal chambers. We'll try to lead from there, but if it doesn't happen, you had better have a good excuse for all this."

"This is the best way," he said, not entirely sure himself. "It will be clear later; I promise." He added, "I swear."

Georgie slung the sword over her shoulder. "Then what are we waiting for?"

~~~

Georgie had been right; they needed Liu. The Windsor complex was a mass of gardens, cottages, and the castle itself, still under reconstruction. The former Regent's intense interest in architecture had not waned when he ascended the throne; they had him to thank for the public parks and the wonder that was Charlton Palace, for those important enough to see it.

We're really doing this, Frederick thought as Liu threw a grappling hook over the wall. Georgie removed her sandals and tied them to her belt, walking barefoot to soften the noise of movement. *They're doing this for me.*

"When was the last time you climbed a rope, Frederick?" she asked. "Let me guess – never?"

He nodded, embarrassed. Georgie only rolled her eyes and said something to Liu in one of the Oriental languages, probably Japanese, and he hoisted Frederick up on his shoulders so he had a clear view over the wall.

Georgie was already up there somehow, kneeling and offering him her hand. "Try to keep your head down."

He was pulled up and Liu followed, and the three of them took in the enormity of their task. The king did not build small, and he liked to fashion himself a king in the old style; hence, his cottage was needlessly well-guarded. Fortunately, the men were more costumed actors than soldiers, or so it was believed.

"When we go down," Georgie whispered, "you follow Liu and I'll follow you. After all, we need you alive at the other end of this." In the distance, they could see what Liu said was likely Windsor Cottage. "Just keep running, whatever you do."

"How are we going to – "

Georgie and Liu answered the question by leaping down into the darkness and landing in the bushes. With a hard swallow, Frederick braced himself and followed them, surprised to find the landing not that difficult. If he'd rolled any further, he observed, it would have been into some painful rose bushes.

No matter how well they were paid, the guards of the garden were not taking their duty of guarding the royal bushes and fountains very seriously. They lingered closer to the cottage, so it was easy to duck in and out of the maze of bushes.

"Duck!" Georgie whispered harshly from behind, grabbing him so hard by his cravat that he nearly choked; but he did tumble down behind the bushes.

"This is insane," he said as they steadied their breathing. A guard was passing by, close enough to hear serious movement.

"It was your idea."

The guard paused at the intersection. The three of them were not well-concealed if he chose

383

to wander down their path. The guard could not have heard their voices, but perhaps he heard them move.

Georgie wasn't taking any chances. She grabbed her sandal by the straps and hurled it. The wood and steel hit the well-costumed guard precisely on his head in such a fashion that he crumpled over. The way now cleared but their time shortened, as he would wake or be discovered soon, she ran and collected her sandal before they moved on.

The light from the lamps outside the cottage now reduced the darkness slightly. Guards barred the two entrances.

"This is it."

"Do you think we can do it?"

"I hope we can do it without killing anyone," Georgie said with such utter severity that he could hardly doubt it was one of her concerns. "Left or right?"

"Right," Liu said.

Georgie turned to Frederick. "I hope you have your apology speech ready."

He nodded, afraid to say anything else.

"We go first, Mr. Maddocsh."

"All right."

There was no stealthy approach. It was too bright at the only narrow entrance afforded to them from this part of Windsor, and the guards attentively faced outward. The guards could, however, be surprised and possibly even terrified as two black-garbed people leapt from the bushes. Georgie drew her sword and cut the guard's long ceremonial spears in half. Xiao had some kind of wooden poles attached to each other with chains, and he could move faster than either man who faced him, striking them with such efficiency that they did not have time to call out.

The warriors had little time to bask in the glory of victory. The spears had fallen, but they crashed to the ground with enough sound to alert the other guards. Georgie gestured, and Frederick ran across the empty walkway to join them, stepping over the bodies of the guards. They swung open the double doors, shut them, and Xiao barred the doorway with the wooden pole from a broken spear. "It will not hold long."

They did not intend to stay. Liu Xiao led the way down the well-carpeted and ornate hallways of Windsor Cottage. There was no reason for stealth now, as the alarm had been rung. Very surprised guards and more trained soldiers seemed to be around every corner, so the three of them passed very quickly.

They turned a corner and came at last to the closed double doors they needed, and before them, two men who did not look just ceremonial in their duties. "Halt!"

Georgie's sword could not break the metal of the soldier's rifle, but it could hold it down. "The door!" But Liu was busy knocking out the man to his right using his wooden weapon. The left guard remained upright, entangled in the metal struggle with Georgie's blade.

There was a din coming up behind them. The remaining guard in front of them used his rifle to hold down Georgie's sword and grabbed Frederick with his other hand. Frederick tore away from him as hard as he could, managed to reach the door, and yanked it open.

"The king! Protect the king!"

They could see into the next room, larger than the others they had seen, nearly the size of a ballroom, though not decorated as such. They did not have time to inspect it, for there were people advancing toward them. The guard who'd held Frederick thrust his rifle into Georgie's chest, and she had to step back to avoid it, choosing to face the men approaching them instead. She managed to stop the tip of a bayonet from reaching her face, the force of her swing knocking it right off the barrel, but the soldier beside him took the opportunity to knock her overextended arm, and her blade fell to the ground. Liu rushed to her side, but he could only disarm the first line, and there were simply too many of them.

Frederick looked at how many guards had reached them. They were surrounded.

"Frederick!" Georgie cried as a soldier made a grab for her. She ducked it and kicked his knees out from under him. This only served to make the others angrier.

Frederick didn't see the pistol fired, as he made a sudden dash for the door, now swinging open. "Please! We need to see the king!"

Georgie was disarmed and clutching her arm, but the look on her face was like a wild animal, and cornered animals were always dangerous. The only thing that prevented her movement was the line of armed implements pointed at her; they had only not yet decided how to go about dealing with them without killing them, if the soldiers still had such intentions.

"What is this?" said a distinguished man in a wig and white gloves authoritatively, emerging from the room,

"Sir William! There has been an attempt on the life of the king. We'd like your permission – "

"No!" Frederick interrupted loudly. "Sir William! I've only come to speak to him. Let me see the king!" Even with a bayonet pointed at his throat, he managed to pull out a card and hand it to Knighton. "Tell him Frederick Maddox is here."

"If he doesn't want to be bothered, I'll have you in irons."

"He will want to be bothered," Frederick said with more confidence than he felt, and Knighton turned away, heading over to the other side of the room. Frederick was distracted when he heard a cry, and turned to see Georgiana falling to the ground, a soldier standing over her with the butt of his sword still facing her.

"Feck, that's a woman?"

"That's my cousin," Frederick said. "Georgie, don't get up."

She grumbled but stayed put on the carpet, with three different spears pressed against her chest. She could fight them off; he knew it. Or she would make the attempt. "Now it's your show, Maddox," she said. "You'd better have a way out of this."

Liu said something he couldn't understand, but he was probably having similar thoughts. Only Frederick was still standing.

"Who is that?" said a loud voice, heavy with a combination of authority and amusement. "Why are my guards attacking a woman?"

Knighton instructed them to pick Georgiana and Liu up. The crowd followed Frederick to the seat of the king.

King George IV barely fit into his massive and well-cushioned wooden chair. He was as fat as the papers imagined him, his bloated body straining just to be upright, but nonetheless he was aware. His eyes were bright, though he was squinting, and he wore a wig to cover whatever hair he had left. "Mr. Maddox."

Frederick bowed. "Your Majesty."

"Who are your roguish companions?" Despite the alarm of his prime minister and other associates, the king was merely amused, leaning forward. He had to hold on to a cane to do it, a beautiful work of art with a silver tip.

"This is Miss Bingley, my cousin on my mother's side," he said, and Georgiana curtseyed. In breeches, she looked rather ridiculous. "And this is her friend."

"I remember him – the Ambassador."

Liu kowtowed to the king, who merely chuckled and turned back to Frederick. "So – what brings you here, and in such a fashion?"

Before Frederick could answer, Knighton tried to explain, "Your Majesty, this man is supposed to be under house arrest, and he just attempted an assassination –"

"I did not! I only asked to speak to His Majesty about my father. I was under the impression that they would not let me do it at the front door -"

"Your father?" said the king.

Frederick bowed again. "My father, your former physician, was called here to be arrested for treason."

The king turned to the foreign man attending him. "Why was I not informed of this? What are the charges? What sort of treason?"

The Prussian man was backing away, but the king put his hand up, and he stopped and urged a befuddled Knighton to continue. "Your Majesty, it has recently come to our attention that Sir Daniel was once in the business of selling intelligence to the Continent during his stay in Austria –"

"He was in prison!" Frederick shouted. "He was tortured! Your Majesty, you might have known –"

"Boy," Knighton snarled, "do not interrupt me."

"You will not speak to Frederick in such a tone!" the king shouted, and his bellow filled the room. Knighton, caught off guard, stammered and did not finish the sentence, giving the king his opening. "Sir Daniel Maddox stands accused of selling state secrets. This would be a more reasonable charge if he knew any, but I don't recall ever discussing troop movements with him so much as him telling me to stop drinking so much. What was his defense when these charges were laid at his door?"

"He struck his accuser."

The king glanced at Frederick and Georgie, who both stood speechless. "Are we speaking of the same Sir Daniel, otherwise known as Dr. Daniel Maddox, now chief anatomist at Cambridge?"

"Yes, sir."

"The *blind* Sir Daniel?"

"Yes, sir. I was present."

"How in the world did he manage it?"

"He struck him with his cane, sir."

The king began to chuckle. It had reverberations throughout his entire body. "I cannot imagine it. That was his defense to the accusation?"

"This was before he was formally accused."

Now the king was not smiling so much. It was amazing how he could seem so frivolous one moment and completely on target the next. "Please have the guards summon Sir Daniel."

"Sir –"

"*Now*," he said, returning his gaze to Sir William. "He struck a man unprovoked? Has his manner changed since I knew him?"

"I don't think my father's ever struck a man in his life, sir," Frederick interrupted.

"Did he explain his behavior?"

Knighton stumbled. "He said he knew the man. From his voice. His accuser – Dr. Engel."

"Dr. Engel?" The king gestured toward the foreigner at his side.

The Prussian nodded. "Yes, sir."

"Did he say anything beyond that? Sir Daniel, I mean, before or after he was accused of treason and hauled off to gaol?"

Knighton seemed reluctant, but he answered. "He said Dr. Engel was a man named Trommler and that he'd tortured Sir Daniel in Austria."

Everyone was afraid – even Knighton and Liverpool – to break the uncomfortable silence that followed. It took the force of kingship to do it.

"Frederick," the king said, "did your father ever tell you of his experiences in Austria? This must have been 1812, for I was Regent, and you were only five years old. I came to visit him after his return, when he was still suffering from the ill effects of his imprisonment, and we met for the first time. Does that jog your memory?"

Knighton cast a look at Frederick, who did his best to ignore the man and focus on the king. "I do remember him returning from Austria, but as we've never discussed it since, I do not know the details of his imprisonment, aside from the fact that it was done by the count who was my uncle's father-in-law."

"Yes, the wayward brother who ruined his fortune. I remember now. Brian, isn't it?"

"Yes, sir."

The king turned back to his advisor. "How do you know our Dr. Engel is not in fact this

Trommler person? Is not the fact that he is seeking asylum at all suspicious?"

A floundered Knighton said, "Sir Daniel cannot possibly identify him properly – with his condition."

"My Uncle Darcy could," Georgiana interrupted, and all eyes turned to her. "He was imprisoned with Uncle Maddox."

"- But he's in Ireland right now," Frederick said. "And ... Uncle Brian and his wife are in France. My mother is under house arrest. Everyone who could positively identify him is conveniently absent."

The king merely turned his eyes back to his advisor. "We will talk to Sir Daniel, and we will know the truth of the matter."

"Sir, I sincerely advise you – this is a private matter."

"Anything that can be said in front me and my ministers can be said in front of my son." After a pregnant pause in which his advisors stood, stunned, he added, "Do not look so shocked. This is not the first bastard issue of the state you've dealt with. It is different only in that this boy's mother was not someone with a highborn position or the means to care for him. Was this one of the 'state secrets' that Dr. Engel claimed to mysteriously know that Sir Daniel had revealed? Presumably under torture?" Before anyone could react, he eyed

Dr. Engel. "How did you come across this information about Sir Daniel's visit to Austria, Dr. Engel?"

The doctor bowed very humbly, ignoring Frederick's glare, as Frederick ignored Georgiana's shocked expression and nudging. "Your Majesty, I was under the employ of a local Transylvanian count – "

"Count Vladimir Agnita of Sibiu," Frederick said. "My aunt is his daughter. Princess Nadezhda."

"I remember them. Your aunt and uncle. They were here for the knighting ceremony, all in ancient costume," the king said. "Did the count have a daughter named Princess Nadezhda, Dr. Engel?"

"Sir, if you would –"

"Answer the question, Dr. Engel."

Still Engel kept his composure. "I believe he did, Your Majesty, although she had left the area before I arrived."

"I am going to presume that this Mr. Trommler is not a phantom of Sir Daniel's imagination, as I've always known him to be the most sensible of men. Therefore, for the sake of argument, we will say that he existed, and all that is to be determined was whether you knew him or you *were* him."

"Either way, Sir Daniel is still guilty of treason," Knighton said.

"I severely doubt that this Austrian count truly cared about my extramarital dalliances, if you would call either of my marriages valid. If he did, he's certainly kept it to himself all these years, even if he could prove something that was said under torture," the king said. "I saw Sir Daniel only a few days after his return. He was barely holding on to life, only maintaining a slight amount of coherence thanks to the drugs they gave him. It is a testament to his will that he was ever restored to a functioning man. If he was asked and spoke of Frederick in some prison cell, I can hardly blame him for it." He gestured to his guards to come. "Release the others and put Dr. Engel under arrest."

"Your Majesty!"

"Knighton, I've had about enough of your complaints," the king said. "This will all be sorted out as soon as they bring Sir Daniel, so there is little to concern yourself with." He ordered the guards to cut the bonds off Liu and Georgie as Engel was carried off. He then turned to his three mischievous guests with a look of amusement. "Now, I believe there is some explanation required, as I would love to hear the tale of how you got here."

"Yes, Your Majesty," Georgie said, staring hard at Frederick. "There certainly is a lot of explaining to do."

CHAPTER 23

The Bloody Tower

With the soldiers dismissed and things more settled, medicinal help was administered. Liu's head was swelling where he'd been struck when he while being tackled, and he asked very politely to be allowed to sit down. Georgie pulled back her long sleeves to reveal a large red spot where the soldier had hit to disarm her, which would be a nasty bruise in a few hours. The servants wrapped a cold compress around it and requested for her to sit in a chair that was brought. They were still a bit intimidated by the intruders, one of whom had royal blood and two of whom were incredibly dangerous. Their weapons were laid out for the king to inspect.

"I've never seen a blade like this," the king said, inspecting the katana with the Chinese hilt. "Where did you acquire it?"

"My teacher, who is from Japan. I do not know who gave it to him."

He held it up admiringly and then allowed the servant to give it back to Georgie. With her available arm, she carefully sheathed it.

"I do not believe we have been properly introduced," said the king.

"Miss Georgiana Bingley," she said and rose, awkwardly curtseying again, wishing, for once, that she wore a dress. "My father is Lady Caroline Maddox's brother."

"You were presented at court?"

She lowered her eyes to avoid the king's. "It was five years ago. Also, my hair was longer."

"And I've seen countless women paraded before me – one of the few pleasures of kingship," he said. "I do know of your father. He has a shipping business in the Orient with Brian Maddox, does he not? I met him at the doctor's knighting ceremony."

"He does, sir."

"Is he aware of your nocturnal ventures?" he said with a little smile on his face.

"...He is now, sir. Though, not this one. Yet. He's in Derbyshire."

"He never went to Austria," Frederick said. "He could not identify Trommler, so I suppose that's why Aunt and Uncle Bingley didn't mysteriously receive summons to go abroad. I asked Geor – Miss Bingley to come because I knew she could get me in to see you. I figured it couldn't be the stupidest thing she's ever done."

"Oh no," she said, "it's the stupidest. By far. Thank you, Frederick."

"My God!" the king said. "You're not engaged, are you?"

Something between horror and hilarity passed between Frederick and Georgiana before they had to stifle their chuckles. "No, sir."

"Oh God no," Frederick added. "She's engaged to her other cousin. Geoffrey Darcy."

"...Good for you," the king said, though it was unclear to whom that remark was intended. "And you risked your life for your royal cousin?"

"I did not know of his parentage," Georgie said. This time, Frederick could not ignore her glare. "He failed to mention it."

"There is that business of it being a state secret," Frederick said. "I'm surprised Geoffrey didn't tell you. He must have figured it out."

"He only had a guess, and he said he wouldn't tell me even if he knew for certain, because he promised you," she said. "Wait – is your mother Mrs. –"

"- Fitzherbert, no," the king answered. "No, his mother was a very beautiful and daring woman named Lilly Garrison. Frederick has her eyes." Frederick squirmed to hear this kind of talk. "And her mischievous smile. I like to think that did not come from me. Fortunately, you did not inherit my gait, for which your father gave me endless trouble."

"Sir," Frederick said, not sure what else to call him, "Where was my father imprisoned?"

"If the charge is high treason, he's likely in the Tower." The king noted Frederick's horror; it must have been all over his face. "No need to worry. For all of the horrors that have happened there, it is not the worst of places to be imprisoned."

~~~

Dr. Maddox came to consciousness some time after they had moved him. Perhaps they hadn't meant to do it, or he was just getting old, but one of the guards had struck him hard enough to put him out.

"Sir Daniel?"

He realized he was not lying on the ground anymore. He was on a mattress, perhaps even a bed. In a moment of confusion he reached for his glasses. First he remembered he'd heard them being smashed against the ground, and then he remembered he had no use for them except in a cosmetic fashion anyway.

"Are you awake, sir?"

"Is it really that hard to tell?" he said. "Where is Trommler?"

"I don't know the answer to your question, sir."

He was not tied down. He could move about the bed and even put his legs over it and stand up. The walls were unadorned, rough stone. "Where am I?"

"The Bloody Tower, Sir Daniel. If you were capable, you might appreciate the irony of the décor, as it is quite nice for a prison, I certainly think."

The man's voice was low, and Maddox could tell that he was sitting, but it was not someone he knew. "Who are you?"

"Mr. Tuten. Watch your step, sir. There is a fire grate before you."

He nodded. "You're my jailor?"

"Yes."

There were passing moments where he still longed for his sight, no matter how resigned he was to his fate. This was not a passing moment. He was imprisoned, and for all the pleasurable accommodations provided, he was in darkness. "Am I to be interrogated, then?"

"In time."

"What about my family?"

"My understanding is they are under house arrest. No harm will come to them."

Except for Caroline's nerves, which would certainly suffer. "May I dictate a letter to them?"

"You may not, sir."

"What is my crime?"

"You were not informed?"

"I am unclear of the terms," he replied.

"High treason against the state and His Royal Majesty."

Maddox nodded again. "For the record, I am not guilty. My opinion may not mean much to you, and I suspect it means less to Sir William, but that is the fact of the matter." He wanted to pace, but he also didn't want to trip over something. "Where is my cane?"

"It was not brought along with you, sir."

"What is his game?" he asked, mainly to himself.

"Whose, sir?"

"Trommler. I cannot imagine what he has to gain by flaunting his connection to me. I assume His Majesty has not lost all reason and still holds my word in some regard. It must be a trade – something with Sir William. But I cannot imagine what."

Mr. Tuten brought him a tray of food, which was rather good, and certainly beyond his expectations while imprisoned. He felt the sun on his skin where it had not been before and gathered that it must be very early in the morning. His head was still throbbing, and he was bruised from where they beat him, so he requested only a little wine before he stripped himself of his outer layers as best he could and climbed back into the bed.

Suddenly he could see again, but it was blurred until Knighton stepped very close to him. "You stand accused of treason. Do you know what the law calls for? Did you really expect it to end any other way?"

Dr. Maddox was cold and wet in his chair, shivering and exhausted. He could not speak.

"All of the terrible things you've done – the people you've killed, the lies you've told, the things you've hidden – such things, God does not let pass by. He does not forget."

He could say nothing. He smelt of singed hair.

"I'm practically your guardian angel," Trommler said in his Prussian accent. He had not changed. "Reminding you of all the sins you must confess before you die. Because surely, you will die. They will hang you if they are merciful. They won't use the knife." He made a gesture around his neck, probably meaning the guillotine.

"You remember their names. Of the man you killed with your own poisons, because he begged it of you."

Walton. That had been his name, he was sure. "Yes."

"And the little girl?"

Dr. Maddox knew which one he meant. He had treated many girls in need, but her image flashed in his mind. He was two and twenty again,

403

broke, and starving. He would take any case – except this one.

"What did she do?"

She came to him a rape victim, not more than thirteen. She wanted to terminate the pregnancy. She said her father would kill her. Even with his stomach growling, his clothing unwashed, and his face unshaven because he could not afford the cream, he refused. How she pleaded with him! The father of the child was their landlord; fuel to the fire. Still he refused. He rattled off some names of fellow surgeons and fled. He never saw her again; all he could think now was that he sent her to her grave.

"And all the lying. To your wife. You told her you were a good man. When she miscarried ,you said you weren't upset, you weren't disappointed, that you didn't need a son of your own blood."

"I – I was upset, but the body miscarries when something has gone wrong and the health of the mother is –"

"More of your textbook justifications!"

"I am not perfect! I am as God made me."

"Yes. A blind, selfish coward."

They came at him with the prongs.

"Oh, please, please don't do it –"

Dr. Maddox felt the flash and then he was awake. He was sitting up in bed, his heart pounding, drenched in sweat. "Hello?" He didn't know where he was. Right, the Tower. He'd never seen it, couldn't visualize it. It wasn't somewhere you went to on a lark.

He climbed out of bed, but his legs were too shaky to hold and he hit the floor. Mr. Tuten did come, help him up, and give him a bit of tea to settle his stomach, but he was barely aware of it. He was alone, and he was afraid.

~~~

The days passed like that. They did not need to torture him. Between his own memories, his visual impairment, and his loneliness, he was in hell itself, no matter how comfortable they made it for him. Mr. Tuten would not answer his questions about his family or let him petition the king. *The king will listen to reason. Now I must be mad to say such a thing.*

It seemed a very long time before the guards reappeared. "You are to see the king."

"Thank Heavens!" Dr. Maddox said and tried to straighten his clothing before they shackled him and led him to the carriage. It was not a long ride to Windsor, or what he assumed was Windsor, but they did not answer his questions, just thrust him down onto the carpet so he was kneeling.

"Father!"

"Frederick?" The voice was unmistakable. His son, presumably, was the one embracing him. Yes, it was. The doctor knew the scented shaving cream his son preferred.

"My God, man," said the heavy voice King George IV. "You look terrible. You, remove his irons."

"I'm usually – I have glasses," he said. He knew his upturned eyes were very unsettling. Caroline said they were more and more a milky white. A man unshackled him, but he was still confused, tired, and uncertain what was transpiring, and he could not bring himself to his feet. "I had a cane. I think it was destroyed."

"Give him mine," the king said to his servant, and Dr. Maddox was handed the cold metal of what felt, from the complexity of the handle, like a very ornate walking stick.

"Thank you, Your Majesty." He bowed in what he hoped was the right direction.

"Had I known of any of this, you would have not have been treated so. Or questioned at all. Apparently, you were at the center of a conspiracy, Sir Daniel."

"They would not help me send word to you directly."

"No – I might not have discovered it until it was too late, or only when I was in some drugged state where I would have said yes to anything this

Dr. Engel or Trommler or whatever his name is said, if your son and niece had not made a very amusing visit."

"What?" He knew Frederick was there, but his niece?

"Hello, Uncle Maddox," came the voice of Georgiana Bingley, somewhere to his side.

"And you've not been introduced to the Chinese Ambassador, Mr. Xiao," Frederick said. "He helped us – get in."

"Get in?"

"*Break* in, technically," the king muttered, but he sounded more amused than angry.

"You broke into the royal cottage?" Dr. Maddox asked. "Are you all right?"

"I'm fine. Georgie's a bit bruised, but that's what you get for swinging a sword at a guard."

"I did that to protect you, Maddox!"

Dr. Maddox couldn't help but smile a little at their argument. "How is your mother?"

"Unharmed. As soon as she gets word that you've been freed, she'll be fine."

"And Emily? Danny?"

"They're with her in Chesterton."

"Danny helped him escape! You would be proud," Georgiana said. "Or, Uncle Brian would."

"Escape? What?"

"Nothing to be alarmed about," Frederick said, hugging his father again. "We're fine."

407

"I expect a full explanation – at some point. Later."

"Yes. Many things require explanation. Like why my doctor and ministers have been arresting people for crimes against me and failing to inform me of it," the king said. "But I've had enough of Knighton for this evening. Dr. Engel is in custody." He paused. "Do you really believe he is this Trommler person?"

"I'm sure of it," he said. "I will never forget that voice, even if I wish to."

"Uncle! You should sit down."

He felt cold. His face had probably gone pale. They brought up a chair for him and a blanket. He still had only his shirt and waistcoat on, and it was a chilly night. "Thank you," he said as his son wrapped the blanket around him.

"Though the topic obviously disturbs you," the king said, "I must sadly inform you that you cannot stand witness against him if the case is involving identification."

"I know," he said. "Mr. Darcy could identify him. As could my brother and sister-in-law, but they are in France."

"Uncle Darcy is in Ireland on urgent business," Georgiana said.

"He planned it," he said. "They're all gone."

"We'll hold him and send for them," the king said reassuringly. "It will all be sorted out."

It was over. The king was trying to tell him that. Dr. Maddox hadn't realized how tired he was, even though he'd done nothing but sit in the same room for days. The stress of merely trying to get a bearing on his surroundings was enough on his mind. Now Frederick was here, and the king knew, and the king believed him.

"Frederick," he said softly. "You put your life in danger, didn't you, to see the king?"

"I wouldn't have gotten past the guards without Georgie and Mr. Xiao."

"They could have arrested you. They could have had you killed for attempting to assassinate the king."

"He told me all he had to do was get to the king," Georgiana said. "Frederick failed to mention his little ace card."

"It *is* treason to imply that the marriage of royalty has been violated," Dr. Maddox said.

"Which marriage? The one to Maria or the one to Caroline?" said the king. "I think they cancel each other out. And between the two of them, my previous and current mistresses, I think the best child might have come from the one who stabbed me."

"What?" Frederick and Georgiana said in unison.

Dr. Maddox felt himself blush. "I feel I am not of the authority to explain it."

409

"Lilly stabbed me when we had an argument," the king said. "Dr. Maddox was called, and he stitched me up. It was a surface wound, but it was how I met your father, Frederick. Embarrassing as it was."

"And it was," Dr. Maddox added.

"It was not the last time I saw her, but we were on less cordial terms after that," the king went on. "During her confinement, I had someone watching her. When you were born, I knew of it, though I had no business being involved with a son outside of the royal line, and all of my other children have turned out terribly. Or they died." His mood swung easily. He might have been thinking of his only legitimate child, Princess Charlotte, who died in childbirth. "When Lilly took ill..."

Something struck Dr. Maddox, even in the darkness. "It was you?" he asked, replaying the events of that night over in his mind. "You called Mrs. Dudley?"

"When it became apparent that Lilly was not going to recover? Yes. You were not the first doctor she saw."

Dr. Maddox had to think. That night was so many years ago, but so unforgettable. He remembered the ride in the carriage – a carriage, looking back on it, that someone of the likes of Mrs. Dudley couldn't afford – to Lilly's flat. He remembered her describing the symptoms. He could diagnose her without seeing her, but he didn't want to. He held that off until he saw the patient, because it was the proper thing to do, and then he sat with Lilly. How long had he been with her? "I read to her – your mother," he said to Frederick. "She said she liked the sound of my voice, and there was nothing else I could do for her." He made it far into *Tristan*, so it must have been longer than it had felt like. The sky was brightening when he left with Caroline and baby Frederick, so certainly, several hours at least. "I was with her until the end. And we called a priest. I paid him. I hadn't even seen you – you weren't my patient and I wasn't looking. The first time I saw you, Caroline had you in her arms. She told me later that Mrs. Dudley had come back to our place to inform her that I would be late. But I never told her to do that." He didn't bother to turn to the king. "Your Majesty?"

"It took you this many years to find me out? And I always thought you a clever man." said the king. "I needed to leave my son with someone responsible, and God knows no one in my circle is responsible."

Dr. Maddox was overwhelmed. "You didn't know Caroline would take him."

"I knew you would. Always going on about duty, honor, and all that. How could you leave a

411

precious child beside his deceased mother? Nonetheless, I was very relieved when you did."

"Frederick?" Maddox asked. His son had not spoken in a while. He had never heard the specifics of his birth down to that sort of detail. Dr. Maddox avoided telling him the agony his mother suffered, slowly dying of childbed fever in a rotten little hovel, with no guarantee that her son would survive or find his way in the world. Could she even dare to imagine that he would grow into a proud young man of means and intelligence? Who would risk his own life to save his father's? When Frederick didn't respond, he reached out and held his arm. "She would be proud of you."

"I was never good at predicting her moods," said the king, "but I would venture a guess that she would be."

CHAPTER 24

Sir Jack

The hour was growing late, and Dr. Maddox was exhausted and needed Frederick to guide him around, even with the cane. The prisoner was officially released and a messenger sent ahead to open up his London townhouse.

"I do not believe you are excused, Ambassador Xiao. Or you, Miss Bingley."

They turned back in horror and bowed to the king.

"It took incredible bravery to beat up my royal guard," he said. "Nor does it say much of them. Nonetheless, I have been informed that none of them are seriously harmed. Otherwise, there would have had to be consequences." He smiled. "Not to say there won't be."

"Father," Frederick said to the king without thinking, "I asked them to risk their lives to get me to you in time to save my father."

"And breaking into the royal cottage certainly is a life-risking action. One could even say it is treason. Strange, then, how I feel the need to reward them for it. Ambassador Xiao, I believe I have been uninterested in the Chinese empire, and I imagine your Emperor is expecting a bit more from you than nothing. It won't be much, but perhaps a little agreement on paper will speed things along. If you speak to my scheduler, we will arrange a more favorable meeting."

Liu Xiao kowtowed to the king. "Thank you, Your Majesty."

The king nodded and turned to Georgie. "I suppose if you are to be the fiercest woman fighter in my kingdom, you should have an established reputation. Or is it to the contrary?"

She looked at her feet. "Sir, I would prefer if as few people as possible know of this."

"So you will be my son's silent benefactor. Can you think of nothing?"

Georgie grinned. "I can think of something, Your Majesty."

~~~

When Charles Bingley heard of his sister's plight, all that could stop him from riding to Chesterton was Jane quite literally holding him back.

"It's my sister," he pleaded.

"She can't receive visitors, that's what house arrest means," Jane said, releasing the tight grip on his arm. The letter from Geoffrey had said so.

Geoffrey and Charles were still at Trinity in Cambridge and had not been approached by any constable concerning themselves except when they were warned away from visiting the house at Chesterton. There was no news of Dr. Maddox. "If something happens, we will hear."

"I don't want to hear in a day! I want to be there." Such bad timing, with Darcy in Ireland and Brian in France. Perhaps one of them would have an idea, while all he wanted to do was camp outside the Maddox house. "I'll go to London, then, and see what I can do there."

"Tomorrow," she begged, embracing him. "There might be news."

He sighed and relented. Jane loved her sister-in-law and the Maddox children, but her first concern was obviously his safety, and he seemed so ready to put it second. Dr. Maddox had been arrested. Who else might be in danger? What was going on? "Tomorrow. You're right. Besides, I've no formal connection to the king. I doubt he even knows who I am."

"But you could be wanted for questioning."

"Then I will have to go and be questioned, if they ask. But I do not believe this has anything to do with me, even as the doctor's brother."

"How can you be so sure?"

Bingley gestured for the servants to leave the study, shutting the doors behind them. He

415

detached himself from his wife and went to the bookcase to pour a glass of wine for each of them. "Sit down."

Confused, she did so.

"Frederick Maddox is the king's natural son."

Jane covered her mouth. Bingley encouraged his wife to drink some of the wine to help treat the shock.

"His mother is some ... courtesan. Was. She died shortly after he was born. The doctor said her name once, but I've forgotten it."

"Does Caroline know?"

"Of course she does."

"Am I the only one who does not?"

"No," he said. "Until today, I'd never told a soul. On the night of Emily's birth, while you were attending Caroline in labor, Brian and I conspired to get Dr. Maddox drunk enough to reveal Frederick's parentage. Eventually, we succeeded, but he made us swear not to tell a soul. The only other person in the room was Mr. Hurst. I'm not sure if Dr. Maddox even remembers that I know."

She was thinking it over. "Those presents he received every year –"

"– were from the king, yes. Or at least sent by his staff, if not directly from him. There was never any signature, but they were such monstrously expensive gifts that I imagine there was a royal benefactor behind them."

"Do you believe this is what this is about?" she asked. "If so, Frederick would have been arrested."

"That is what I was thinking." He swallowed his wine. "Tomorrow, I'll go to Town, see if I can do *something*. If Georgie's fine where she is, I'm not wont to mess that up."

"Unless she does something incredibly foolish."

He smiled. "And why would you think something like that?"

"*Charles.*"

The typical reaction let them share a moment of laughter, which temporarily set their minds at ease.

They did not have to wait for the next day for something to happen. Though there was no news, the very harried-looking Darcys and Grégoire Bellamont unexpectedly called, having hurried home immediately from Ireland, worried that something had happened in Derbyshire.

"Not in Derbyshire, no," Bingley said and explained the situation as best he knew it, even showing them the letter from Geoffrey.

"Someone called me away," Darcy said, explaining his side of the story. "It seems as though

Dr. Maddox was arrested almost to the day that we arrived in Dublin."

"This could not have been a coincidence," Grégoire said.

"But what connection do you have to the doctor that Charles doesn't?" Elizabeth said to her husband.

"I ... don't know." Darcy and Dr. Maddox were close, but they were not directly related by blood or marriage and were not involved financially in any way except both having shares in Brian and Bingley's company. "You said Brian is also gone?"

"He is still in France, yes."

"Assume then, there is a connection. What connects all of us but not yourselves?" Darcy said to the Bingleys.

There was a moment of silence.

Elizabeth had it first. "Austria."

"Mr. Bingley, Mrs. Bingley, you are the only ones in this room who were not, at some point, in the Austrian Empire," Grégoire said.

"And Dr. Maddox did ... possibly commit treason in Transylvania. If you consider confession under torture treason, and if he'd known something about His Majesty that was worth political gain."

"He always said he stayed out of politics," Jane said.

"Perhaps that is what is being determined by his arrest," Bingley suggested.

"But the count is dead, is he not?" Elizabeth said. "Who does that leave that we would all know?"

"Trommler," Darcy said, but his voice did not sound like itself, but was lower, more restrained, and distracted. He sat down, and Bingley, seeing all of the color go out of Darcy's face, raced to get him some wine, which he accepted. He did not offer further explanation.

Elizabeth did it for him. "Dr. Trommler was the count's advisor during their imprisonment." She turned. "This does not necessarily involve him. Or even Austria."

"No, not necessarily" Darcy said, his voice still subdued.

"So we're to London, then?" Bingley said, as Darcy seemed unusually to not be taking charge.

"Yes. Or do you want to go to Chesterton?"

"We believe we might do more in London," Jane explained, and it was agreed. The Bingleys would go on ahead, and the Darcys would take the morning to rest from their journey before continuing on.

Edmund and Eliza begged to go, but one harsh look from their parents told them it was a hopeless case. They hugged their parents, who then climbed into a carriage bound for London.

Two days later, after making exceptional time on the new roads, the Bingleys arrived in Town to open their townhouse, only to find it already occupied.

"Papa!" Georgie came charging down the stairs. "Mama!" She hugged her mother and curtseyed to her father. She was dressed properly, except she had a heavy gold chain around her neck. "Why didn't you tell me about Fred's father? I practically made a fool of myself!"

"What did you do?" Jane asked. "What are you *doing here?*"

"And why are you wearing a knight's regalia?" Bingley added.

"I would tell you, but I don't think you would believe me," she grinned. "Uncle Maddox will tell you."

"You know that Dr. Maddox has been –"

"– released. Where have you *been?*"

~~~

"Mr. Bingley. Mrs. Bingley. I am so glad you've come," Dr. Maddox said, welcoming them into his townhouse. He seemed well despite his captivity, which presumably had been short, though Frederick protectively stayed very close to his side. "Miss Bingley, *most* knights do not

420

commonly wear their vestments. Especially ones who do not have their real names on the list."

"How did you know?"

"I heard the chains," Dr. Maddox said, and they proceeded to the sitting room, where they could all be more easily settled and refreshed before the whole tale was recited to the Bingleys, from Dr. Maddox's arrest to Frederick's escape to Georgiana and Liu's escapades and the confrontation with the king. It all seemed unbelievable, but if Dr. Maddox was telling it, including the side of the story he was not present for, there was no reason to doubt it. "Caroline and the other children are on their way. Word had to be sent, and she's likely just received it. I was not expecting to see you here before that."

"I wanted to come earlier, but we waited a day, which was lucky, since the Darcys arrived from Ireland. Apparently, they received a false note from a bishop to lead them astray."

Dr. Maddox just nodded. "I've written my brother. If he is still in Paris, he will be home as soon as possible. Nothing can proceed ... before then. Though, I suppose, Darcy can stand witness."

"But – there was no witness to –"

"My niece being knighted, no," the doctor said. "The king had to get the servants out of the room for that one, though they've doubtlessly seen worse things." There was now a man named Jack Wolfe on the rolls as a new member of the knights

421

of the realm, though it was unlikely he would ever make a formal appearance, and no announcement would be made of this particular elevation. "Nor was Sir William present for much of the proceedings. I suspect there will be an investigation concerning his involvement in this entire scenario, though I do not know the extent of it. I only know that Trommler was seeking asylum, and the way he presumed to get it was to offer up a traitor to the crown. I must be the only traitor in England he knows or is willing to give up his connections with."

Dr. Maddox seemed to tire with the very discussion of the man, and Frederick excused his father from their gathering, explaining that he had been under stress for a long time and needed his rest. Bingley caught him only briefly, in the stairway. "Are you all right?"

"I am thankful to God for many things, Mr. Bingley," the doctor said. "Among them is that when I face Trommler again, I will not *see* him. I do not ever want to look upon his face ever again."

~~~

When Georgie inquired as to whether she was in trouble or not, the honest response from her parents was that they were entirely unsure. Thus, the three of them returned to their home to write many letters assuring people that the matter was going to be resolved.

The next day brought the dual arrivals of the Darcys and the rest of Dr. Maddox's family, minus his brother and sister-in-law. When asked very politely how Darcy had privately taken the news that it was Trommler behind the arrest, Elizabeth said to her sister, "Not well." They saw very little of Darcy.

Caroline's reunion with her husband was more dramatic. "You would not believe what your son did."

"Which one?"

"Danny. Who else did I mean?"

"Frederick. Oh, and our niece. I believe we should be shocked about that."

"I stopped being shocked at anything Georgiana did a long time ago," she whispered to him, and he hugged her. "And where is our little warrior!"

"I'm not little!" Danny Maddox said as he charged into the room.

"You are indeed, runt," Frederick said, putting his hand down on Danny's head, which his brother knocked away. "But thanks for providing the distraction." He raised his head to see his 'twin' sister join them. "Emily."

They embraced. She was already in tears. "As soon as you'd gone – I was so worried about you." She added, "I wanted to help."

"Did you comfort Mother?"

"I tried."

"Then you helped," he said. "She needed someone –"

"Frederick Maddox!" came Caroline's booming voice. "The fright you gave me! I expect this kind of nonsense from Georgiana, but a *Maddox* –"

"I *am* in the room," Bingley said.

"I withdraw nothing," she said to her brother. "Though it is good to see you."

"I was worried," he said, "but Geoffrey wrote that we –"

"– couldn't visit, yes. Your time was better spent getting to Town." She kissed her brother on the cheek. "Though, if you'd gotten here sooner, you might have stopped my niece from making a fool of herself." She paused and considered the outcome. "I suppose I must only be grateful that you didn't."

~~~

Only Elizabeth had been witness to the brief meeting earlier of Darcy and Maddox, and only because they seemed to forget she was in the corner of the room when they spoke.

"Is it really him?"

"Yes."

"But you can't testify that it is."

"Yes. That was his plan, Darcy. To have me tried for treason while you were absent."

"There's no – chance it could be anyone else?"

Maddox shook his head. "No. If you truly wish to be uninvolved, my brother –"

"No," Darcy said harshly, "I want to make sure he hangs."

Elizabeth made their excuses, and they left the Bingleys and the Maddoxes and returned to their own house. Grégoire offered to rejoin them later. Alone in the house, with no children or relatives, Darcy could relax. He did not speak, and she did not ask him to. She had no fond memories of Trommler, either, but her first concern was her husband, whom she held until, exhausted from the road, he finally fell asleep.

She was still up when Grégoire returned; it was not very late, only just getting dark. "Dr. Maddox is a very strong man to present such a face to the world when he suffers so much," Grégoire said. Darcy had more of an excuse to seek privacy for any reason he wanted — everyone was accustomed to his habits. Dr. Maddox was more sociable.

"I have a question for you," Elizabeth said, to which Grégoire nodded. "Is it terrible that part of me wishes someone dead?"

"You feel guilty about a natural instinct to pure evil," he said. "It is a vicious cycle. I experienced something similar with Caitlin's first husband."

"Darcy said you asked the judge to give him a private execution."

"I thought every man deserved a moment to consider his fate and repent. I even have the farfetched notion that Mr. Trommler might repent. This is because I am a foolishly eternal optimist." He paused and then continued buttering his bread. "It is not bad to wish someone gone from this world that truly deserves not to be in it. With that said, I would not wish the fires of hell on anyone. Life is temporary - the afterlife, eternal."

"And if you do want him to burn in the fires of hell?"

"Then he must have done something truly worthy of it."

~~~

426

The next day, Darcy's presence at the Tower was requested by the Prime Minister. Lord Liverpool was there to greet him. "Mr. Darcy."

"Lord Liverpool."

"This is to be done as expediently as possible," he said. "We only need you to identity Dr. Engel as the man known as Mr. Trommler before we can continue the investigation."

Darcy nodded and was ushered into the Tower. Walking across the Tower Green in the sunlight was actually pleasant, not like the terrible debtors' prisons and asylums. *A man ill or insane might be better off committing a lesser crime against the state*, Darcy mused as the guards checked his pockets and then ushered him into the ominous-sounding Bloody Tower. The room that was unlocked before him was no prison. It was tastefully decorated in wood, even if the windows were closed up with wiring and the door was locked. Chained to a chair was a man, the sight of whom briefly made Darcy's heart almost stop.

"Sir," Lord Liverpool said, "do you recognize this man as Mr. Konrad Trommler?"

"Yes," Darcy said, his mouth so dry the words hurt him.

"This is the same man that was an advisor to Count Vladimir Agnita of Sibiu during your imprisonment in Transylvania?"

"Yes." He could not look anymore. Trommler's expression was neutral, as if he were trying not to recognize him. He was neither gloating nor frightened.

"Dr. Engel, would you address this man so that he may hear your voice?"

"Yes," said that horrible, horrible Prussian accent. "Sir, I hope you are doing well."

You bastard! "It's him." Darcy turned away.

"Thank you, sir," Lord Liverpool said, and Darcy was escorted out. Now the grass of the green did not look so bright, no matter how the sun shined on it. Nothing about the place looked pleasant to him; it was a façade to mask a terrible thing.

~~~

Letters arrived within a few days from Geoffrey and Charles at Cambridge and from the girls at Pemberley, happy that Dr. Maddox's name was cleared and that all would be well. They did not know the extent of it, nor did anyone feel compelled to explain it. The task at hand was keeping up the spirits of Maddox and Darcy. Both of them were asked to report, not to the Tower, but to Windsor to give depositions to Lord Liverpool and a clerk. They did not see Knighton, the king, or Trommler during any of these sessions, and they

428

were grateful for it. Other than that, they were asked to stay in London until the trial, but their time was their own.

Lady Georgiana Kincaid was in Scotland, and though they informed her of the proceedings, she was told not to race down, for there was nothing she could actively do. Having Grégoire there was an unexpected comfort, and Darcy openly lamented that he did not spend more time with his brother. They played chess with the carved set Grégoire had given him for Christmas.

Grégoire was also asked to Windsor and returned without incident. The next day, the Prime Minister made a visit to the Darcy house to listen to Elizabeth Darcy's side of the encounter with Trommler in Austria before doing the same with Lady Maddox. Alone in the room with him and a guard, she finally dared to ask, "Why is Sir William not conducting the investigation?"

"Sir William is not an official member of the government and not authorized to conduct such investigations," he said.

"He conducted one against Sir Daniel."

"He was not supposed to," he said. "Sir William has decided that a visit to Brighton would be good for his health."

"So he will not stand trial."

"He is not on trial. That he knowingly or unknowingly may have been an accomplice is not enough to bring him to the gallows, and he knows it, Mrs. Darcy."

"But he will not testify against Mr. Trommler."

Lord Liverpool sighed. "There is reason to very privately believe that Mr. Trommler may have been holding something over Sir William to make him a bit more compliant in his designs, but not enough to convince the king that Mr. Trommler was worthy of asylum. The man has a number of enemies abroad, it seems."

"Sir William was being blackmailed by the man he was working with?"

"Precisely," he said, his voice lowered. "Mr. Trommler is a very clever man. When Dr. Bertrand – who has now been reinstated – was dismissed, Mr. Trommler stood to take the position of the king's main physician, despite only a limited known medical experience. And who knows what disasters that would have brought about."

"So the king will let Sir William go?"

"He is not interested in pursuing him on this, no. Though that is not official and you understand that this is said in confidence, do you not?"

"I just would like some understanding of the situation that has wrecked so much havoc."

"Is the story true? About Lady Maddox and the cup of blood?"

Elizabeth nodded.

"Trommler will hang. Be assured, Mrs. Darcy."

Grégoire was right. The upcoming death of a human being was not something she felt terrific about, no matter how assuring.

~~~

The trial began quickly and privately. As it was a state matter of the highest order, and the king put special precedence on it, not a word of it appeared in the papers, especially important due to all of the secrets Trommler seemed to have on everyone.

He had surprisingly little to say in his defense. "Your counsel is determined to hang me, so you might as well go about it; elaborate rituals that presume to create some kind of notion of justice bore me. You are killing a man for something, he said and that is the beginning and end of it."

In their seats, Elizabeth felt Darcy's hand ball into a fist, and she tightened her fingers around his. Called before the council, Dr. Maddox testified that yes, he had given away personal information about the king under torture (done by Trommler's instruments) many years ago in Austria, but to his knowledge, all of that information had been concerning the king's health as it was when he was Prince Regent.

There were no spectators beyond those called as witnesses and their wives. Sir William Knighton was not present. A minister read a speech prepared by the king, who was not present, denouncing Trommler and supporting Maddox's claims and demanding the harshest punishment for the man on trial.

The council was still reading through depositions when the clerk announced, "There are visitors demanding entrance."

"Who?"

"Prince Brian and Princess Nadezhda Agnita of Sibiu, Lord Liverpool."

"My brother," Dr. Maddox said to the question before it could be asked, "and his wife. Her father was the count in question."

Lord Liverpool said, "Admit them."

Fresh from France entered Brian and Nadezhda Maddox, not in Japanese but in their noble Transylvanian garb, complete with crowns. People belatedly realized they had to stand and bow to the prince and princess.

"Lord Liverpool," Brian said, "we have only lately become aware of these proceedings and came as soon as we heard. I assume a trial has taken place to the satisfaction of finding this man –" he pointed to Trommler, looking altogether too comfortable seated in the chair with the cage around it, "– guilty?"

"Who is this man to you?"

"You know who this man is to us," Nadezhda said. Women did not speak in court unless asked first, but no one stopped her. Her heavy accent was intimidating. "This man pretended to be my husband's manservant during our wedding and the year that came after it, but he was my father's spy. He pretended to speak only Romanian, but he spoke English, and in this way he could listen to our private conversations."

"When we fled to escape the count's wrath, he followed us and attempted to blackmail me in Russia," Brian added. "When I refused to give him the monies required, he attacked me, and I barely escaped with my life. He then conspired to capture my brother and hold him for ransom. By Transylvanian law, he is guilty of any number of capital crimes. Therefore, instead of allowing him the comfortable death of an English hanging, we request of this council that he be extradited to Sibiu and face trial under the current count."

"No!" Trommler jumped up to his feet as much as his shackles would allow. "This man has no authority to say that! He is a Prince only by marriage, and only to some backwater country –"

"Do not upset me further, *Andrei*," Nadezhda said.

"– for the love of God, do not send me back to Transylvania!"

Trommler's change in mood was startling. His eyes were wide, and he was struggling against his irons to stand and be heard, where he had, just a few moments earlier, been so passive.

Lord Liverpool was impressed. He turned to the noble couple with new eyes. "You truly wish to make this an international concern?"

"The crimes that were committed were committed in my country first, Lord Liverpool," Nadezhda said. "Therefore it is fitting that he is tried there first."

"I am a subject of the English crown! Sir William made sure of it!"

"That ruling does not necessarily stand," Liverpool said. "However, would this not just be delaying the inevitable?"

"No, I assure you, it is quite different in Transylvania," Brian said coldly.

There were murmurs in the council. Finally they seemed to reach a consensus among themselves. "Prince and Princess Agnita," Liverpool said, rising, "if you would accept the terms, we are willing to offer an opportunity to deliver your Austrian justice, but it must be done here, in privacy, in the Tower."

"No!"

Brian smiled. "Those terms are acceptable, Lord Liverpool."

"Then we will make our ruling. If you would be seated, Your Highnesses."

Brian slid into the seat next to his brother and gave him a pat on the back. "Hi, Danny."

"What is Austrian justice?"

"You don't want to know."

He simply nodded in response.

After minor deliberations, the court rose, and so did everyone else. "For the crimes of blackmailing members of His Majesty's government, falsely accusing members of the knightly order of treason, and lying to His Majesty King George IV, we find the defendant guilty and, according to prior agreement, will extradite him to a section of the Tower, where he will be met with aristocratic authorities from Austria who will decide his fate. This court is adjourned!"

~~~

Three full days later, Darcy and Dr. Maddox were sitting in the doctor's study, quietly drinking tea and trying to make conversation when Brian was announced. Now dressed in his normal (Japanese) clothing, he said simply, "It's done." He did not gloat or make jokes. He did not inform them that Trommler's head was currently on a spike outside traitor's gate at the moat entrance to the Tower. He bowed to his brother and Darcy, and left.

The two men remaining parted ways with a firm shake of their hands – Darcy's numb hand and Dr. Maddox's hand with a missing finger – and they both went back to their wives and said, "It's over."

Beyond that, nothing needed to be said.

CHAPTER 25

Light Shines Again

After weeks of gloom, the family was finally revitalized. Before they turned to go their separate ways, they decided to have some kind of celebration – not of the conclusion of the terrible events, but of something else to lighten the deadened mood. Fortunately, one was readily available.

On the day of her twenty-first birthday, Georgiana Bingley seemed to be the only one not smiling. The Bells had not been thrilled with her sudden departure, no matter how apologetic Heather was for her, and now she had no excuse to be in the Cambridge area, where Geoffrey still was. Even her birthday letter from him did not assuage her feelings, though he did promise to make it up to her when he saw her next. He had a brief break in April, and he would be in Derbyshire for it. Included in the letter was a small, simple seal – not his official seal for Pemberley, but one that simply had the letters "G.D." impressed into the metal. It did not require explanation.

"Ladies shouldn't be grumpy on their birthdays," Bingley said as he entered the sitting room where Georgie had her feet up on the settee and was playing with her locket.

"Why not? Is this yet another unwritten social rule?"

"No, because I don't like to see you frown," he said. "What can I get you? Being reasonable."

"When are my requests ever reasonable?"

He grinned. "I have something planned anyway."

Those present in Town appeared at the Bingley's house, including Dr. Bertrand, newly reinstated as physician to His Majesty (though still not clear on the *entire* story behind it), and his wife and children.

"Is it true?" Joseph Bennet asked nervously. He sipped his brandy with Frederick and Georgiana as they waited for dinner.

"You can call me 'Your Highness' if you'd like," Frederick said with a wicked grin.

"Of course, that would be treason, but who in this room is not guilty of it other than yourself?" Georgie said. "I still would not offer any more encouragement of his outrageous opinion of himself."

"Then I won't be calling *you* by any titles either," Frederick said. "Speaking of what we generally have the good sense to leave unspoken, will you settle the rumor for us about the mysterious Italian?"

"Frederick!" Georgie shouted.

Joseph just blushed. "He's ... I believe he is a bishop now. Mr. Grégoire told me." He added, "There was a rumor?"

"That he was promised to the church, yes," Georgie said. "But we were all trying to be *polite* about it and not ask you." Her glare met Frederick's grin.

"Well ... the rumor is true. He met my mother when she studied in France. There was a settlement. I – don't have anything else to say about it."

"You don't have to say anything else about it," Georgie said.

"Aren't you supposed to be in a pleasant mood for your last birthday as Miss Bingley?"

"How can you be begging me for help one day and the jerk the next?"

He raised his glass. "Give me credit. There were a few days in between."

Supper was called, and the strange mix of Darcys, Bingleys, Maddoxes, and Bertrands sat at the table to honor not only the milestone in Georgie's life but also what they had all unwillingly but successfully gone through. Only Brian and Bingley succeeded in getting drunk, with Darcy watching with his rueful stare at both of them.

439

It was only in more privacy, retired in the sitting room with most of their guests gone, that Bingley and Jane revealed their gift.

"Please promise not to make us regret this, but Dr. Maddox and Caroline have graciously offered to host you at Chesterton from next week until the end of the term."

She squealed in unrestrained delight and hugged both of her parents, a considerable feat considering both of them were sitting, kissed them, said her thanks, and excused herself excitedly to pen a letter. Charles Bingley, still a bit in the cups, pulled his wife closer to him on the settee. "I told her not to make us regret this, did I not?"

"You did."

"Do you think she will?"

"Make us regret it?" Jane said. "I have the dress sewn. I took her measurements when the engagement was announced. Your Indian veil has only to arrive back from the tailors."

He giggled, and leaned into her. "I love you. And I love our daughter, though I've learned to be cautious with my trust. Though, perhaps not cautious enough."

"We did not anticipate our vows."

"We certainly tried."

"*Charles.*"

"In the basement stairwell?"

She kissed him. "I remember it."

~~~

Georgiana Bingley's reception at Chesterton, no less than a week later, was done by a dutiful aunt. "You're to be chaperoned. Properly, this time."

"Edmund was a proper chaperone," Georgie said. Edmund had returned to Chatton House shortly after his sister took off to London.

"Edmund was a *boy*."

"Still, we were properly chaperoned."

Her Aunt Maddox rolled her eyes, and Georgie was shown to her quarters and left to prepare for supper. She was not halfway unpacking her trunk when a maid entered. "Master Daniel to see you, marm."

"Send him in, then."

Daniel Maddox Junior bowed. "Miss Bingley."

"Danny. I heard about your fight with the guards. That was very brave of you."

"Mother didn't think so at the time," he said. "Or at all. She thinks I spend too much time with Uncle Brian."

She smiled and continued unpacking. "She would think that, wouldn't she?"

"May I ask you a question?"

"That in itself is a question," she said. "So, properly, I must say you may ask another one."

"Aren't there things you want to do ... before you get married?"

She paused, but did not turn to him. "What do you mean?"

"Mother says once you get married, you'll finally have to show some good sense."

"I hope those were her words."

"They were." He did not know what he was saying, really. Or maybe he did. "I think she meant you'll be having children and all that, and you won't get to travel and fight and all that."

"Life does not end at the altar," she said. "Hopefully. Why do you ask?"

"I have a cataract." He pointed to his right eye. "Next year sometime, it will have to be removed. I'll have to be very lucky if the eye isn't damaged by it. Father almost died once, when his eye was infected. It's why he doesn't like bleeding people. They almost bled him to death until Uncle Brian sent the doctors off, and then he recovered."

She set aside her bonnets. "Who told you that?"

"Father. I asked. I asked whether it hurt, the surgery, and he didn't say yes, but he didn't say no."

"He avoided the question."

"Yes."

Georgie sat down on the edge of the bed, inviting him to join her. He was still just a boy, even though he had very mature concerns. "You're not necessarily going to go blind just because your father did."

"That's what everyone keeps saying. What if it's not true?"

She paused. What was he asking? "What do you want to do before you go blind?"

"I want to learn to fight."

"Your father, the physician, would be pleased."

Danny put his head down.

"You want me to teach you?" she asked. "You know my style is very different from Uncle Brian's. Bushido is so linear."

He looked up, his eyes brightened. Nothing about them seemed off. "You would?"

"Normally, I would do it for free," she said, "but I am very much in need of a few favors."

~~~

When Geoffrey arrived for supper, Georgiana was on the front steps waiting for him before he could even be called in properly.

"I was worried about you," he said as they embraced.

443

"Get used to it," she said, and he laughed and kissed her on the cheek before they were called inside.

Dinner with the Maddoxes was pleasant, though trying as well, for both of them. Dr. Maddox was in a subdued mood, and that left Lady Maddox to do all the talking, and she was a far more severe questioner than her husband. Geoffrey was doing well in his final months of University, and had little else to say about University life in front of Lady Maddox. Emily, who read extensively like her father had done, was able to ask him about some of his curriculum, though not the mathematics that were so heavily favored.

After dinner, the young couple was allowed their time on the veranda, out of earshot of their watchful cousins.

"I liked your gift," she said, referring to the wax seal. "Not that I can use it."

He stroked her hair. "Only a few more months." He groaned. "My God. That is a long time, isn't it?"

She giggled. "It is."

Geoffrey stood. "Frederick!" To which Frederick looked up, and Geoffrey tossed him a coin.

"Come on, kid," Frederick said to his brother, taking Danny around the corner.

Georgie laughed. "It is that simple?"

"I am not sure how he got Danny away so easily."

"I took care of that," she said, and he replied with a kiss. In fact, he replied with so many kisses that they lost count. At the same time that it was becoming evident that he was going to have to pull away, Georgie did the same.

"Can you hear them?"

"Hear what?"

"The bells."

"You can hear them all the way from here?"

She nodded.

"The pitch is too low," he said. Even with Georgie, it was still an uncomfortable subject. He heard the bells at Cambridge, but not outside. It was a moment that served its purpose of distracting him from his reaction to being pressed against Georgie for so long.

Geoffrey turned away with a sigh.

"What is it?" Georgie said. When he didn't respond, she tugged on his shirt. "*What is it?*"

"I can't do this."

"Having an attack of conscience?"

"It has nothing to do with conscience."

She could imagine his frustration; she shared it. "You know you're adorable when you're grumpy and irritated?"

"I'm so glad you think that," he said.

She kissed him. "Maybe we could try again."

"No."

"I won't be as extreme."

"I won't let you hurt yourself."

"I won't. You have my word; I will not take anything even remotely harmful." She added, "We've been lucky before."

"You promised your father you would be good."

"How do you know that?"

He grinned, finally settled enough to turn back to her. "Uncle Bingley took the trouble to write to me, informing me of your sacred oath."

Georgie blushed. "He did? It was hardly a sacred oath. Do you want to listen to my father or me?"

"You know the answer to that." He kissed her before standing up and straightening his coat. "My birthday is Tuesday."

"Try not to get hit in the head by any more Radicals."

"That was the day after my birthday. As I was about to say, George is hosting a party at his apartment so that you may come. I even managed Dr. Maddox's consent, seeing how your brother will be there and George will be there."

"So we have to get them both exceedingly drunk."

"Precisely. See you there?"

"You have my promise," Georgie said. "And this one I intend to keep."

~~~

The weekend passed uneventfully for Geoffrey. He saw Georgiana only for a meal on Sunday after services at the Maddox house and otherwise remained within the world of Cambridge and the walls of Trinity College.

"Where are you off to?" he said to Charles, who was emerging from his room with an especially large bag. Frederick was in the armchair by the unlit fireplace, taking a late afternoon nap to sleep off a midday hangover. They had given up worrying about disturbing him long ago.

"If I report to you, you would be required to report to me," Charles Bingley the Third replied, "and I do not believe I would always want to know the answer, come to think of it."

"George was much worse than me." The three of them had been roommates the previous year.

"George wasn't betrothed to my sister," was Charles's reply. "If you really must know, I promised I would donate my old shirts to the drama club at King's."

Geoffrey poured himself a glass of wine. "If you become an actor, your father will have an apoplexy."

"Good thing I act as well as I fence."

"You fence terribly."

"My point exactly. That does not mean I cannot have an appreciation for the theatrical arts."

"You Bingleys do have your strange obsessions."

"I'll tell Georgie you said that."

He grinned. "She'd be pleased."

Charles rolled his eyes and left just as Reynolds entered with Sir Gawain, who did not walk so easily in Cambridge's dark hallways and sometimes needed assistance, for which Geoffrey was not always available. "I found him roaming the park, sir."

Geoffrey knelt before his old hound. "I've not been a very attentive master, have I?" Gawain looked at him with green eyes clouded by the cataracts of old age. He didn't hear very well either, and Frederick often joked that Geoffrey heard as well as an elderly dog. Geoffrey glanced at Frederick, still sound asleep and snoring, and scratched Gawain behind the ears. "Are you hungry?"

Gawain dropped his head, and the little tube that was held in his jaw dropped to the floor. Geoffrey scooped it up and unrolled the scroll

inside. It was an address from off-campus. "Huh."
He lifted Gawain up. "I promised you a meal,
didn't I?" He turned to his manservant. "The
bacon, please."

Reynolds opened the top case and removed
the jar of dried bacon strips, one of which he
handed to Geoffrey.

"Let's get back at Frederick, shall we? For all
those mean things he said about us?" Geoffrey
removed a piece of the strip, scraped it across
Frederick's face, and rubbed it into his hair. The
rest of the strip he tossed to Gawain, who nearly
swallowed it whole.

"My overcoat," he said to Reynolds. "The
grey one, please."

"Yes, sir."

He emerged from his room, straightening
said coat, when Frederick cried out, "What – Oh
God – What is this damned mutt doing on me?"

"Licking your face."

Frederick, who knew better than to hurt
Gawain in Geoffrey's presence, pushed the hound
away from him. "And why is he doing that?"

"Because you smell of bacon, Mr. Maddox."
He doffed his hat. "Good day."

"Geoffrey? Geoffrey, why do I smell of
bacon? You get back here!"

~~~

Geoffrey knew the street well enough, though he had never frequented the particular commercial buildings, except once to force the matter on poor Charles. He didn't know what he was doing there or why, but since he recognized the handwriting, he went, trying to hide his face under his hat. The particular address he did not know. It did not seem to be an establishment of any kind, merely an apartment building in the same district, and he tried to avoid recognizing the gowned students he saw scurrying along the same streets.

He felt guilty knocking on the door with the top of his walking stick, but he did it nonetheless, and the door opened. "This had better not be a joke..." He stepped in, and the door shut behind him, and someone jumped on top of him. Someone whose small figure and slight weight were very familiar to him. "Georgie!"

"Hello," she said, kissing him on the side of the head. He had to swing around a bit to get her off and into a proper embrace. "Thank God you've come. I've better things to do with my day than spend it in a flat on this street. My opinion of Cambridge and its students has gone down considerably, Mr. Darcy."

"As long as it hasn't affected your opinion of one student –"

"I still love my brother very much, yes."

He kissed her.

There was little else to the place but a bed and a few pieces of furniture, but it was surprisingly neat and clean. "How did you –"

"George's mistress. He can call her whatever he likes, but that's what she is."

Geoffrey frowned. "And how do you know her?"

"He accidentally told me her name when he was giving me some medical advice," she said. "She won't tell. She thinks it's amusing."

"Oh," he said. "And you're –"

"I promise I'll be careful."

"Because I don't want –"

"Geoffrey Darcy, did you come to the lair of a courtesan to talk all day?"

He did not want to question her as to how she had managed to escape all of her chaperones, how she had managed to find George's 'mistress' and form some kind of friendship with her, or anything else that was not the answer she particularly wanted to hear. Georgie was respectably dressed, and that was more concerning to him, because she was overdressed and so was he. It was hard to undress while kissing, but they were getting better at it, and the bed helped.

"Do you even know how to unbutton your own shirt?" she said as he struggled.

"Can you lace a bodice?"

"I'm not wearing one."

"Can you?"

"I can lace the tachi of a sword," she said, whatever that meant.

"Excellent avoidance of the question," he said, kissing her neck as she pulled down his shirt for him. "Is this a bad time to tell you how much I worry about these stunts you pull?"

"Yes!"

"Because I wouldn't want anything to happen to your ... lovely ... body," he said, trailing his kisses down her chest.

"If it does, I'll yell it into your *right ear*."

"You're lucky I'm in love with you," he said.

"I know," she said, letting him remove the last of her garments. "I wanted to show it."

He had no argument with that. His first instinct was the well-trained suppression of his emotions, or more precisely, his body's responses to them. Then he remembered where he was, here and now. There were no such requirements. He could take his time, and the clarity of that thought allowed him to do so.

Georgie was still wearing the Indian locket. "Does it still work?" he asked.

"Of course." She freed one hand to hold it up. "Geoffrey Darcy." She hit the little knob, and an array of colors played against both of their chests for several seconds before going out. "You've no idea," she said, her voice suddenly heavy.

"No idea of what?"

"How many nights I've done that, alone in my room," she said, and he wiped away the beginning of tears from her eyes.

He shushed her with a soft kiss, and then there was no more talking, and no more crying, though there were some moans. No, he would not give in to the temptation of a physical frenzy. He wanted to touch her; he wanted to touch all of the parts of her that had never been touched slowly, or perhaps at all. She had calloused hands, not soft like his sisters' hands when he'd held them when they were little and would tag along by his side. She had worn feet, not protected by slippers and stockings as much as he could only imagine women who wore shoes and not wooden sandals had, but she was utterly feminine to him. He could not hold back anymore and entered, and it was quiet and beautiful and there was nothing wrong with anything in the world for those moments.

Georgie did not seem to be on a particular schedule. She was playful, and she seemed to know some things. "The whore?" he asked. "Excuse me. Mistress."

"No," she said. "My father has a locked drawer in his study with a book –"

"God, no –"

She laughed. "When I first discovered it, I thought they were Indian two-headed monsters."

"You realize we are talking of your *father's* study?"

"I know. Disgusting, but I'm passed it. Besides, do you want me to stop?"

"*No.*"

She had a wicked grin. "Good, because it's your birthday present. Do you like it, or do you want me to exchange it for some wrapped gift?"

"No," he replied. "This will be fine."

CHAPTER 26

Milestones

"Where's the booze?" was the first thing out of Frederick's mouth as he came in the door of George Wickham's apartment. Then he noticed Georgie sitting in the armchair. "Oh. So it's that kind of party."

"What does he mean?" Georgie said to her host, who was quickly pouring Frederick a drink.

"He means there won't be women here," George said. "Besides yourself, of course."

"Why did I come?" Frederick said and finished the glass in one gulp.

"To celebrate your relative's birthday?" George suggested.

"Free booze?" Georgie added.

Frederick lifted his empty glass to her as the servant struggled to refill it. "Precisely! Oh, and possibly gambling. We can still gamble in front of a woman, can't we? George, do you own a carriage?"

"Even if I did, I wouldn't lend it to you. I saw the wreck you made of the last one."

Before Georgie could question that statement, the door burst open and Geoffrey entered, being dragged in by the more rowdy Charles and a man about their age that Georgic didn't recognize. Charles and the stranger were clearly already drunk.

"Georgiana, this is Guy Peterson," George said. "Guy, Miss Bingley."

She rose to curtsey, and he bowed to her. "So you're the dramatist."

"And you're the fiancée who is preventing us from other female company. But, for the birthday boy's sake, I will forgive you. Just no snogging in front of –"

Geoffrey stepped forward. "Georgie." He kissed her, but on the cheek. "I apologize in advance for our drunken friend."

"*Hey! I said –*"

"What about my drunken cousin?" Georgie said, gesturing with her head in the direction of Frederick.

"I don't make apologies for him," he grinned.

"Happy Birthday," she said, even though she had wished him it – verbally and physically – many times the day before.

"Thank you. How was your birthday?"

"I watched our parents try not to be miserable about all kinds of things, and Papa got cup shot with Uncle Brian. What else is new? Oh, and for your information, Emily and Danny very much wished to come, but for some reason, when George came to pick me up, Aunt Maddox would not let them out the front door. I can't imagine why."

"And Edmund's in Derbyshire. That leaves ... who? Lady Littlefield?"

"Is she single?" Guy said.

"This isn't her type of party," Frederick said. "Georgie's ... well, mannish." He faced the triple stares of Georgie, Geoffrey, and Charles without hesitation. "Well, she dresses like one."

"Only when I'm fighting. Which could be right now, if you'd like?"

"If you two are going to bicker the entire evening, I may actually drink something," George lamented.

Charles nudged his sister, "Say something mean."

"Why?"

"We *never* see George drunk."

"That doesn't mean we want to," Geoffrey said. "He's a moody drunk, I assure you."

"Is this all you talk about in University?" Georgie said. "Spirits?" She did, however, take the offered wine.

"We're trying to refrain from the subject of women," Charles said.

"Or gambling," Frederick added.

"Or any assortment of vices," Guy said and gave Georgie a smile. "Does anyone have a carriage?"

Frederick piped up, "You need *two* for a race."

"You race carriages? On these streets?" Georgie asked Geoffrey. The streets of old Cambridge were more cobbled than paved and as narrow as any formerly medieval hamlet.

"I only did it once," Geoffrey said. "That was enough. Though I won, actually."

"Pure, blind luck," Frederick said. "Also, I never thought he would fill the whole sewer afterwards with his vo –"

"Enough!" Guy said. "I didn't care for the story the first time. Or the second. Besides, we could say why *you* gave up racing, Mr. Maddox."

When Frederick did not offer up the explanation, Geoffrey chipped in for him. "He lost a bet of three months allowance, and that was about as long as he could go without his father figuring out he was gambling."

"You think my father is a nice old man," Frederick said, "who cleans your skinned knee. Let me dispel that rumor for you. Mention gambling in front of him, and it's like you've become the Antichrist."

"I didn't say I thought he was old," Georgie said. "Does anyone study?

458

"George."

"George."

"George."

"I study," Guy said in his defense.

"I hardly think memorizing Lear's lines is on the same taxing level of a Tripos exam," Frederick said.

"I don't see you doing it."

"Give me an hour and the script. I'll bet you –"

Charles looked to his friend. "Don't take the bet. He'll vanquish you and take your money."

"He's that good?"

"Let me put it this way," George said, "Were it possible, I would pay Frederick to excise his brain and swap it with mine."

"I don't want the Darcy family madness."

There was silence in the room. Only Guy looked around in confusion, but no one offered up any explanation. Even Frederick sort of shrunk in his seat and disappeared into his glass of brandy before uttering, "My apologies."

"Accepted," George said quietly and finally took a drink for himself.

~~~

Georgie had to be home by midnight, but they still managed to teach her their card game, and

Guy even knew a couple of card tricks, though he had more and more trouble doing them as he was increasingly in the cups.

Geoffrey escorted her out into the brisk night, pausing before the waiting carriage. "I would say they were subdued, but really, George is usually like this, and Frederick talks a bigger game than he plays."

"It's good to see you whiling away the hours of your education," she said. "Is Guy a good friend for my brother?"

"Charles seems to like him," Geoffrey said, which meant a lot. Charles had an easy smile and loved to dance, but he was shy around the company of tougher men than him. He needed friends that weren't relatives. "I don't think they've been in any serious trouble."

"Good." She kissed him. "Make sure of it."

"I will do my best. After that, it will be up to George and Frederick, because I intend to spend the rest of my twenty-first year in more feminine company." He kissed her, which seemed a satisfying enough answer before he saw her off. It was not until the carriage had disappeared entirely from sight that he was hauled back into the apartment.

"Darcy!" George said, grabbing him.

"What?"

"George is smashed," Charles informed him.

"Darcy, promise me we'll never be like our fathers."

Geoffrey did his best to keep from smiling as he stared George in the eyes and said, "I promise not to stab you if you promise not to shoot me."

"Capital!" George shouted, and collapsed in his chair.

"Did your parents not like each other?" Guy asked.

Geoffrey took another glass from the servant. "They did the things we just mentioned. My father survived." He looked at George, who now miraculously seemed to be sleeping. "I hope that was a 'yes.'"

~~~

The next day, Georgie got a note that no one was available to chaperone her on the University end, as they all had bad hangovers (and, inexplicably, Frederick had a black eye and George had a bruised hand – neither of which, he assured her, were connected), and so it was Friday before she saw Geoffrey again.

"Charles?" he said when told of their chaperone. "Charles Bingley? The third?"

"Yes."

461

"Your brother?"

"Yes."

"Why?"

She laughed at him. "Because this is that time of the month when you won't find me a very suitable partner."

"Indisposed?" They always had to talk around it.

She nodded. She said a brief hello to her brother, and he left them to walk out in front of them as they walked along the park road. The flowers were coming in, bright colors against his black robe and her white dress.

"I apologize for invading your little club," she said, holding onto his arm.

"Hardly. I think the bigger issue was who George thought to assemble. As you can see from the attendance, George Wickham is not the socialite. Not that I necessarily wanted a large crowd. Or anyone besides you, really." He gave her a peck while Charles was chatting with a passerby.

"You only turn one and twenty once."

"You only turn all of your birthdays once."

"I cannot disagree with that epiphany, Mr. Darcy," she said. "At my party there was far more civility, so it was far less interesting."

"That will be us someday, you realize."

"Geoffrey."

"I've never heard a single story from my

father's University days," he said. "My mother once confessed that he never cared to tell her. I can draw two possible conclusions from that: either it was utterly boring, or something he would not want his wife to know occurred. If I went to King's, maybe I would find out, no matter how little I would wish to." He continued, "Grandfather Bennet says that *your* father was quite the charmer."

"Be quiet!"

"Grandmother Bennet would not stop talking about him before he even officially arrived in the neighborhood."

"Hush. I don't want to know. Why are you so fascinated with such a disturbing subject?"

"Because it shows our parents were human once, too," he said.

She huffed. "*Once*." But she couldn't hold it. "If I accept your proposition that we are destined to imitate our parents in some fashion, will you stop talking about them?"

"I promise."

Geoffrey had an unfinished paper due for his tutor, so he regretfully said his goodbyes, leaving Georgie with her brother.

"When are you due back?"

"When you escort me," she said. "Or send someone. Why?" Before he could answer, she said, "I've hardly seen you."

"I know perfectly well why you don't want me as a chaperone." He didn't sound offended, just concerned. Charles was her little brother, the one *she* protected, though he was not so much younger, and perhaps it should have been the other way around. Maybe if Geoffrey hadn't lived so close by, she would have had that relationship with Charles. Instead, their siblinghood was more nebulous, without a clear hierarchy.

"I'm living with the Maddoxes. I'm perfectly available most of the time." She added, "Eliza complains that you don't write."

"I do write."

"Not as often as you did."

Charles sighed. "This is my second year. All four of us are here, even if George is a Fellow. I'm not as homesick. But you are correct; I should be more dutiful to my sister."

"Are you in debt?"

He blinked. "What?"

Something was troubling him. That much, she knew. "It's all I can assume. You're not constantly in the cups, you are in good health, and from what I hear, your marks are perfectly acceptable. You've not tried to kill yourself in this drunken carriage racing business, so that leaves me only with the conclusion that you and this Guy and the others from Trinity are in debt together."

"No," he said. "I am not. Guy is from a very respectable family in Sussex and never gambles past his allowance. Some of the others do – another fellow named George – not our George – got himself into trouble and his father has passed so his uncle had to bail him out. By Cambridge standards, certainly nothing serious. And I don't want to gamble. Father worked too hard for that money. He went all the way to India." He went on, "Why do we name everyone after the kings, anyway? The last one was mad, and the current one is a laughingstock."

"I met him, you know."

"And?"

"He was sort of ridiculous looking, but he had moments of incredible clarity and brilliance."

They began walking down the path, the way they had come. Charles idly picked up a flower and began plucking the petals out. "So, like you-know-who?"

"Like Frederick, yes. Except Frederick just *acts* ridiculous."

"When Fred told me the story, I didn't believe a word. But Geoffrey never lies, at least not about this sort of thing, and their stories were the same. I knew you'd gone because Lady Littlefield came by looking for you to see if we had any news."

"She did?" Her interest was piqued. She'd written to Heather, and her friend was invited to dinner on Sunday at Chesterton, but that was not mentioned. "How nice of her to see you."

"No matchmaking!" he said. "She only asked about you and Frederick and that was it. We didn't want to arouse suspicion, so it was a very brief call." He added, "Geoffrey was in hysterics. You should have seen it."

"My being there would have contradicted the entire notion, and there would have been nothing to see."

"True, but nonetheless he was. And I was worried as well, but I was far less dramatic about it."

"Says the friend of the dramatists."

"Well, he's smitten. As he's always been, but I didn't want to look." He finished off the flower, and tossed it into the pond. "I suppose it's not all different."

"What is?"

"When sisters go off and get married, it's like they're gone. Why do you think Father is so nervous?"

Finally, what was on his mind! "Papa is very close with Aunt Maddox. He always wrote to Aunt Hurst and he still writes to Uncle Hurst now and again."

"He took care of them both after our grandfather died. Even though Aunt and Uncle Hurst were married, they lived with him until he married Mother. But when you get married ..." He gave one of his sheepish grins, identical to his father's. "I suppose you'll only be a few miles away. Or you'll have your own place, won't you?"

It was more than likely. They had, in passing, more often in their letters, discussed it. There was no particular reason for Geoffrey to live at Pemberley immediately after he graduated, and she couldn't imagine married life with her aunt down the hall. With her inheritance, they could set up nicely however far away they wished, then sell when the time came to move back to Pemberley. "We won't leave England. Geoffrey's such a homebody. But yes, it will be different."

"'Life is impermanence.'"

"One of Papa's books?"

He nodded.

"Try the one he keeps locked in the desk in his study."

"Good heavens! Those pictures are locked in mind forever now. I hope Eliza hasn't seen them."

"Or Edmund."

"Edmund wouldn't know what to do with them."

They shared a laugh together, and continued their way back to the square.

~~~

March passed into April, and even under the critical eye of her aunt, Georgiana found enough ways to escape her various chaperones entirely, whether by bribery or trickery or the brevity of her needing to excuse herself from an activity.

"Frederick's rates went down," Geoffrey told her. "Did you threaten him in some fashion?"

"No, but I did commit treason for him," she answered, putting her bonnet back on. "Or he's just so amused by us that he's not even pretending to resist."

It was not hard to find other activities to occupy her time, with helping Danny with his training (his footwork needed the most work, and that was both simple enough and less violent-looking), visiting Heather Littlefield, or shopping trips with her aunt and cousin Emily. She was overwhelmed by the things her mother had already bought her for the wedding, but Aunt Maddox was not satisfied by the descriptions. "You already have a dress, but that doesn't mean we can't add some finishing touches to what I'm sure is your mother's masterpiece." Georgie was almost amused; Aunt Maddox could be downright mean and sarcastic when she wanted to be, and she paid more attention to fashion than any woman Georgie had ever met. *Uncle Maddox wasn't always blind*, she reminded herself.

At last, she pried the truth from Uncle Maddox in his study one lazy Saturday afternoon. "When I met Caroline, she was still on barely decent terms with your mother and despised Mrs. Darcy."

"What did they do?"

"The Bennet sisters were country girls with no dowries and an overbearing mother. Your father fell in love with your mother because their temperaments matched, but as I was told, it was Mrs. Darcy who really triumphed. Caroline had been pursuing Darcy for years."

She put her hand over her mouth. "Aunt Maddox was in love with Uncle Darcy?"

He smiled a bit uncomfortably. "No, not precisely, but remember we were all much younger, and foolish, and she was a bit ... concerned with the Ton's opinion, and in the Ton's opinion, a tradesman's daughter would do well to marry Mr. Darcy of Pemberley and Derbyshire. Instead he married a country girl, and since Darcy and Bingley were good friends and the sisters very close, Caroline was constantly thrown into Mrs. Darcy's company during the engagement and after the wedding."

She could imagine it – Aunt Maddox was concerned with fashion and appearance and keeping a good home – but not all that he was talking about.

"It was a long time ago," her uncle said in response to her silence. "We've all changed. Caroline grew to love Jane as she does her own sister Louisa, and she even formed some sort of friendship with Mrs. Darcy. I think it was while they were rescuing us from Austria, the two of them. Yes, that's right. Cassandra was born shortly after that. You'll experience it too, when your sister marries, or your brothers marry, perhaps."

"Experience what?"

"Not liking the intended or their family. It can tear families apart – but only if you let it," he said. "There is nothing more important in life than family. I would have had every reason to disassociate myself from my brother, but he was still my brother; he never would have regained his fortune, married Her Highness, or begun all of this obsessive nonsense with the Orient. So you have a lot to be thankful for, Miss Bingley." He stood up. "Now, no more embarrassing stories about your relatives. At least for today."

She curtseyed to him, even though she supposed she didn't have to. Shortly afterwards she saw him out to the veranda, where he sat in the sunlight on pleasant days such as this. She often read to him until he nodded off in the chair. "If you would be so kind ..."

"Of course, Uncle Maddox. Do you want to continue with Chaucer?"

"Yes, please." He sat down as she picked up the book from the pile set out for him. "I've heard it said that upstanding women shouldn't read Chaucer or Shakespeare, but I suppose it's better than Fanny Hill or those torrid women's novels. You don't read those, do you?"

"Very rarely, Uncle Maddox. A lot of girls in the seminary did."

"Rubbish, all of it. What's wrong with the father of English literature? Or the greatest playwright of all time?" He shook his head. "The Knight's Tale, if you would."

She sat down and began. It was amazing how he would often correct her, having memorized the book long ago, but he still wanted to hear the stories again, over and over, just as he had read them himself when it had been possible. Somehow, he found a way.

~~~

"Your aunt is so different from your mother," Heather Littlefield said. "Oh, look at that!"

"Well, they're not sisters. Why would they be alike? And what am I looking at?"

"That purse, there."

There was nothing extraordinary about the purse other than the jewels, but she had seen many bejeweled things in her life, and purses were no exception. "The last thing I need is another purse. Let's go to the bookshop."

"Your uncle must already own everything they sell there."

"I want to buy Charles something. Maybe a set of plays. He seems so down about my wedding, of all people."

"Perhaps we should, then. Maybe he'll miss you."

"As if I'm off anywhere so distant." They went into the bookshop, but they couldn't tell one play from the next, other than the more famous ones, which he likely already had. She bought a copy of *The Mysteries of Udolpho* and asked for the purchase to be wrapped and sent to Trinity. After that, Heather dragged her into a fabric store, not for Georgie but for herself, because she wanted to see the new blues that were supposed to come from the colonies in South America.

Georgie had separated from her and was looking at the various Indian fabrics in the back corner when Geoffrey burst in from the backdoor, his mortarboard barely on his head. "Georgie –"

"Geoffrey!" she said in a surprised whisper. His face was flushed. "You're drunk."

"Wine party."

"It's not past two yet."

He grinned at her. Why did she have to find it so charming? "Early wine party. But I had to see you."

"And you have just been running in and out of shops?"

"A cup shot student embarrassing himself? They're used to it," he said, pulling her into the back room. "I missed you."

"So have I," she said, "but excuse me for demanding an explanation of sorts."

"Of sorts," he mimicked and removed his cap. "George gave me one of those lectures – like he's my father. Worse. My father just has to look at me and it's as good as done. But George goes into details. About how I should be careful, about how I don't understand anything –"

"Geoffrey."

"– and I have to consider all of the serious things that come with marriage. Like fatherhood, setting up a family, and acting like a gentleman and not a boy. What does he know? He just sees whores and holes himself up in libraries. If they come there, he would never leave those places –"

"*Geoffrey.*"

"I'm a little scared, all right. He's making me feel scared. But I love you, and I don't believe I could do anything besides what I've done and what

I'm doing, so what? I wouldn't have it another way." He kissed her.

She couldn't help but respond. Her only uneasiness came from the fact that they were standing up, and dressed, and in the back room of a fabric shop. Only Geoffrey could get her so riled up with a single kiss, but damned if he could do it well.

He was already aroused. There was very little space, so it was impossible not to feel it. And they had all that fabric to pad them. He was not terribly in the cups, just a lovesick fool, so he had enough sense to manage to get his breeches open without having to remove his gown entirely. She was lost. Her main concern was that they didn't make too much noise, and the second was that they didn't break the wall down behind her. But it did hold, and he released, and it was awkward and wonderful at the same time.

With a contented sigh, Geoffrey relaxed and removed himself carefully from their entwined state. She helped him with the buttons on his breeches, and he straightened her gown. They didn't speak, having nothing for the moment to say, as nothing else seemed to exist. There was nothing but their heavy breathing before Georgie finally swallowed and said, "Heather – is ... probably missing me."

"Women ... you wander around," he said, wiping the sweat off his brow before putting his cap back on. "I love you. I don't want to leave you again."

"There'll come a day when you'll be sick of me and all of my craziness."

"Never," he said, and kissed her. "I'm sorry if I –"

"There's nothing to be sorry for," she said. "I love you."

He smiled, and they parted, him out the way he came, leaving her alone in that tiny room with nothing in it but stacks of garments on rolls. She needed to sit down. And yes, Heather would be looking for her. Even in her contented daze, she could tell there was some immediacy to that.

She opened the door, hoping she was not overly flushed and disheveled, and sat down on the nearest available bench, numbly staring at the fabrics hanging across from her until Heather returned. "Where have you been?"

You've no idea. "Do you have moments where life just gets away from you?"

"I suppose that's what it's like, to be in love." She took Georgie's hand. "Do you want to shop?"

"No," she said. "I think I've had enough for the day."

~~~

She next saw Geoffrey for supper the following day. It was not nearly as uncomfortable as she thought it might be. He just smiled at her, and she smiled at him, curtseyed, and they went in to the Maddox house. The soup was her favorite, but she was so interested in the person sitting across the table that she hardly touched it, and only ate when Aunt Maddox insisted she not let her food go cold. Uncle Maddox gave a knowing chuckle at this; how in the world did that man know everything?

"Are you all right?" Geoffrey asked her, the only mention of it, at the end of the night and after more mundane conversation.

"Yes. Do you remember it?"

He blushed. "*Yes*. I wasn't that drunk."

"Good to know."

"I love you."

"I love you, too," she said, and he climbed into the carriage.

~~~

As for Geoffrey, he finally had something to do with his spare time. He didn't gamble, drink excessively (by other people's standards), wasn't in any debating clubs, and he was not a scholar. He did not find the material too difficult, but it was so obtuse to him to be studying calculus when he

476

already knew the math he would need for his life as master of Pemberley. Some students used their tutors to engage in personal studies. He studied up a bit on medieval literature, as everyone around him seemed so obsessed with it, and some Shakespeare. He polished his French, a bit rusty from Eton, and he went to lectures, but he was an outdoorsman, and Cambridge had little to offer in that regard. In his third year his father let him bring Gawain, mainly because the hound was reaching the end of his very noble life. A few tosses of the ball tired him, but he was still as loyal as ever, and it was good to have another warm body in his bed, though Gawain was no longer the one he preferred. The first two years had passed easily enough, but until his engagement he was restless, and until Georgie officially came to lodge near Cambridge, even more restless. His days were consumed in figuring ways to see her, supervised or not.

George Wickham lectured him at every chance about responsibility. At first he was just annoyed, but there had to be a reason, and in his frustration Geoffrey had time to think. George might have all of the benefits of female company in the strictest sense, but not true companionship. Nor was he likely to have it soon, as he was a Fellow and aiming for a doctor's license, so he could be sitting in the libraries for almost a decade if he took his time about it.

He's lonely, Geoffrey mused. Of course, George always had been. They all knew it, but they didn't talk about it, or at least didn't talk about the real reasons for it, beyond being shy. Even Frederick knew better; one of the first times Geoffrey actually heard Frederick apologize for something was at his birthday party. Georgie was right; George needed a good woman, and he was not likely to have one unless he fell hopelessly in love, and he was not the type to do so. Father hadn't married until he was nine and twenty – maybe there was a reason for that. It was by no means unusual, but Uncle Bingley had been younger than that. Perhaps someday, Geoffrey and Georgie would conspire to give their poor cousin a hand, or someone else would take the lead on that, but he certainly needed it.

He saw Georgie off and on for the next few weeks, but the calls were mainly social. She was increasingly nervous about the wedding, and it was only April! What would she be like in July?

Or maybe she was hearing too many speeches about it like he was. At least she was away from home and her mother and aunt and sister. She had that. They had a chance for a more intimate arrangement, but she said she just wanted to be held. He prepared himself for the worst, but she relaxed in his arms and they finally made love, as he was told to call it around the fairer sex. It was a weird sort of term, but he was fine with that.

~~~

Geoffrey was studying (legitimately) to prepare a paper when, somehow, she had managed her way into the quad – she had a gown and a wig on – and practically dragged him into a corner. Her eyes were red from tears. She just stared at him, as if assessing him, and didn't speak.

"What is it? Georgie?" he begged. "What happened?"

She stared at the ground before his feet. "Do I have to say it?" Her voice was a hoarse whisper. "Please don't make me say it."

He looked at her posture, so frightened. He suddenly understood. "Did you see a doctor?"

"I live with a doctor."

"Are you sick?"

"I was ignoring it. But then I fell."

"You fell," he said. "Are you all right?"

"I'm fine. I was teaching Danny about posture, and it was so simple – but I tipped right over. At first I was just embarrassed, but then I was sick. And I never fall. I was just so dizzy –" She still couldn't look at him. "I knew something was wrong."

479

"Georgiana," he said, cupping his hands around her cheeks and raising her eyes to meet his. "Are you carrying my child?"

She nodded. "I'm so sorry –"

He couldn't, upon retrospection, describe his feelings at that moment. There were so many of them, most unexpected. "Georgie," he said, pulling her into his arms, "we're going to be married, and we're going to have a child. There is *nothing* to be sorry about."

"I didn't want this to happen," she said. Her voice was so muffled by her face buried in his robes that he barely heard her, but he felt her fear.

"It could not have been entirely unexpected." He laughed. "Despite all of the tremendous planning our family has been doing, we're going to be married of our own speed," Geoffrey kissed her head, her hair tickling his face. "You'll be my wife, and we can dispense with this nonsense of pretending otherwise."

"You'll have to tell your father."

"I love you. Though I do not relish the idea of doing it, you are fortunate to be the one person in the world I would gladly stand up to my father for." He wiped away her tears with his thumb. "I'm to London, then, for the license."

Her voice was still uneven. "Yes."

"I suppose I should leave as soon as possible – after I write the letters home." He scratched his head. "But – it's too much."

"It is." She said it much more seriously.

"I want to stay with you. I need a moment – I need more than a moment." A child. He was going to be married, and he was going to be a father. Just an hour before, he was merely an affianced undergraduate. "I want to be with you."

"We should probably –"

"What does it matter?" He laughed. "In a few ... days ... you're going to be my wife in a very respectable manner, and if you interpret it as damage, it's already done. So what should we do that does not involve being together?"

She could not properly answer him, so he took it as a yes. He knew no one was in the apartment except Reynolds, and he just gave him a particular nod of the head and the man made himself scarce.

Georgie was scared. She didn't have to say it, and he didn't have to ask. At first, she retracted from his touch, so subtly that she likely didn't intend it, but he was insistent. It wasn't so much as he wanted to ravish her as much as she needed to know that even though everything had changed, nothing had changed. She needed to know that before he went and did anything else.

"This is nice," she said. "Not worrying about it."

He lay beside her. "It is," he admitted. She was still tense; it was returning in the passing moments of no activity. He invited her with his arms to curl against him, nuzzling into the crook of his arm.

"I'm not ready," she said.

"You are."

"I'm good at fighting and upsetting my parents. I can't do ... lady things."

"Even in my limited experience, I'm quite sure that having a child is a different sphere than making fashionable conversation at a ball," he said. "You have never once failed at anything you truly cared to do. So my faith in you is assured."

That he was sure he was ready to be a father was not so true. His father and uncle had both taught him of the happenstance of fate, and it was best to accept it and continue on. Georgiana was with child, they would be married, and with God's help, he would be a father before Candlemas. Since he had no say in the matter, he felt little need to concern himself with those sorts of self-castigation. In the coming days, he would have little time for it. All he had was this moment, when it was just the two of them, with their new…addition, and no one else to intrude or interrupt or offer counsel. That was not time he wanted to waste.

The rest would just have to come later.

CHAPTER 27

The Second Lesson

Bingley was still reading the morning papers, but had retreated to his study when the dishes were put away, putting off work for the day, which involved many announcements. There was a knock at his door, and he bid them to enter. The door swung wide.

It was Darcy at the door, holding up a letter. "The strangest of correspondences has arrived today."

"Really?"

"Really," Darcy said, betraying no emotion. "It seems my son is to be married to your daughter within the week. I was under the assumption that the ceremony would not be until at least July."

"Also my assumption," Bingley said, "but it is not to be." He sighed. "I suppose – I shouldn't have entrusted the watch over my daughter's virtue to a blind man? Or at least learned the lesson the first time?"

Darcy could no longer hold back his smirk. "Perhaps."

485

"Caroline could offer to have the wedding at their manor. For convenience's sake."

"Nonsense. Both of the families hail from Derbyshire, and my son is the heir to Pemberley. He will be married in the church at Lambton as my father was –"

"– but you weren't –"

"– No, wait, I believe he was married in Kent." Darcy frowned. "No matter. There's no harm done delaying it another week to have it here. I'm sure Professor Maddox could write some sort of physician's note for the absences of three students –"

"He does owe us."

"Yes, he does," Darcy said, sitting down in the chair at last. "How did Mrs. Bingley take it? Is she sewing the wedding dress as we speak?"

"Nonsense. She had it ready by December." Bingley crossed his arms. "The flowers aren't all ready yet. That's a shame, but there's nothing to speed *those* along. Unlike everything else, apparently."

Darcy paused. "We should be angrier, should we not?"

"I suppose we've grown complacent in our old age."

"Maybe you have," Darcy said. "I still intend to have Geoffrey explain himself at length to his humiliation as punishment for this."

"Those are details you may not want to know." But as Darcy dropped the letter on the table, it finally hit him. Marriage would have to be pressing not because they'd run off to Gretna Green, or because Geoffrey was now one and twenty and could do as he pleased, knowing full well his Uncle Bingley would give his consent to the marriage even if his father wouldn't, but because Georgiana was increasing, and the baby could not be born too early.

The baby. His daughter, with child. His daughter, carrying his grandchild, forcibly, because of the man who couldn't hold himself back.

Darcy was playing with the fireplace poker and the ashes from the previous night. "I was wondering when you would see the facts before you."

"She must come to Derbyshire," Bingley said. "It must happen at Pemberley. Or Chatton House. Or the church. But she has to be here –" She had to be here so he could give away *his* baby to another man. He choked. He could barely speak. "How can you be so calm about this?"

"Because," Darcy said, "I have already thoroughly defined the plan in which I intend to make my son suffer for this massive breach of propriety." He added, "Would you like to be part of it?"

Numb, he nodded. "Do tell."

487

~~~

Darcy's behavior while informing Bingley was unnatural for him; he was practically performing, and the demand for the little play to soften the blow of the news was by the only person who could ask that of him.

But an hour earlier, the Darcy family breakfast had been interrupted by a courier from Geoffrey. Though it was addressed to Darcy, when he excused himself to read it, Elizabeth decided it was best to follow him. "Papa," she said respectfully to her father, leaving him at the table with his granddaughters. If it was nothing, all the better. Geoffrey wrote them every once in a while, but never by special courier.

Her husband did not stop her from intruding on his privacy. He was consumed in the letter. He paced as he read it, his face visibly tensing and his jaw clenching. Then, with a suppressing calm, he said, "He's gone to London for the license."

He handed the letter to her. It was quite short, only a few lines (Geoffrey was probably embarrassed to say more) explaining that the marriage could no longer be put off and they should prepare for an immediate ceremony as soon as he returned from London. Her son gave his apologies at putting them out but added that he loved Georgiana, and despite "everything" (as he put it), he could not be happier.

Of course, it had been nonsense to send Georgie to Chesterton. No matter how tight the thumb pressed over her to keep her in place by Caroline, the girl was simply a master of doing what she wanted when she wanted to. Elizabeth had not been so brazen in her engagement, though perhaps if she already knew the pleasures of the marital bed and was subjected to half a year's wait, she might have contemplated some walks around the paths behind Longbourn where very little walking was done. She grinned at the idea, to which Darcy demanded, "What?"

"Nothing. I was just contemplating what could have been," she said, "had we been forced to wait ten months instead of three weeks to be married."

"That hardly excuses –"

"When did you grow so cold?"

He stammered, "I've always been cold."

"Yes, I know, dearest, but now it seems you are also incapable of remembering that you were once a headstrong, sometimes foolish man. And that you still are, but you were once a lovesick fool as well."

"We did not –" He straightened himself as he digested her words. "You think I'm not in love with you because I will not tolerate rash behavior from our son?"

"I did not say that at all. I would not have laid my blessing upon it had they asked," she said, "but I cannot say, if I were them, I would have done so much better, given the oppressive circumstances. And if you insist that you would have, then you've no memory of our engagement."

Darcy looked out the window, but his non-answer confirmed that his memory was in fact intact.

"Our son is getting married," she said, holding the letter with trembling hands. "To our niece, I might add, a young lady of good breeding with a suitable dowry, whom he loves beyond all reason. And he is doing it within the week." She cried out, not in sadness, but in joy. "It's too soon."

"Yes," he said, but not for the same reasons. Still, Darcy was softening. He took Elizabeth into his arms as she ran to him.

"You would feel this way if it were Anne," she said. She thought she could even feel his heart skip at the idea. "Promise me you'll let Bingley down easily. None of this grave presentation."

"Only if you tell Mrs. Bingley."

She kissed him on the cheek. "Deal."

~~~

They decided that everyone at Pemberley could wait – the Bingleys had to be told about their daughter's condition. Darcy went off to tell Bingley, and Jane rolled her eyes at the news and said, "Well, of course."

"Jane."

"My daughter is not a wanton woman … I assume," Jane said. "She is, however, highly adept at getting what she wants, which is why I had the dress sewn before Christmas."

"Jane!"

Her sister gave her a knowing smile, and they hugged. "I am worried about her."

"I know," Elizabeth said.

"When she was younger, before it was so obvious about Geoffrey – that she wouldn't –" She stumbled with her needlework. "Now she'll settle down. Now she has someone. She was such a lonely child. And now –" She began to cry, and she just let the tears roll down her cheeks. There was no use fighting them. "Now she'll finally be happy." If Geoffrey had sent the letter, Georgiana's could not be far behind. "There's so much to do. She's not even here! But the flowers are coming in, at least."

"The what?"

"The flowers. Charles is positively obsessed with this Indian wedding he once saw, and said it was beautiful with all the flowers. He even brought home seeds and planted them right away."

Elizabeth smiled. "It sounds like something he would do."

"Oh Lizzy, I must see her. Though I suppose, perhaps, I should tell the rest of my family."

"It might be prudent."

Darcy entered. "Mrs. Bingley." He turned to his wife. "I believe we must be off to tell our daughters of the news. The staff of Pemberley would appreciate knowing they are hosting a wedding feast with some advance."

Bingley followed him. "Mrs. Darcy. Jane, dear." He kissed his wife, and there were congratulations all around. Yes, the circumstances could be better, but this was a wedding of *their children*. Elizabeth and Darcy invited them for dinner, and they left to return to Pemberley.

While Darcy arranged for his daughters to be summoned to the study, Elizabeth found her father, in the same chair he always was in, reading by the fire. He liked a roaring fire, even during a mild day. "Papa," she said, "Geoffrey's to be married."

"Of that I am aware," Mr. Bennet said, taking the pipe out of his mouth. "Though you look as though it is a more imminent event than I assumed it was. Was I mistaken?"

"Things have changed."

"Well." Mr. Bennet paused and smiled and let his daughter kneel next to him like she used to and kiss his hand. "I suppose I'm to see yet another thing I never thought I would see – my grandchildren, married. Your mother would be so pleased."

"I'm sure she's watching over us," she assured him. He mentioned her mother more and more often now, what she would have liked and disliked.

"I do hope so, my dear Lizzy. She would truly hate to miss a wedding."

She kissed him on his head and excused herself to join her husband in the study, where her daughters were waiting. They took the explanation with a stunned silence, which Cassandra broke to say, "*Why* can't they wait?"

"Because sometimes it isn't possible," Darcy said in the tone he used to end a line of questioning.

"Can we go to the ceremony?" Sarah asked.

"Of course," Elizabeth responded. "Geoffrey would be upset if his sisters weren't there."

"We don't have a proper present," Anne said.

"Whatever you find in Lambton will be fine," Elizabeth said. She was sure it was the last thing on Geoffrey's mind.

The girls were dismissed and Mrs. Annesley called in.

"Our son is to be married, likely within the week, and if at all possible, the wedding breakfast will be held here," Darcy said. "Please alert the staff. Mrs. Darcy will help you make further arrangements."

She nodded. "Yes, Master Darcy. Mrs. Darcy." She very politely hid most of her shock and went about her business.

"I think she took it well."

"The butchers of Lambton will have a far more visible reaction," he said.

~~~

Georgiana arrived the next day, very late in the afternoon, in a carriage with Emily and Sir and Lady Daniel Maddox. She ran to her mother's awaiting arms, already sobbing. "I'm sorry. I'm so sorry."

"Shhh," her mother said. "We're not angry. You're getting married. It's a wonderful thing."

But Georgie was hysterical, and Jane nodded to her husband and took her inside as the Maddoxes climbed out of the carriage, and Dr. Maddox took his wife's arm. "Mr. Bingley."

"Dr. Maddox. Caroline. Miss Maddox."

"Uncle Bingley," Emily curtseyed prettily and followed her cousin inside so the 'adults' could talk.

"How is my daughter?"

"Four weeks along, we think. Or, she is fairly sure," the doctor said.

"She's emotional," Caroline told him. "More than usual, I mean."

Bingley debated about being the protective father and scowling at his sister but decided against it. "She cried the whole way?"

"Only started when we reached Derbyshire. She is terrified of your reaction."

"You seem to have taken it well," Caroline said.

"Our apologies, of course. We did try –"

Bingley put his hand up. "While I'm sure you did everything in your power to protect your niece, she is a knight. Or so I hear."

"Yes," Dr. Maddox smiled. "She is a little ill, more than she'll admit, but mainly she's had a bit of a fight over it." He coughed. "Geoffrey was very apologetic."

"I'm sure he was." This he was a bit sterner about. "We've decided on his punishment, but we might require your aid, Dr. Maddox."

"I'm not much of a fighter."

He couldn't help but grin. "Nothing of the sort, I assure you."

~~~

Georgie was in no condition to face her brother and sister. She only gave them a weak smile before Jane shooed them away and helped her daughter into her chambers. Georgie suddenly went pale, and the maids ran to bring her a chair and tea. Jane ordered ginger for it.

"I fouled it up," Georgiana said in a whimper. "I ruined everything."

"You did nothing wrong," Jane said. She was about to explain how the responsibility was truly solely Geoffrey's, but she didn't have the chance before her daughter started speaking again.

"I'm not ready. I can't do this. Mama, I can't. I don't know how, I can't. I just –" She looked up, her eyes saying everything. *I'm scared.* "I'm not ready."

"Darling, we don't get the choice," Jane said, taking a seat on the ottoman across from her. She held Georgie's hand, which was shaking. "When I married your father, I thought I wasn't ready. I had months to think on it. It was almost a year before I even became pregnant, and still, I was sure I was not ready. I thought I was so silly. A married woman, not ready to have children? I thought myself to already be a terrible wife and parent for just thinking it. Why did it not come naturally? And do you know what your father did?" Of course, Georgie didn't. She shook her head. Jane continued, "He held me and told me it was going to be all right, with little authority on the subject. I think he was as terrified as I was. But then I talked to Lizzy, and she said the same thing. She was frightened, her husband was frightened, but of course he wouldn't say it. We were all pretending to not be scared, and we were scared that everyone else would find out, all four of us. Your father made a bet with your Uncle Darcy just to relieve the tension, and you were born first and your father won five pounds. Darcy was flummoxed, but two weeks later he had other concerns, and he was the happiest I'd ever seen him." She looked into Georgie's eyes. "You used to smile so much as an infant. You loved stuffing your hands in your mouth. When your teeth came in, you bit yourself constantly and always were somehow surprised at the same outcome." This, at least, got a bit of a smile out of her daughter. "When I was in my last months with Charles and Eliza, we didn't know about both of them and I just thought I was a whale, and you loved crawling on top of me. I couldn't get you off. I thought it was the most wonderful time of my life."

"Thought?"

"Yes," Jane said, "but it turns out it is only a very close second to seeing a daughter marry."

~~~

It was a while before Bingley dared to approach his daughter's chambers, much less enter. He parked himself on a stool outside the door and waited for Jane to emerge.

"She's shaken, but it will pass," she said. "She told me about Geoffrey's reassurances."

"What did he say?"

"That he would stand up to even his father's disapproval for her sake," she said. "He was not upset in the least. She couldn't believe it."

Bingley said nothing.

"He'll be good for her. A proper husband." She added, "We've nothing to worry about."

"Then why is my daughter crying?"

She sighed. "I suppose she finally found a situation where hitting things is not the answer, and therefore she has no idea what to do."

CHAPTER 28

The Groom Errant

Slowly the relatives began to trickle in. First, Charles Bingley the younger and Frederick returned from Cambridge, completing the Maddox and Bingley clans, and finally George, his head still in his books. Brian and Nadezhda were faster than anyone else from London. The Bertrands came, and apparently Geoffrey had written an invitation to the Bradleys, as he wanted to include Isabel Wickham. The Townsends of Netherfield had not been this far north in a while, at this time of the year, but they managed.

Fortunately, Grégoire had left London previously to go to Scotland, where his wife and son had joined him, so they were traveling south with the Kincaids. Reynolds, who did not accompany Geoffrey to London, explained that the list was quite comprehensive. Unfortunately, it did not seem to include the groom, who was busy securing a license.

The next carriage at the Bingley house was not Geoffrey, as expected, but another surprise. Mr. Bingley was there to greet him. "Mr. Hurst."

The widower Hurst, who lived in Wales, had come a great distance to see his niece married. "Charles. It has been a while, hasn't it?"

"I'm rarely in Wales."

"And I'm rarely in India or China or wherever you go." They shook. "Where is my niece?" Georgiana Louisa Bingley had been named after her Aunt Hurst, and he was quite fond of her.

"I would guess at the moment she is being attended by many well-meaning relatives, or, more likely, running from them. She'll be happy to see you."

"We're not having an Indian wedding, are we?"

"Of course not. We need liquor, and the Mughals preach temperance."

Mr. Hurst, older and even fatter now, could only walk with a cane, but he still showed his good humor and slapped Bingley very hard on the back. "Thank God for that!" He turned to walk up the front steps and passed a man he did not recognize. "Now sir, I must ask you two questions: Do you speak English, and what country are you from?"

"Yes, sir, and China," Liu Xiao said, and bowed.

"Goodness."

"This is Ambassador Xiao," Bingley said. "Mr. Xiao, this is my brother-in-law, Mr. Hurst. He was married to my sister Louisa. The ambassador has offered to help with the flowers."

"The flowers?"

~~~

"Why are we doing this?" Brian said, kneeling in the dirt with his kimono sleeves tied up, clipping at the stems of thousands and thousands of tiny flowers. They were still in the 'red' section. The servants were on the other end, in the green section. There simply were not enough of them to handle the job.

"Because it's Georgie's wedding," his wife, similarly attired, said.

"She didn't say anything about flowers."

"Mr. Bingley did, and you listened to him."

"He had those stupid sad eyes on. Please, please won't you do this for me? I'm a sucker for it." Brian looked up. "Hello, Danny."

Dr. Maddox was standing on the grass. "Am I trampling on anything important?"

"Not unless you go about two feet forward, no. Then it will be my wife and I'll have to kill you."

"Dr. Maddox," Nadezhda rose.

He bowed. "Your Highness." His head was often slumped, as if he lacked a reason to hold it up. "It does smell like flowers."

501

"It should. He's been growing them since India," Brian said.

"Where is he intending to put them, exactly? I don't recall that the church is very large."

"How should I know? Maybe he'll set up a tub and we'll bathe in them."

"Stop complaining," Nadezhda said, and turned to the doctor. "The heat makes him grumpy."

"Like an infant," Dr. Maddox said.

"I am armed, you know."

"You'd never hit a man with glasses."

"They're cosmetic."

"Brotherly love," Nadezhda said. "Truly a wondrous thing."

~~~

"It's going to look so bare," Georgie said, staring out her window at the workers in the little field.

Jane shook her head. She could hardly believe that the flowerbed was at the top of Georgie's list of concerns. She was probably trying to distract herself until Geoffrey returned. Then there wouldn't be any time for worrying about the garden she never cared a whit about before.

"Where does Papa think he's going to put them?" Eliza said as she sorted through all of the ribbons with Anne. Georgie seemed content to leave those decisions to them.

"At Pemberley, I suppose," Anne answered. "For the luncheon."

"I do hope he has informed *your* Papa," Elizabeth said to her daughter as she entered. "Or at least someone at Pemberley."

Georgie said nothing. Jane had watched her moods swing more than usual, which could easily be simple nerves or that on top of the strain of increasing. She was ill in the mornings, and sometimes in the afternoons, but she was remarkably stoic about it, at least in front of her mother. She passed on the scones that were offered to her and took only the tea, in which she showed little interest.

"Miss, the seamstress is here," her maid announced, and Georgie frowned.

"You'd best have it over with," Jane said, "or Geoffrey will come and you won't be able to see him because you'll be stuck full of pins."

That was enough incentive for Georgie.

~~~

The full party of guests was not quite complete when the lone bachelor strode in, still walking unsteadily from many hours on a horse, looking haggard from the road. A host of servants

503

nearly smothered him with their attendance as his coat and hat were removed, his walking stick taken away, and his bags removed but for one, a satchel of documents that he would not relinquish. He barely had time to collect himself before facing the master of Pemberley.

"Father," he bowed. There was genuine fear in his eyes; Darcy couldn't help but feel some pangs of sympathy. Geoffrey had done wrong, but had done his best to tend to it in every way possible, and he looked it. He had whiskers and a layer of dust on him.

Darcy did not wait for Geoffrey to begin explaining himself. He did not need to say it, and Darcy did not need to hear details. Instead he embraced his son, who simply looked at him with utter confusion. "It's good to have you home." He released him and smiled. "Your mother is at Chatton House, and before you ask, it is not your place to intrude on that brood of women. Not looking like that, at least."

Geoffrey managed a smile. "I got the license."

"So I gathered. Then we are just awaiting the Kincaids and the Bellamonts."

Geoffrey looked overwhelmed. "Everyone else is here?"

"I suppose with more planning, the guest list would have been a bit wider, but everyone important is here. Now, you should hurry up the stairs and make yourself look proper before your loving relatives rush you. Before my wedding, I couldn't get a moment's peace." He let his son start up the stairs. "Oh, and Geoffrey? Try to catch a nap if you can. You should be ready for tonight."

That statement his son didn't even dare to question; he just darted up the stairs like a madman.

~~~

When Elizabeth returned from Chatton House to get ready for supper, she was not pleased to learn her son was soundly asleep and to be left undisturbed. She could not resist the urge to peak into his room, letting light fall in the darkened room with the shades drawn, where he slept limp like a rag doll on his stomach, his head to the side. Gawain had been brought home by Charles and Frederick as a sort of gift to Geoffrey and the hound could no longer climb up on the bed himself, so Geoffrey must have lifted him up, because he was curled up beside him.

She was lucky. Geoffrey would always be her son, even if he lived elsewhere. He would always be Geoffrey Darcy, and she would never give him away. He might go away for a while, but he would always come home to Pemberley. Jane could not say the same thing of her daughter.

She shut the door as she heard Darcy approaching. "He grew up so fast."

"He's one and twenty."

"He's marrying."

This, Darcy could not contradict. "My sister's carriage was spotted. We should greet them."

"I suppose we should." She forced herself away from the door and took her husband's arm as they descended the stairs to meet the caravan that was the Kincaids with their two children and the Bellamonts.

"Brother!" Georgiana Kincaid (née Darcy) could not resist the urge to hug him.

"Aunt Darcy!" shouted the young Viscount Kincaid and Patrick Bellamont in tandem. Aunt Darcy was the aunt who had unfortunately decided to give them treats when they were young for good behavior, but they'd failed to connect it to the good behavior and therefore ran to her whenever they saw her.

"Oi wus gran' al' de way 'ere!" Patrick said.

"Aunt, aam sae guttin'. Ah barely hud anythin' oan th' road!" Robert said.

"Yer wee liars. Yer both 'ad galore," Caitlin said as she stepped in, and there were embraces all around.

"We did feed them," Lord Kincaid said very insistently, and the boys were dragged off to the nursery, and Elizabeth got to sit with her youngest niece before it was time for her nap.

"So the wedding is –"

"Tomorrow would be best," Darcy said, "but I suppose it can wait another day to give the cooks some preparation time. Bingley has all kinds of things he wants to bring over, apparently."

"What kind of things?" Grégoire asked.

"How should I know? I'll ask more specific questions when *I'm* the one giving a daughter away," he replied.

~~~

When Geoffrey woke, Reynolds was ready and quick to understand that Geoffrey wanted everything in his appearance to be absolutely perfect for dinner, when he would see his bride for the first time in days. Reynolds was still making the last adjustments when there was a knock at the door. "Come."

George Wickham entered. "The errant groom returns."

"George."

George raised his glass to him.

"When is the wedding?"

"The plan is the day after tomorrow. The staff needs a bit more time. The heir to Pemberley must be married in style."

"How is she?"

"I've not seen her, but I hear she is well and being assaulted by cousins and aunts with all kinds of advice. Speaking of which ..."

"George, save it."

"We were told you would be occupied tonight, but tomorrow night, we'll have some time and Frederick and I can give you embarrassing advice in front of Charles about what in the world to do with his sister."

Geoffrey smirked. "As if you would know."

~~~

After avoiding the torrent of relatives when he first arrived, Geoffrey now had to face them all as the Bingleys and Maddoxes arrived with the party being hosted at Chatton House and, finally, Georgiana. He had no interest in anyone else, or having anyone else around for this moment in time, but it was not to be. He could only kiss her hand. "Miss Bingley."

"Mr. Darcy." She looked better than she had been when he left Cambridge, but she was pale.

"It's good to see you," he said.

"I would hope so."

So she had retained some of her good humor, if one would call it that. "Two days." In two days, she would be his. It seemed so very far away, and yet, they would manage. "How are you feeling?"

"Sick of that question."

"Better, then."

She gave him a little smile. It helped through the long meal, when they had little chance to speak to each other and none of it in any privacy. Getting some privacy was the only thing on their minds, and it seemed as though there would be none of it. There was not much entertainment after supper, as herding the children around and getting the right people back to the right place was enough work that it hardly left any time. They barely got to say good-bye to each other before Geoffrey was given a glass of wine and dragged into the drawing room. He had been drinking fairly steadily during the dinner to make it pass, but it was no wine party.

It was late, he realized. The others were gone. The fire was lit, and his father, Uncle Bingley, Dr. Maddox, and Mr. Maddox gathered around him.

"If we're going to do this, I'm going to have a drink," Brian announced and opened up a new bottle of port. "Or a few."

"Do what?" Geoffrey asked. His father and Uncle Bingley stood over him.

"Geoffrey," his father said, "you are about to enter the very sacred and noble institution of marriage. Therefore, we think it best that you be educated in it the same way your uncle and I were – forcibly."

"That was horrible, wasn't it?" Bingley said.

"I never wanted to know so much about the Hursts' bedroom antics," his father said. "Still, Mr. Hurst insisted that I, the young bachelor, know all of the details of the marriage bed. As if I didn't already."

"It was one girl!" Uncle Bingley said, taking a proffered drink from Brian.

"You weren't there the term I lived with Wickham," Darcy said.

"Don't be ridiculous. Your middle year was your worst," Dr. Maddox said. He was the only one sitting.

"How do you know?" Bingley asked.

"Austria," he replied. "There are only so many ways to pass the time. I probably know more than you do, Mr. Bingley. I know all about that time –"

"*We're not talking about that*," Darcy snarled before Bingley could say anything.

"Darcy will kill you," Bingley said.

"He's threatened such," Dr. Maddox said.

Either Geoffrey was very drunk or not drunk enough. "Are you all talking about what I think you are? Because there's no need –"

"We are, and you're going to sit and listen to it. Maybe if you'd made it to the altar in the traditional way –"

"Darcy, please. No gentleman goes to the altar without something in their history," Brian said, to which Bingley coughed and took a moment to right himself again, having swallowed badly. "Oh God. Really, Charles?"

"Give the man a break. He was five and twenty," Darcy said.

"*I* wasn't a virgin at five and twenty," Dr. Maddox said.

"When did you have time? You were doing double terms in France!"

Dr. Maddox grinned. "I found time. Granted, it was nothing compared to my honeymoon. I'd never seen so little of a city I came to visit."

"Doctor!" Bingley shouted. "That's my sister!"

"And my wife," the doctor countered. "Oh, this should be informational. Geoffrey, should you ever be so unfortunate as to lose the remainder of your hearing –"

"God forbid," Geoffrey breathed.

"– you will find your other senses much enhanced. Which, I will say, will give a whole new life to your bedroom. If I'd gone blind any earlier, we'd surely have more children by now."

Geoffrey could not possibly sink any lower into his seat.

"This was perhaps not information I wanted to know, Maddox," his father growled.

"Well this was your bloody idea, what do you expect?" Brian said. "Not that I was particularly interested in that fact, either. Thanks, Danny."

"Glad to be of service."

"Can we stop talking about my sister now?" Bingley demanded.

"We could have invited Mr. Hurst," Darcy replied.

"Either sister!"

"Can I go?" Geoffrey begged.

"No. You're not properly embarrassed."

"Since Bingley here was apparently as pure as fresh snow and Darcy's sordid tale is old news, I'll add something, I suppose," Brian said, and knocked back another glass after clinking it with Darcy's. "I once paid a prostitute to pretend we had sex."

"Why in the world would you do that?"

"Technically, my father-in-law paid her. What a bachelor party that was." Brian shook his head. "I was cup shot on vodka, and the count essentially tosses me in this room with a veiled dancer; wanted to test my virility. As much as my virility is very intact, I assure you, I had no inclinations to betray my lovely fiancée, so I gave the girl a tip to scream in ecstasy occasionally as we told stories for a few hours. I think we ended up playing cards."

"I'm sure that was the only reason," Dr. Maddox said skeptically.

"I don't need your insults, Danny. You're in dangerous territory. Remember that nurse you really liked but I had to dismiss one day and I wouldn't give you the reason?"

"Miss Henderson. Why, what did – Oh my God."

"Relax. Nothing came of it, and she got a nice settlement. Besides, it was mutual."

"That was Miss Henderson! She changed my linens!"

"That wasn't the only thing she changed." Brian grinned. "Darcy? You all right?"

Geoffrey turned to his father, who had collapsed in the chair to his right. His father's face was flushed from the port, and Geoffrey was shocked—Mr. Darcy never drank. He came out of his trance to say, "Geoffrey was conceived on the desk of Bingley's study in Netherfield."

"*What?*" Geoffrey and Bingley said in concert.

"Well, we're not entirely sure, but it's most likely," Darcy said calmly, his speech a little slurred. "Anne was in the little villa we had outside Rome. Lovely wines there. I think Sarah and Cassandra were both somewhere in Pemberley."

"My desk!"

"Smashing job." Brian raised his glass to Darcy, who raised his in return.

"Smashing is what he'll be doing to that desk, I think," Dr. Maddox said with a chuckle.

"*My desk! Darcy, you bastard!*"

"And of course, the evening must at some point steer towards Bingley threatening Darcy's life. He never goes through with it, but it always goes that way."

"It does go that way, does it not? I think he punched him once." Dr. Maddox said.

"When? Where was I and why did I miss it?"

"You were stabbed in the chest," Dr. Maddox said, "and we were all smashed with Lord Kincaid. To celebrate our victory."

"We should have let him come. He could have told us some wonderful stories about his life as a married man," Bingley said directly to Darcy.

Geoffrey looked at his father, who swallowed away another glass and said. "That's my sister, man."

"I know very well who she is. You wanted me to marry her."

"I did not. That was Caroline's idea."

"Father," Geoffrey interrupted. "I am embarrassed enough, I assure you. May I please go?"

"You should be careful, Darcy," Brian said. "He might start telling us things about your nephews."

"Posh. Charles never dates, George sees a whore every week, and my son's been chasing around that Head's daughter. Fortunately, he managed to select the daughter of a Head of a different college. What's there to say?" Dr. Maddox said.

"Wait," Darcy said. "George Wickham?"

"Yes."

"With whores?"

"He only has one, to my knowledge. Per location."

To which Darcy merely raised his eyebrows and said, "I suppose George Wickham has a little Wickham in him after all."

He was saying that because he was drunk. Geoffrey had never seen his father like this. He didn't want to see his father like this and tried to get his attention unsuccessfully.

"I wish my father had been around for my engagement," his father moaned, not listening to Geoffrey's pleas at all.

"He might have told you about your bastard brothers," Bingley said, still fuming.

"He should have told me that ... a long time ago. Could have avoided Ramsgate. Oh my God, Ramsgate!"

"What is he talking about?" Brian asked.

"You don't want to know," Bingley said.

"I do!"

"You don't," Darcy said. "Oh God!" He shook his head. "Where were we?"

"Mr. Darcy is marrying Miss Bingley," Dr. Maddox offered.

"Yes, yes. Who would have thought? The little shrew set her cap on me thirty years ago."

Now it was Dr. Maddox's turn to be offended. "Little shrew?"

"She certainly isn't little," Uncle Bingley said. It was true; Lady Maddox was the tallest of the women in the family. "But she was acting a bit of a shrew. Oh, and how she used to talk of Elizabeth before you married. And after you married! Why do you think we ran all the way to Derbyshire?"

"To get away from Mrs. Bennet," Darcy said.

"That, too."

Geoffrey took another drink. If it served to wipe this night from his memory, so much the better.

His father leaned over, brandy on his breath, and whispered in Geoffrey's ear, "So now you know what your foolish behavior has gotten you into. And with a wild woman, no less."

"Hey!" Bingley said from his chair, as he could no longer stand.

"Be careful, Geoffrey," Brian said. "I heard she bites. But you probably already know that."

"My daughter. Do I have to remind you that this is –"

"Your daughter, yes, Charles, we know. We're very aware. That said, she's mad and we love her all the more for it," Dr. Maddox said. "And she is to be mistress of Pemberley."

"Oh God," Geoffrey's father moaned. "What is the item they use to make the walls thicker?"

Geoffrey was seriously wondering if he could possibly bribe Uncle Brian to take his place as his father grew increasingly drunk so he could escape. He looked grimly at his Uncle Bingley for help, but his uncle just responded, "This is what you get ... get for getting my daughter with child!"

Brian broke out into hysterical laughter, and eventually Dr. Maddox joined him. Geoffrey looked to his father, who was staring very intently at the empty cup but seemed unable to focus on it. Geoffrey stood and said, "I'll be going, then."

He only took a step before his father grabbed his arm and clutched it tightly, probably tighter than he meant to. "Don't use a desk."

"What?"

"No matter how desperate you get, it's not comfortable. Especially if there are still papers and tablets on it. Your mother nearly ruined her dress. We were worried we would have to explain a suspicious ink stain. Don't do it."

He blushed harder. Apparently it was possible. "I will keep that in mind."

"Good. Go ... go with God, my son."

"He can't go! He has to explain himself! Or I have to explain myself. I can't remember," Uncle Bingley moaned.

Stuck in place, Geoffrey was assessing his options when the door opened. Thankfully, it was only Mr. Bennet. "Grandfather Bennet, thank God."

"Who are these people bothering my grandson?" Mr. Bennet said. "I won't stand for it. Geoffrey, come with me."

At last! He escaped the room, but only after Brian slapped him so hard on the back he almost lost his balance.

"Once again, I am a groom's savior," Mr. Bennet said.

"That you are, Grandfather."

"You'd best behave yourself when your children are to be married, because I won't be there to save them from you," he said with a twinkle in his eye. "Up to bed with you, young man! You've a long day tomorrow."

To that he did not disagree. "Good night, Grandfather." After a bow, he ran up the stairs as fast as his legs could still take him and into his room, behind a safely-locked door.

CHAPTER 29

This is the Wedding Chapter

The earliest riser opened the day with incantations to a greater God, all alone in the Pemberley chapel. It was still night to the rest of the world, and he lit the candles before he began, even though he had the prayers memorized. Grégoire Darcy-Bellamont was nothing if not precise.

He was also not unaware, despite the hour, of the guest. He finished Vigils and turned to his nephew, who rose. "Uncle Grégoire."

"George." He took a seat beside the very patient George Wickham. "What wakes you at what some would call an awful hour? Or did you not sleep?"

"I don't always sleep well," he admitted. "It is convenient for my studies."

"Yes, of course. Though I am sure your cousin appreciates you taking time from them for his wedding."

"I'm to be groomsman," he said, some hint of pride in his voice. "Charles gets to be godfather. We decided."

Grégoire nodded. "I am to understand that though the circumstances were different, Darcy stood up beside your father at his wedding."

"I didn't know that. Uncle Darcy's never mentioned it."

"Mrs. Darcy mentioned it once to me when I asked about your father."

George was silent. Grégoire didn't push him. George could lock himself up better than anyone. He chose when to speak. "I read a book on the lives of saints recently. It was in the library, a devotional from before the Dissolution. There were so many of them – mostly the early ones – who lived alone. In caves and whatnot."

"Saint Augustine. But he went on to found a monastic order of brothers. There are very few who lived truly alone their whole lives. I don't think they would have been saints if they did. All of them tended to the community in some great way."

"The wedding won't change everything," George said, taking a different tack. "They'll still be my cousins, and we'll still see each other. Maybe Georgie might even calm down, though I think perhaps not. Or perhaps I simply can't imagine her any other way." He went on, "It was inevitable, wasn't it? I was predicting it for years. And now it's happening. They marry, have children, I study for my license, see that my sister marries well. It's so simple."

"It does appear so, does it not? But maybe it isn't." Grégoire looked up at his anxious nephew, who was taller than him. "You've left out your own happiness."

"I like school. I have everything I need there."

"Then why are we having this conversation?"

George had no response at hand, nor did he attempt to formulate one.

"In the case of our more ascetic saints," Grégoire said, "the pattern is that they achieve some kind of connection with the divine in their solitude and then leave it, lesson having been learned, to share with others. Saint Augustine wrote his confessions. Saint Jerome translated the bible into Latin from Greek. Saint Francis wandered the woods before emerging to teach the values of poverty and charity. None of them were alone."

"I thought we were never alone. We always have the Lord."

"This is true, but a physical presence is always helpful. When I was cast out of my order, it was the first time I had ever felt truly alone. When my mother died, I had my brothers at the monastery surrounding me. When I left that monastery, it was to go with Darcy and Elizabeth. When I was lost in Bavaria, I had Sebald with me, and again my family found me. But when I returned to England no longer a monk, I was truly lost. The family did bring me cheer, but they were not the companionship I was seeking. I did not know its name until I met Caitlin." He added, "You will find someone."

"That's not what I meant."

"Because you do not desire it, or you think it impossible?"

George sighed. "For so many reasons. You can't understand it. You couldn't possibly understand –" He looked up to look away from his uncle. "Who would want me, anyway?"

"Apparently, both your father and your uncle were, at one point, very desirable bachelors, if for different reasons. And they had their own challenges. Your uncle overcame them and is a very happy man. Your father, I must believe, did what he was meant to do on this earth, and if one of those things was to help bring you and Isabel into the world, then I cannot find fault in him. I also know that when he died, he was not alone, nor did he express any wish to be."

"Women – they have expressed an interest. Even though I'm a Fellow. But I don't want it. Not now."

"Not now," Grégoire repeated. "The time will come, nephew. It is just that in the case of

Geoffrey and Miss Bingley, it could not be soon enough. But your time will come."

"How do you know?"

"Because I have asked God for so many little great-nieces and nephews," Grégoire said, "and I cannot expect them all to come from the Darcy side."

"*Uncle!*" George said, but laughed anyway.

~~~

It was to be a long day. Geoffrey Darcy was roused early to begin selecting his suit with Reynolds. He drank an excessive amount of coffee and had little time to nurse his hangover before he was summoned into his father's study, where both parents awaited him.

"Father. Mother. I apologize for the brevity, but I am very busy." Geoffrey realized as he said it that he came off as cross, but his stomach was upset from nerves, and he had little patience for anything that did not involve the woman who would be, in four and twenty hours, his wife. "Father, I can barely look at you after last night."

"What did you say to him?" his mother said, but Mr. Darcy of Pemberley did not give himself up too easily. He sat back in his chair and gave a little shrug.

"That is not the matter that concerns us," his father said. "And unless you do not wish a wedding gift, you should sit with your parents for a moment."

Geoffrey sat down very quickly. His father still said little (perhaps nursing a hangover of his own) and passed a paper across the table. Geoffrey unrolled it. It was the unsigned contract for a lease on a country house in Lancashire. Actually, one of the signatures was already filled in, the other empty.

"We thought your rooms at Pemberley might prove to be inadequate," his mother said.

It was not terribly far from Pemberley, perhaps a day's journey, but he did not recognize the places mentioned. "Have you seen it?"

"Yes," his father said. "We needed something to do while the Bingleys were busy gardening."

"Darcy!"

His father smiled at his mother but continued, "It would need some renovations if you decided to extend the lease past a year, but as it is, it is ready for living. It's a bit smaller than Netherfield and in a very remote area."

"The grounds are especially beautiful. And it is close to the shore."

Geoffrey was overwhelmed. He had thought about getting their own house, even discussed it a bit with Georgie, but never gone this far. "When will it be staffed and ready?"

"I would say ... in a day or two. Provided you want it."

In truth, he didn't care where he went with Georgiana as long as they were together and away from their family, but it seemed as though his parents were willing and even eager to see that he would be properly settled. He would have to return to school by the end of the month, but he could be in and out until he sat for the degree exam, and then he was free. Of course, he'd not seen the place, but it could truly be a shack for all he cared. "I should ask Georgie first."

"Then you will make a better husband than most men if you've already learned *that*," his father said.

"I am ... overwhelmed," Geoffrey said. "Thank you so much."

"We would not have it any other way," his mother said.

~~~

Georgiana Bingley was late in rising – or, more precisely, she was late in opening the door of her chamber to visitors. So it had been almost every day since her return, owing to her uneasy morning

527

stomach, and her maid tended to her until she was well enough to face the day.

As most of the wedding plans involving her directly were finished or could wait until the next morning, all Georgie had to do was pack. "The Darcys have something in mind," was all her mother would say.

Georgiana sipped her tea as she directed the servants. "Don't touch that," she said as they went for the red trunk. "That'll go later. Besides, it's already packed. And heavy." One more day and she would be done with all of this, and it would just be her and Geoffrey, if they could make it through the celebrations. It was all she wanted, and yet there were so many things standing in her way.

"Marm, your father is here."

She nodded and rose to curtsey as he entered. "Papa." He looked a little sleepy-eyed, like he had just risen despite the hour.

"I was supposed to be at Pemberley an hour ago," he said. "If the gazebo doesn't get set up now, it never will. I just wished to see you before I went."

"Papa," she said in a slightly scolding tone, "you're not destroying Pemberley for this wedding, are you?"

"Parts of the outside will be a little messy," he said. "Your uncle's forgiven me for worse." He kissed her on the cheek and left, bowing briefly to the people standing outside the door. "Jane. Your Highness."

Her mother and aunt entered. "The hairdresser is here."

"I'm to be married *tomorrow*."

"Nonetheless she might need a look today to generate some ideas," her mother said.

"Nothing involving wax," Georgie said. "I don't want to be burned again. And no wigs."

"No wigs," Nadezhda promised.

"Hopefully it won't come to that," her mother added.

Georgiana sighed and prepared herself for a long day.

~~~

"Patrick? Patrick, you get down from there! What if your mother sees you?"

Deciding that Uncle Bingley's demands were not encouraging enough, Geoffrey Darcy decided to take the lead while he was passing by and reached up to grab Patrick Bellamont, who had climbed up onto one of the wooden poles that made up a tent of red gauze and flowers. "Oof. Patrick, you're getting too heavy for this."

"You're not de 'eadbombadare av me," Patrick said as he was set down on the ground. "Me

ma said I can chucker whatever I want as long as I
don't 'urt meself."

Trying to pretend he'd understood that,
Geoffrey replied, "I won't have you hurt at my
wedding, no matter how many surgeons are
attending." He felt something drop on his head and
then in front of him. It was a bunch of tiny flowers,
matching in color to the gauze around the tent.

"Sorry," said the voice of Brian Maddox
somewhere up on the beams, which hardly made
up for Patrick laughing at him for being covered in
flowers. Well, laughing was better than climbing.

"Where's your mother?" he said to his
cousin. "I would be very interested in her
whereabouts at this time, Mr. Bellamont."

"She's at Chatton House," Uncle Bingley
answered before the boy had a chance, reappearing
from the other side of the tent flaps. "Doing ... well,
whatever it is women do the day before a wedding.
I've never been invited. What about you? I'd
imagine your schedule is packed."

"Father sent me to check that you hadn't
destroyed the front garden."

"Did he tell you to use that precise phrase?"
"Yes."
"He knows me too well. You can be off. All
we're doing is putting up a few tents." There were a
half dozen of them, all with different colors and

530

covered with bundles of correspondingly colored flowers.

"I will be sure to tell him," Geoffrey said. Lowering his voice, he asked, "How's Georgie?"

"Fine. And that's all you get from me. Now go."

Geoffrey smiled as he was shooed away.

~~~

The post arrived with letters of congratulations from those not in attendance and other friends Georgie hadn't even thought of or sent letters to. Lady Littlefield had just arrived and settled in when the package of letters came. "She must have read about your engagement in the paper," she said after Georgie inquired about one of their schoolmates from the seminary.

"And they all said I would never marry."

"They didn't *all* say that."

"Some of them said I would never find a man who would put up with me."

"Very few of them said that."

"To my face."

"Only one person did that."

Georgie smiled.

"What did they decide about your hair?"

"How should I know? The woman shrieked and ran out of the room." Georgie opened the next one. It was by far the largest and written in calligraphy, even though it was merely a congratulations. "Oh. How about that." She handed it off to Heather.

"I didn't know you got a message from the Crown when you married."

"Let's just say our family is well connected."

~~~

Dinner could not arrive quickly enough for the bride or the groom. The very last of the guests were arriving, including Lord Richard, Lady Anne, and Viscount Henry Fitzwilliam. The table at Chatton House was longer than anyone could ever remember it being while the Pemberley staff was preparing for the meal the next day.

It was hard for anyone to get a word in except to the people beside them, so Geoffrey was very glad that he was seated with Georgie on his side. Unfortunately, it was his right side (that part had been overlooked), but he spent most of the meal staring at her anyway, and everyone was willing to overlook his small breach of etiquette. "My parents have gifted us a house in Lancashire, if you want it."

"That's quite a wedding a gift."

"Unless you're not inclined to take it."

She smiled. "When can it be ready?"

"Tomorrow."

She smiled and looked at her food, which was mostly untouched. "Who's standing up with you?"

"George."

"Not Charles?"

"Charles is going to be godfather." He put his hand over hers. "George can be godfather of the next one."

"Next one? *Next one?*"

"What did you say?" George shouted from across the table.

"Something I should have thought about first," Geoffrey answered and looked down at his soup. Georgiana pecked him on the cheek, which showed him her shock had been feigned and raised his spirits considerably.

After many toasts and congratulations, Geoffrey was released to return to Pemberley. "One more day of this nonsense," he whispered to her before they parted. "I love you."

"I love you. And try to wear something nice. We're getting married tomorrow."

He kissed her and climbed into the carriage. Back at Pemberley, the rest of the boys (well, young men) were disappointed to learn that he did not in fact want to spend his last night as a bachelor soused. That didn't stop them from passing the wine around, but he just waved it off. "I'm still recovering from last night."

"What did they say to you?"

"Charles, pray they never do the same to you, because it's nothing you want to know."

Frederick raised his glass. "To taming the craziest woman in the kingdom. Hopefully. God help you if you fail."

"Your kind words are always appreciated, Mr. Maddox."

"My sister is not the craziest person in the kingdom," Charles said.

"Name one person."

"What?"

"Your other candidate for the admirable title," Frederick said.

Charles stumbled in his answer, as if he thought he had a name on his tongue, only to realize he had none. The silence that followed was broken by laughter that even Geoffrey and George felt compelled to join.

~~~

Georgiana woke not to illness, which usually didn't strike her until she attempted to rise from bed, but to the sensation of a weight on her stomach. She opened her eyes and was soon protecting her face with her hands from an invasion of even smaller ones. "Monkey – no. Not my face." She pulled him into a more comfortable embrace as he clung to her nightgown. "What are you doing here? Are you going to miss me?" Monkey chirped. "You're Papa's, so you have to stay here. Maybe you shall visit." He had soft fur, softer than a dog or a cat's. "Though I don't know where I'm going, precisely. Somewhere far enough away from all these people." Monkey howled. "Not *you*. You're not a person. Be glad for it."

The cock crowed again, and she sighed and pulled herself up into a sitting position. Her stomach reeled, but she sat motionless. Monkey put his tiny paws on her rumbling belly.

"I know. I don't much care for it either at the moment. If only it would behave." She swallowed very definitively. "This had better be a child, or else there might be something truly wrong with me."

This was not the morning to wait around for her system to calm itself, so she slowly put her legs over the bed and rang for her maid to draw the curtains. "Geoffrey, you are obliged to make this worth my time," she said as she grabbed the chamber pot.

Her mother did not politely wait for her to recover herself. She knocked several times and inquired after her until Georgie finally let her in. "Darling." Her mother was crying. Already.

Nonetheless, Georgiana accepted the embrace, however unsteady she still was on her feet. "Look at you. I don't know how we'll manage without you."

"I always thought I was more trouble than I was worth."

"Never," her mother said more seriously and started bringing in more servants as Georgiana went to bathe. When she was dry, she mindlessly went to brush out her hair, which was precisely all she had to do with it on an ordinary day. She still had the brush in hand when she reentered her chambers. They brought the box in for her to stand on as she was, more accurately, tied and sewn into her dress. Though the style was rather flowing, she breathed a sigh of relief that she was not yet showing.

"Monkey," her mother said, swatting him away from climbing on Georgie's dress. "No!"

"Mama, he's just going to miss me."

"He's a monkey, darling. I do not think the idea of marriage is within his comprehension."

"Maybe he just knows I'm leaving."

"Then he can express it in some way that does not involve your dress." But Monkey was already working on Jane's hem. "Or mine. Off!"

The seamstress finished with the lacing on the back, making Georgie wonder how she was to ever get out of it, short of destroying it (an option she would likely consider) or having Geoffrey do so. The very thought of that moment distracted her such that the seamstress had to scold her back to attention as she put silk gloves over her calloused hands and scarred arms.

"None of that," her mother said, taking the brush out of her hands. "Your father has a surprise for you."

She told the maid to call for the master of the house, who promptly entered carrying a box with a bundle of fabric over it. He stopped abruptly in the doorway, startled.

"Papa?"

Monkey climbed up on the leg of his very nice breeches, but he did not notice. "My goodness," was all he said. He set the box down and gave the bundle to the seamstress. "Now," he said, his voice wavering, "it has been a while, but I should remember, hopefully, how this goes..." He opened the box to reveal a set of Indian jewelry with sapphires set into the gold.

"Papa!" Even Georgie was overwhelmed. "You got that in India?"

"One for you and one for your sister, but don't tell her," he said. There were multiple bracelets for each arm and multiple necklaces for her neck to go with her locket necklace. "I'm not sure the vicar will approve of such heathen practices, but it will hold the veil in place," he said as he put a golden set of tiny linked chains on the top of her head, with one golden bead hanging down on her forehead. He took the veil from the seamstress. "Now – how in the world did this go?"

"I told you to practice on something," her mother said.

"I was busy. Here." He literally tossed it over her head. "I think it is supposed to wrap around – Georgie, hold you head still – No, not like that – Damnit, how did it go? If Brian – well, I suppose we shouldn't call Brian in here just yet."

"Charles..."

"I – there!" He readjusted one of the edges so it hung like a scarf on her shoulder and instructed the seamstress to pin that down. Her hair was very effectively covered by the Indian silk. "Why don't you take a look?" He pushed the mirror out in front of her.

Georgiana took one look at herself and gasped. She looked like a princess in one of her father's books. "Papa." She turned back to him, and his eyes were watery. "I love it."

"You look like a princess," her mother said. "Hopefully not the violent kind."

"She does do that. We cannot deny it."

"Charles."

He kissed her mother. Georgie tried to look away, but it was too quick as he said, "You will always be my angel. My daughters are princesses."

~~~

"Nervous?"

"What kind of question is that?" Geoffrey grumbled. "Of course I am."

George gave him one of his rare smiles as they stood together at the altar. The guests were almost assembled, and the vicar was preparing his notes at his pulpit as if he did not have the simple service memorized.

"Do you think she'll like the ring?"

George was the only one he'd shown it to. "I don't presume to know her as well as you, but I will take a guess and say she will love it."

Geoffrey was glad to have sensible, calm George by his side and not Charles. Charles was a good man but protective of his sister, and he had not George's maturity. "What if I forget what I'm supposed to say?"

"You have two lines."

"They are long."

"Never been in a play, have you? You could utter the thing drunk and backwards and she wouldn't care," George said. "Just try not to faint."

"Now you have me thinking of it!"

If George had a response, it was cut off by the music starting. Geoffrey turned and realized why George had warned him about fainting. Perhaps that was why they had groomsmen – to

539

catch the limp bodies of grooms, faced with a bride either too hideous or too beautiful (in this case, the latter). His uncle had done her up in some kind of Indian fashion, complete with more jewelry than he had ever seen on her. Geoffrey had seen Georgie dressed as a debutante, as a man, as a wild warrior, and not dressed at all, but he had never seen her so beautiful. Playing the female part really did her more justice than she was willing to admit.

He had only a moment to look at Uncle Bingley as he gave his daughter away, and the face that he saw was a man with bittersweet emotions and flowing tears, though he did his best to ignore them. What would his own father be like when it was time to give Anne away? He couldn't imagine his father crying, but he could imagine him upset. Uncle Bingley was giving Geoffrey something very great and all he could do was give him a reassuring smile before returning his attentions back to Georgie.

The ceremony began as the vicar reminded them why they were all there, as if they'd forgotten, then gave his cue.

Geoffrey did not forget. "I, Geoffrey Darcy, take thee, Georgiana Bingley, to be my wedded Wife, to have and to hold from this day forward, for better or for worse, for richer or for poorer, in sickness and in health, to love and to cherish, till death us do part, according to God's holy ordinance; and thereto I plight thee my troth."

He released her hand, and she took his.

"I, Georgiana Bingley, take thee, Geoffrey Darcy, to be my wedded Husband, to have and to hold from this day forward, for better or for worse, for richer or for poorer, in sickness and in health, to love, cherish, and to obey, till death us do part, according to God's holy ordinance; and thereto I give thee my troth."

The vicar gave the ring to Geoffrey, who placed it on Georgiana's finger. She gave a little gasp. It was his signet ring, the one with the initials "G.D." that she had given him for his birthday. Now, there were diamonds added to the circle around it that had been hastily beaten in while he was waiting for the license in London. On that ring, with all of the strange Irish letters, both of their blood had been spilled in what now seemed like so long ago – his when he was struck and raised his hand to protect himself, and she when she was carrying it around her neck and was shot. With a trembling voice he said, "With this Ring I thee wed, with my Body I thee worship, and with all my worldly Goods I thee endow: In the Name of the Father, and of the Son, and of the Holy Ghost. Amen."

He heard a woman's sobs; he was fairly sure it was his mother's, but it was hard to tell.

The vicar continued, "I pronounce that they be Man and Wife together, In the Name of the Father, and of the Son, and of the Holy Ghost. Amen."

~~~

She was his. She was Mrs. Geoffrey Darcy, and he wanted to make that perfectly clear in the basest way possible. The only thing that stood in his way was a horde of relations and acquaintances that wanted to wish him well, none of which interested him. He managed only a single kiss with her on the steps as they left the chapel after he had removed the front of her veil (or what he could manage of it – it seemed to be pinned). It would have to hold. "I love you, Mrs. Darcy."

"I love you, Mr. Darcy. Now, don't you dare call me that again unless you have to."

He grinned and took her hand as they were showered with flowers. It was only a short distance back to Pemberley for the wedding breakfast. "I suppose we owe it to our parents," he said in the gig. "Uncle Bingley for putting up all those ridiculous pavilions and my father for putting up with them."

"I wish we didn't have to," she said, leaning on him.

"You are preaching to the converted," he said, and kissed her.

They arrived to gathering crowds under the beautiful gauze tents, covered in flowers, which was all indeed very Indian and very colorful, and the guests were most intrigued. Everyone who was anyone in Derbyshire had been invited, and then some, to congratulate the heir of Pemberley on his marriage to a woman of fortune and certainly good relations. Since there was no way to prevent them sneaking in, some of the townsfolk who knew the younger generation since they were babes were invited not to the ceremony but to the massive meal, served in the tents on many trays. Geoffrey must have been kissed by every female relative – willingly or unwillingly – whereas his wife was an untouchable beauty. Except, of course, to Patrick Bellamont and Robert Kincaid. "They'll ruin the dress," he whispered to his wife as she struggled with the two boys hugging at her, begging to see her many bracelets very close up.

"So? I've no intention of marrying again."

He laughed. Someone offered him a tray of pastries, but he was too distracted to be hungry. The next person before him was not a servant but a tenant, clearly dressed in the best clothes he owned.

Geoffrey bowed. "Mr. Jenkins."

"Mr. Darcy." He bowed to him and his wife. "Mrs. Darcy. I'm so glad –" He was fingering his old sunhat. "I'm very happy for you both. And that Mr. Darcy saw fit to invite me –"

Geoffrey gave the old, shaking man a smile and a pat on the arm. "Enjoy yourself. Without you, the two of us might not be here, and I doubt my father will ever forget that."

"Or us," Georgiana added. "You have our thanks, Mr. Jenkins."

The old farmer was too overwhelmed to respond. He bowed himself away from them, clearing the path for Frederick and Emily Maddox.

"Fred hasn't been saying things about my wife behind our backs, has he?" Geoffrey asked Emily.

"He never says anything bad about either of you!" she said, apparently genuinely surprised at the notion.

"I only say it to your faces," Frederick said, draining another glass of wine. "I think that's a bit more honorable. It gives Mrs. Darcy here a chance to take a swipe at me. Yet somehow, she never does."

"I wouldn't know how to even touch you without having to explain to Uncle Maddox why you were a bruised pulp, sobbing like a little girl."

"That's the reason," Frederick said. "Prepare to face the mob."

Before Geoffrey could ask what he meant, the Maddox 'twins' made way for the Darcy sisters, who all hugged their brother and new sister in turn. "You should have seen it," Anne said, "Papa looked like he was ready to cry. Have you ever seen that?"

"Once, but under less desirable circumstances," Geoffrey said, remembering when he woke after being comatose for several days. "Besides, my attention during the ceremony was elsewhere."

"Mama was crying," Sarah said, "but we expected that. Papa never cries."

"He did after my coming out ball," Anne said. "Oh, I wasn't supposed to say that!"

"I'm sure Sarah will find out soon enough," Georgiana said.

"Your bags are all packed," Cassandra said. "Will you visit us?"

"I imagine I'll be around," he said with a smile.

After each of the sisters wished them well, Georgiana mentioned she was hungry, and snagged a loaf-shaped object from a passing tray. "Very sweet."

They were approached by the other Georgiana, formerly Darcy herself. Lord and Lady Kincaid offered their congratulations on what was a most fitting match. Apparently, they were not the only ones to predict the marriage – it was a compliment the two of them heard several times.

Princess Nadezhda was especially emotional. "You will take care of her," she ordered Geoffrey in her very intimidating accent. She turned to the frowning Georgie and said, "And you will protect him."

"I'm not sure what you're implying here," Geoffrey said, "but thank you, Your Highness."

"I find it is best not to argue with her," Brian Maddox said.

Because of the complicated set-up, which included pillows for lounging on the grass, Dr. Maddox was being led around by his wife. "So," Lady Maddox said, "I see Charles hasn't failed to do something wild and foreign. This time, he seems to have done a beautiful job for a change."

Dr. Maddox nodded. "Your appearance has been quite universally admired, Mrs. Darcy."

Georgie looked at her husband, who gave a nod of approval as she took the Doctor's hand and guided it to her wrists, then her forehead, where the gold headset still hung and kept part of her veil in place.

"Very nice indeed. Gold, is it?"

"Yes."

"Very fine. Perhaps, on that awful but wonderful day that I am obliged to give my daughter away to some husband who had better deserve her, we shall –"

"No," Lady Maddox said, cutting him off.

He just chuckled. "I've been overruled on this matter. Somehow, I am not surprised."

"You *are* beautiful," Lady Maddox said.

"Thank you, Aunt Maddox." Compliments on garments did not come easily from their fashionable aunt, so it meant all the more.

Geoffrey still wasn't hungry, but Georgiana had wolfed down three more sweet cakes by the time Charles and Eliza found them. "Congratulations."

"Remember our promise," Charles added.

"Of course," Geoffrey said.

"You were made for each other," Eliza said. "Is it true our parents planned the wedding while you were still in the cradle?"

"I don't think so. I think it just happened."

"Also, Papa is a good guesser," Georgie said.

Edmund Bingley came next. "So you're to Lancashire, then?"

"For a bit. Eventually, I have to be back at Cambridge, and Georgie will stay with the Maddoxes while I sit for my degree examinations."

"So your father just gave you a house?"

"They might have wanted to give us a little privacy."

Edmund just shrugged. "Good luck." He bowed and left.

He was the youngest Bingley and would have been the youngest between their families if not for Cassandra, and he had not yet really reached an interest in or understanding of women. "He'll come around," Geoffrey said.

"If it's not the two troublemakers!" came a voice from behind them.

"Grandfather Bennet," they said in unison.

"What a pair you two will make. Or have made. I'm not sure of the arrangements, precisely. Perhaps you will keep each other in some sort of balance," Mr. Bennet said. "I would say I intend to live to see a great-grandchild, but I'm better off predicting my death. I seem to live longer that way, and then perhaps I will see that great-grandchild."

Georgiana kissed her grandfather on the cheek and Geoffrey shook his hand. Mr. Bennet could still walk on his own, if it was more of a hobble, and he made his way back to the food.

"You attended a heretical ceremony," Georgiana said to Grégoire. "What was it like?"

"Like most of those I've been to," he said. "A little boring and not enough Latin, but it serves the same purpose." He looked up to his nephew, who was taller than him. "I remember when you were a little boy who thought Jesus was a fish."

"I thought that?"

"You did, and it was adorable. It was one of my first conversations with you. You also asked me why I wore a dress once. Now, look at you."

"And you're no longer wearing a dress."

Even just greeting everyone once seemed to take forever. There were so many well-wishers and they felt themselves well enough wished. Geoffrey had a glass of wine and Georgiana ate more cakes, but they were merely biding their time.

"You look beautiful."

Georgiana turned to her papa. "You made me that way."

He embraced her and held her for longer than anyone else had held her as Mrs. Bingley came up beside him. "You take care of her. If not, we'll be more expedient and just send Mr. Maddox after you."

"I will make a note of it, Aunt Bingley."

Jane Bingley kissed her daughter good-bye. That left only his parents, who had predicted their desires and were waiting by the carriage. Mr. Darcy of Pemberley always made sure everything was properly done within his grounds. He gave his son a firm handshake, from man to man. "You can do as you wish to the house, if you want to keep it."

"We'll be there in Cambridge in July," Elizabeth said. "Write us."

"We'll have time."

Elizabeth exchanged a knowing smirk with her husband, who did not seem too happy about their private joke but was willing to acknowledge it. "Try to *find* time." She kissed her new daughter and then her son. "My baby."

"Mother!"

"Sorry, but you will always be that, so you might as well resign yourself to it," she said. "Good-bye."

"Good-bye, Mother. Father."

"Aunt Darcy. Uncle Darcy."

At long last, they boarded the carriage, overstuffed with their things. Even with the closed door, they could still hear the cheers of the crowd as they departed, headed west for Lancashire and their new home.

Georgiana succeeded in removing the many pins that kept her veil straight and then the veil entirely.

"They didn't brush your hair."

"Didn't even try. Some parts of me just can't be tamed."

"Good," he said, and pulled her into a kiss. "Those are the parts I like."

~~~

Two fathers, now brothers in every possible way, watched the carriage disappear into the

550

horizon. When it was only a speck in the distance, they finally lowered their hands from waving.

"So," Bingley said.

Darcy grumbled and removed coins from his breast pocket, tossing them to Bingley. "Five pounds. Why did I ever agree to that bet?"

"I like to think I have more foresight," Bingley said, "but the truth is I'm just a very lucky man."

CHAPTER 30

The Book

The drive went through the night, with only brief stops to change horses and some delays on account of mud. Geoffrey and Georgiana Darcy slept through most of it, their feet up on the opposite cushion where Gawain was curled up. It was dawn when they arrived at the old stone house with a very gothic front. The road to it was barely more than mud, and there was no other house in sight. Geoffrey nudged his wife awake and climbed out of the carriage in time to offer his hand to help her out.

Everything at the house was ready for them. The new master and mistress were greeted by the local staff as their trunks were sorted by their own servants.

"Are you hungry?" he asked. His stomach was growling.

Georgie put a hand on her stomach. "No. But I could use a cup of tea."

"Tea it is, then." His mother had told him she would be reluctant to eat at times and it was best not to press her, but it made him anxious nonetheless. When they did sit down, she managed some bread with her tea as he wolfed down the meal prepared for their arrival. Still tired from the road and an uncomfortable night's sleep, they were little aware of their surroundings, noticing only that the staff was quick, the place seemed clean and pleasant, and, more importantly, they were alone. The silence was delightful; they hardly said a word over their meal or as they went up to their chambers. They chose the mistress' chamber to retire, and Geoffrey gave brief instructions for food to be left in the outer chambers before they shut the door entirely. Reynolds would not arrive for another day, and Georgiana was perpetually between lady's-maids, but they did not accept the offers to help them undress.

"Your clothing is much less complex," Georgie complained good naturedly as she undid his buttons for him. He always had trouble with the buttons. The poor man was so rich he couldn't always dress himself. "Except for the cravat."

"Something has to require a manservant," Geoffrey said. She turned around, and he stared at the lacing of her gown. "I'm afraid I might ruin it."

"I have no plans to need this dress again, so don't let it worry you."

He smiled and kissed the back of her neck as he began to untie the lacings and anything else he could find that kept her gown up. It fell away and she unceremoniously dropped it to the floor, leaving only her chemise beneath it. There was only one problem left.

"Gawain," Geoffrey said, shooing the dog off the bed he had only just succeeded in climbing on. "Shoo." He opened the door and pushed the dog out, shutting it to the whimpering.

"You didn't even say you were sorry."

"No," he said, removing his shirt. "Because I'm not." With a wicked grin, he pushed her in the opposite direction, onto the bed, and climbed on top of her. He wasn't *that* tired.

~~~

Geoffrey loved waking up to the sun's rays peaking through the drapes with Georgie curled up against his side. Her hair was so beautiful in the afternoon light, even if he had only a few minutes to appreciate it before she hastily woke and ran to the chamber pot.

"I hate being with child," she said after she had cleaned up and returned to bed. "You did this to me, you bastard."

"I recall the actions on my part were heavily requested."

"But not – argh," she leaned into him, and he kissed her on the head. She always smelled of the wild, of flowers and grass, even when she had not ventured outside as of late. She was so tiny in his arms – perhaps that was why she was so fiercely defensive.

Give it up, Geoffrey, he thought. *You'll make your head spin trying to understand her. And then you'll both be ill.*

"What is it?"

"What?"

"What are you thinking?"

"Oh," he said. "I – was just contemplating your complexity."

"Was that meant as a compliment?"

"Would you prefer that I say you're a simple, shallow girl instead of the most mysterious and confounding woman in Britain?" He pulled her in. "*My* most mysterious and confounding woman in Britain?" He kissed her on the forehead. "Mrs. Darcy."

"Geoffrey, I love you, and am most happy to be your wife," she cooed. "That said, if you ever call me that again before your mother passes to the next world, I may take extreme measures."

"Such as ...?"

"Ones too terrible for you to contemplate."

He laughed. "You will have to get used to it."

They spent little time beyond their bedroom, managed to explore the house a bit, noting what would need to be renovated, and on one particularly bright and beautiful day, they wandered the grounds. They were nearly surrounded by woods, reminding them both of Derbyshire. As far as Geoffrey was concerned, it was a quiet little piece of heaven, with only the two of them to explore it and one faithful hound to trail behind them. Even Gawain was giving them distance.

"We don't have to stay," Geoffrey said, "if you truly wanted something else."

"We could be in a mud hut for all I care," she said, and he laughed. "Fortunately for you, I love it."

"I'm fortunate indeed."

The next day, they brought a blanket and some food and stayed out longer, returning only when their hair was messed up and some of Geoffrey's buttons were done incorrectly. Georgie teased him about not being able to put on his own clothing if it was anything more complicated that a gown.

"Promise me you'll take care of yourself," he said.

"I have Sir Gawain to protect me," she said.
"Nothing too strenuous."
"I'm barely two months along!"
"I stand by what I said."

Georgie frowned and shook her head. "What does it matter? All my balance is gone since it happened. I might as well sit and be useless."

"You're not useless," he insisted, and kissed her. "Trust me when I say you are laboring very hard and to a very wonderful outcome."

"Yes. I am *laboring*."

"Would that I could take some of it off your back. Shoulders." He frowned. "Stomach."

The wedding gifts arrived shortly, though they paid them little heed at first. It was only on the first rainy day that they gave them any proper attention. Aside from the normal books and jewelry and everyday items that were common wedding gifts, they received a number of things from Brian and Nadezhda that Geoffrey didn't even recognize.

"It's an ink brush set," she said. "For drawing."

"And the sand?"

"I don't know. Read the card."

He undid the wax. "He says it's for the 'Zen Garden,' whatever that is. Are we going to have to write him to explain it, or do you already know?"

"I'll write."

Grégoire gave them a wooden chess set, with kings and queens that looked unmistakably similar to themselves and some sort of dog or wolf hybrids as pawns. Lady Maddox sent them a very elegant painting for the sitting room, and Dr. Maddox included a small pamphlet on pregnancy and a book wrapped up in paper.

Georgiana blushed as Geoffrey unwrapped it. "Oh my God. He didn't."

"What?" There was a note in the inside cover, which he plucked out. "'I'm quite sure neither of your parents have it in them to give you a copy, though they both own one.' What's this?" The title was unfamiliar. He only needed to open it to one illustrated page to see precisely what it was.

"My papa has this book. He keeps it locked in the bottom drawer of his study."

"Which didn't prevent you from – Oh dear."

Georgie picked up the note and flipped it over. "'Try chapter fourteen.'"

"What? All right." He flipped to the page. "Oh my God." He slapped the book shut. "No, no, no. Oh, we have some very disgusting relations."

"What? I want to see it."

"You don't. You really do not-" But his pleas were useless. Georgiana easily got it out of his hands and opened it to the correct chapter and briefly scanned the description. "No, please," he said.

"Chicken."

"Georgie, please –"

"It might not be so bad."

"I beg of you –"

"Beg as much as you please," she said, and pulled him back into her bedroom. "When you're finished, I can remind you about all of those lectures concerning the eternal happiness of one's spouse."

Geoffrey groaned but did not contradict her. "Next time, I pick the chapter."

~~~

They had two perfect weeks together before there was a mild nudge of a letter from his father, reminding him that he had to prepare to sit for his exams, and that the books he needed might perhaps be chained to the library shelves at Cambridge. Unfortunately, the town was a few days ride from Lancashire. For his first absence, Georgiana did not come with him and stay with the Maddoxes. He tried very hard to stick to his studies and not count the minutes until he would be back on his way to his new wife and his new home.

He returned two weeks later, his head full of mathematics, to a very joyous greeting that she could not give until she put down the wooden rake she'd been studiously using. When he finally let her down (and she was a bit heavier than he remembered her), he took the time to look about in the courtyard. "Why is there sand everywhere?"

"I told you. Zen garden." She kissed him.

"It's hardly a garden." He looked at the square box that had only a few stones in it. She had been sculpting the sand with the rake to form neat, unnatural lines.

"It's a Zen garden."

"What does that mean?"

"I've no idea. I'm just following Uncle Brian's instructions. But it is very relaxing." With that said, she showed no more interest in the garden business or anything else that they possibly could have wanted to discuss until supper, the time for which was defined by when they were too hungry to stay in their room for any longer.

The days were getting longer and it was still light out, so they walked, arms entwined, down the path that led to the forest. He noticed that more of the ivy had been taken down and that the front had generally been fixed up more than he remembered it. "It looks lovely."

"I know we have to return to Pemberley for the confinement –"

"That's months away." He kissed her, and they continued their walk. "After that, we can return for as long as we like. We might want to fix up the guest rooms, though."

"You're not eager to live at Pemberley?"

"I'm Mr. Darcy. When my father passes, I will *be* Pemberley. But until that day, I have the choice to remain there and worry about making too much noise or being dragged into another meeting discussing the ledgers, or I can stay here and have little else to do that does not directly involve my wife. I choose the latter."

"I've always admired your ability to make wise decisions," she said.

Though she would not admit to being lonely, it was more obvious to him the second time that splitting his time between Cambridge and Lancashire would not be enough. Two months had passed since their wedding before he finally invited Brian and Nadezhda Maddox to visit for a few weeks, some of which he spent at Cambridge. He swallowed the unexpected bout of jealousy of sharing his wife with anyone. She needed someone to talk to, and she had always gotten along with the Princess best. It was only after they arrived that it occurred to him that Princess Nadezhda was lacking knowledge in the very key realm of being with child, but Georgie took to the idea of having her about anyway.

He was surprised at the way Brian Maddox spoke to him. There was a notable difference that at first he could not define, but he liked it all the same. Only late at night, when he said it to Georgiana, did she look at him as if he was brainless and said, "You're a married man now with your own home.

Of course he's going to treat you more like an adult."

What Geoffrey did not tell her (at that moment, anyway – he would find one) was how he had always wondered how the Maddoxes stayed so close to each other without children of their own. He could not believe how extensive their relationship was and how he had never seemed to notice it before. He never looked at his parents as companions (and he tried very hard not to think of them as lovers), but Brian and Nadezhda obviously were. If they felt anything lacking, after all, they could have taken a ward.

"There's no one in this world like Nadezhda," Brian said when he asked. "I hope to God there's no one out there like me. Therefore, it's us against the world. We might as well be friends, at the very least."

Geoffrey had another question. "I didn't want to say it to Georgie, and I've never been good at approaching Her Highness, especially about this."

Brian nodded when he heard the explanation. "Jorgi-chan already knows. No fighting. No practicing. She's not that foolish."

"No one's ever succeeded in getting her to give it up before."

"Apparently, you did it without too much trouble."

563

Geoffrey blushed.

~~~

Each time Geoffrey returned to Cambridge, he was reminded that it was not the same. Though no one outside the family knew of his marriage, neither of his roommates bothered to invite him to parties. Most of his time was spent studying for a change, so he saw little of them, though he saw a bit more of Charles, who asked after his sister's health constantly.

"It is the same as it was yesterday," Geoffrey said. "I presume." He opened a letter from Georgiana, which confirmed it. It was one of his longer absences, and he was a bit surprised to learn her mother was visiting, though Aunt Bingley was gone when he returned.

"I want you all to myself," was her response to his questioning of that.

May became June, and June became July, and they were marking off the days on the calendar until his exams. He did indulge himself in some good-bye parties with friends, but nothing excessive. He was not surprised at the appearance of his parents – many graduations were family celebrations – but he was surprised to see his father smile to say, *I'm proud of you*. He didn't have to verbalize it, and Fitzwilliam Darcy never said anything he didn't have to. Geoffrey's mother said it for him when the results were posted. "We're so proud of you." He did not take the honors exams, but he passed for his degree, which was all he wanted or would ever need, and happily discarded his mortarboard, tossing it into the river before heading to the party at Chesterton.

"Will you miss anything about Cambridge?" Georgiana asked him on the way. Her gowns could be let out so her condition wouldn't be obvious in public, though there was a slight bump hidden under her gown where there had not been one before.

"The fabric store," he said with a wicked grin.

~~~

The rest of the summer passed peacefully. Georgiana was feeling better and eating more (much more). She was still fit to travel, though he had no intentions of doing so. That changed when a certain letter arrived.

"What is it?" She looked up from her breakfast to see his expression.

"Mr. Collins," was all Geoffrey said, his tone conveying everything else.

Mr. Thomas Collins, having married off two of his four daughters and paid in full for his house in Hunsford, died suddenly. A heart attack was heavily suspected, given his chest pains earlier in the summer and his considerable size. Geoffrey's parents would be attending the funeral; Elizabeth and Mrs. Collins had been friends since childhood to his knowledge, and his father had once been Mr. Collin's patron. For some reason, his father wrote that his Uncle Grégoire was coming and bringing his family, so Patrick and Aunt Bellamont would be there, and he was suddenly more interested in going.

Upon arriving, they were surprised to see the crowd that came to mourn the Vicar Collins, or at least to see the other mourners. A strange smattering of the old Bennet family was there based on their schedules and connection to Mr. Collins. The Bertrands were there, and Joseph Bennet, who would begin at Cambridge in October and probably be ordained himself. Since their daughter was going, the Bingleys came and brought Eliza and Edmund to Kent as well.

It was very hot, and considering all of the heavy black clothing, the service was mercifully short. Mrs. Collins and her four daughters sat, dressed in jet, beside the grave as Grégoire spoke after the current vicar finished his prayers. "Mr. Collins was a man who took prodigious care of his beloved wife and daughters," he said, "On those merits alone, nothing bad can be said of him in good faith."

And he had. Two had married well, and inheritances were set for the other two. Their renovated house in Hunsford was theirs until they died, if Mrs. Collins was not inclined to remarry or her daughters to marry at all. Many of the guests went to walk along the vast gardens that he had so meticulously cared for during his life.

The greatest surprise was the arrival of Mr. Bennet. He had not made such a long journey since the death of his wife, nor had he been known to care for this cousin in the least. Nonetheless, he sat by the graveside and listened to the speech, very quiet and respectful. There was no open discussion, at least at first, of the massive change this brought about. The entail on Longbourn would now die with Mr. Bennet. It would be put up on the market and its value split equally among Mr. Bennet's daughters, though it went without saying that Joseph Bennet had every intention of purchasing it.

"We had the decency to not begin discussing it in front of Mrs. Collins," Mr. Bennet said to Geoffrey's unasked question when they had retired to their guest rooms at Rosings.

"I did wish to speak of it," Joseph Bennet said. "My mother and Dr. Bertrand are looking for a summer place. Would it be possible to reopen Longbourn for them?"

"Reopen Longbourn?" their grandfather said. His face seemed to light up. "Yes, yes. Of course. Why should the house not see some new life? Though, respectfully, I much prefer a certain chair in a certain library that is not in Hertfordshire."

Elizabeth Darcy kissed her father on the head, and it was settled.

~~~

Geoffrey Darcy experienced his first idle autumn when he was one and twenty, and he loved every minute of it, aside from a few scares with his increasing wife. She had cramps and headaches, but the local midwife was very reassuring that everything was progressing normally.

"*This* is normal?" Georgie said with a hand on her belly, back in the privacy of their bedchamber. He smiled and kissed it.

The child kicked for the first time in Lancashire, merely a week before her confinement was set to begin in Derbyshire. She woke him out of a sleep. She was shaking, and he held her until she was sensible again, and then *he* felt it as well and could only laugh when he realized what it was. "It's our baby," he said, kissing her. "It wants to come out."

"It doesn't care for its current quarters?"

"I imagine they're a bit cramped."

Georgie giggled and covered her mouth. It was so strange to see her smile over the prospect of a child, and so wonderful.

But he could not fully soothe her and was somewhat relieved to return to Pemberley, where she would be surrounded by relatives who knew better about this particular subject. He did not find it as stifling as he thought it would be. Since he'd left, they had fixed up his rooms so that they were far more suitable to a female companion. Gawain seemed happy enough to lie down on his old cushion, now accustomed to spending his nights alone.

Georgie took to it better than he would have imagined. He expected her to be clawing at the door within a day, but instead she was content to have her mother and aunt with her by day and her husband by night. She was eager to see her sister and her brothers. Charles returned for his final Christmas as a University student just days before the holiday and celebrated his birthday with Eliza among a large gathering of family. There was a detectable air among the servants this holiday. A possibility of an heir to Pemberley was not something to take lightly.

Two months into her confinement, it was not a light thing to Geoffrey, either. Not when she woke him in the middle of the night. He turned over. "Is it kicking?" He squinted in the darkness. "Are you crying?"

"Geoffrey," she said, digging her nails into his wrists, "I think the baby's coming."

CHAPTER 31

The Littlest Darcy

The midwife was summoned, along with the local doctor. Dr. Maddox was still at Chatton House, but he would be of no real use. The master and mistress of Pemberley were roused from slumber with all expediency, and someone was sent to wake Chatton House.

Geoffrey was dressed and told to wish his wife the best. It pained him to leave her in such a state of distress, but propriety demanded it. "I love you," he said with his parting kiss. "You'll be fine."

She rolled her eyes. "Come back in a few hours and we'll see how fine I'll be."

"I'd do it, but I don't know if Mr. Maddox brought his armor."

He left only when his mother entered to replace him. When he emerged, it seemed all of Pemberley was up and ready, and his father was assuring Anne and Sarah that it would be a long process and they ought to go back to sleep. Still in her bedclothes, Anne caught sight of her brother first. "Geoffrey!" She hugged him. "This is so exciting!"

"Yes," he said in a far more muted tone. He bowed. "Father."

His father gave him an encouraging smile. "It's a bit early to start drinking, but you might as well take up the traditional position in the study." Unusually affectionate, his father patted him on the back and escorted him to the study. Uncle Bingley arrived shortly, even though it was still dark outside.

"Uncle Bingley."

His uncle went straight for the liquor cabinet. "How is she?"

"I've nothing to compare it to, but Mother said she was doing admirably."

After a bit of nothing happening, Geoffrey's body gave in to the desire to return to sleep despite his tension. When he woke, he noticed that the sun was up and that he had been dozing in the armchair without his knowledge or consent.

"The doctor wishes to speak to you," Suddenly Reynolds was at his side, nudging him.

"What? Is everything all right?"

"He did not seem alarmed, sir."

That didn't stop Geoffrey from worrying as he raced ungracefully into the hallway, where Dr. Dunhill was waiting for him. "What's wrong?"

"Nothing," the doctor said. "I just wanted to inquire if you are certain of her calendar."

"Yes." He knew of only one event it could be. "So that would make her three weeks early. How bad is it?"

"Not entirely abnormal, especially for a first child. At the moment, there is nothing of great concern."

"How is she?"

"She managed to get some rest in between contractions, and I believe they have her walking about her room now."

"What?"

"It is good for the progression of labor."

Geoffrey just nodded. He had no idea. No one had told him, and it aggravated him that something of such great magnitude was not shared with him because of his sex. "Please keep me informed."

"Sir."

The doctor left and George Wickham replaced him, still yawning away sleepiness. He had been visiting with his sister for the holiday. "As no one bothered to wake me, I assume the screaming I heard was not in fact a fire but merely Georgiana's time."

"I apologize for not telling you. I was distracted."

George gave him a little smirk. "Of course you were."

A very informal breakfast was laid out, with women running to and fro. Geoffrey was initially too nervous to eat and satisfied himself with a cup of coffee, but his stomach got the better of him and he had a muffin. His father cast him a knowing glance as the other relatives began to trickle in.

At noon, he started more actively looking at the clock in the study and paid little attention to what his relatives were saying to him, no matter how well-meaning they were being. The one time he was allowed to stray in the vicinity of the stairs, he heard her screams and had to be held back from going upstairs.

An hour later, he was again called to speak to the doctor in the hallway. This time his mother was there, and her expression said everything. "What's wrong?" he said.

"The baby appears to be breech," the doctor said. "It's not entirely uncommon in early labor, though we do have reason to believe that the baby is still alive."

Still alive. As if there was a possibility that it wasn't? What then?

"What – what happens now?"

"I can attempt to use forceps, but I think we ought to give it more time."

"What does my wife think?"

"Georgiana is not entirely coherent at the moment," his mother said. "She's very tired." She was trying to play it down, he could tell. "It would be better if we gave it a little more time before using forceps."

"All right." He just then realized he was being asked a question which he was not qualified to answer. The doctor bowed and left to see his patient. Geoffrey turned to his mother. "Dr. Maddox just arrived. Can we ask him?"

"He's not been fully updated, but if you'd like his opinion, we can do that."

"Is she all right?"

Elizabeth nodded. He didn't know what else to say. His mother kissed him on the cheek. "She's a fighter," she said. "And I imagine the child is, too."

He was not comforted – not enough. He ignored his sisters' questions when they assaulted him. If only he could be there for her... "Dr. Maddox," Geoffrey said to the doctor, who was sitting beside his brother in the parlor. "If you would – Dr. Dunhill would ask your opinion."

"Of course." Geoffrey returned to the study and delivered the news, then collapsed in his chair. His father tried to look encouraging, but Uncle Bingley had gone pale. George offered him a glass of wine, and he took it.

He had finished a second by the time Dr. Maddox reappeared and took him aside. "I think you have your wife in very capable hands with Dr.

575

Dunhill. Another few hours and he can probably avoid forceps."

"They're that dangerous?"

"They could be. Any medical intrusion on the natural process is a risk on Georgiana's health. And the infant's."

He had a lump in his throat that made it almost hard to speak. "Do breech babies live?"

"They have a lower rate of survival than a more uneventful birth, but yes, they certainly do live. That it is still alive after so many hours is already a good sign."

He was willing to cling to anything as the minutes ticked off. He sat quietly and drank, mostly oblivious to any attempts to distract him or cheer him up.

"Master Geoffrey." Eventually, a servant spoke directly to him, which got him out of his stupor. "Your presence is requested."

"Is she –"

"Your wife is very ill, sir."

Geoffrey did not stay and listen to anything anyone else had to say. He pushed past everyone and ran up the stairs, nearly crashing into his mother, who was crying.

"What is it? It's dead, isn't it?"

That was when he heard the cry, one distinctly not of a grown woman's.

He charged into his chambers. Georgiana lay either asleep or unconscious, and Aunt Bingley was wiping clean her brow with a wet towel. Dr. Dunhill was turned away, his interest on the table, wrapped in a blanket. He seemed alarmed at Geoffrey's intrusion. "Mr. Darcy, I don't advise –"

"Let me see my child!" he said, pushing the old doctor away far more roughly than he intended. He did not apologize. Instead, he took the very tiny bundle in his hands. The child – his child – was alive, but very small, and quite blue.

"She's underweight," the doctor said, picking himself back up. "It's not recommended –"

"I have a daughter," he said, the lump in his throat returning. "What is not recommended?"

"That you grow too attached. It's unlikely – "

"That she'll survive?" He turned, his child in his arms, and faced the doctor. "This is my daughter, and I've no intention of giving up on her because of a few pounds."

He said it with such ferocity that the effect on both Dr. Dunhill and Mrs. Bingley was visible. Neither of them could say anything.

"Georgiana," he reminded impatiently.

"The birth was very taxing, though I believe she is unharmed by the process. She was not very large to begin with, so she is still in some danger."

"You don't know Georgie," he said, and sat down on the bed beside his wife. "Aunt Bingley."

She gave him a tired smile. "She's just gone to sleep."

He didn't care. He tugged on her hand, which was cold and clammy. "Georgie."

She did wake, though not easily. Her eyes were glassy. "What?"

"Your daughter wants to see you."

"Mr. Darcy –"

He ignored the doctor and put the infant in Georgiana's arms, positioning them both with pillows so that she did not have to do any actual work to hold the baby. The midwife returned to the room with a bowl of clean water. "Mr. Darcy!"

"Look at her," he said with a smile, ignoring everyone else. In Georgie's arms, the baby finally murmured and stretched one of her very tiny arms.

Georgiana looked down at the little child in her arms, blue and pink except for the top of her head, where she had a little tuft of red hair. "Why … why did I ever think I couldn't do this? Why was I so scared?" She looked up at Geoffrey. "She's perfect." She didn't have the strength to laugh.

The midwife brought broth for her to drink. "Mrs. Darcy, you need your rest. For both of you." Georgie didn't put up an argument. She was already fading. Her eyes had never fully focused, but she still had a grip on her daughter as Geoffrey carefully pried the child out of her hands.

"My God," he said to his daughter, "What in the world am I going to do with you?"

~~~

The doctor left, and while Geoffrey was basking in his newfound fatherhood, a very different conversation was taking place between Darcy, Bingley, and the doctor, with Grégoire standing by.

"What are its chances?"

"A breech baby, three weeks premature – maybe a few days," Dr. Dunhill said. "It's best if he understands that. It's much harder afterwards."

"Baptism?" was all Darcy could manage.

"If you want to do it, it should be as soon as possible."

This wasn't how it was supposed to be. It was supposed to be a wonderful ceremony, well-planned and well-attended, not some rushed thing in the night with the nearest available Rector. Darcy instinctively turned to his brother. "I know you're not ordained –"

"I can't do it. I do recommend that it should be done, though, for the child's soul."

"Of course." But to go through the whole ceremony, naming it and everything, for someone they were about to lose? "They will have to decide on a name for –" Darcy faltered. "Do I have a grandson or a granddaughter?"

"Daughter," Dunhill answered.

Granddaughter. It was impossible not to hear that word without feeling pride and joy. The doctors were right. This would be even further tragedy if they began to associate with the child, but how could they not? He was a grandfather, and he wanted to revel in it. He wanted the child to live so she could grow up and run around him and call him 'Grandpapa.' The temptation was there, so loudly and clearly.

"How is Georgiana?" Bingley asked, his voice cracking.

"Very weak. If she rests, she should recover, however slowly. We briefly feared for her life, but I believe that moment has passed."

Bingley nodded and looked down at the floor, drained by the few simple sentences that had been spoken. "She – I think she should be baptized. The child."

"Yes," Darcy said.

The doctor said grimly, "Then do it quickly."

~~~

Geoffrey would not leave his wife or child's side, and since Georgiana needed all of the rest they could afford her, there was remarkably little activity in the upper halls of Pemberley. Darcy focused his attentions on finding the Rector. When Mr. Reed assured him the task was being handled for him, he ran to his wife, who was white from exhaustion. He did not need to respond verbally to her greeting, just to hold her.

The news was very quietly circulated that a daughter had been born to Master Geoffrey and Mrs. Georgiana, but the child's health was not yet assured, and celebrations were not appropriate. As the sun fell, the appropriate relatives went to the chapel.

Dr. Maddox remained behind on a bench just outside. "Dr. Maddox," Geoffrey said as he approached. "Here," Geoffrey said, holding the child up in front of the doctor. "You hold her. Just – I'm being presumptuous, I know –"

"It's all right," Dr. Maddox said, and held out his arms for the baby. She did make those sounds that were not quite whimpers, but something more adorable, and she did not cry as he ran his hand gently over her face and eventually found her hands, then her feet. "She's very light. What does she weigh?"

"Three pounds."

"She's very lively for a newborn," he said. "If she gains weight, she may live."

"They want to baptize her tonight. They don't expect her to survive."

Dr. Maddox raised the baby, indicating for Geoffrey to take her back. "I thought it was cats that always landed on their feet."

"What?"

"Cats, not wolves. A whole different class of species. Did you really think your daughter's birth would be anything but extraordinary?" he said. "She has hair. What color is it?"

"Red. Like her mother's."

"Did she kick a lot?"

"She did."

The doctor nodded. "If she is her mother's daughter, she will hardly give up without a fight. On the other hand, she will be a handful for the rest of her life."

Geoffrey smiled, his heart so lightened by the doctor's assurances. "That I will gladly endure."

~~~

The Rector arrived in good time and made informal inquiries as to the gender of the child and the intended godfather, whereupon Charles Bingley the Third raised his hand.

A hushed silence fell over the group as Geoffrey entered, proudly bearing a bundle containing the child few had dared to lay eyes on for fear of growing an attachment. The baby announced herself quite loudly as Geoffrey shushed her, "I'm very sorry, but your mother isn't here." He looked up at the Rector. "They've never been separated for very long. I'm sorry."

"It's quite all right," he replied. "Her name?"

"Alison," he said proudly, and brought the baby to the stone.

Somehow, the memories of Geoffrey's birth did not come so easily to Darcy, and when they did, they were so hard to believe. That he had once been so small, and so utterly pink and helpless. Now *he* was a father and would remain so for the time being at least, though Dr. Maddox was very carefully hopeful. The baby had already gained a quarter pound since her birth. It was an encouraging sign.

"Do you want to hold her?" Geoffrey said, and Darcy sensed from the tone of his voice that his son might have asked the question once already. Darcy was lost.

"– Yes," he said and accepted the child, who flailed her arms around a bit, her tiny hands snagging on the buttons of his waistcoat, which were of about equal in size. He laughed. "She's so small." He remembered the girls being small but not so vividly, and of course, none of them had been quite as small as this baby. Bingley was standing next to him, but he would not relinquish this child for anything in the world, and fortunately, Bingley did not ask.

The formalities were dispensed with as casually as possible. Charles Bingley the Third reaffirmed his Christian faith as the godfather to his niece and could not have looked prouder. Alison Darcy, who by so many impossibilities managed to grace them with her presence, was quiet at least for the actual baptism. Her entrance to heaven now assured, she immediately became restless and whimpered again, and there was only a small amount of passing around before she was given back to Geoffrey.

It was the shortest baptism Darcy had ever been to and the only one where every woman in the room was silently crying. Not particularly dry-eyed himself, Darcy waited until most of the others were gone and the Rector dismissed to embrace his wife, and he did not let go until they were too tired to keep standing there, in the cold of night.

~~~

Every morning was a terror for the Darcys – to wake to the possibility that their granddaughter had died in the night, until it was confirmed that she had lived. And every morning she was very much alive, and by the end of the week she had gained half a pound. Georgiana was recovering but still had not left her bed. From there, she received her visitors for very short visits, because after the baptism she would not let her child out of her sight, except for a few moments when they were able to sneak the infant away while she was resting. It was a full week and two days before the doctors declared Georgie fully out of danger, but she did not recover her color. They recommended that she not nurse, which she of course refused.

Darcy and Elizabeth could not imagine the terror Geoffrey was going through, as his daughter's life still hung in the balance. He was overwhelmed by fatherly emotions, but beneath the exterior, the worry was obvious. Georgiana, however, was entirely dismissive of the concerns. She was still able to assert herself, if weakly, to say, "She's my daughter, and I'll be damned disappointed if she does not survive." No one dared to contradict her.

Slowly, with each passing day, the morning panic became more of an expectation of good news, not bad. Another night, she had survived. When two weeks had passed, Geoffrey took note of her eyes, which were blue like his own, and absolutely mesmerizing. It was on that day, when she was two weeks old and weighed nearly two pounds more than she had at her birth, Dr. Dunhill began to sound more openly hopeful. She was by all appearances healthy, if on the small side. The first month, the first year – those would all be a dangerous time, but they were for any infant.

"If she's no longer premature," Georgie said, "what does that make her now? A mature baby?"

"Yes. She'll be out in society by next month, at this rate," Geoffrey said with an encouraging smile.

The doctors conferred, and at three weeks of age, Alison Darcy was proclaimed a healthy infant with a good chance of surviving a normal period of infancy. It was then that those who had not seen her were paraded in to sit with the child.

"Why did you choose Alison?" Darcy asked his son as Eliza Bingley sat in the chair with her niece.

"In honor of Grégoire's mother, Alice."

"Yes, of course," Darcy said, too embarrassed to admit he had forgotten the name. Grégoire rarely spoke of his mother, who was buried in Mon-Claire. "It is a lovely name."

"Thank you."

When his father had departed, Geoffrey went behind the screen that had been set up to give

Georgiana some privacy as she rested while the guests saw the new addition to the family, asshe would not let her baby out of the room. "Why did we name her Alison?"

"Oh?" Georgie said, opening her eyes. "I always liked that name. Some very respectable women have been named Alison."

"Name one."

"I know of one whom I particularly liked," she said. "Her husband promised to do whatever she said, and she was beautiful in his eyes and loyal to him to the end of her days."

"Did she really exist, or is this a character in a story?"

"Does it truly matter?"

He grinned. "I suppose it doesn't."

CHAPTER 32

Epilogue

6 Months Later

Charles Bingley the Third graduated in style. The gathering at Chatton House celebrated not only the completion of his studies, but also offered a last glance of the man who would soon depart on the traditional tour of the Continent. He would be the first of his generation to take it; George stayed in school, and Geoffrey got married. Frederick pestered him to bring back names and locations of beautiful women for his own trip the following year. Emily pestered Frederick about being so jealous. George Wickham and Joseph Bennet ignored them all and retreated to their texts, George in medicine and Joseph in his undergraduate studies. Edmund had entered Oxford, where men intending a profession and not a living went, and returned with excellent marks, nearly rivaling Frederick.

The second bit of excitement was the arrival of Mr. and Mrs. Darcy of Lancashire, who had not been seen since Georgiana had been well enough to depart in March. Alison was twice the size and becoming an adept crawler. She was also very talented at stuffing things in her mouth, to the amused consternation of her parents and her nurse.

"She's so much like you," Elizabeth said to her son. "Georgie liked to explore, but she was so quiet." Alison, on the other hand, readily announced herself in incomprehensible babble. Geoffrey smiled and passed his daughter to her grandmother. Alison responded to this action by grabbing the tie to Elizabeth's bonnet and chomping down on it before either of them could stop her. She would have stopped the baby, but she was too distracted. "Papa!" She rose to curtsey to her father.

Mr. Bennet, now eighty years of age, hobbled across the paved walkway towards the object of his interest. Geoffrey bowed and ran to him. "Grandfather Bennet." He helped him the rest of the way, and Elizabeth gave up her seat.

"Now, now, there's no need for a fuss," he said as Alison was placed on his lap. She could sit upright now, which was a help. "Well, perhaps some fuss. This is my great-granddaughter." The child responded by putting the first available thing in her mouth, which in this case was his forefinger. "Thank goodness she does not have any teeth."

"Yet," said an embarrassed Geoffrey, who produced a coral teething ring for his daughter and replaced Mr. Bennet's finger with it, and she seemed satisfied by this. She made a giggling sound when Mr. Bennet kissed her cheek but otherwise remained focused on the ring.

"Yet another sight I never imagined I would see," Mr. Bennet said with delight. "I remember when Jane was born. I remember all of my daughters' births, but the first one is special. Though, I would add, the second was special as well." He looked up at his daughter. "You were an endless frustration to your mother, though a very happy kind, for she did delight in her children when there were fewer girls and more prospects of a boy. Jane was adorable, but she had always been a sitter. You would climb everywhere and bite everything. We were afraid you would cut your teeth on the furniture in the dining room." He looked down at Alison. "That Mrs. Bennet could see this."

They had no response to that. Fortunately, Georgie Darcy (née Bingley) broke the silence as she approached from behind. "Grandfather. Aunt Darcy. Is my daughter causing trouble?"

"Not in the least," Mr. Bennet said.

They let Mr. Bennet sit with his great-grandchild for as long as he pleased, even when Alison reached her nap period and drifted off in his arms. There was no one who did not have some affection for Alison, excepting Monkey, though that had been her fault. Her attempts at a good-natured friendship began with pulling his tail with her very sticky fingers, which delighted her far more than it did him, and he spent the rest of their time together perched safely up in the chandelier. Though Georgie offered Monkey a comforting word or two, her allegiance was to her daughter.

Only after Mr. Bennet was soundly asleep himself did Georgie carefully detach her daughter from the slumbering great-grandfather and carry her onto the blanket in the shade beside her husband, who was enjoying the view of Pemberley's lake with Charles. When he had the chance, Charles Bingley III doted on his goddaughter. "I'm not going to wake her, am I?" he said as she was passed into his arms.

"She naps when she wants to, regardless of anyone else's opinion," Geoffrey explained. "Also, she could sleep through anything."

"*You* could sleep through anything," Georgie said. "You sleep on your left side and miss all of her crying. I know you do that on purpose!"

Geoffrey grinned and kissed her. "If the only benefit of poor hearing is a good night's rest, then at least let me enjoy it."

Gawain, who had been sleeping, picked his head up, signaling to them the arrival of another person. Isabel Wickham curtseyed and joined them. "May I ask a terrible imposition of you, Mr. Darcy?"

"I doubt it is, and you may," he replied.

"Can you talk to George? *Please?*"

"What's this about?" Charles asked.

"Izzy has a suitor," Georgie said. "And of course, her brother is terribly critical of him."

"What's wrong with him?"

"Nothing," Isabel said. "He's just being George."

"Am I at least to have an argument in your favor?" Geoffrey asked.

"His name is Mr. Franklin, and he's an American."

"I said *in* your favor."

"You can't be prejudiced against someone because of their origins. He's lived in London for two years now, and he loves it. He thinks it's quaint."

"Quaint? You can barely breathe in the market on a hot day."

"Because it has history. His country has so little. He's traveled to more places in the kingdom than I have. Including Derbyshire – he saw Chatsworth last summer."

"I am partial to a man with an appreciation for Derbyshire," Geoffrey said. "What of his fortune?"

"His father had a plantation in Virginia, and he inherited it, but he couldn't stand owning slaves, so he freed them all and sold it and decided to tour Europe and see where his ancestors came from. Franklin *is* an English name."

"Has George met him?" Georgie asked.

"You know how he is, locked up at Cambridge. I wrote him to say I had met a nice fellow, and he sent me a long letter about the responsibilities and duties of marriage. Made it sound dreadful. No doubt pulled it from one of his books."

"If I were him," Geoffrey said, "I would no doubt be concerned that this Mr. Franklin has no intentions of returning to his home country, which he may very well do in the future, and that would terrify any brother or father."

"Nonetheless, it's unfair to make out the character of someone you've never met," Georgie said.

"True." He turned back to Isabel. "I'll speak to him. I don't imagine what I can do that you can't, but I can hardly refuse you."

"Thank you!" She hugged her cousin and ran off.

After a few moments of peaceful silence, Charles said, "He did sell all of his property in America. Not exactly a sign of patriotism."

"This is true. But George is going to be a bit stubborn when it comes to giving away his sister. I suppose I should at least –" But he was interrupted as Alison began to cry. "She's probably just hungry."

"She can't be; I fed her an hour ago."

"Then she just wants some attention," he said, taking her out of Charles's arms and lifting her up. "Who missed her papa? Who did? Was it you? Do you want a kiss?" He brought her down to kiss her right between the eyes, then raised her back up again. Alison giggled. "Yes you do!" He brought her up and down, and she was thrilled about it.

"Are infants that easy to handle?" Charles said to his sister, who stared back at him.

"*No*," she said. "He just makes it look like it, because *he* slept through the night last night."

"Does Alison have a kiss for her jealous mama? I think she does!" Geoffrey bumped Alison's face into Georgie's, who kissed her daughter. "I knew she did."

"Fine, fine," Georgie said with a smile and took her child into her lap, letting Alison grab the locket around her neck. "Ow, ow. I love you, but it may be lessened when you're actively hurting me."

As the two parents struggled with their infant, *their* parents looked on from the wide windows of Pemberley's great hall. More specifically, Darcy took up his normal position by

595

the window and watched pensively, and Elizabeth came up from behind and put her hands around his shoulders. "They're naturals."

"They're young. They have that ... playful spirit."

"I remember someone chasing his son all around the study to keep him from hurting himself, and without a word of complaint. You even seemed to enjoy it."

Darcy smiled. "We were all young once."

"Who are you calling old?" Bingley said, approaching from behind with his wife.

"Fortunately, we still have Mr. Bennet to claim that title," Darcy said.

Jane smiled as she watched Georgie try to get Alison on her own tiny feet, which the infant was incapable of doing at this stage, however much she wanted to. "I had only dreamed that our daughter would reach this happy stage."

"Speaking of daughters," Bingley said, "have you set a date for the ball yet?"

"No." Darcy answered in his usual monosyllabic way.

"Even chosen a month? I thought I'd heard you promised Sarah that she'd be out by next winter."

"No."

"Stop chiding him," Elizabeth said to Bingley. "He can't even think of it yet." She turned to her husband. "You're not intending to do this with all of our daughters, are you?"

"Yes. Yes, I am."

"So you will abide by the old custom of making sure Anne is secured in a good match before Sarah is allowed into society? Your Aunt Catherine would be proud. Now we must hurry to find a wife for Anne –"

"*Fine.* I'll consider it." He added, "Maybe."

Elizabeth kissed her husband, and Bingley gave him a knowing smile that Darcy did not very much appreciate but was ready to accept as a fact of his existence.

~~~

Geoffrey found George some ways away, leaning against a tree with a large tome in his hands. Upon closer inspection, it was not a medicinal manual, but a copy of the works of Malory. "George."

He nodded. "Geoffrey. What do you want of me now?"

"You always assume the worst."

"Am I wrong?"

"Perhaps not this time," Geoffrey said and sat down on the grass next to him. "Isabel spoke to me of a Mr. Franklin."

"I will not tolerate a lecture from you."

"You should at least meet the man."

George huffed and looked down at his book.

"She's out in society and has been for years. She is not who she was at fifteen; even you will acknowledge that. How long does she really deserve to continue to split her time between Gracechurch and the Maddoxes? There is something to be said for having a home of your own." When George didn't respond, Geoffrey continued, "She would never do anything you would disapprove of. She is desperate to please you. She wants you to be happy –"

"I'm not unhappy. Just because I'm not Britain's greatest father and husband does not mean I am not content with my studies."

Geoffrey chose not to contradict him. "I am saying I do not think she will abandon you when she marries. She cares for you too much."

He gave his cousin time for a response. "I'll see the man with intentions toward my sister, honorable or not," George said.

"Hopefully the former."

George skeptically rolled his eyes and returned to his book, effectively dismissing Geoffrey. It was rude, but that was the way George was in a foul or overprotective mood, so it was not a surprise.

Geoffrey imparted the news to Isabel, who hugged him and ran to talk to her brother (presumably). He then returned to his wife and cousin. Charles said to Alison, "When I return, you will be able to stand and run all around me."

"Hopefully," Geoffrey said. "You intend to spoil her rotten, don't you?"

"Isn't that what godfathers are for?"

Geoffrey picked his daughter up. She was still light enough that he could hold her in one arm without any trouble and offer the second one to his wife so she could get to her feet. They excused themselves from Charles and walked out towards the woods, following the path that his mother loved so much. Geoffrey had sensed that Georgie was tiring of all the attention she was receiving as a new mother – not all of it kind, in that it was inquisitive without openly or intentionally being so. There had been some speculation as to how the mighty warrior woman would become a mother and a sigh of relief when it seemed to go well, but the very unconscious process of it tired Georgie in a way that didn't need to be spoken.

"What did George say?"

"He was not interested in talking or listening to me, though he was polite enough to do so anyway."

"Isabel is reaching that age."

"So is Anne. It doesn't mean I'm thrilled about it."

"Anne has your father to watch over her."

"Yet there is a tradition in our large family of daughters managing to do as they please, regardless of their father's intentions."

Georgie smiled, and he leaned over and kissed her. Alison giggled, and they continued their walk.

"Have I pleased our parents?"

"We have not even had to discuss it."

Of course, there were things their parents didn't know and didn't need to know. Lancashire was remote, their servants were loyal, and he rarely invited guests. None of them needed to know about Georgie's dark moods or the days where she could not bring herself to rise from bed at all and said only depressing things as she cried into her pillow and ignored Alison completely. They had a wet nurse, and the moods always passed, but Geoffrey was determined that, for the health of both his wife and his daughter, if there was slack, he would pick it up. When Alison cried and Georgie was not capable, he held and cared for their daughter until it passed.

In the third month, when it had been especially severe, Geoffrey consulted privately with a local midwife, who explained to him that while uncommon, it was not unknown for a new mother to be in a sunken mood, and it did not reflect on anything except what her body had endured. She loved Alison; she could not always express it. "It will pass," the midwife assured Geoffrey, and it did. When Georgie reemerged from her stupor, she felt guilty nonetheless, but he was there to assuage her fears.

They had veered off the path. He was familiar with the woods enough to know precisely where they were, but not where they were going. Georgiana did not seem to be wondering.

"Mr. Darcy. Mrs. Darcy."

They turned to the huntsman, a new hire at Pemberley. For years, he had worked for the Duke of Devonshire but had been dismissed when the staff was decreased. "Mr. Matthews."

He bowed to them. "I was going to say, you'd best not be heading down to that waterfall, sir. They say it's haunted."

"Is it?" Geoffrey looked at his wife, who shrugged. "I've never known it to be. I swam there as a child."

"There is a story – but I'd best not say it in front of Miss Darcy."

"She can hardly understand you, so I do not believe it will be a problem," Georgie said. "I would be interested to know the story of this waterfall."

He swallowed. "They say – and I heard this from a reliable source – that an old spirit haunts this place."

"Really. A ghost?"

"No. A spirit, like them magical beasts. A wolf."

Georgie covered her mouth. "A wolf?" Meanwhile, Geoffrey buried his smile in his daughter's hair.

"A terribly fierce creature; comes out of nowhere to attack its enemies. Sometimes, you can still hear the howl, even if it ain't there. The barkeep who told me said he knew a man who saw it with his own eyes. Told him to get off his land. This place is might' sacred to it. You ought not to be trespassing." He added with another bow, "Though it's not for me to say where you go, Mr. Darcy. This is your land."

"My father's land," he corrected. "And it has always been lucky to us. Mrs. Darcy, I believe you once swam here?" She hadn't swum as much as sunk, but she smiled at him anyway.

"I did," she said.

"You be careful, Mrs. Darcy. I know forest creatures – they protect their own. I don't mean to frighten you, marm, but I heard they'll come from the shadows to defend this place."

"I heard about a wolf that was attacking people," Geoffrey said. "It died. Someone shot it with a silver bullet."

"Spirits don't die, Mr. Darcy. They just disappear to this place inside the world and return when they are needed."

Georgie turned back to the waterfall behind them, which they could see in the distance. "Perhaps you're right."

THE END

Bibliography

Distinction, Lady of. Regency Etiquette: The Mirror of Graces (1811). Mendocino, CA Fort Bragg, CA: R.L. Shep Distributed by R.L. Shep Publications, 1997. Print.

Garrett, Martin. Cambridge: a Cultural and Literary History. Northampton, Mass: Interlink Books, 2004. Print.

Green, E. S. A Concise History of the University of Cambridge. Cambridge, England New York, NY, USA: Cambridge University Press, 1996. Print.

Kelly, Ian. Beau Brummell: the Ultimate Man of Style. New York: Free Press, 2006. Print.

Leff, Gordon. Paris and Oxford Universities in the Thirteenth and Fourteenth Centuries. New York: John Wiley & Sons, Inc, 1968.

Murray, Venetia. High Society in the Regency period, 1788-1820. London: Penguin, 1999. Print.

Pool, Daniel. What Jane Austen Ate and Charles Dickens Knew: From Fox Hunting to Whist: the Facts of Daily Life in Nineteenth-Century England. New York: Simon & Schuster, 1994. Print.

Acknowledgments

Between when I started this book in November 2007 (thanks, Fanfiction.net, for keeping track) and now, I've had a lot of help. Most of those people have been thanked in other books. Now, in alphabetical order to make it fun, the people I am thanking again:

Alex Shwarzstein
Alter Reiss
Brandy Scott
Cherri Trotter
City College of New York, the
Dad
Deb Werksman
Diana Finch
Facebook fans
Fanfiction.net
Fanfiction.net fans
God
Grandma
Grandma's various friends
Hannah Scott
Howard Morhaim
Ian Kelly
Jason Morman
Jane Austen
Jeff Gerecke

Jessica Kupillas
Joanna Mansbridge
Katie Menick
Kate McKean
Kelly Scott
Leanne Eastman
Lindsey Doren
Madalyn Kaufer
Margarita Simonetti
Mark Mirsky
Madison Scott
Michelle Woods
Mom
Naomi Libiki
Rachel Gutin
Sensei
Steven Scott
Sylvia Chan
Talia Goldman
Tamra Prior

CHAPTER 1

1828

"You have no more pressing matters than this?"

Isabella Wickham smiled at her cousin and host and laid a gentle hand on hers. "I wanted to see you. I might not see you again until after the child is born."

Georgiana Darcy (née Bingley) put her other hand on her much expanded belly. Only a lot of pressure on Geoffrey's part had convinced their parents that they would remain in Lancashire until the last month of confinement and then return to Pemberley for the birth. But this was Isabel's day. "What romantic adventures has your beloved planned for you?"

"France, then Spain, Greece, and Italy. Maybe we'll see Charles. Is he still in Naples?"

"He might well be. Last we heard, he had not yet decided if he was to move on. He very much prefers the coast there. He does send his best and his apologies about missing both of us at this time. But he seems happy there. He had an unexplained melancholia at Cambridge that even Eliza couldn't explain, though I confess my attentions were elsewhere. Alison! No!"

"What?" Geoffrey Darcy charged in the room, bowing quickly to Isabel and his wife. "Miss Wickham. Georgie. Where's she gone now?"

"She's on the bed."

He turned to his daughter. Alison Darcy, aged seventeen months, was still unsteady on her feet but steady enough to make everything her playground and had succeeded in pulling herself onto the mattress, high up as it was. She was throwing the sheets around to the best of her ability.

"No harm done. What safer place for a child is there than a bed?" Geoffrey took his daughter's tiny hands as she got to her feet on the uneven mattress, and she giggled at him. "At least it's cushioned."

"Until she bounces right off it."

"She's yet to do that. Maybe she just wants a better view of her mother. Do you, darling?" He picked her up almost sideways and let her arms fly out to her mother. "Who's that? Say 'Mama.'"

"Mama," she said. "Mama!"

Georgie couldn't resist a smile and a kiss for her daughter. "Your very whale-ish mama."

"I never said you resemble a whale."

"Just because you didn't say it doesn't mean it isn't true."

He leaned over and kissed her. "I'll put Alison down. Izzy, I'll see you at the wedding."

His cousin blushed. "Yes, thank you, Geoffrey."

He left, taking his daughter with him and leaving the two young women alone together.

"I hope Mr. Franklin is half the father Geoffrey is," Isabel said. "I would be quite satisfied with just half."

"Some fathers do dote on their daughters. Others take pride in their sons. Mr. Franklin seems to be the sort of man who will do at least one," Georgie said. Mr. Saul Franklin, Isabel's betrothed, had gone through great lengths to dazzle her very discerning brother, and in the process the larger family had met him at least a few times. He was judged to be a very amiable and sensible man (even for an American), and he showed no desire to return to his home country, but longed to set up a house in Brighton or some other picturesque place and still keep his fashionable house in London, which would suit Izzy admirably. George would be welcome there when he was in London, which was most fortunate, as the Bradleys now had four children and there was little room for him with his mother and stepfather on Gracechurch Street. He stayed mainly in Cambridge, but this year he would be studying at the famed University of Paris medical school, a very advisable course of action for future doctors who wished to have a license before they were thirty. It was that or St. Andrews, but Dr. Maddox encouraged him to pursue studies on the Continent, and he was persuaded once he knew his sister would be in the care of a husband. The particular future husband in question he'd withheld his approval on until even his Uncle Darcy was ganging up on him with the rest of the family to see sense and let his sister go.

The servant knocked. Isabel did not have much time, and she really ought to be in London, doing last-minute preparations. Almost all of her family were there, excepting those abroad and Geoffrey, who would accompany her back. "I should be readying for the journey." She hugged Georgiana as best she could, and they said their goodbyes and dual congratulations. On her way out she passed Geoffrey, who shut the door behind him.

"My trunk is packed, and Alison is asleep," he said. "By all logic, I should be ready to go."

"I will be fine," she said, leaning back onto the pillow placed behind her in the armchair. "And if I am not, you will hear me scream your name all the way from Town, so there's no need to worry."

"I wouldn't go if there was no obligation," he said. Geoffrey was groomsman. Saul Franklin was not from London, and most of his friends were only acquaintances, but he had formed an easy friendship with Geoffrey over the year of the courtship and engagement. Geoffrey knew that when Saul asked him to stand up with him, it was a show of good faith for George, and Geoffrey was happy to take part in it. "We would try getting George drunk before the ceremony to keep him calm, but he's such a moody drunk."

"He is. A cheap one, though. It wouldn't cost you much wine."

He grinned and kissed her, letting it linger. "I will be back as soon as I can."

"Try at least to stay for the entirety of the ceremony. Mr. Franklin would appreciate it." She added, "I will be fine."

"I love you."

"I love you, too."

Geoffrey left with a smile on his face. Georgie, despite her uncomfortable situation, was able to settle in enough to doze in the chair more peacefully than she had been previously.

~~~

The Darcy townhouse was full of unease – particularly in the certain corner of the study where a window gave a good view of the street.

"He's late."

"There is a long Darcy tradition of late arrivals to weddings," Darcy said, still focusing his attention and his pen on the ledger in front of him. "He was nearly the last person to arrive for his own. What do you expect of him?" He added, "And you are standing by my window in a very aggressive manner, Mr. Wickham."

George Wickham huffed and looked to his uncle. "What do you mean?"

"That is my window, and if anyone is going to sulk by it, it should be me. Yet I have found more sensible things to do with my time, boring as some might find them."

"I don't find mathematics boring."

"There is more to life than facts and numbers." He looked up. "I never imagined I would be saying that."

"You're turning into Grandfather Bennet."

"George Wickham, don't you dare!" A grey-haired Fitzwilliam Darcy, wearing spectacles for reading, might be looking older but was still very imposing. "Well, at least it got a smile out of you. I haven't seen one in a decade."

George raised his glass to his uncle.

"One would think that you would be relieved about your sister being removed from the mortal peril that is the marriage market," Darcy said, closing his massive ledger and ringing for more tea. "All of those odious dances you now must only attend in hopes of someday finding a bride for yourself."

"*Uncle.*"

"The day will come, I assure you. Just try not to insult your future bride while she is within earshot, as you may come to regret it." He looked up as the door opened. "Grégoire."

"Uncle Grégoire."

"So glum in here," Grégoire Bellamont-Darcy said, "just days before a momentous occasion."

"If the groomsman ever arrives and brings the bride," George mumbled and took another sip from his glass.

Darcy gestured to the open wine bottle for his brother, but Grégoire picked it up, inspected the label carefully, and set it back down. "Not a good year for that vineyard."

"I was assured it was very good."

"Perhaps by our English standards, yes," George said.

"I am honored to be part of this family, but I feel no obligation to swear allegiance to English standards of wine selection," Grégoire said as his son came charging into the room. Patrick Bellamont was nearly nine and quite capable of escaping the grasp of anyone who was watching him.

"Saint Barnabas!"

"Saint Barnabas is not present with us; however, he may be in the kingdom of heaven. Address the others first."

His son groaned impatiently and bowed. "Hello, Uncle Darcy. Cousin George."

"Master Patrick," Darcy replied. "What is this about?"

The boy turned to his father. "Saint Barnabas!"

"Yes, yes, I suppose it is."

"Can I have candy?"

"Ask your mother."

"She always says no!"

"Because you'll ruin your teeth." But he quickly buckled under the weight of his son's displeasure and kissed him on the head. "Fine. One sweet – and you brush your teeth with the powder afterwards."

"Tanks, Pa!" With no further explanation, he excused himself by darting out of the room as quickly as he came.

Grégoire sighed and settled into one of the chairs. "I used to give him sweets on Saints' Days and had the misfortune to make a game of having him guess whose it was. Now he's gone and memorized every Saint's Day on the calendar, even the most minor, if it means a candy. I cannot decide what is better – having great knowledge of religion or having teeth."

"Teeth," Darcy answered.

"Teeth," George said just as quickly.

Grégoire just smiled and shook his head.

~~~

At the Bradley house, quiet grumbling was not the order of the day.

"How could she! The nerve of that girl," Lydia Bradley (née Wickham, née Bennet) shrieked, pulling her shawl out of the reach of Isabel's cat. Fortunately the creature was quite old and did not put up much of a fight. "Running out on her own wedding. What will Mr. Franklin think?"

"I hardly think she would do such a thing," Elizabeth said with a knowing look to Mary. The Bennet sisters had gathered at Gracechurch Street at Mr. Bradley's request to help with the children as Isabel's last things were packed for storage. The only one missing was Jane Bingley, who was on her way to Lancashire to care for her daughter for the duration of the wedding. Mr. Bennet himself was similarly excused, as he'd been advised that unnecessary traveling was not good for his health. "She's just gone to see her cousin."

"And a fine time she picked to do it."

"Izzy's getting married," Kitty Townsend said. "How can you not be excited?"

"I'm sure Jane would assure us that there are different types of excitement when it is time for the first daughter to be married," Elizabeth said. She looked down at the cat, who merely purred at her. "Besides, the groomsman is also required for the ceremony."

"Oh, he could find another groomsman. What is she doing to me?"

"Lydia," Kitty said, "you are in danger of turning into Mama."

Lizzy giggled, and Mary merely said, "Indeed, you are."

Lydia did not find it so funny, and it was hard to keep her in a contained mood, much less a good one.

"Mama," Julie Bradley, the eldest of the Bradley children, appeared at the door. "George is home. Oh, and another gift's come."

Her mother sighed. "I don't know where we're going to put it. Why would they send it here and not to Mr. Franklin's like sensible people? Tell George to put it in his room."

"I saw it. It's all frilly with a lace bow. It'll get all dusty."

"Then tell him to find somewhere else!"

"There is still some room in the green trunk by the stairs. You can put it there," Elizabeth suggested, and Julie curtseyed to her aunts and ran to do her mother's bidding. The walls of the

Bradley house were not very thick, and they could hear the sound of heavy boots ascending the stairs. Finally, George Wickham appeared at the open door and bowed. "Mother. Aunt Darcy. Aunt Bertrand. Aunt Townsend."

"When are you due back at the Darcys?" Lydia said in a very measured tone.

He gave her a look. "I'm not." George was known to spend most of his time in town elsewhere, but he always slept at Gracechurch. "Aunt Darcy, I am to inform you that you're to dine with Uncle and Aunt Kincaid tonight."

"Thank you, George." She was secretly grateful for the excuse to leave, though her sisters would likely begin squabbling again without her supervision – but when had she been any good at that? Now that it came time to do it in the traditional, drawn-out way, Lydia was a bit more sentimental about giving her daughter up, which in this case translated to nerves that were approaching a Mrs. Bennet-like scale. There were too many details for her to be unsatisfied with; maybe Isabel had had an ulterior motive for going to Lancashire.

On the way out, Elizabeth encountered Mr. Bradley and Brandon Bradley behind him.

"How bad is it?"

"Not as bad as it could be," she said with a little smile, and was gone.

~~~

"I hope Mrs. Bradley doesn't smash the package I sent," Lady Caroline Maddox said to her husband. "Queen takes rook."

Sir Daniel Maddox smiled. "Knight takes queen." As usual, his wife moved the chess pieces for him. "And I'm sure she won't."

"You trapped me into giving up my queen!"

"You always overuse it," he said.

"There's nothing wrong with liking the queen over her far less useful companion. Knight to 4h."

"Until you've lost her. Bishop to 4a. And check. Possibly mate; I forget." He was no master, but simply being able to play based entirely on his memory of moves was impressive. It also gave him something to do with his day.

She toppled her own king over for him. "Am I really that predictable?"

"You are quite capable of surprising me," he said. "Just perhaps not at chess." Caroline huffed and stood up, but he caught her passing hand and kissed it. "What time is it?"

"Nearly six; and your brother is still making a ruckus in the courtyard." She turned to the window, where she could watch Brian Maddox, armored, dueling her younger son, who was in similar costume.

He chuckled. "The smell of food will bring him in. Put a dish by the door."

"Like a hungry dog."

"I'd never thought of it that way. Nor will I admit it to him."

"He's turning our son into a maniac."

"Danny has permission to choose his recreations as he pleases, provided they do not involve drinking, gambling, or anything else that would get boys like him into trouble. That limits it to reading or fighting, and the latter provides a great deal more exercise." He stood up and took his wife's arm as they left the study, only to hear their daughter's voice in the distance.

"It's not fair."

"What isn't fair?"

She turned to them and curtseyed. "Papa, Mama, Frederick is bragging about all of the fine places he's to visit on the Continent. Why does he get to tour and I do not?"

"Isabel Wickham is to tour the Continent after her wedding, I understand," her mother said. "When you do find a husband – and Daniel, don't say anything – make sure to mention it as part of the celebratory travels."

"Frederick doesn't have to get married."

"Frederick studied for three years in a prestigious University," Dr. Maddox said. "Or, I assume he did something else with his time, but he was there for a full three years, and courtship is much shorter than that. If you look at it that way, your trip requires far fewer hours of anticipation."

"Provided you ever consent to her being courted, much less letting her marry someone," Brian Maddox said, announcing his entrance as he pulled off his helmet, his breathing still heavy. "That'll be the day."

Emily curtseyed quickly, mumbled an acknowledgment to her uncle, and ran back upstairs.

"Now look what you've done," Caroline said. "You go and reassure her that Daniel is a sensible father and she will find someone she loves and is a suitable match, or there'll be no dinner for you."

"What am I, a dog?"

Caroline put a hand over her mouth, but Daniel Maddox didn't bother with the attempt to contain his laughter.

About the Author

Marsha Altman lives in a world inside her head. So far, this has been working out pretty well for her. Probably to the surprise of historians reading this series, she has a BA in History from Brown University and an MFA in Creative Writing from the City College of New York. When not writing, she is generally wasting her time, because she should be writing.

Look for her online at MarshaAltman.com

27449622R00344

Made in the USA
Lexington, KY
14 November 2013